Also by Ian O'Neill:

'Jimmy First and Destiny's Watch'

'Jimmy First and the Time Conflict'

'The Elf Boy Trilogy, Book One –
The Heritage Bloodstone'

'The Elf Boy Trilogy, Book Two –
The Waterswood Rebellion'

To Isabelle,

Elf Boy Book Three

The Hunt for Graydon Leah

Ian O'Neill

Ian o'Clii

In memory of Mick Mercer

Once again, a special thank-you to Michele Anne for another wonderful cover illustration and another massive thank-you to Caroline Byrne for her editor's eye and Gill Gravenstock for the proof reading, and to Yvonne Baker for the final read through.

Chapter One – A Time for Healing

Jack sat in the bay window of Lomund's cottage looking out across the deserted lanes of Waterswood. He felt bereft; he felt lost. In fact, he'd never felt so lonely in his whole life. Yes, he had his good friends Elensar and Rory with him, but they couldn't possibly begin to understand the loss he felt at that moment.

How could they?

Everybody experiences loss in their life at some time but to watch your whole community fade away in front of your very eyes was more than any one individual should have to witness. He could still see the fear and anguish in his mother's face as she slowly melted away in his grasp. It was an image that would stay with him forever.

He'd known her for only a few months and was already facing the heartache of separation. His life that had once been so mundane had changed from the moment he knew of her existence. When Jack saw that burnt frame of his cottage back in the early spring, he had no idea of the enormous effect it would have on him. It sent him on a journey that was beyond even the wildest imagination.

His sedate life with his grandfather when he lived in that cottage was a dim and distant memory. The drama of that single event had coloured his life ever since, and no more so than the previous two days. That day he found out he was an Elf was life changing and despite the initial shock, he was made up. He had never felt he fitted in the traveller world even though he loved his grandfather dearly.

But even that wasn't true.

He was neither Elf nor human; he was what Grimley gleefully described, a mongrel. There was never going to be a pleasant way to hear that news but to be told by a triumphant Grimley was as bad as it got. Now he was in the spirit world along with the rest of the community. It was a thought that gave Jack no satisfaction; it was anger he felt towards the former head of the Council of Elders for what he had inflicted on the people of Waterswood.

And the irony was that if he wasn't part human he would have joined his friends in the spirit world. He could guess what his grandfather would say if he was sat in front of him now: *'What is meant to be will be, Jack lad. No good complaining just get on with it and make the best of the hand you're dealt.'* The thought made him smile. He would visit his grandfather when he returned to the human world.

And now he was faced with the almost impossible task of finding the gold dust and returning it to the valley communities. He first had to find his father; then a Dwarf and a Pixie. And there was this mystery character Graydon Leah to deal with. Even the Faery Queens didn't seem to know anything about him. And the task was made even more difficult by the absence of his Koehtia. The lack of gold dust made it barely detectable within him.

Rory placed a mug of Roseleaf on the windowsill in front of him. 'A penny for them, Jack me lad,' he said cheerily.

'Thanks Rory,' said Jack forcing a smile and reaching for the mug.

Rory pulled up a chair and sat next to him and stared out onto the lane that led to the village centre. 'Lomund has a grand place, all right. With those lovely hills behind and a fine view down the lane, what more could anyone ask?'

'I loved it as soon as I saw it,' said Jack. 'I couldn't believe it was going to be my home … and now it may never be.'

'Aw come on Jack me lad, I know things look a little bleak at the moment, but I'm sure we have enough about us to find this Leah fella and get the gold dust back.'

Jack loved Rory's optimism. It had kept him going during the dark times when they were searching for his mother. The glass was always half full for Rory McNory.

'The shock of seeing the people of this village disappear into thin air, well … it just leaves you numb.'

'I know, Jack lad. I have to say it left both Elensar and I with a huge lump in our throats when it happened. I can't begin to imagine how I would feel if it happened to the people of Cill-Arney.'

Jack quietly sipped his tea for a few moments. 'I didn't see Elensar leave this morning.'

'He was up with the birds and said he was going out for a run. He must have run to Cill-Arney and back for he's been gone for hours,' smiled Rory.

Jack looked down the lane to see Elensar striding purposefully towards the cottage. He suspected there was more to Elensar's outing than just a run. Rory stood up and walked over to the table and filled another mug with Roseleaf. He handed it to the Captain as he walked through the door.

'Expert timing as ever,' smiled Elensar as he took the tea and sat at the table.

Jack sat down across from him and asked the question that he wasn't sure he wanted to hear the answer to. 'What did you find in the village?'

'It's deserted,' said Elensar solemnly. 'I checked all the buildings in the main square, as well as the gaol and the surrounding area. We are definitely the only Elves left in Waterswood.'

Jack wasn't surprised. Maybe a little disappointed but he'd seen the other villages in the valley after their gold dust had been taken.

'So, what's your plan?' asked Elensar.

Jack shrugged his shoulders disconsolately. 'I haven't had time to think. I'm still having trouble taking it all in. A few days' rest would be welcome.'

'And who would deny you that,' said Rory.

'Nobody,' agreed Elensar, 'but Morning-Dew said we may only have six months to return the gold dust. I'm afraid time isn't on our side.'

Jack knew Elensar was right, but he needed time to gather himself. Just a few days would help. 'We'll rest here while I work out what we need to do. I'll be ready within the week, I promise.'

'We're here to support you, Jack,' said Elensar. 'You

take as long as you need, and Rory and I will be ready when you are.'

*

Jack spent the next few days exploring the village and the surrounding countryside. Rory and Elensar asked him if he wanted company but he politely declined. And they both understood why – this was something that Jack had to do on his own. He'd never had the time or opportunity to get to know his home village before. Sometimes he sat with the Tickle Tree as he pondered the challenges that lay ahead. Other times he just stared longingly at his friends' cottages wishing they were there, so he could call in and share a mug of tea with them.

In many ways he was dealing with his grief; he was attempting to come to terms with the loss of his family and friends. His heart ached as he wandered in lonely isolation through the lanes. It was a painful process, but it was a healing one. He had to draw a line under what had happened to him over the previous months to prepare himself for the challenges that lay ahead.

He slept deeply for over twelve hours for three nights running. It was what his grandfather called the sleep of the dead. His body was replenishing its exhausted reserves. But on the fourth night he dreamed lucid dreams. His mother came to him. She stood just a few feet in front of him and told him she was safe and well, and that the Faery Queens were looking after them all. Lilac, Tyler, Lomund, and Crystal all came to him with the same message.

Then Shane came into focus, standing tall and erect like the proud warrior he was. Jack could see the fear in his eyes had gone. He didn't speak but held out his hand in the manner of a warrior. Jack reached forward to grasp it, but Shane was gone. Jack woke what seemed like a moment later and the tears streamed down his face. It was the release he needed, and he immediately knew that he was healing. He rolled out of his bed and immediately woke Elensar and

4

Rory. As they rubbed the sleep out of their eyes, Jack said two words, 'I'm ready.'

*

Jack sat in front of a breakfast that only Rory McNory could muster. The appetite that had deserted him for the previous four days had returned with a vengeance. He waded through a plateful of mushrooms, tomatoes, scrambled eggs, oat cakes and several slices of oatmeal toast.

'That's a grand sight to see,' said Rory as he sat down in front of his own breakfast, 'Green-Jack doing what he does best … making short work of a Rory McNory special!'

'I haven't enjoyed a meal like that for a long time,' agreed Jack.

'Let's hope I get the opportunity to make it a regular feature,' smiled Rory.

'So, do you have a plan, Jack?' asked Elensar.

'Of sorts,' said Jack. 'We need to go to the human world first. I have a friend we need to see. She lives in Grasslake Village which is where my father comes from. I'm hoping that Becky knows the family or at least knows of them. I'm not sure where else to go if she doesn't.'

'I have no experience of dealing with humans so I'm not going to be much help,' said Elensar.

'Nor me,' said Rory. 'I see them from time to time around the lakes of Cill-Arney, but I've never had any sort of serious conversation with them.'

'There's good and bad as there is in all races,' said Jack, 'but their world is a lot different from what you're both used to. I can go on my own if you'd prefer.'

They both looked offended. 'I said that I would accompany you throughout this quest and I see no reason to change my mind,' said Elensar firmly.

'And that goes for me too,' agreed Rory.

Jack smiled in resignation. 'I'm glad you're coming with me but just as long as you both know it's going to be a huge culture shock for you.'

'So, when we've found your daddy,' said Rory moving on, 'what happens then?'

'That's when it gets difficult,' said Jack. 'First of all, I'm going to have to persuade him that I'm his son and that I'm an Elf. That's even before I have to ask him to help us on our quest.'

'Ah,' said Rory, 'I see what you mean. But you have great powers of persuasion, Jack me lad, so I'm sure you'll find a way.'

'Let's hope so,' said Jack, 'let's hope so ...'

'Then I assume we come back here?' asked Elensar.

'We do indeed,' said Jack, 'and then I'm going to be relying on you to find us a Dwarf and a Pixie.'

'As I said, Jack, I'm sure they'll find us. We just have to put ourselves in their general vicinity.'

'I didn't find the two dwarves in Korrian's castle over friendly,' said Jack. 'They both seemed intent on cracking my head open with their axes.'

'We have fought wars for years,' said Elensar, 'but we have learnt to be more accepting of each other. Let's hope the Dwarves we meet are open to our request for help.'

'Maybe I can help there,' chimed in Rory. 'I'm nearer their height so I won't be so intimidating.'

Elensar laughed and slapped Rory playfully on his back. 'I've never tried diplomacy before, but you may be right.'

'Morning-Dew said that Graydon Leah resides in the eastern lands way beyond the Fireridge Mountains. I asked Lomund and he had no knowledge of these lands. No Waterswood Elf has ever travelled there,' said Jack.

'We will rely on our instincts, Jack,' said Elensar. 'You will be able to tell when we get nearer to Leah as your Koehtia will guide you.' He placed a reassuring hand on Jack's shoulder. 'We all have our roles to play, Jack, and I have no doubt that the new members of our company will play their parts too.'

'I'll be the cook on this journey,' chirped Rory. 'No good things are done on an empty belly!'

'You're right,' as always,' laughed Elensar, 'your role

will be a key one.'

Jack already felt the bond between them. It was as if they hadn't been apart for all those months. He felt energised and ready to confront the raft of challenges that faced him. Rory grinned from ear to ear as Elensar placed his arms around them both.

'We are the core of the company and the success of our quest rests squarely on our three pairs of shoulders. But I couldn't think of two people with whom I would rather share this amazing journey with.' He removed his arms from their shoulders and picked up his mug of Roseleaf: 'To my friends Green-Jack and Rory McNory and to the success of our quest.'

'To the success of our quest,' repeated Jack and Rory as they both joined him and raised their mugs of tea.

'So, when do we leave?' asked Rory.

Jack placed his mug back on the table. 'I don't see any point in delaying any longer. Let's pack our rucksacks and go.'

*

Chapter Two – A Shock for Jack

Jack, Elensar and Rory emerged one by one from inside the wishing-well at the Faery Crossing in Heywood Forest. Jack and Elensar checked the surrounding area for humans as Rory marvelled at the scenery.

'I love cold and frosty mornings. We only get the odd one in the winter months back home in Cill-Arney. I'm just glad that Auntie Bridie made me wear my warm coat and woollen hat. Just wish I'd brought my mittens as well.'

Rory pulled up his collar and blew his misty breath onto his cold hands to warm them. The ground was as hard as granite and silver threads of frost glistened across the grass and the trees. Jack and Elensar quickly finished their reconnaissance and re-joined Rory.

'There's a Faery trail that leads across the middle of the forest that Lilac told me about. It shouldn't be too hard to find. Then we just have to cross a field to the barn where we'll be staying while we're here.'

They strolled across the clearing towards the frost covered beech trees and Jack immediately found the Faery trail. 'I've lived in this forest for fifteen years and never noticed this before,' he said shaking his head.

'And that's because you weren't looking,' said Rory. 'Once you know something's there it's easier to find.'

That was classic Rory McNory logic which sort of made sense to Jack, but he was more relieved they could cross the forest without any prying humans seeing them. They followed the trail through the midst of the undergrowth and chatted as they strolled along.

'I always think the forest looks sad in winter,' said Rory. 'It's like it's been stripped of all its beauty.'

'It needs the winter to rest,' said Elensar. 'It's when it replenishes itself which is why it will always come back as beautiful and colourful as ever.'

'I spent my childhood here,' said Jack. 'I shared a cottage on the edge of the forest with my grandfather. I have many fond memories of living here. He would teach me all about nature as we strolled through the trees and undergrowth. And many of the animals who live here are my friends.'

'You've got animal friends?' said a surprised Rory.

'It was one of them, Cyril the Squirrel, who led me to Waterswood.'

'Now he sounds like a character I'd like to meet,' said Rory.

'I don't see much of him in wintertime,' said Jack. 'He spends most of it asleep.'

'Well I'll have to come back to see him in the spring,' said Rory.

Jack was the first to emerge from the Faery trail on the edge of the forest and was taken by surprise when somebody called out his name.

'Jack! Where did you spring from?'

He looked along the path and saw Becky and Sonny running towards him. She wrapped him in her arms as Sonny leapt upon him. Elensar and Rory stepped from the Faery trail and suddenly appeared behind Jack. Both Becky and Sonny were startled, causing the latter to bark. Becky stepped back from Jack and looked a little coy.

'Oh, I didn't realise you had company.'

Jack knelt down and fussed Sonny. 'It's all right, boy, they're my friends.' Sonny stopped barking and tentatively sniffed them both. Jack stood up and pointed to them in turn. 'This is Captain Tathar Elensar and Rory McNory.' He walked up to Becky and put his arm around her shoulder. 'This is Becky – she's my girlfriend.'

Becky looked at Jack with a beaming smile. Rory took her hand, kissed it and bowed low. 'It's grand to meet you, Becky.'

Elensar was a little less formal and shook her hand. 'A friend of Jack is a friend of mine.'

'You seemed to appear out of thin air,' said Becky. 'I was walking along the path and all of a sudden there you were.'

9

'We followed a Faery trail through the forest,' said Jack. 'They're a little difficult for humans to see.'

'Well I'm just pleased you're here; and it's Christmas Day which makes it even more special.'

'Christmas Day!' said Jack. 'I had no idea. I've been a little preoccupied for the last few months.'

'Are you planning to stay a while?' asked Becky.

'A few days,' said Jack. 'I'm hoping you can help me.'

'Me, help you? I'm intrigued,' said Becky. 'But let's get you back to the barn as it's freezing out here. I've kept it clean while you've been away, and I managed to find an old gas heater in our shed at home. You'll be as warm as toast!'

They took a relaxed stroll across the field and Becky told Jack all about the presents her mum had given her that morning. Jack had many fond memories of the Christmas's he'd spent with his grandfather in the cottage. Noah would always buy him a small gift and they'd start the day with a huge breakfast. Noah would cook a goose over the fire and try to persuade Jack to try it but of course he never would. He made up his mind that he would surprise his grandfather later that day and visit him at the camp.

The barn was indeed very clean although freezing cold, but Becky lit the calor gas fire and it soon warmed up. Rory made it known he needed a cup of tea.

'I don't suppose you have a kettle as I need a sup of tea to warm me inside.'

'Of course,' smiled Becky and produced an old steam kettle and a primus stove from a cupboard. 'I found these in a second-hand shop in the village.'

Rory looked at the primus and said, 'I have no idea how to use this. Would you mind showing me?'

'Here,' said Jack, taking the stove from Becky and placing it on the bench. He turned the gas on and lit it with a match.

Rory looked bemused. 'Are you using that magic of yours again, Jack me lad?'

'Just human technology this time,' smiled Jack.

'I'll pop home and get some water,' said Becky. 'I won't

be two minutes,' and ran out of the door with Sonny.

'She's a grand colleen,' said Rory. 'And I would say she's more than a little smitten with you, Jack, as you are with her.'

'Did you know her when you lived in the forest, Jack?' asked Elensar.

'I only met her the day before I left,' said Jack. 'I found her face down in the pond … she was … she was dead.'

Neither Rory nor Elensar responded. Jack could see the shock on their faces. 'I know it shocked me too once I realised what I'd done … I thought she'd just stopped breathing when I reached her. But she didn't respond to conventional heart massage and mouth to mouth, so I used Koehtia to bring her back to life, although I didn't know that was what I was doing at the time.'

Elensar unbuttoned his coat and sat down on the bench. 'When did you tell her you were an Elf?'

'The last time I was here a few months ago. She told me that she had feelings for me and I thought it could be down to the Koehtia. So that's when I told her.'

'And she believed you,' said Elensar.

'Not at first but when I held her and shared my Koehtia with her she realised that I was different. But it was these that finally convinced her,' he said pointing to his ears.

'And you trust her?' asked Elensar.

'Aw Elensar, you can see that she worships the ground Jack walks on. I have no great experience in dealing with humans, but I can tell she's a grand young lady.'

'Rory's right, she is special. I felt it as soon as I met her. I wouldn't have told her about me if I didn't trust her.'

'You have sound instincts Jack and I shouldn't doubt you. Besides, you have lived in the human world and I know nothing about it,' said Elensar.

Becky and Sonny returned after ten minutes - she was carrying two bottles of water and filled the kettle before placing it on the primus. 'It should boil in around ten minutes and then you can make your tea.'

'Are you going to join us, Becky?' asked Rory.

'I would love to,' said Becky, 'but my mum is going to be serving up our lunch soon.'

'Well you know you're always welcome,' said a smiling Rory.

'Jack, can I see you outside for a minute?' asked Becky.

Jack followed Becky outside while Sonny checked out if there was any food available from either Elensar or Rory. They strolled over to the wrought iron fence and Becky pulled out a small box and handed it to Jack.

'I bought you a present for Christmas. It's only something small but I hope you like it.'

Jack took the box and was momentarily lost for words. 'I, er, I … I didn't buy you anything.'

'Don't be silly,' said Becky. 'I didn't expect you to. I'm sure you've had a lot more important things on your mind.'

Jack opened the box and found a silver ring inside. He held it between his thumb and index finger and studied it. 'It's beautiful.'

'I found it in that second-hand shop in the village. Look on the inside; it's got Elven runes written on it.'

Jack studied the inside of the ring and sure enough there was Elven writing. 'How do you know about runes?'

'I've been studying all about Elves on the internet. I found it really interesting.'

Jack tried to slip the ring on his little finger, but it was too tight. 'I'll keep it in the breast pocket of my shirt.' He removed the flattened gold coin that Cara had given him. 'I'll keep it alongside this coin that a Leprechaun colleen gave me.'

'Oh my goodness!' said Becky putting her hand to her mouth. 'I've just realised! Rory's a Leprechaun?'

'Sorry, I should have told you when I introduced you both.'

'I didn't really think. I …'

'It's a world I never knew existed until just over six months ago,' said Jack, 'and I live in it, so it must be difficult for you to accept.'

Becky tenderly touched Jack's face. 'If it wasn't for you

being an Elf I would have died.'

Jack covered her hand with his and kissed her tenderly on her lips. 'Maybe destiny had a hand in the way we met.'

Becky smiled and kissed Jack back. 'I'd better go or my mum will come looking for me. I'll come back after lunch if that's OK?'

'I'm going to visit my grandfather so why don't you call in later this afternoon.'

*

Jack walked into the camp and was greeted by the usual yapping dogs. Curtains twitched in the caravans, but no-one came out to greet him. He was really looking forward to seeing his grandfather especially as it was Christmas Day. It would be a nice surprise for him, thought Jack.

He strolled casually up to Dimey's caravan and knocked twice. The door opened and a stout lady with jet black permed hair stood there.

'Hello Dimey, I've come to surprise my grandfather for Christmas Day.'

'Oh Jack, I'm glad you're here. Noah was taken into hospital last week.'

'Taken into hospital! What's wrong with him?'

'He had trouble breathing one night and started to cough up blood. I called the ambulance and he was rushed into Glenchester General.'

'What do they say is wrong with him?'

Tears welled in her eyes. 'He has the lung cancer, Jack. I'm afraid it's inoperable.' The tears streamed down her cheeks. 'He's going to die.'

Jack slumped against the caravan and held his head in his hands. *This can't be happening*, he thought. His grandfather was tough and was going to live forever.

'He's smoked the roll-ups since he was ten years old,' said Dimey. 'The cancer was going to get him sooner or later.'

'What ward is he on?' asked Jack recovering his

composure.

'Twenty,' said Dimey, 'but visiting doesn't start until three in the afternoon.'

Jack didn't care about visiting hours and immediately ran from the camp and out onto the road to Glenchester.'

*

Chapter Three –
The Dark Shadow of Death

Jack ran the two miles to Glenchester hospital. When he arrived he almost crashed through the automatic doors and went straight up to a woman sitting behind the enquiries desk in the reception area. 'Ward twenty – where is it?'

The woman pointed towards a corridor behind them. 'Down there, up the stairs and last on the right.'

Jack ran down the corridor and up the stairs. He ran all the way down to ward twenty and through the double doors. A nurse stood behind a desk.

'Noah Green – where is he?'

'Visiting doesn't start for another hour. We're in the middle of serving lunches. You'll have to come back,' she said curtly.

Jack's instincts were to grab her by the lapels of her uniform and force her to tell him, but he managed to catch a hold of himself. 'Please, he's my grandfather. I've been away for months and I've only just found out he's ill. I've been told he's dying.'

The nurse's harsh exterior softened a little. 'He's in a private room. He's sleeping and is very weak. You can go and sit with him if you promise to be quiet.'

'I promise,' said Jack.

She pointed to a door just across from them. 'He's in there.'

Jack rushed over to the door and pushed his way through into the side-room. His grandfather lay in bed with an oxygen mask over his mouth. His normally tanned face was pallid and grey, and his chest barely moved when he breathed. Jack sat on the bed and took a hold of Noah's hand. He closed his eyes and searched for the Koehtia in the soles of his feet. He waited and waited but there was barely a mild tingle.

Jack stood up and punched the cushion on the chair in frustration. The magic that had been with him all his life had deserted him just when he needed it the most. He gritted his teeth in frustration. But it hadn't deserted him; the means of channelling it to him had been stolen by this Leah character. He sat in the chair next to the bed and held his grandfather's hand again. He leant back and closed his eyes.

Jack had held Noah's hands many times over the years, but they had never felt as cold and lifeless as they did at that precise moment. He didn't need to summon his Koehtia to know that his grandfather's life was hanging by a thread.

Then he felt a hand on top of his. He opened his eyes and saw his grandfather smiling at him. Jack leant forward and kissed him on his cheek. 'Look what happens when I leave you on your own.'

Noah tried to pull his oxygen mask off, but Jack stopped him. 'You're too weak, Grandfather. 'I'll just sit with you while you rest. I won't be going anywhere, I promise.'

*

A distraught Jack eventually left after three hours when the nurse persuaded him to go. She said that she had Dimey's mobile number and would call her if anything changed. Jack took a slow thoughtful walk home. He tried to come up with ways he could summon the Koehtia that would save his grandfather, but none were forthcoming.

The light was fading and darkness fell by the time Jack arrived back at the shed. Becky and Sonny were waiting there along with Elensar and Rory.

Becky instantly knew that something was wrong. 'What is it, Jack? You look worried.'

Jack sat down on the bench next to her. 'It's my grandfather – he's dying.'

'What's happened?'

'He's got lung cancer. I've just been to the hospital and sat with him, but he couldn't even talk to me.'

'Which hospital?' asked Becky.

'Glenchester – they'll ring Dimey at the camp if anything happens.'

Becky reached into her pocket and pulled out a mobile phone. 'I'll ring them from this and give them the number. You're his next of kin and should be told if anything changes. I'll leave it with you tonight just in case they ring.'

'I can't believe it, Becky' said Jack. 'He's always been so strong. I can't ever remember him being ill.'

Becky held Jack's hand as Sonny sat in front of him and laid his head on his lap. He looked up at him with his dark soulful eyes. He knew Jack was hurting.

'I can't lose him, Becky, not at this time. I've lost my Elf friends and my mother; this would just be too much.'

'You lost your mother?' said Becky.

'She's not dead … it's difficult to explain. The Elves from my home village have faded back into the spirit world.'

Becky looked bewildered. How could she possibly take in what Jack was telling her? But it didn't stop her showing her love and empathy to him. 'I'm always here, Jack. And I'm sure Rory and the Captain are too.'

Rory sat down the other side of Jack and placed his hand on his shoulder. 'The three of us are here for you, Jack me lad.'

Sonny-boy barked in protest.

'I think you'd better make that four, Rory,' said Becky.

*

'So, explain to me again how that thing works?' asked Rory as he munched on a piece of toast and examined the phone Becky had left. Jack sat on the bench opposite him and sipped his tea. Elensar had gone for a run in the forest.

'It's called a mobile phone,' said Jack. 'It uses radio waves to communicate with other phones.'

'It makes no sense to me,' said Rory. 'It seems like more powerful magic than yours.'

'That's just it,' said Jack. 'I don't have any magic at all …'

Rory raised his right hand apologetically to Jack. 'Sorry,

that was insensitive of me.'

'Don't worry, Rory,' said Jack, 'I know you didn't mean any harm. I just feel so helpless as I can't use my Koehtia to help my grandfather.'

The door to the shed opened and Becky and Sonny walked in. Sonny trotted up to Jack and rested his head on his lap. Becky put a plastic carrier bag down on the bench. 'I brought you some food. The local shop doesn't open until tomorrow, but this should keep you going until then.'

'You're a life savour, Becky,' said Rory. 'I'm afraid I get grouchy when I'm hungry.'

Becky turned to Jack. 'Have you heard any more from the hospital?'

Jack shook his head. 'Nothing – I'll go over there this afternoon.'

'I thought you might like to go for a walk. The fresh air will do you good.'

'I'm not in the mood, Becky. I think I'll wait here by the phone.'

'We can take it with us,' said Becky. 'I still get a strong signal in the forest.'

'You should go, Jack,' urged Rory. 'You two youngsters need some time on your own. I'll make us all a bowl of porridge while you're out.'

Sonny barked his agreement and Jack relented so they went to the forest. Jack strolled alongside Becky as Sonny-Boy explored the sparse undergrowth with his nose semi permanently glued to the ground.

Jack loved Heywood Forest; it was and would always be his home. The happy childhood memories were tempered by the sadness he felt for his grandfather lying at death's door in that hospital. How he wished he could do something to arrest that terrible illness.

Although he knew it would add to his pain, he found himself inextricably pulled towards his cottage. He felt the tension as he approached the clearing where the cottage was situated. His heart ached as he looked longingly at the burned-out skeleton of what was once his home. Becky squeezed his hand as she stood sympathetically next to him.

'I read about this in the local paper. They said it was a feud between the Travelling communities. I didn't realise it was where you lived.'

'It was nothing to do with the travellers. The former head of my Elven village had it burnt down,' said Jack forlornly.

Becky looked horrified. 'Why would he do such a terrible thing?'

'Because he was trying to kill me.'

'I … I don't understand. What could you have possibly done that would make him want to kill you?'

Jack turned to her and tried to force a smile. 'He didn't like the fact that my father is a human.'

Becky looked astonished. 'But I thought you were an Elf?'

'Only part it seems,' said Jack. 'My father comes from your village.'

'My village! What's his name?'

'Roger Thorne. I know very little about him. He may not even still live there.'

'It's not a name I recognise,' said Becky, 'but my mum has lived here for all of her life – I'm sure she'll know him, or at least know of him.'

Just at that moment Elensar came running into the clearing. Even though it was a cold, crisp day, he'd worked up a healthy sweat. Sonny ran up to him wagging his tail in the hope he'd found someone to play with. Elensar stopped and crouched down to ruffle Sonny's ears.

'This is a fine place for a run. I followed a path all around the perimeter of the forest.'

Becky looked surprised. 'That's miles. You must have been gone for ages.'

'A couple of hours at the most,' panted Elensar catching his breath. 'Any news on your grandfather, Jack?'

Jack shook his head. 'I'm going to the hospital this afternoon.'

'Is there nothing the human Healers can do for him?' asked Elensar.

'It seems not,' said Jack. 'The doctor said that his lungs were riddled with cancer. It's just a matter of waiting for him to …' His words trailed off into a sad and uneasy silence.

'Perhaps we could take him to Arminas? Baelsar and his Healers can work miracles.'

'He'd never survive the journey,' said Jack solemnly.

'He doesn't have to go on a journey, as such. Morning-Dew brought Rory and I here in a flash. One minute I was in Arminas the next I was in the forest overlooking Waterswood, and it was the same for Rory.'

A flicker of hope lit in Jack's heart. 'Do you really think she would do it?'

'What have you got to lose by asking her?' said Elensar.

'Asking me what?' said a voice from behind them.

They all turned around to see Morning-Dew standing on the edge of the clearing. Sonny bounded up to her, his tail wagging like a windmill. She crouched down on one knee and playfully stroked him. 'Sonny-Boy, it's good to see you.'

Becky looked surprised. 'You know him? More to the point, he seems to know you.'

'Ahh,' said Morning-Dew mysteriously. 'That's because we've met before.'

'Well in that case I should know you and I've never seen you before in my life,' said Becky pointedly.

Morning-Dew walked over to them. She reached out and gently touched Becky's face. 'Still so beautiful, Becky Grainger …'

'Who are you?' asked Becky taking a backward step.

'I'm your friend, Becky, and always will be …'

A confused Becky turned to Jack. 'Do you know this woman?'

'I do indeed, but she isn't a woman. Let me introduce you to Morning-Dew – she's a Forest Faery.'

Morning-Dew gathered her frock and curtsied. 'It's my pleasure as always.'

'A Forest Faery?' repeated Becky shaking her head.

'There's a whole world out there that I know absolutely nothing about.'

Morning-Dew smiled reassuringly. 'There will always be new things out there, Becky. That's what makes life so much fun.' She turned her attention to Jack and Elensar. 'So, what is it you have to ask me?'

'It's my grandfather, Noah. He's dying, Morning-Dew. I have no Koehtia to help him. Elensar suggested that you could take him to the Healers at Arminas.'

The smile faded from Morning-Dew's lips. 'You ask for something that I am not able to give.'

'Why not?' asked Elensar. 'Our Healers would gladly help him.'

'Of that I have no doubt, but the Faery lore does not permit me to interfere in such a situation.' She looked tenderly at Jack. 'It is Noah's time, Jack. It comes to us all eventually. Even Faeries have to die.'

Jack couldn't believe what he was hearing. Anger flickered inside him. 'You said that it was the Faeries who woke Noah the night my cottage was burnt down. What is that if it isn't blatant interfering? If they hadn't done that we would have both been burned to death.'

Morning-Dew absorbed his anger. 'And it most certainly wasn't your time.'

Jack stood in front of her and stared deep into her dark brown eyes. 'You're asking me to undertake the biggest challenge of my life; a challenge that even the Faery Queens don't fully understand. And you expect me to be able to do this while I'm grieving for my grandfather?'

Morning-Dew couldn't hold his stare and lowered her gaze. Sonny-boy sat in between them alternately staring up at them. He sensed the tension in the air. Elensar stepped up beside Jack and placed his hand on his shoulder.

'Jack makes a good point, Morning-Dew. You are asking too much of him.'

Morning-Dew looked up and Jack saw tears in her eyes. For the first time since he'd known her she looked sad. 'I can't take Noah to Arminas, Captain. The Faery Queens won't allow it. We are all governed by the laws of life and death. As much as I may want to help, I can't.'

Becky stood the other side of Jack and took hold of his hand. 'Please Morning-Dew - the pain inside Jack is as plain as the nose on his face. I don't know the nature of the challenge that he faces, and I doubt I would understand it even if I did, but how could anyone undertake any task when they're consumed by grief. Please help Jack – I can't stand to see him hurting so much.'

Morning-Dew wiped a tear from her eye and stood silently staring into space. She sighed deeply, stepped forward and embraced Jack and whispered in his ear, 'I will meet you in your shed at midnight.'

*

Chapter Four - Resurrection

Jack sat on the bench next to Elensar sipping his Roseleaf as Rory snored rhythmically in his sleeping bag. He picked up the mobile phone that Becky had left him and checked the time - it was just coming up to midnight. He'd been to visit his grandfather that afternoon and was saddened to see that he was getting worse. He wasn't even aware of Jack's presence. The nurse said that he would eventually slip into a coma and then it would only be a matter of hours before he died.

Where was Morning-Dew?

The door to the shed opened and Morning-Dew stepped inside. Her usual smile and happy demeanour were missing. Jack thought she looked troubled and a disturbing thought suddenly struck him. *Had the Faery Queens got to her and changed her mind?*

'Don't worry, Jack, I haven't changed my mind about helping you,' she said sensing his anxiety.

'I saw my grandfather earlier. He's clinging to life by a thread. I'm not sure he can survive any sort of journey.'

Morning-Dew took hold of Jack's hands. 'I promise you we will do our best for him. Now close your eyes.'

Jack did as she asked.

'Now open them again.'

Jack opened his eyes and he was standing next to his grandfather's bed. The oxygen mask was still strapped to his face, but Noah's chest barely moved. Jack was sure they were too late.

Morning-Dew picked up Noah's hand and felt his pulse. 'It's very weak, Jack. He hasn't got long.'

'It could kill him if we try to move him,' said Jack anxiously. 'What are we going to do?'

Morning-Dew took hold of his left hand. Jack looked to her for guidance and she smiled reassuringly.

'Feel it, Jack,' she whispered.

He was about to ask what she was talking about when he

felt a familiar tingle in his fingertips. It travelled into his hand, along his arm and into his body.

It was Koehtia.

He looked at Morning-Dew and she smiled again. 'You know what to do from here.'

Jack placed his right hand on his grandfather's chest and closed his eyes. The Koehtia flowed from his hand and into Noah's body. It headed straight for the tumour that was entwined within his lungs. Jack couldn't see it but he could feel it. There was a strong life force in this diseased tissue and it was strangling Noah's lungs.

His grandfather was on the cusp of life. Jack could barely detect his presence. The Koehtia had to ease its way around his lung and into the tumour. All of Jack's experiences with Koehtia had been delicate operations but this was going onto yet another level. The shock of removing the tumour could kill his grandfather.

Jack heard Morning-Dew's voice in his head. '*Let the Koehtia find its own way. Trust in it, Jack.*' The same words that Meredin had told him in Arminas. The Koehtia wrapped the tumour in its healing glow. Nothing happened for what seemed like minutes but was probably only a matter of seconds. The Koehtia slowly but surely cut off the blood supply to the diseased tissue. Jack kept monitoring Noah for signs of life and his grandfather was still hanging on.

Jack spoke to him through his thoughts. 'Keep strong grandfather. The tumour will soon be gone, and you'll be able to breathe easier again. I will be with you throughout, I promise.'

Bit by bit, millimetre by millimetre, the tumour fell away from Noah's lungs until it became totally separated. The Koehtia seemed to close in on the tissue and squeeze the life from it. Within a matter of minutes, the tumour had gone. Jack sensed Noah's lungs moving easier and filling with air.

The Koehtia repaired the damaged tissue in Noah's lungs before flowing through the whole of his body searching for other tumours. It ran from the top of his head

24

to the tips of his toes but came back immediately to Jack. He sensed that its job was done. Jack withdrew from his grandfather and took an unsteady step backwards and was glad that Morning-Dew was there to steady him.

'Rest, Jack. You have drained yourself.' She helped him onto the chair next to Noah's bed and gently stroked his hand.

'Do you think I've done enough?' he asked.

Morning-Dew knelt in front of him and cupped his face in her hands. 'You have given him a chance.' She kissed him tenderly on his cheek and Jack saw the tears welling in her eyes. 'You love him with all your heart, Jack, and you have done all you can. It is now down to Noah and his will to live. If I know anything about him it is that he loves life dearly and it is that desire that will heal him.'

'You channelled the Koehtia into me,' said Jack. 'Will you get into trouble for that?'

'The Faery Queens understand. We are asking a lot of you, Jack, and it would have been cruel to expect you to help us while you were grieving for your grandfather. Yes, I have broken our lore concerning life and death, but the circumstances demanded it.' She swallowed deeply; her facial expression darkened. 'This is the last time I can help you in this way, Jack. The Faery lore must be obeyed for all our sakes. The Faery Queens will always be with you in spirit …'

Jack nodded that he understood and leant back in the chair breathing deeply. He was exhausted as he always was after using Koehtia. 'So, what do we do now?'

'I will take you back to your shed so you can get the rest you need and leave Noah to heal.'

*

'Wake up, Jack me lad. I have a nice hot sup of tea for you.'

Jack opened his eyes to see the smiling, freckly face of Rory staring down at him. 'What time is it?' he croaked.

'Just after midday.'

25

Jack panicked and dragged himself from his sleeping bag. 'I have to get to the hospital to see my grandfather. I have to go now.'

'Not before you drink your tea and eat the breakfast I've cooked for you.'

'But I have to …'

Rory waved away his protests. 'The hospital rang this morning and Becky spoke to them. Apparently, your grandfather is sitting up in bed and drinking tea. The person who spoke to Becky said it was something akin to a miracle.' Rory grabbed Jack in a hug and held him tightly. 'You've only gone and saved your granddaddy, Jack. Today is a day to celebrate!'

Jack dropped onto his knees and fell into Rory's embrace and let his tears flow. The last few days had drained him in so many ways, but his grandfather was well and that was all that mattered.

'Let it out, Jack me lad,' said Rory. 'I always feel better after a good ole weep. And what better way to follow it than with a Cill-Arney breakfast!'

Jack surprised himself by making short work of the breakfast. Becky and Sonny entered the shed as he sipped his Roseleaf. A broad smile covered her face and she sat down next to Jack and hugged him

'Your grandfather's going to be fine. The hospital is totally at a loss to explain his recovery.'

'I'm just relieved,' said Jack. 'He was very weak when Morning-Dew and I arrived last night. I was worried that he wouldn't be strong enough to survive.'

'Well survive he did, Jack me lad, and it's all down to you. When are you going to see him?' asked Rory.

'As soon as I finish my tea,' said Jack. He turned to Becky. 'Would you like to come with me? I think it's time you met my grandfather.'

'I would love to,' beamed Becky.

'And don't worry about Sonny-boy,' said Rory. 'He and I will be fine here.'

Jack and Becky stood in the corridor outside Noah's room waiting for the nurse to finish making him comfortable.

'I feel quite nervous,' confessed Becky.

'There's no need,' said Jack. 'He'll love you just like I do.'

The nurse popped her head through the door. 'You can come in now, Jack.'

Jack squeezed Becky's hand and said, 'wait here. I need a few minutes on my own with him.'

Jack stepped into the room. Noah was sat up in bed drinking tea from a plastic cup. His face lit up when he saw Jack.

'Oh Jack, it's good to see you. Come and sit on the bed next to your old grandfather.'

Jack sat on the bed and kissed Noah on the side of his head. 'You're looking much better.'

'And I'm feeling much better, no thanks to this awful tea they serve in these horrible plastic cups. I can't wait to get home and get a decent sup of tea in a mug.'

A doctor walked into the room and stood at the end of the bed. 'Are you Noah's grandson?'

Jack stood up and reached forward and shook his hand. 'My name's Jack. I can't thank you enough for saving my grandfather's life.'

The doctor smiled enigmatically. 'As much as I'd like to take the credit for your grandfather's miraculous recovery, I have absolutely no idea what's happened. When I finished my shift yesterday he was slipping off into a coma and I fully expected that he wouldn't last the night. I came in this morning to find him sitting up in bed drinking tea. We X-rayed him and the tumour has gone.'

Jack looked at Noah and smiled. 'He comes from good travelling stock, Doctor. He's not going to let a tumour beat him.'

'Well something totally beyond my comprehension has happened and I have no explanation for it. But the good news is that your grandfather can go home tomorrow. We just want to make sure we haven't overlooked anything.'

'Thank-you very much, Doctor, for all you and the nurses have done for me. But if you don't mind, I won't be rushing back,' smiled Noah.

'Good luck, Mr Green,' said the doctor, 'and I'm sure we'll be reading all about your case in the Lancet one day!'

The doctor left the room and shut the door behind him. Jack sat back down on the bed and hugged his grandfather close. 'You don't know how good it is to see you looking well again.'

'I'm feeling on top of the world,' said Noah, 'but could I ask you a favour?'

'Anything,' said Jack.

'Could you bring me my baccy tin as I'm desperate for a smoke?'

Jack shook his head and smiled. 'I suppose it was too much to think that you'd give up! I'll ask Dimey to bring it over later.'

'Yer a good lad, Jack. You know that it's too late in the day for me to stop.'

'It would probably do you more harm than good,' agreed Jack.

'I had a very strange dream last night,' said Noah changing the subject. 'It's a bit vague but I can remember some of it.'

'Go on,' said Jack.

'I was in a tunnel … a long tunnel and I was walking towards a bright light. I felt strangely at peace. As I was about to disappear into the light I heard you calling me. I turned around and you ran up to me. You didn't speak … you wrapped me in your arms and I felt this warm sensation moving through me. You stayed with me for a while and then left. When I looked back down the tunnel the light had disappeared. The next thing I remember was waking up in this bed.'

Jack squeezed Noah's hand. 'It wasn't your time, Grandfather.'

Noah smiled at Jack. 'I think we both know what happened. I was dying, Jack until you came …'

Jack dropped his gaze for a second before looking back up at Noah. 'I couldn't lose you, not at this time …'

Noah looked concerned. 'What is it, Jack? Are you in some sort of trouble?'

Jack sighed deeply. Trouble didn't begin to describe it. 'There is a serious threat to my homeland and I have been tasked to find the person who is behind it.'

'It sounds dangerous, Jack. Make sure that you look after yerself.' Noah didn't attempt to disguise his anxiety. He'd spent most of his life worrying about Jack.

'I have two of the truest friends you could ever imagine with me,' reassured Jack. 'And I have to find my father.'

'I often wondered who he was. Yer mother never mentioned him to me. Surely she can help you there.'

The sadness Jack felt about his home and friends resurfaced. He breathed slowly and kept his emotions in check. 'My mother has faded into the spirit world along with all of the other Elves from my village. The gold dust that sustains our world has been stolen and it's my job to find it.'

Noah shook his head. 'I don't begin to understand it, Jack, but it sounds awful sad. A huge responsibility has been placed on yer shoulders?' Then something suddenly occurred to him. 'Hasn't your father disappeared along with the others?'

'That's just it,' said Jack. 'My father isn't an Elf. He comes from Grasslake village.'

'He's human!' said a surprised Noah shaking his head again. 'I'd never have guessed.'

'He's the reason I stayed here and didn't fade away with the rest of the village.'

'Because you're part human?' asked Noah.

'So it seems,' confirmed Jack.

'What's this fellah's name?'

'Roger Thorne,' said Jack.

'And he still lives in the village?'

'I don't know,' said Jack, 'but I'm hoping my friend can help me.'

'And who would that be?' asked Noah.

'She's outside,' said Jack. 'Would you like to meet her?'

'I would indeed,' smiled Noah.

Jack opened the door and called out to Becky. She nervously stepped into the room and stood at the end of Noah's bed. 'Grandfather, this is Becky.' He swallowed hard before carrying on. 'She's my … she's my girlfriend.'

Noah held out his hand. 'It's grand to meet you, Becky. I hope Jack is taking good care of you?'

'Yes he is,' said Becky as she took his hand and sat on the side of the bed

Noah winked at Jack as he sat the other side of him and whispered in his ear, 'she's a grand looking lass, Jack lad.'

*

Chapter Five - London

Jack sat alongside Elensar and Rory as they ate their porridge.

'I must say I love a bowl of porridge in the morning,' said Rory. 'Auntie Bridie always says that it lines the stomach.'

'My grandfather used to say that it warms you from the inside,' said Jack.

'And your grandfather is a wise man,' said Rory, 'it's grand that he's back home again.'

'He's driving poor Dimey mad,' said Jack. 'She has to take him outside for a smoke every hour or so as he can't manage the step down from the caravan.'

'Well I'm sure he'll get his strength back again thanks to you,' said Rory through a mouthful of porridge.

The door to the shed opened and Sonny-Boy came bounding in, quickly followed by Becky. Sonny sat down next to Rory and hopefully slapped his paw onto his knee.

'This is too hot for you, Sonny lad,' said Rory. 'You'll burn your mouth.'

'That won't stop him,' laughed Becky. 'He'll eat anything!'

Rory reached into his pocket and pulled out a biscuit. 'Here you are, Sonny. You'll enjoy that more.'

Sonny snatched the biscuit from Rory's hand and made short work of it and was soon back in the begging position. Becky put the carrier bag full of food down and sat opposite Jack.

'I've got some good news for you. I told you that I would mention Roger Thorne to my mum. Well it turns out she knows the family. Roger left the village over ten years ago and is now living in London. She's sure he works for an environmental campaign group called 'Save the Planet'.'

'Do you know whereabouts he lives in London?' asked Jack.

'No,' said Becky, 'but we don't need to. I'll ring the

agency in the New Year and ask to speak to Roger. I'll tell him that I'm interested in doing some volunteer work for his agency and try to persuade him to meet me here in the village. If not, we can always go down to London to meet him in his office.'

Jack had never been to London; it was a place he had no interest in visiting. Noah had told him that it was full of cars and people and was to be avoided. 'Let's hope that you can persuade him to come here as I really don't relish the thought of going to London.'

'It's only an hour on the train, Jack, and I'll come with you.' She leant forward and playfully squeezed his knees. 'It will be fine, I promise.'

*

Jack spent the next few days visiting his grandfather and was relieved to see him getting stronger and stronger each day. Noah was made up when Jack took Rory and Elensar to visit him. They all got on like a house on fire and they were transfixed by Noah's tales of when Jack was growing up.

It was the day after New Year when a beaming Becky came into the shed with Sonny and sat down next to Jack. 'You and are I going up to London tomorrow to meet Roger in his office. I said we'd be there by midday.'

Jack didn't respond and sat quietly as the conflicting feelings fought battles within him. He wasn't even sure that he wanted to meet Roger and he had absolutely no idea of how he was going to persuade him that he was his son. And that was before he had to persuade him to join the quest to save the Elven land.

And he had to go to London.

'Would you like me to come with you, Jack?' asked Elensar.

As much as he would have liked the Captain's company could he really ask him to come to a place that would be a complete anathema to him? Elensar had great strengths but they were more suited to the Elven world. 'I think this is something that I'll have to do with Becky, but I appreciate your offer.'

'We'll only be gone a day,' reassured Becky. 'Hopefully we can at least persuade him to come back with us. I'm sure you'll convince him if you take him to Waterswood.'

Rory nodded his agreement. 'It makes sense, Jack. As much as Roger may have trouble believing what you tell him, he's not going to be able to deny what he sees with his own eyes.'

'So that's settled then,' said Becky grabbing Jack's hand. 'You and I are going to London tomorrow.'

*

An apprehensive Jack stood on the platform at Glenchester station alongside Becky. She'd been to a local charity shop the day before and bought him jeans, trainers and a warm jacket. As much as he might have looked the part, he most certainly didn't feel it. He'd never travelled in a car, or a bus or a train in his entire life and was about to enter a world that, if he was honest, frightened him.

Becky reassuringly held his hand and whispered words of encouragement. 'It's only an hour, Jack. We'll be there before you know it, I promise.'

Jack fidgeted from one foot to the other. 'I don't think I felt this nervous before I rode on the back of a flying horse.'

'You've flown on a flying horse!' said Becky. 'How cool is that?'

'That's how we travelled to Rory's home village Cill-Arney,' said Jack. 'Troy is just the most beautiful horse I've ever seen.'

'Will I ever get to meet him?' asked Becky hopefully.

'When all of this is over, Becky, and Waterswood is safe and secure, I'll take you there and share this magical world I've discovered with you … and that's a promise.'

Becky looked delighted. 'I'll hold you to that.'

Just at that moment the train rumbled into the station and

the fear that had been lurking deep in the pit of Jack's stomach threatened to overwhelm him. He heard his grandfather's voice in his ear. *Fear isn't yer enemy, Jack. It's yer friend. Let it rest within you and don't fight it.* The train pulled to a stop in front of Jack and the carriage doors slid open.

'Come on,' encouraged Becky and they both stepped into the carriage along with the other travellers. They found two seats together and sat down. Becky snuggled up to Jack and whispered in his ear, 'just sit back and watch the scenery. You might surprise yourself and enjoy it.'

I doubt that very much, Jack thought to himself as he attempted to slow his breathing.

As the train slowly pulled out of the station, the knot in the pit of Jack's stomach tightened. They were soon out into open countryside and Jack did his best to concentrate on it. But as the speed increased, so did Jack's anxiety.

'Why does it have to go so fast?' he asked.

'It has to get to London on time,' laughed Becky, 'otherwise it will hold up all of the other trains and we may have an …' She stopped herself completing the sentence as she didn't want to add to Jack's already increasing anxiety and mention the word accident.

'That's what I've never understood about humans,' said Jack. 'They're always in a hurry. They never take time to enjoy things. You can hardly appreciate the countryside as it's flashing by so fast. And it's the same when they come to the forest – they're always in a rush.'

'You might have a point,' agreed Becky. 'It's just we all get caught up in it. The pace of life is even faster in the city.'

'Even faster!' gasped Jack. 'No wonder they're all falling over with heart attacks.'

'Well there is one advantage of the train going faster,' said Becky.

'And what's that?' asked a sceptical Jack.

'We'll get to London quicker, so your ordeal will be over sooner.'

By the time the train pulled into Paddington Station, Jack was ready to get off. He hadn't enjoyed the experience in the slightest. They joined the throng of people as they disembarked and queued to get through the ticket barriers. They left the station and followed the underpass through to Marylebone Road.

'It's about a ten to twenty-minute walk along this road. It's near a place called Madame Tussauds,' said Becky.

'My grandfather told me about that. It's where all the waxworks are isn't it?'

'I went there on a school trip years ago,' said Becky. 'It's OK if you like that sort of thing.'

It was a cold, crisp winter's day but it made for a pleasant stroll along the Marylebone Road. A mixture of tourists and commuters crowded the pavement, but Jack was so relieved to get off the train that it didn't bother him too much.

'How do people do this day in and day out?' asked Jack.

'I don't know,' said Becky. 'I like coming to London for the odd day out, but I wouldn't like to work here.'

'I couldn't think of anything worse,' agreed Jack.

Just at that moment someone pushed past Jack and ran up to a young girl and slashed at the shoulder strap on her bag with a knife. They pulled the bag from the screaming girl and ran off into the crowds. Their head and face were covered by a hood but Jack didn't hesitate and sped after them as they dodged in and out of the people walking along the pavement.

The attacker was fast, but Jack was faster and managed to catch hold of his hood and pulled him back. He found himself holding onto a young teenage boy who slashed at him with his knife. Jack stepped back and momentarily lost his grip on the boy but as he tried to run away again, Jack tripped him up. The boy stumbled to the ground but quickly got back to his feet but this time he didn't try to run he confronted Jack.

'OK, you wanna be the hero. Try this!' And lunged at

him with his knife.

But Jack was too quick and easily stepped back out of the way. 'Just drop the knife and the bag and I won't hurt you.'

'Dream on,' sneered the boy. 'It's you who's gonna get hurt if you don't get out of my way.'

A crowd had gathered, and Jack heard Becky screaming in the background. 'Let him go, Jack! He's half crazed on drugs. Let the Police deal with him.'

Jack looked into the boy's eyes and could see a mad, vacant stare, but he couldn't let him get away to do the same to someone else. The boy was getting more and more agitated and lunged at Jack with his knife again. Jack neatly side stepped him and grabbed his hand that was holding the knife. He banged the boy's hand against a wall and the knife fell away from his hand and the boy screamed out in agony. Jack kicked the knife away and held the boy in an arm lock.

'Aghhhhhh! Get off me!'

'Stop struggling or I'll break your arm,' hissed Jack and snatched the bag from his hand and dropped it on the pavement. He turned the boy around, pushed him to the ground, and pulled both arms behind his back. He took out some leather twine from his pocket and tightly bound his wrists together before tying him to the pole of a traffic sign. He picked up the girl's bag and handed it back to her.

She grabbed him in a hug and said, 'thank-you so much. My phone and credit cards are in there.'

The bystanders burst out into a spontaneous round of applause as Becky ran up to Jack and embraced him.

'Oh Jack! Are you hurt?'

Jack shook his head. 'I'm fine.'

An elderly man came up to him and said, 'I've called the Police. They'll be here in five minutes.'

Jack turned to Becky and whispered, 'time for us to go. I don't want to be around when the Police turn up.'

People came up to Jack and shook his hand and patted him on the back as he tried to make his way through the crowd gathered on the pavement.

'Well done son,' said an elderly lady. 'It's about time we stood up to these thieving toe-rags.'

Jack nodded and grabbed Becky's hand and pulled her through the crowd. They walked as fast as they could along the pavement towards Madam Tussauds. A Police car with its lights flashing and siren blazing wound its way through the traffic towards where they'd just come from.

'I didn't want to be around when they turned up,' said Jack.

'Why not?' asked Becky. 'You'll be a hero.'

'My grandfather always told me that the Police were best avoided. The travelling community have a huge distrust of them.'

As they fought their way through the crowds, the green dome of Madam Tussauds loomed large in front of them.

'Which way is it?' asked Jack.

'It's called Chiltern Street. Roger said that it's just across from Madam Tussauds.'

They crossed the road, dodging in and out of the traffic and turned into Chiltern Street.

'It's number 14a,' said Becky. 'It's the first block of flats on the right.'

They walked up the steps to the flats and studied the line of buzzers by the side of the door. The words 'Save the Planet' were displayed next to one of them and Becky pressed the button. A woman's voice came out of the speaker; 'can I help you?'

'It's Becky Grainger – I've come to see Roger Thorne.'

'Push the door, Becky. We're on the third floor.'

Becky pushed the door open and they stepped inside. They walked up three flights of stairs and found the 'Save the Planet' office on their right. Becky rang the bell and a young woman came to the door.

'Becky, please come in. Roger's on the phone. He won't be a minute. Can I get you a tea or a coffee?'

'We're OK, thanks,' said Becky.

'Well take a seat. Roger won't be long.'

The woman went back into the office and they both sat

down. Becky reached across and grabbed Jack's hand. 'Are you OK?'

Jack did his best to smile. 'I'm a little nervous.'

'I'm still shaking from that knife attack. I can't believe how brave you were.'

'I didn't really think about it, Becky. I just reacted when I saw what that boy had done.'

The door opened and a tall dark-haired man walked into the reception. 'Becky Grainger? Roger Thorne – nice to meet you.'

Jack couldn't believe his eyes. He was looking at an older version of himself. He'd always put his looks down to his mother, but Roger could have been his twin if they were the same age.

Becky stood up and shook Roger's outstretched hand. 'I brought a friend along. This is Jack Green. He lives near me.'

Roger shook his hand warmly. 'Nice to meet you, Jack. As you two have very kindly come up to London to see me, the least I can do is buy you lunch. There's a really nice pub just along the Marylebone Road.'

*

Chapter Six – Roger Thorne

'I can recommend the vegetarian lasagne,' said Roger. 'That is if you both like vegetarian food,' he qualified.

'That's fine by me,' said Jack not having a clue what lasagne was.

'And me,' agreed Becky.

Roger ordered the food and drinks and they sat down at a quiet table in the corner.

'This place gets really busy at around one o'clock so it's good that we beat the rush.' He took a sip of his water and placed his glass back on the table. 'So, you both come from Grasslake.'

'I do,' said Becky. 'Jack used to live in the old gamekeeper's cottage in Heywood Forest.'

'I know your mum, Becky,' said Roger. 'She used to go to the same school as me, although she's a couple of years older. How is she?'

'Really well,' said Becky.

'And you lived in the forest, Jack. I love that place. I spent so much time there as a kid growing up. It's still one of my favourite forests, especially at bluebell time.'

Jack instantly liked Roger. He could see why his mother cared for him. He was charming and attentive, and most importantly of all, seemed genuine.

'I think you know my mother too,' said Jack tentatively.

'Really?' said Roger. 'Did she go to Ridgeway as well?'

'Er no,' said Jack coyly. 'You met her in the forest. Her name is Ciara.'

Roger was about to sip his drink but stopped mid movement. 'Did you say Ciara?'

'Yes I did,' said Jack.

Shock didn't begin to describe Roger's facial expression. 'Ciara's your mother?'

'Yes she is,' said Jack.

Roger momentarily seemed to be lost for words. 'I er, I haven't seen her for over, let me think … for over sixteen years … how is she?'

How did Jack answer that? She'd faded away into the spirit world. He avoided the question. 'She was fine the last time I saw her a few weeks ago.'

'I never got the chance to say goodbye to her,' said Roger sadly. 'I used to meet her every day in the forest and then one day she didn't turn up and I never saw her again.'

'That must have been when she went travelling,' said Jack.

'Travelling? Where did she go to?'

'She met some friends and ended up going to Ireland,' said Jack staying as close to the truth as he could.

'Wait a minute,' said Roger. 'You said that you lived in Heywood Forest. Surely I would have seen Ciara around the forest as I didn't leave Grasslake for two years after I lost contact with her.'

'She was away for a good while,' said Jack. 'You would've left the village by the time she returned.'

'I often wonder about her,' said Roger sadly. 'I have to admit to being heartbroken when she disappeared without saying goodbye.'

'I think it was circumstances at the time,' said Jack. 'She talks fondly about you.'

That seemed to cheer Roger up. 'Really – please give her my very warmest regards the next time you see her.'

The next time I see her … If I ever see her.

'So, are you both interested in volunteering for 'Save the Planet'?

Jack and Becky exchanged uncomfortable looks.

'We may have misled you slightly,' said Becky. 'We are talking about saving the planet but not quite in the way you might think.'

The waitress interrupted them and placed three plates of steaming hot lasagne on the table.

'Let's eat first,' smiled Roger. 'I always think it's better to discuss things on a full stomach.'

Jack sensed that Ciara was still a source of pain for Roger – that much was obvious from the way he reacted when he mentioned her name. And he understood why, because Roger loved his mother and then she suddenly disappeared without any explanation. He probably hadn't heard a word about her until Jack brought her name up a few minutes previously.

Jack was pleased to find that the lasagne tasted delicious. It consisted of aubergine, mushrooms and onions, all smothered in a creamy tomato sauce and topped with melted cheese and pasta. He had no idea what lasagne was but he didn't like to say when Roger suggested it, but he was glad he went with his choice.

Once they'd finished eating, Roger pushed the plates away to the far end of the table. 'Would you like anything else? They do an amazing treacle sponge and custard. Can I tempt you?'

'I'm stuffed,' said Becky. 'I couldn't eat another thing.'

'Me too,' said Jack.

'Well in that case I'll give it a miss too,' said Roger patting his stomach. 'I could do with losing a few pounds. So, how can I help you?'

Becky looked at Jack and smiled her encouragement. He sipped his water and breathed slowly to relax. He reassured himself that Roger seemed a nice person and would hopefully be open minded about what Jack was about to tell him. It was going to be a case of trusting his instincts and going for it.

'My home village is under threat. I've got six months to save it.'

'Under threat?' said Roger. 'An environmental threat?'

'You could describe it that way,' said Jack.

'Is this a village near to Grasslake?' asked Roger.

'In a manner of speaking …'

'What's the village called?'

'Waterswood.'

Roger thought for a moment. 'Waterswood? I don't think I've ever heard of it.'

'I would have been surprised if you had,' said Jack. 'You're going to find what I'm about to tell you very hard to believe, but I can assure you it's the truth.'

Roger sipped his drink. 'I'm listening.'

Becky gave Jack's hand a reassuring squeeze under the table. He took a deep breath and continued. 'The reason you haven't heard of it is because it's an Elven village and doesn't exist in this world. It's in a … a sort of parallel world. It's hard to explain …'

'An Elven village?' repeated Roger as if doubting his ears.

'Yes,' said Jack, 'and yes, I am an Elf.'

Roger didn't react, much to Jack's surprise – in fact he didn't say anything. Jack pulled his hair back and showed Roger one of his ears. 'I think you'd have to agree that my ears are a little different.'

Roger seemed to be stunned into silence. Jack wasn't sure what else he could say to convince him. Becky stepped in.

'I know it seems far-fetched and you're probably thinking we're a pair of crackpots but Jack's telling you the truth. I found it hard to believe when he first told me, but I can promise you it's true.'

'If I'm honest, Becky, I'm not sure what I'm thinking. What I do know is I've got a huge pile of work waiting for me at the office and I need to get back there to make a start on it.'

'Please!' urged Becky, 'Jack desperately needs your help.'

Roger remained unmoved. 'I've travelled the world, Becky. I spent a year in the Amazon and visited some of the remotest parts of Australia and Africa and I've never come across anything other than human beings or members of the animal kingdom. Now you're trying to tell me that the forest I grew up near to is full of Elves.'

'What about my mother?' asked Jack. 'Wasn't she real enough for you?'

'Now you're telling me that Ciara was an Elf,' said Roger impatiently.

'She's my mother,' said Jack. 'What else would she be?'

Roger got up from the table and walked over to the bar. He took out some money from his wallet and paid the bill. He came back over to Jack and Becky but didn't sit down. 'I'm not sure what you expect me to do but I don't believe in Elves and Faeries and I have absolutely no idea why you have brought this to me, but as I said previously, I have a lot of work waiting for me back at the office and that's where I'm going now.'

Becky stood up and grabbed his arm. 'If it's proof you want, why don't you come to Grasslake this Saturday? Then Jack can take you to Waterswood so that you can see it with your own eyes.'

Roger remained unconvinced. 'I work most weekends and really don't have time for wild goose chases.'

Becky persisted. 'Please Roger – it's only an hour on the train and a short walk to Grasslake. I live in Gables cottage on the edge of the village. Your mum will tell you where it is. What have you got to lose?'

'My mother's and all of my friends' wellbeing are at stake here,' pleaded Jack. 'Just give me a chance to show you that we're telling the truth.'

Roger buttoned up his coat and put on his gloves. 'I wish you both well, but I'm afraid I have more than enough problems of my own to get on with. I really hope you both have long and happy lives. Now I must go,' and marched out of the pub.

*

'Well you tried your best, Jack,' said Rory. 'You can do no more.'

Jack, Rory and Elensar sat on the bench holding mugs of Roseleaf while Becky sat on the beanbag with Sonny dozing at her feet.

'But Morning-Dew said I needed him to join us. We can't undertake the quest without him, 'said Jack.

'I think he may surprise us,' said Becky. 'I could see in his eyes that he was shocked when we told him about Ciara

43

being your mother. I don't think he really took in any of the other stuff we told him about. When he thinks about it, his curiosity about your mother will get the better of him.'

'I hope you're right, Becky,' said Jack, 'but I'm not quite as confident as you are.'

'Well in my experience, the female of the species usually gets it right more than us, Jack me lad, so my money's on Becky.'

'Did you tell him he was your father?' asked Elensar.

'I decided not to. He already thought I was mad so if I'd have told him that, I think it would have frightened him off completely. No, I just hope that Becky is right and that his curiosity gets the better of him.

*

The next few days dragged by for Jack. He just wanted Saturday to arrive so that he would find out if Roger would come. As much as he admired Becky's optimism, his own instincts were telling him that he wouldn't show. Elensar had tentatively suggested that if Roger couldn't be persuaded then they should take Becky, but Jack dismissed that immediately telling him that there was no way he would put Becky in such danger.

Jack could sense Elensar's restlessness. He was a warrior and being cooped up in that shed day in day out was driving him to distraction. The Captain went out every morning for fresh air and exercise and sometimes would be gone for as long as four hours. But what really frustrated Elensar was that he knew that they only had a finite time to succeed in this quest. Morning-Dew had suggested that they had six months at the most to save the Elven land and they had already taken the best part of a month to achieve very little.

The silver lining for Jack was that his grandfather was getting stronger by the day. His appetite had returned and Dimey had even persuaded him to cut down on his smoking much to Jack's amazement. On the odd occasion he would take Rory and Elensar with him and that always cheered

Noah up. In fact, he and Rory got on like a house on fire and they would share a drop of whisky every time they met no matter the time of day.

But Jack's mind never drifted far from Roger. Would he turn up? By the time Saturday came, Jack had gone through the complete spectrum of emotions, ranging from hope to despair. Becky waited at home just in case he turned up but when she and Sonny came to the shed unaccompanied that evening, Jack had his answer. Roger wasn't going to help.

Rory tried to look on the positive side but even he was struggling. 'I have to admit we're stuck without your daddy. Perhaps I should try to persuade him? Surely he'll see that I'm a Leprechaun.'

'I appreciate the offer,' said Jack, 'but I don't think Roger is able to be persuaded.'

'Then we'll have to force him,' said Elensar.

Jack was shocked by his suggestion. 'I'm not sure I could do that. And the last thing we want is the police getting involved.'

'We're dealing with high stakes here, Jack,' said Elensar asserting himself. 'I'm not suggesting we use violence but the threat of it may be enough.'

Then Becky surprised Jack. 'I think he's right, Jack. Roger has made it clear he's not going to help us voluntarily, so we have little choice other than to force him. Once he sees Waterswood he'll realise that you've been telling the truth.'

Jack leant back against the bench wrestling with his conscience. He needed Roger, but he really didn't like the thought of having to threaten him.

'Sometimes, Jack, to achieve your goals, you have to do things that you neither like nor approve of. You may tell me that it's not ethical to kidnap Roger, but do we just sit back and watch your land destroyed.'

Jack was about to argue with him but Elensar continued.

'And are you prepared to run the risk that you will never see your mother or friends again?' Elensar squatted in front of Jack and held his gaze. 'Morning-Dew never told us the full effects of what happens when the magic goes but I'm sure it doesn't make pleasant hearing. These are high stakes, Jack, and high stakes require bold decisions.'

'Roger said that he works weekends,' said Becky. 'I can take you and the Captain to his office tomorrow morning on the early train.'

Jack felt trapped. Elensar's arguments were strong and Becky seemed willing to go along with them. 'OK, we'll go. But promise me that there'll be no violence involved.'

'You have my word,' said Elensar.

*

Jack, Elensar and Becky stood outside Roger's office block. It was ten o'clock on the Sunday morning and the street was empty.

'You know what you have to say?' asked Becky.

Elensar nodded. Becky pressed the buzzer and waited. A voice answered – it was Roger. 'Hello, how can I help?'

'I have a special delivery for you,' said Elensar in a flat tone.

'On a Sunday?' quizzed Roger. 'OK, I'll let you in. We're on the third floor.'

There was a loud buzz and Becky pushed the door open. They quickly ran up the three flights of stairs and pressed the bell outside the 'Save the Planet' office. The door opened a few seconds later and Roger appeared. His face dropped when he saw Jack and Becky. Before he could react, Elensar pushed past him and held the door open. Jack and Becky followed him into the reception area and Elensar shut the door behind them.

'I really haven't got time for this,' said Roger not disguising the irritation in his voice. 'If you don't go I'm going to have to call the police.'

Elensar was wearing a long thick coat that he'd borrowed from Dimey. He took if off and threw it over the desk. He was dressed in his full Border Guard uniform. 'What do you think I look like?'

Roger frowned and turned towards the desk and went to pick up the phone. Elensar snatched the phone and pulled the wire from the wall. He dropped it on the floor and repeated his question. A bemused Roger sat back on the desk.

'Why me? I'm just an ordinary guy who's trying to do some good for our planet. Can't you go away and annoy somebody else?'

'All we're asking is for a day of your time. If you still don't believe us at the end of it, I promise we'll leave you in peace,' said Elensar.

'I fly out to New York for a conference next week. I'm meant to be giving a paper which I haven't even started yet and you're asking me to give you a day.'

'Did you love Ciara?' asked Elensar pointedly.

'What sort of question is that?' asked Roger.

'A very simple one. Did you love her? Yes or no?'

Roger looked uncomfortable. He glanced, first at Becky, then at Jack. 'Yes, I did. I loved her very much.'

'If Jack and I are unsuccessful in our quest, then she will be lost to us forever.'

Roger looked horrified. 'Are you saying she will die?'

Elensar's face reflected the seriousness of their situation. 'As good as …'

Roger held his face in his hands and groaned in resignation. 'If I agree to come with you today, will you give me your word that you will leave me alone to get on with my life?'

'If you remain unconvinced, then I promise you that neither Jack nor I will stop you from leaving.'

'Very well,' said Roger. 'I'll come with you.'

*

Chapter Seven –
A Journey of Enlightenment

Roger sat on the bench sipping the tea that Rory had given him.

'It's called Roseleaf,' said Rory. 'It's Elven in origin. I have some shamrock tea that I brought from Cill-Arney with me. We can try that another time.'

'I'm not planning on spending any more time with you than I have to,' said Roger bluntly. 'I agreed to go to this village and then I will be returning to London.'

'Whatever you say,' said Rory cheerily, 'but I have a feeling that you'll be trying the shamrock tea sooner rather than later.'

Jack walked into the shed with Becky and Sonny. 'The coast is clear. We need to leave straightaway.'

Rory and Elensar packed their rucksacks and threw them over their backs. Sonny wagged his tail in anticipation of the walk that he knew was about to happen.

'OK,' said Jack. 'Let's go,' and led them all out of the shed and across the field to the wrought iron fence. He pulled the corner of the fence back and checked there was no-one about and stepped through. He turned to Elensar and said, 'I don't want to spend too much time out in the open. We'll use the Faery trail across the forest again.'

Jack set a healthy pace and poor Rory had to trot behind them. Roger walked silently alongside Elensar, not commenting or asking any questions, just as he did on the train journey from London. Jack prayed that the experience of entering the Elven land and seeing Waterswood would be enough to convince him to join his quest, but his doubts persisted.

They entered the forest and made straight for the Faery trail. Roger again made no comment and continued to follow Jack in silence. They emerged at the far end of the trail just across from Faery Crossing. Jack stopped by the wishing-well and spoke directly to Roger. 'We'll be going down the well.' He turned to Becky and whispered. 'I'll see you back at the shed later when I bring Roger back.'

Becky looked disappointed. 'Don't you think he'll be going with you?'

'He'll have things to attend to even if he is coming with us.' Jack hugged her and kissed her cheek and ruffled Sonny's ears.

'Elensar, if you go first followed by Rory. Then Roger, and I will go last.'

Elensar stepped onto the wall of the wishing-well and carefully lowered himself down into the dark hole. Rory followed him and then Roger and Jack. Once at the bottom Jack found the torch in its holder and lit it with a match. He led them into the tunnel and eventually through the crevice in the wall and into the small stone chamber. They climbed the stairs and hesitated at the top in front of the wooden door.

Jack pointed to the panel on the door and said to Roger, 'put your hand on the panel.'

Roger did as he asked and nothing happened. Jack handed the torch to Elensar and grabbed Roger's shoulder. He then placed his hand on the panel and the two of them were instantly standing under the Arch of Peace looking across Golden Meadow.

Roger turned a full circle and looked behind him. He looked lost; in fact, he looked bewildered. 'How did you do that?'

'This is the Elven land. That door stops anyone but Elves entering. When you put your hand on the panel it knew that you were human and didn't let you in. It knows that I'm an Elf which is why we're standing here.'

'But we're no more than a mile from the crossing. I know Heywood Forest and the surrounding fields like the back of my hand. I've never seen any of this before,' said Roger.

They were joined by Elensar and Rory. 'So, Roger, welcome to the Elven land,' chirped Rory. 'Isn't it beautiful?'

Roger walked a full circle around the arch shaking his head. 'It's just not possible,' he muttered to himself.

Jack put a friendly hand on his shoulder. 'Why don't we go straight to Waterswood? We can rest there and get some refreshments and I will do my best to explain to you what's happening in our world.'

They followed the path that wound its way through the middle of Golden Meadow and when they came to the brow of the hill, there was another shock waiting for Roger. He stood mesmerised looking down into Woodgate Valley and then up at the towering Fireridge Mountains.

'How can it be? This landscape is more akin to Switzerland than England.'

'That's just it,' said Jack. 'We're no longer in England. This is an Elven land and it's not the only one on this planet. Captain Elensar comes from the Elven homeland which is entered via the mountains on the west coast of Ireland. Just absorb the beauty and enjoy a pleasant walk on a cold winter's day.'

They followed the path down the hill into Waterswood and made straight for Lomund's cottage. Once inside, Jack lit the range and Rory filled the kettle from the hand pump at the sink.

'I'll soon have a sup of tea ready,' said Rory. 'Roger, why don't you take a seat and allow everything you've just experienced to sink in?'

'I'm going to check out the village,' said Elensar. 'I'd like to see if we have any company, welcome or not.' He walked out of the door and Jack sat down at the table opposite Roger.

'So now do you believe me?'

A baffled Roger shook his head. 'To be honest, Jack, I don't know what to believe. I'm a scientist, I have a degree in geology. There's no way we could just step from one world to another.'

'Well that's just it,' chimed in Rory, 'there isn't always an explanation for everything, especially in the world of magic.'

'But there's no such thing as magic,' said Roger.

'And that's where you're wrong, Roger lad. What else would you call it when Jack puts his hand on that wooden panel and takes us into this amazing world?'

Roger tried to speak but the words wouldn't come. He ended up shaking his head in exasperation.

'Don't worry yourself, Roger lad,' said Rory patting him on his shoulder. 'Sit back and relax while I pour the tea.'

As Rory filled three mugs with Roseleaf, Jack leant across and whispered in his ear; 'would you mind leaving Roger and me on our own? I have some things that I need to discuss with him.'

'Of course,' said Rory. 'I'll go and find Elensar in the village.'

Jack picked up two mugs of tea and placed one in front of Roger and sat down opposite him.

'I'm going to get some fresh air,' said Rory as he discreetly disappeared out of the door.

Jack studied Roger as he sat quietly staring into his tea. He remembered his own excitement the first time he came to Waterswood. But there was one major difference – he wanted to be an Elf and wanted to find a magical land. Roger didn't believe in either.

'I'm sorry that we had to almost kidnap you, but it seemed the only way to get you here,' said Jack. 'You are still free to return to London at any time but I'm hoping you can give me a chance to tell you what's been going on here.'

Roger looked lost and totally disorientated. 'I'm thinking that I'm still lying in bed at my flat, in the middle of some bizarre dream. This is just too fantastic to take in.'

'I couldn't believe how beautiful it was when I saw it,' said Jack. 'I first came here last spring at night-time. Golden Meadow was awash with bright yellow flowers and the lanterns glowed on the trees. And then I had my first view of Waterswood and I instantly knew I wanted it to be my home.'

Roger nodded his agreement. 'Who wouldn't want to live here? I can feel the peace and tranquillity of the place even though I'm in shock.' He sipped his tea. 'Although this seems to be helping.'

'Roseleaf has healing properties according to Crystal Oak.'

'Crystal Oak?' asked Roger.

'She's the local Healer; she runs a clinic in the village centre. I met her when I first came to the village.'

'I'm intrigued as to how you found this place as you previously told me that you grew up in Heywood Forest.'

Jack smiled at the memory. 'A friend brought me here. His name is Cyril and he's a squirrel.'

Roger looked disbelievingly at Jack. 'Are you being serious? You have a squirrel as a friend?'

'And a fox called Reggie,' said Jack proudly.

Roger leant back in his seat shaking his head. He folded his arms and smiled warmly at Jack. 'I can see I'm going to have to readjust the way I look at our world.'

'My grandfather has always taught me to be open minded. I think there's a lot more to animals than we think, which is why I can't bring myself to eat them.'

Roger nodded his agreement. 'I stopped eating meat when I was around fifteen much to my parent's disapproval.'

'And that's one area where my grandfather and I disagree.'

Roger finished his tea and placed his mug back on the table. 'I couldn't help noticing that we didn't see any other people as we walked through the village. Where is everybody?'

Jack picked up his tea and took a healthy sip. He held the mug in his hands and felt its soothing warmth. 'Are you ready to hear my story?'

Roger nodded. 'As ready as I'll ever be, I guess.'

Jack cast his mind back to the previous spring and reflected on his former life. Each and every day had been the same. It had been safe, secure and simple. His grandfather had provided a solid foundation for him on which to build his life; a life which had changed beyond anything he could ever have imagined after the attempt on it by Grimley. No two days had been the same since.

He leant back in his chair, breathed deeply and began his tale. 'As I told you in London, I was brought up in Heywood Forest by a traveller called Noah Green. I grew up believing he was my grandfather.'

'Why weren't you brought up by Ciara?' asked Roger.

'She left me with him because she was frightened for both of our lives. She had to get away from Waterswood and thought that it wouldn't be fair to live a life on the run with a young baby. As much as it tore her apart doing it she figured that I would be safer with Noah.'

'Is that when she went travelling?'

'She met Rory's friend Seamus in a forest to the west of Heywood. He took her to his home village of Cill-Arney in Ireland, or to use its Faery name, Emerald Island. Seamus told her about the legend of the Elven home land being hidden in the mountains of the west. My mother went in search of our homeland along with Seamus and his friend O'Reilly, in the hope of persuading the Elves there to help her.'

'Help her to do what exactly?' asked Roger.

'To get rid of the dictatorship in Waterswood.'

'Dictatorship? Was it really that bad?'

'Pretty much,' said Jack.

'And did she find your homeland?'

'No,' said Jack sadly. 'The Elven homeland lays on the other side of a mysterious place called the 'Mist of Time'. She wondered lost for years through different lands on the other side of the mist, and eventually ended up in a land called Lestrada, where she and the Leprechauns were imprisoned by an evil sorcerer called Korrian.'

Roger stood up and walked over to the bay window and rested his hands on the sill as he gazed out onto the lane. He didn't say anything for at least a minute before turning back to Jack and sitting down on the sill. 'I don't mean to appear dismissive, but your story is like a Faery tale. Leprechauns, 'Mist of Time', evil sorcerers; it sounds like a story my mother would have read to me as a child.'

'And twelve months ago, I would have agreed with you, but I've seen it all with my own eyes – I've lived it.' He refilled the two mugs with tea and handed Roger's to him. 'I've ridden on the back of a flying horse; danced with Leprechauns at a ceilidh, and engaged in magical combat with a sorcerer.' He leant towards Roger, his eyes on fire with passion. 'I know that it must sound like I've lost my sanity, but surely you can't deny the reality of where you're sitting now?'

Roger dropped his gaze and picked up his mug of tea. Even though Jack was doing his best to persuade him to join their quest, he felt for Roger. The magical world that was now Jack's life must have seemed like a bizarre Faery tale to Roger. He was probably doubting his own sanity at that precise moment, but Jack had to find a way to convince him.

Roger looked up at Jack through tired eyes. 'You said that you were brought up in the forest by your grandfather. When did you learn that you were an Elf?'

'It was last spring,' said Jack. 'Strangers came in the night and burnt our cottage to the ground. They were trying to kill me … and they would have succeeded if my grandfather hadn't been awake and we both escaped through an underground tunnel.'

'Who would want to kill a young teenage boy?' asked a horrified Roger.

'A young teenage Elf,' corrected Jack. 'It was Elves from this village that tried to kill me.'

'You knew that yet still found your way here? Why would you do that?'

'My grandfather told me about my mother, about how she was frightened which is why she ran from Waterswood and left me with Noah. I made up my mind to find out who I was and where I came from.' He reached inside his shirt and pulled out his Bloodstone. 'Before I left him, my grandfather gave me this.'

Roger's jaw dropped when he saw it. 'Ciara used to wear that around her neck. I remember telling her how beautiful it was.'

'It's our family Bloodstone. My mother and I are descended from one of the five high Elven families.'

Roger stood up and joined Jack at the table. 'Can I have a closer look at the stone?'

Jack lifted the chain over his head and handed Roger the Bloodstone. Roger studied it carefully for a few minutes and Jack saw tears welling in the corners of his eyes. He handed the stone back to Jack and wiped his eyes on his coat sleeve.

'It brings it all back - the times we spent together, wandering through the forest hand in hand. I've never been happier. Then she stopped coming – no warning, no explanation, she just disappeared. I went back to the forest every day for months, but she never showed. I threw myself into my schoolwork and eventually went to University. I left for London straight after University and worked for 'Save the Planet' and I've been there ever since. I've never had any serious relationships, in fact, my last girlfriend said I was married to my job,' he said smiling weakly. He looked at Jack with sad eyes. 'I really loved her, Jack. I would give anything to see her again.'

How did he tell him that she had just faded away into thin air?

Jack breathed deeply and continued his story. 'When I arrived in Waterswood I was arrested by the authorities. I found out then that it was the head of their ruling Council, an evil Elf called Grimley, who had tried to have me killed. And it was him that my mother was running away from. With the help of friends, I managed to escape and went on an adventure that took me to this mystery land of Lestrada. I rescued my mother and we both came back to Waterswood to challenge the Council. But Grimley brought in a band of mercenaries to stop us. What he didn't know was that these mercenaries were in the pay of a mysterious character called Graydon Leah whose sole aim was to steal our gold dust.'

'I assume by your expression, that is significant,' said Roger.

'It's the gold dust that sustains this world. Without it,

this Elven land cannot exist as it is,' said Jack solemnly.

'And the people who live here?' asked Roger.

Jack hesitated - the words momentarily stuck in his throat. 'They've faded back into the spirit world ...'

Horror didn't describe the look on Roger's face. 'Please tell me that Ciara isn't one of them?'

Jack swallowed down the emotions that were threatening to overwhelm him. He knew that this was going to be difficult, but he hadn't expected this reaction from Roger. 'Yes, she is, along with all my other friends from Waterswood.'

Roger looked distraught. 'But that means that she's dead, or as good as.'

'No, it doesn't,' said Jack firmly. 'If we can track Leah down and get our gold dust back, they can all return.'

Confusion and pain in equal measures numbed Roger. 'How can I possibly help with this? What skills do I have that could possibly be of any use to you?'

'A Faery called Morning-Dew has told me that I need a human to join us, along with Elensar, Rory, a Dwarf and a Pixie. She called it the 'Unification of a Common Purpose.'

Roger stood up again and wandered aimlessly around the cottage shaking his head and muttering to himself. Jack hated to see him like that, but he had to tell him what had happened to his mother. Roger returned to the table and sat down opposite Jack. 'So why haven't you faded into the spirit world alongside your mother and friends?'

'Because,' said Jack, 'I'm half human.'

'Half human?' repeated Roger in disbelief. The truth of what Jack had just told him slowly sunk in. 'Are you telling me that your mother had another relationship with a boy?'

Jack's throat was as dry as a desert. He took a large mouthful of tea and swallowed. He put his mug back on the table. He hadn't wanted it to turn out like this. But he had no choice, he had to tell him. 'No, I'm not ... I'm telling you that you're my father ...'

*

Chapter Eight –
An Unexpected Turn of Events

Roger shook his head again but this time not in bewilderment. 'Now I know that's not true. There is a certain thing that has to happen to make a baby and Ciara and I most certainly didn't do it,' he said adamantly. 'We loved each other very much but it was innocent in as much as we held hands and kissed, but I can assure you that was all.'

'And I believe you,' said Jack. 'But it's not quite as simple as you say.'

'Oh, I think it is,' said Roger. 'Let me put it more succinctly, your mother and I never had sex, so I am definitely not your father.'

'When I say that it's not that simple, it's different in the Faery world. It's more of a spiritual conception rather than a physical one.'

'Jack, I am not your father, so that's the end of it, OK?'

'Just let me explain?' urged Jack.

Roger stood back up and started to button up his coat. 'There's nothing to explain. I need to get back to London and make a start on my paper.'

'Please,' said Jack. 'I'll take a few minutes of your time at the most, I promise.'

Roger finished buttoning up his coat and slung his bag over his shoulder. 'Can you take me back to the forest?'

Jack was about to remonstrate with him when the door burst open and Rory came running in. 'Jack! Elensar has captured three Elves in the village centre. He's holding them in that large building in the square. He needs you to come now.'

Rory noticed Roger was ready to leave. 'Are you going back to get your things?'

Roger didn't answer Rory …He stared down at the floor…

'Roger won't be coming with us,' said a dejected Jack.

'He's going back to London.'

'What do you mean you're going back to London? Hasn't what you've seen here convinced you?' said Rory assertively.

Roger fidgeted with the bag strap and didn't look at Rory. 'I have to get back to London. I have a conference to attend next week.'

Rory walked over to Roger and looked up at him so Roger couldn't avoid his determined stare. 'The future of this community and all of the other communities in this valley are under threat. If we fail in our quest, then this land will be lost forever, and you're just going to walk away.'

Roger didn't answer and swallowed nervously.

Rory pointed to Jack. 'This young Elf is still to see his sixteenth birthday and yet he accepts this huge responsibility that's been given to him. Elensar and I live across the water and our communities will not be directly affected by what happens here, but we couldn't wait to come and help Jack.'

Rory looked up at Roger, his eyes blazing with passion. 'And do you know why? Because he's our friend and if either of us were in a similar predicament we both know that Jack would be the first to help. That's what friends do, Roger, they help each other.'

Rory turned away from Roger and walked over to the door. 'Come Jack, we'll go and question these Elves Elensar has captured. Roger, go back to your world and don't worry about us, we'll be fine.' As he walked out of the door he muttered to himself, 'now I know why the Muldoon never wants us to have anything to do with humans …'

Jack went to follow Rory and hesitated by the doorway. 'Can you find your own way to the arch?'

Roger nodded.

'I'll have to take you through. I'll be there in an hour.'

Jack shut the door behind him and hesitated as he caught his breath, then he and Rory marched down the lane towards the village square and Rory did his best to console him.

'We'll find someone else to help us. Surely not all

humans are that selfish?' He corrected himself immediately. 'Of course they're not; Becky and your granddaddy are fine examples of care and compassion.'

'The problem is, Rory, I have absolutely no idea who else we can turn to.'

'Don't worry, Jack me lad,' said Rory with his usual optimism, 'something, or more to the point, someone will turn up.'

They climbed the steps to the community centre, opened the large double wooden doors and stepped into the lobby.

'They're in the main chamber,' said Rory striding over to the door and pushing it open. Jack walked into the chamber and his mood lifted instantly when he saw who was sat on chairs in front of Elensar.

'Albert! Herbert! How good is it to see you?' Jack strode over and shook them both warmly by their hands.

'What brings you here?' asked Jack.

'A friend of yours told us that you would be in need of some warm clothing,' said Herbert. He pointed to several packs on the floor. 'Fred very kindly put these together for you.' Jack recognised the packs that only Fred Fumble could put together.

'A friend?' asked Jack. 'What was their name?'

'She didn't say,' said Albert. 'But she was very pretty?'

'What did she look like?' asked Elensar.

'She had long, brown, wavy hair and eyes like dark pools and was wearing a long, flowing maroon gown,' said Albert.

Elensar, Jack and Rory looked at each other and said simultaneously, 'Morning-Dew!'

The third Elf sat crouched on the chair shrouded in a dark robe. A hood covered his head and face. He said nothing.

'And who are you, my friend?' asked Jack.

The stranger lifted his head and pulled his hood back. Shock didn't begin to describe what Jack felt on seeing his face.

'Green-Jack – we meet again.'

It was Stran Vander.

'I didn't think I would be seeing you again,' said Jack coldly. 'Especially so soon.'

Stran's piercing grey eyes studied Jack forensically. 'May I suggest it's more a case of you not wanting to?'

'You can suggest what you like' said Jack not attempting to disguise the contempt he felt towards the mountain ranger. 'What are you doing here?'

'Albert and Herbert said that they were bringing you mountain clothing. It didn't take too much of an effort to fathom that you're going on a journey. I thought you could use a guide.'

Jack laughed dismissively. 'You think I would ever trust you again?'

Stran stood up and removed his cloak. 'I'm glad I've seen you again as I owe you an apology. I should have told you my reasons for taking you to Willy Venn. I am sorry for what I did.'

It was Jack's turn to study Stran. The apology seemed sincere but how could he ever trust him again?'

'I would fully understand if you refuse my offer, but I am an experienced mountain ranger. My knowledge of the Fireridge Mountains could prove invaluable.'

'What makes you think we're going to the Fireridge Mountains?' asked Jack suspiciously.

'It didn't take a lot of working out,' said Stran. 'You need mountain clothing. I somehow don't see you coming back to the Purple Mountains, so it can only be the Fireridge range.'

Stran was sharp, Jack already knew that, but his deception on the Purple Mountains had left a deep scar on him. He turned to Elensar. 'Captain, can we talk outside?'

Elensar followed Jack out into the lobby and shut the door to the chamber behind him.

'What is it, Jack?' asked the Captain sensing Jack's unease.

'You've probably gathered that I know Stran. He was our guide when we went in search of Willy Venn on the Purple Mountains.'

'Shane told me that Willy led the 'Raven'.'

'He wasn't a very nice character,' said Jack. 'He was a callous brute. I planned to ask him for help in removing the Redwoods from Waterswood and if that didn't work I was going to challenge him to unarmed combat. Stran encouraged me in this and even wanted me to use my magic to defeat Willy. What I didn't know was that if I beat Willy in front of his warriors that he would lose face leading to all out anarchy in the 'Raven' until one of them eventually won through.'

'So, it was a waste of time challenging him,' said Elensar.

'Stran knew what would happen. He was using me to exact his revenge on Willy because he killed an Aelf who had helped Stran in the past.'

'Do we need him on this trip?' asked Elensar.

'His knowledge of the mountains could be useful. He could save us a lot of time.'

'Then we should take him,' said Elensar. 'I will keep an eye on him and if he even thinks of playing any games … then let's just say he will live to regret it …'

Jack nodded and smiled his agreement. Just as he went to open the door to the chamber Elensar put his hand on Jack's shoulder.

'I'm assuming that you defeated this Willy Venn without resorting to magic?'

'I didn't intentionally use magic,' said Jack. 'He grabbed my bloodstone amid the combat and shall we say he received a slight shock off it, but I used everything I'd learnt from your training to defeat him.'

A broad grin spread across Elensar's lips. 'I knew you had what it takes to be in the Border Guard.'

They re-entered the chamber and strode up to Stran who was now sitting down fiddling with his clay pipe. Herbert and Albert were engaged in conversation with Rory.

Jack stopped in front of Stran. 'I will accept your offer to guide us in the mountains, but I warn you not to try any of your tricks.' He pointed to Elensar. 'This is Captain

61

Tathar Elensar commander of the Arminas Border Guard in our homeland who will be joining us. He is not an Elf to be crossed, I promise you.'

Stran put his pipe in his pocket and rose slowly to his feet. He didn't speak at first and locked his piercing grey eyes, first on Elensar, and then on Jack. He spat on his hand and held it out to Jack. 'No games this time, I promise you. You have my absolute loyalty, on that I give you my word.'

Jack grasped his hand and shook it firmly. Stran turned to Elensar. 'It will be a pleasure to travel with an Elven Captain from our homeland.' Elensar followed Jack and grasped Stran's hand in a firm grip.

'Well I'm glad all that's sorted,' chirped Rory. 'I think the least we can do is repay our friends' kindness with a hot meal back at Lomund's.'

'I have to escort Roger through the Arch of Peace first. I'll join you afterwards,' said Jack.

'Roger's not coming with us, even after seeing Waterswood?' said Elensar.

'Apparently not,' chimed in Rory. 'Let him wait, Jack. I'll feed us all first then you can send him on his way with a strategically placed foot up his ...'

'OK, Rory, said Jack interrupting him. 'I get the message. We'll eat first.'

*

Jack opened the door to Lomund's cottage and was surprised to find Roger still sitting at the table. He'd taken his coat off and was sipping tea from a mug.

'I hope you don't mind but I made another pot of Roseleaf,' said Roger lifting the pot. 'I've only had one mug – I'm sure there's enough there for you all if you want one.'

Jack wasn't sure what was going on. He looked alternately at Rory and Elensar before sitting down opposite Roger. 'I thought you were going to wait for me at the arch?'

'I was,' said Roger hesitantly, 'but I used the time on my

own to do some thinking.' He filled a mug with tea and pushed it towards Jack. 'Rory made me realise how selfish I was being. I don't begin to understand what's happening here, but I do know that it's serious. A paper on climate change to be read in front of a bunch of boring academics, well, suddenly it doesn't seem quite so important.' He hesitated before continuing. 'I'd like to join you on your quest if you'll still have me.'

Jack couldn't begin to describe the feelings flowing through him at that moment. At last things were starting to come together. 'Of course I still want you to come. What are you going to do about work?'

'I'll travel back to London tonight and go into the office in the morning. I'll ask one of the others to present the paper and I'll arrange compassionate leave.'

'You do realise that we could be gone for months?' said Jack.

'They'll just have to understand that it's an open-ended arrangement. I'll be back when I'm back.'

Rory skipped over to Roger and planted a kiss on his cheek. 'I knew you were a good sort as soon as I met you. All you needed was a bit of Leprechaun logic to help you on your way. I'll make a pot of my vegetable stew for everybody as a way of celebration.'

*

Chapter Nine – The Seeds of a Plan

'He just changed his mind?'

'After Rory told him a few home truths,' said Jack.

'So, there's a bit more to Rory than first meets the eye,' smiled Becky.

Jack and Becky sat next to each other on the bean bag. Sonny lay on the floor in front of them, quietly snoozing with one eye occasionally flickering open.

'He's always made me laugh ever since I first met him,' said Jack. 'He may be small, but he is mentally strong. There were so many times he kept my spirits up when we were searching for my mother.'

'Did Roger say what time he would get here?' asked Becky.

'He's got a lot of sorting out to do in his office before he leaves. Hopefully he'll be here by seven.'

'Will you be going back to Waterswood tonight?'

Jack nodded. 'Elensar wants to set off tomorrow. We'll need to get back to discuss our plans.'

Becky looked a little disappointed. 'Won't you find it spooky travelling through the forest at night?'

'Don't forget I lived there for most of my life. I think I could find my way through it with my eyes closed.'

Becky snuggled up close to Jack and rested her head on his shoulder. 'I'm trying hard not to worry about you going away again but I have to admit I'm struggling. You will take care, won't you?'

Jack wrapped his arm around Becky and hugged her reassuringly. 'Elensar is Captain of the Border Guard and they are the best warriors in the Elven world. And with Stran Vander joining us we have one of the most experienced guides in the Elven land. He kissed her forehead. 'And you can guarantee that Rory won't let any harm come to me. I really do have some of the best friends you could ever wish for.'

Becky kissed him back. 'I'm starting to realise that.'

Sonny-Boy suddenly raised his head and his ears pricked up. A deep growl rumbled through his entire body. Jack guessed that it was Roger approaching the shed. He stood up and walked over to the door and opened it just as Roger reached it.

'I'm managed to get away a little earlier than I thought.' He stepped inside the shed, removed his backpack and dropped it on the floor.

'Were your work colleagues OK with you taking time off?' asked Jack.

'Not really,' grimaced Roger as he sat on the bench. 'I sort of dropped the guy who's going to present my paper right in it, although I did stay up most of the night writing it.'

'Will you be able to go back there?' asked Becky.

'I should think so,' smiled Roger. 'I've been there over ten years and very rarely taken all of my holiday entitlement, so I think they owe me.'

Jack sat down on the bench opposite Roger. 'I really appreciate what you're doing, not just for me, but my people.'

'In a strange way, it's liberating,' said Roger. 'I've always cared about our planet and how we as humans are destroying it slowly, so this is my chance to really do something to redress that balance.'

'Are you ready to leave now?' asked Jack.

'I'm ready when you are,' said Roger.

Jack put on his jacket and buttoned it up as Roger strapped his backpack on. A sad looking Becky stood up and wrapped her arms around Jack. 'Please be careful.'

'I promise,' said Jack. 'And try not to worry; we'll be back before you know it.'

*

Jack and Roger stepped through the arch into a clear, star filled night. Frost had already started to coat the trees and the grass on Golden Meadow. A radiant moon rested over the Fireridge Mountains, shedding its warm glow across the landscape, caressing its natural beauty.

'I never tire of this view,' said Jack as he walked alongside Roger.

'Why would you? I've travelled the world, and this rivals anything I've ever seen.'

'I know so little of the human world,' said Jack. 'I spent most of my time in the forest with the occasional trip into the surrounding towns and villages. My grandfather wanted to protect me as I was an Elf. I really hated the trip into London when we came to see you. There were so many people – I felt crowded in.'

'I know what you mean,' said Roger. 'I struggled with it when I first worked there but I got used to it in time, although I could never say I enjoyed it. I'm like you, I prefer the countryside.'

They reached the brow of the hill and looked down into a shady Woodgate Valley. No lights flickered in Waterswood. An air of sadness hung over it like a dark cloud. The despair that had been lying deep within Jack threatened to surface again but he swallowed it down concentrating on the task in hand.

He turned to Roger. 'The first time I saw Waterswood, the whole village was alive with flickering candlelight. It looked amazing. I knew that my mother had run away from it and I couldn't understand why. It breaks my heart to see it so empty and lifeless.'

Roger placed a reassuring hand on his shoulder. 'Although I'm not quite sure what use I will be to you, Jack, I will do whatever I can to help you save Waterswood. Anything as beautiful as this valley should be preserved and most definitely shouldn't be left to decay.'

'I appreciate that, Roger. We will sit down with the others as soon as we arrive at Lomund's and I will do my best to explain to you what our task is. But be warned that it's going to stretch your view of the world as you know it.'

'I'm sure it will,' smiled Roger, 'but in a strange way, I'm really looking forward to it. As much as I love my work,

I can only bring the Earth's plight to the attention of the public and governments. I can't actually do anything practical to change things, but this … well it's being thrown right into the deep end.'

Jack looked across at Roger and acknowledged his comment with a nod. He'd only known him a short while but was already starting to feel a bond with him. Roger hadn't mentioned anything about their relationship, so Jack decided to follow his lead and leave that discussion for another time.

They strode through a dark and eerily quiet Waterswood and headed straight for Lomund's cottage. Jack was pleased to see the welcoming candle burning bright in Lomund's bay window. As they lifted the door latch and entered the cottage, they were greeted by the enticing aroma of a Rory McNory stew. Elensar, Stran, Rory, Herbert and Albert sat around the table drinking tea.

Rory's face lit up when he saw Jack and Roger. 'Ah, Jack me lad, Roger - it's grand to see you both. I have the stew ready; I'll dish it up now.'

Rory served up large bowlfuls of his trademark vegetable stew with huge chunks of oatmeal bread. Roger enthusiastically ate his stew and bread followed by a large slice of apple pie and cream for dessert. Once the meal was finished, Albert made a pot of Roseleaf and they all sat around the table ready to discuss their plan.

Jack was pleased to learn that Stran and Elensar had already been talking.

'I've outlined to Stran what's been happening in the valley and he's given me an idea of the lay of the land beyond the Fireridge Mountains. He knows several passes through them and that will save us time. Morning-Dew has said that Leah lives in the eastern lands, but did she give any idea where?'

'I don't think either she or the Faery Queens know much about him,' said Jack. 'We're going to be following our instincts, unless you know of him, Stran.'

'Very little,' said the mountain ranger. 'I've never met

him, but I've heard stories.'

'What sort of stories?' asked Rory.

'He is a character that's cloaked in mystery. He appears and disappears like a ghost in the night. Some say that he is of the spirit world but …'

None of this was reassuring for Jack but if he'd learnt anything from his travels it was to keep an open mind. 'How well do you know these eastern lands?'

'I have travelled the Fireridge Mountains many times. There are vast plains the other side of the mountains that stretch for many hundreds of leagues. They're known as the Running Plains and from what I've seen of them from the mountains, they are bare and desolate. I personally have never travelled them, but I'm told that they are skirted by a range of tall, rocky mountains to the east.'

'Do you know anything of these mountains?' asked Jack.

'Mountain rangers call them the Dwarf Mountains,' said Stran. 'I'm sure you can guess why.'

Stran stood up and walked over to the fireplace. He took out his clay pipe, tapped it on the brickwork and emptied the grey ash into the fire, before refilling it with tobacco. He held the pipe up towards them. 'Does anybody mind if I smoke?'

They all shook their heads simultaneously. Stran crouched down in front of the fire and lit his pipe from a wooden spill. Plumes of grey smoke surrounded him as he sat down in the armchair by the fire. 'Dwarves like nothing better than to fight with Elves, and when there are no Elves, they fight each other.'

Jack looked at Elensar. 'So, we know where we can find our Dwarf.'

'Finding them is one thing; stopping them from cracking our heads open with their axes is another,' said Stran. 'We approach them with caution and respect.'

'Do they ever cross the plains?' asked Jack.

'Never,' said Stran. 'They hate open spaces. They live in the caves and underground most of the time and are experts at fighting in confined spaces.'

'They're as strong as Wood Trolls but not very mobile,' confirmed Elensar.

'Well I'm hoping that we don't have to resort to combat,' said Jack. 'I'm pinning my hopes on a diplomatic approach.'

'They may even know of this Leah's whereabouts,' speculated Rory.

'Let's hope so,' said Jack.

Stran emptied his pipe on the hearth and replaced it in his pocket. He joined them at the table, his piercing grey eyes narrowed as he focused on Jack. 'The magic in this valley is fading. Your magic is fading, Green-Jack. How do you expect to challenge a person as powerful as Leah without any magic to protect you?'

'The Faery, Morning-Dew, assures me that my magic will return as I near the gold dust. She has also told me that I need to be accompanied by a Dwarf, a Leprechaun, a human, an Elf and a Pixie. She called it the 'Unification of a Common Purpose.'

'I have no idea what that means,' said Stran. 'Did she explain it to you?'

'I think it's intended to provide a united front to Leah. Quite how it works I'm not sure.'

'This Faery asks much of you, Jack,' said Stran grimly. 'How are you expected to confront such a being with so little knowledge?'

'Because, Stran, the alternative is much worse. If we don't at least try, this beautiful land will be no more.'

Stran dropped his gaze and sat quietly for several moments. When he looked back up, Jack saw the steely determination in his eyes. 'Then we must do as you suggest. What little skills I possess are yours.' He reached behind him and picked up his rucksack. He took out a bottle of Peardrop and placed it on the table.

'Now that's an Elf after me own heart,' chirped Rory. 'What better way to seal a deal than to share a drink? I'll get the glasses.' He almost danced over to the cupboard by the sink and retrieved several glasses and placed them on the table. Stran half-filled each glass with the golden liquid and Rory pushed them around the table in front of each one of his friends.

He picked up his glass and looked at Jack. 'I know you don't drink, Jack me lad, but I think that this is one of those occasions that warrants one. Let me propose the toast. If you would all please be upstanding.' They all stood and raised their glasses. 'To the wonderful people stood around this table; I wish them all good health and happiness. But most of all, I wish the 'Unification of a Common Purpose' the success it so desperately needs.'

Jack held his breath and downed his Peardrop in one. He looked at Roger as he emptied his glass and wondered what strange and intriguing thoughts were circling through his head at that moment.

*

Jack found Roger sitting on a bench outside the front of Lomund's cottage. He shut the door behind him. 'Do you want some company?'

Roger looked up at him and smiled warmly. 'Of course - it's such a beautiful evening I thought I'd get some fresh air.'

'I've had precious little chance to enjoy this view,' said Jack sitting down on the bench next to Roger.

'I've always liked the outdoors,' said Roger. 'It's in my blood. It's surprising that I ended up working in London.'

They both sat quietly looking out onto the moonlit Waterswood. Although Jack didn't know Roger that well he sensed his unease. He would have been amazed if Roger had taken everything that had happened to him over the last few days in his stride.

'This must all seem pretty strange to you,' said Jack.

'Just a little,' said Roger. 'But at least I now realise the scale of the challenge we face.'

'You can still change your mind,' said Jack. 'We would all understand.'

'I wouldn't dream of it,' said Roger, seemingly a little offended. 'Besides, I know that you need me as part of this 'Unification of a Common Purpose'.'

Jack nodded his agreement. 'I do …'

'Although there is something I'd like to ask you.'

'You can ask me anything,' said Jack.

'Stran mentioned that you had magical powers. What did he mean?'

'It's probably one of the most difficult parts to accept when you enter the Faery world, but I can assure you that magic exists. The energy originates in the Earth's core and is channelled into the atmosphere by the gold dust we were talking about. The gold dust is one hundred per cent pure. This energy is an elemental power, or to use the Elven name, Koehtia. The word Koehtia actually translates as 'Earth Magic'.'

'And you can summon this Koehtia?' asked Roger.

'Yes, I can,' said Jack.

'When were you first aware of it?' asked Roger.

'I told you about my fox friend called Reggie. The first time I met him was just after he had been hit by a car and he laid lifeless in the gutter. He didn't have a mark on him but when I felt his chest I couldn't detect a heartbeat. I tried heart massage for several minutes, but he didn't respond. I was desperate to save him and worked feverishly massaging his heart.

It was then I felt this energy run through my whole body. It's difficult to describe but it surged into my hands and into Reggie's body and he jolted back to life. I sat back in a daze not really aware of what I'd done but Reggie made a full recovery and he's still prowling Heywood Forest to this day.'

Roger shook his head in amazement. 'That is powerful,' he said emphasising the word 'is'.

'I also saved Becky's life when I first met her,' said Jack. 'I found her face down in Millar's Pond. I didn't realise at the time that she was dead but the Koehtia brought her back to life.'

71

Roger didn't respond. He sat in stunned silence.

'My Koehtia is barely detectable now because of the missing gold dust and our land will be destroyed if we don't find it.' He stood up and drank in the image of Waterswood as if he was frightened he might not ever see it again. 'So, the stakes are pretty high.'

Roger stood up beside Jack and followed his gaze and breathed, 'I'm slowly beginning to realise that …'

*

Chapter Ten – The Journey Begins

Jack stood alongside Elensar and Rory next to the wishing-well in the main square. Stran was helping Roger with the one of the winter backpacks that Herbert and Albert had brought for them. They had all indulged in a breakfast earlier that only Rory McNory could muster and were preparing to start on the first leg of their journey.

Herbert quietly walked up to Jack and whispered in his ear. 'I'm sorry that Albert and I won't be joining you, but I really think we'd be more of a hindrance than a help.'

'You've been a great help already,' replied Jack. 'None of us expect you to come on this trip. Go back to Mountpass and prepare the people for our return. This is the start of a new era in our land.' He shook them both warmly by the hand before strapping on his backpack. They were all packed and ready – a combination of anxiety and anticipation surrounded them like the approach of a thunderstorm.

Jack looked at Stran as he cleaned his clay pipe with a penknife. 'I'm assuming you're happy to lead us on the first leg of the journey?'

Stran put his penknife and pipe back in his pocket and nodded his agreement. 'There's a trail that takes us directly east. We'll follow that to the foot of the mountains and through a pass I know that will bring us out onto the plains on the other side.'

'No mountain climbing?' asked Rory.

'Not yet,' said Stran curtly, 'but I'm sure there will before this journey is over.'

'We'll worry about that when we get there,' said a visibly impatient Elensar. 'We need to leave now. If the weather is kind to us we can make good progress across the plains by nightfall.'

They all said their farewells to Albert and Herbert before Stran set off across the square and onto the lane that led eastwards out of the village. Elensar had helped himself to a longbow and sword that had been taken from the Redwoods by Shane and his warriors. Jack took only a short sword and dagger which he strapped to his belt. Rory had a short sword and Roger had to be persuaded to take a dagger.

'I have no idea how to handle a weapon,' he protested.

It was Elensar who insisted that he take the dagger as a safeguard. 'We have no idea what dangers we may face so you need something to protect yourself or save one of your colleagues should the need arise.'

Roger nodded that he understood but still felt uneasy as he sheathed the dagger in his belt.

It was a freezing cold, dull grey day which did little to lift their spirits. And as soon as they exited the cover of the village, they walked headlong into a chilly, easterly wind.

'Holy mother of Leprechauns,' complained Rory as he blew on his hands. 'I'm not used to such biting winds. I think my fingers are going to drop off.'

'Get used to it,' said Stran in his usual direct manner. 'This is mild to what we can expect when we get to the Dwarf Mountains.'

Jack put a friendly hand on Rory's shoulder and whispered, 'don't take him to heart, it's just his way.'

'I think he must have missed out on charm school as he was growing up,' winked Rory.

They entered the pass through the Fireridge Mountains two hours after leaving Waterswood and emerged onto the Running Plains by midday. Rory hinted at stopping for lunch but neither Stran nor Elensar would hear of it. They continued their trek into the biting wind until the light started to fade as evening approached.

Elensar looked all around him for any sign of cover but the landscape was bare. Stran stood to his side looking disinterested.

'If you're looking for shelter don't waste your time because there isn't any.'

'I hope you're kidding,' said Rory, 'as this wind is cutting through to my bones.'

'Do I look like an Elf who jokes about anything?' asked

a stone faced Stran.

Rory turned away and whispered to Jack, 'ask a stupid question.'

Stran and Rory were total opposites, thought Jack. Rory saw the humour in everything while Stran had no sense of humour whatsoever. But Jack knew that the company would have need of diverse qualities during their quest.

Elensar dropped his backpack onto the ground and opened it. He unstrapped a cylindrical pack and unfurled it. 'This is heavy canvass, we can use it as a windbreak.' He turned to Jack and Roger. 'Can you help me stick the poles into the ground?'

It was a struggle against the constant wind, but they managed to get the break up. Elensar had them all collecting dead wood to make up a camp fire. Jack couldn't call on his Koehtia to generate a spark, so he had to resort to more traditional methods and used matches to light dry tinder. It took several attempts with the wind swirling around but they eventually had a fire blazing and Rory soon had a pot of Roseleaf brewing. He handed out mugs of hot tea to everyone before sheltering behind the windbreak.

'I've always hated the cold,' he moaned. 'I think I'm going to miss that warm bed in Lomund's cottage tonight.'

Stran sat to the side of him and lit his clay pipe with a burning twig from the fire. 'I suggest you stop complaining and save your energies for the journey ahead.'

'I'm not complaining, I'm just saying,' said Rory. 'And don't have any worries about my ability to suffer hardship because I survived the 'Mist of Time' and take it from me, Stran, this is like a pleasant stroll in the countryside in comparison.'

'Rory is a seasoned traveller, Stran,' said Elensar. 'He's the most loyal friend anyone could ever wish for. He will play his part as we all will.' Stran studied Elensar without replying. 'And make no mistake, if I had any doubts about him he wouldn't be here.'

Rory nodded his appreciation to Elensar and smirked triumphantly at Stran. 'And just to show I don't bear grudges I'll even cook your supper tonight.'

*

They all huddled in their sleeping bags after the supper things had been cleared away. The stew was hot and filling and they all felt the better for eating it. But it was going to be a cold night, especially as the fire was now reduced to a small pile of glowing embers, and there wasn't any more wood to be found on the empty and desolate plains.

Jack lay next to Roger as they both looked up into a star filled sky. Stran puffed quietly on his pipe as Rory and Elensar tried to sleep. Jack used the opportunity to speak with Roger.

'How are you finding it so far?' he asked.

'I've never been keen on the cold,' said Roger. 'That's why I always avoided the polar expeditions. I tended to volunteer for the hotter climes when it came to travelling.'

'I may be wrong,' said Jack, 'but I don't think we're going to see much sun on this trip.'

'I'll survive,' said Roger. 'I'm used to hardship on my trips. When I was in the Australian outback there was little food and water at times, but I got by.'

'It can be quite surprising how little you can survive on,' agreed Jack.

They sat quietly for several minutes. The only sound being the whistle of the wind as it flew around the canvas break.

Roger broke the silence. 'I've just realised that the stars are the same here. There's the North Star and the Plough.'

'And why wouldn't they be,' said Stran abruptly. 'You're in a different land not another planet.'

Rory sat up and glared at Stran. 'Why do you always have to be so smart? Roger was only saying.'

'I say it as it is, Rory. I have little truck for small talk.'

'Well don't ever visit Cill-Arney then, because we spend our days just chatting away ... And a fine time we have too.' Rory slumped back down and pulled his sleeping bag over his head. Jack reached across and gave his shoulder a reassuring squeeze.

Roger leant over towards Jack and whispered. 'Will Rory be OK?'

Jack nodded and smiled. 'It will take more than Stran Vander to wipe the smile from Rory McNory's face.'

*

The weather didn't ease over the coming days and nights. In fact, it took a turn for the worse as they were subjected to periodic bouts of icy rain, sleet and snow, with no shelter to speak of. Even Rory's natural optimism started to wane after the fourth day of continuous wind, rain and snow.

'Remind me to never complain about the rain in Cill-Arney ever again. I can't remember what it's like to feel warm.'

Jack looked across at Stran but even he was too cold to make a sarcastic comment. They'd all changed into their mountain clothing after the second day. Without it, Jack was sure they couldn't have survived the constant onslaught. They could never find enough wood to keep a fire going for more than a few hours. Sleep only came in fits and starts because of the biting cold and their energy levels suffered as a result.

The bleak plains seemed to go on forever. Seven days after leaving Waterswood they were still trudging through a bland and barren landscape. Jack could feel the resolve in the company weakening. Nobody said anything but that made it even worse. Jack needed them to express their anxieties and concerns, but it was virtually impossible as the wind whistled by them and they were subjected to alternate rain and snow showers. And by the time they stopped for the night they were all too exhausted to talk.

But halfway through the second week a remarkable change in weather happened. The wind stopped suddenly during the night and the rain and snow disappeared with it. For the first time since they left Waterswood they woke up to relative peace and tranquillity.

Rory almost leapt out of his sleeping-bag and did a jig of joy around his friends. 'Come on, get up. The wind has gone, and it's taken the snow and rain with it. I'm minded to make a good ole Cill-Arney fry for everybody.'

Elensar dragged himself out of his sleeping-bag and surveyed the horizon for the first time in days. 'It's clear for as far as I can see. I think we may have a chance of making some real progress today.' He turned to Rory. 'I'm sorry to disappoint you but I really think we need to have a light breakfast and get on our way. We may not get many more chances to cover some serious ground.'

As much as Rory wanted the cooked breakfast, he understood. 'OK, Elensar, but promise me we'll have a good fry as soon as we reach the mountains.'

Elensar smiled warmly. 'I promise.'

They were packed and on their way within half an hour and the mood in the company had lifted noticeably. Stran kept his own council while Rory jabbered away to Elensar. Jack and Roger walked quietly behind them. Low grey clouds filled the sky and did little to brighten up the dull landscape, but the absence of the wind was reward enough for them all.

Roger leant across to Jack and whispered, 'Stran is so different from you all. How do you know him?'

'I met him a few months back when he guided us on the Purple Mountains in the north. I'm not sure I still fully trust him but his experience as a guide could prove invaluable. Elensar will keep his eye on him as will I.'

'He hasn't said a word to me since I arrived,' said Roger. 'I don't think he likes me.'

Jack smiled with a mixture of irony and amusement. 'Stran doesn't like anybody, Roger … and that includes himself.'

'Elensar seems to be very focused and Rory makes me laugh. You have two loyal friends there.'

'I'm very lucky,' agreed Jack. 'Elensar is not just a great warrior but he is a fine Elf. Rory will keep us all going when we're tiring. I couldn't wish for two better friends.'

'I just hope I can prove my worth on this quest. It's so far removed from anything I have ever done in my life before. My friends at 'Save the Planet' were asking me where I was going and why I had to leave at such short notice.'

'What did you tell them?' asked Jack.

Roger hesitated before answering and looked across at Jack. 'I told them there was a crisis in the family.'

Family – he used the word family. Does that mean that he accepts I'm his son? Jack decided to leave it and nodded a smile. He was glad that Roger was with him.

The plains continued to stretch for a far as the eye could see. There was nothing else other than sandy dirt for miles and miles. Jack wondered what Tyler would have made of it. There was absolutely nothing of beauty to catch his eye but Tyler professed to find beauty in anything. He smiled to himself. *I think even you, Tyler, would struggle to find beauty in this!* But he was relieved that the wind had dropped and the sky, although cloudy, didn't show any imminent signs of rain or snow.

It was early afternoon when they came across a cluster of huge boulders sat large and lonely in the middle of the plains, which provoked a comment from Rory: 'It's only taken ten days for us to find something to look at.' He turned back to Elensar. 'Please say that we can stop for a sup of tea and a snack. My throat is as dry as the inside of a Leprechaun's boot and I'm weak with hunger.'

Elensar surveyed the sky all around them and reluctantly agreed. 'It looks like the weather is going to hold but I don't want to waste too much time.'

'Aww, I've always said that you're a grand Elf, Captain Elensar.'

They gathered some wood for a fire and Rory soon had a pot of Roseleaf brewing. He reached inside his rucksack for the food to make their lunch.

'You seem to have an endless supply of food in that rucksack?' said Roger.

'It's what we call a Cill-Arney rucksack, Roger me lad,' winked Rory. 'Jack's friend, Tyler could never quite believe how much food we could pack inside. We Leprechauns can't do a thing if we're hungry so when we go travelling we make sure we have plenty of grub to keep us going.'

Roger helped him to prepare a snack of bread, cheese and dry fruit, and they were back on their way again within the hour. The food had given them a much-needed energy boost and they set off with renewed vigour.

They'd only covered a few hundred metres when Elensar suddenly stopped. Jack walked up beside him and said, 'what is it?'

Elensar didn't respond and turned a full three hundred and sixty degrees, his eyes carefully studying the horizon. Stran appeared by his side. 'What can you see?'

Elensar shook his head. 'I can't see anything but listen carefully.'

They all listened intently and scanned the horizon for whatever it was that was bothering the Captain, but nobody saw or heard anything.

'I can hear a faint rumble in the distance – probably a league, or a bit less, from here. I think it's coming from the north.'

'Aww, Elensar, please don't tell me it's thunder, because if it is, there'll be a rainstorm following it,' said a despondent Rory.

Elensar lay on the ground and placed his ear on the sandy dirt - the others silently looked on. He lay there for several seconds before raising his head and turning to Stran. 'I'm sure I can sense a vibration. Do you have any idea what it could mean?'

Stran shrugged his shoulders; 'it could be anything.' He carefully studied the northern horizon. Elensar and Jack stood either side of him and followed his eye line. The three of them didn't speak but then Jack spotted something in the distance.

He pointed towards it. 'Look! There's a dust cloud. It must be a storm coming in.'

But Elensar wasn't convinced. 'The ground is definitely vibrating – I've never known a storm do that, no matter how severe.'

They all stood quietly watching the cloud slowly come towards them. It was only a matter of seconds before they all heard the faint rumble and felt the vibrations in the ground.

'It could be an earthquake,' said Roger. 'I experienced one when I was in Japan some years ago.'

'An earthquake!' said Rory not disguising the alarm in his voice. 'Does that mean we're all going to get swallowed up?'

'Let's not jump to any conclusions,' urged Elensar. 'We'll calmly assess the situation and then decide what to do.'

The dust storm continued to move steadily towards them. The tension caught them in its vice-like grip. Nobody spoke – they stood rooted to the spot like statues. They all carefully scrutinised the approaching dust cloud looking for any clue of what it could be. The rumble grew in intensity as the white cloud drew nearer and nearer.

'Elensar,' said Rory in a trembling voice, 'shouldn't we do something?'

'Like what!' snapped Stran. 'There's nowhere to run too so we're as well standing here until we know what it is.'

The words were barely out of his mouth when they heard a shrill squeal beneath the rumble. Realisation followed by a look of alarm spread across Elensar's face like a rash. He turned to his friends and screamed: 'Run for the boulders!'

Jack was about to question him but Elensar roughly pulled him around and pushed him back towards the boulders. The rumble built in intensity to the point where they could barely hear each other speak and the dust cloud was less than half a kilometre away.

They all ran as fast as they could but the heavy packs they carried slowed them down. Jack focused on the boulders and didn't risk looking towards the fast approaching dust cloud. More shrill squeals penetrated the

81

deep rumble and Jack suddenly realised what it was that was coming towards them. The last time he heard a similar cry it was Troy bidding him goodbye.

He looked towards the moving cloud and could make out a herd of jet black wild horses stampeding towards them and Jack and his friends were in their direct line of travel. If they didn't make the cover of the boulders they would all be trampled to death. Jack ran as fast as his legs would carry him and tried to dismiss the screaming horses from his mind. The noise of their hooves pounding the dusty plains reached deafening proportions and Jack knew that they were only a matter of a few hundred metres away.

But Jack's legs ate up the ground and carried him to the safety of the boulders with time to spare. He threw himself down in between them and was quickly followed by Roger, Stran and Elensar. Jack threw off his backpack and looked for Rory. He was horror struck when he saw him sat on the open ground clutching his ankle.

Jack didn't hesitate and ran from out of the cover of the boulders towards Rory as fast his he could. Despite the deafening noise of the stampede he heard Roger and Elensar call after him, but he didn't hesitate and covered the fifty metres or so in seconds and lifted Rory in his arms. But the herd of black horses was nearly on them and there was no way he and Rory would make it back to the cover of the boulders.

He dropped Rory to the ground next to him and stood proud and erect, staring straight at the stampeding black stallions. They were so close he could see their flared nostrils and ivory teeth. They were creatures of beauty but in a matter of seconds he and Rory would be trampled to death under their pounding hooves. Jack reached inside of his shirt and pulled out his Bloodstone and held it tightly in his right hand. He wrapped his other arm around Rory and pulled him close.

He stared directly into their dark eyes as he caressed the Bloodstone between his fingers. Rory shook uncontrollably next to him and buried his head in Jack's coat. But Jack continued to stare at the stallions as they bore down on him. Each stride bringing them nearer and nearer.

But Jack felt no fear.

The Bloodstone felt warm and alive in his fingers – it was going to protect him, he knew it. The stallions were only a few strides away when they appeared to go into slow motion, and instead of running over Rory and him they parted and ran either side of them. Wave after wave of jet black stallions stampeded past them, not touching a hair on either of their bodies. The noise of their hooves slamming into the dusty ground drowned out the outside world; their squeals of excitement rang in Jack's ears as they galloped past.

And just when it seemed as if it would go on forever, the last of the stallions left them in their wake and galloped off towards the southern plains. The deafening sound of their hooves on the ground trailed off as they disappeared into the horizon. Rory looked up to him, his eyes portraying the fear that coursed through him.

'Are we dead, Green-Jack?'

Jack put the Bloodstone back inside his shirt and knelt by him and cupped his freckly face in his hands. 'Well if we are, Roger and Elensar have joined us.'

Rory followed Jack's gaze and saw Roger and Elensar sprinting towards them. Roger fell upon Jack and wrapped him in his arms and Elensar did the same with Rory. They all held each other as Stran casually strolled over to them.

Roger eventually let go of Jack and looked as if he couldn't believe his eyes. 'I thought you'd been trampled to death …'

Jack was bemused, maybe even shocked by Roger's reaction, but he was relieved that he and Rory were OK. Rory dusted himself down and said, 'Well at least now we know why they're called the Running Plains.'

*

Chapter Eleven – The Dwarf Mountains

Rory leant against a large boulder as Elensar bandaged his ankle. Stran tended to the fire he and Roger had made when they returned to the shelter of the boulders. Roger sat down next to Jack and handed him a mug of Roseleaf.

'Here drink this – they say that hot sweet tea helps with shock.'

Jack took the tea from him and slowly sipped it. Elensar finished binding Rory's ankle and poured himself a mug of tea and sat down by the fire.

Rory felt his ankle and smiled at Elensar. 'You've done a grand job, Captain. Is there no end to your skills?'

'It was just a slight sprain,' said Elensar. 'You'll be back to normal in a day or so.'

'I'm not sure what happened,' said Rory. 'I was running after you all when my ankle turned over. I went down so quickly that I bumped by head. I think it was the extra weight I was carrying because of my backpack. But Jack saved the day. If he hadn't have come back for me I'd be a mangled mess on the plains.'

'I don't understand why you're both still alive,' said Roger. 'Why didn't you both get trampled to death?'

'Ah, that's down to Jack,' said Rory. 'I just closed my eyes and hung onto him for dear life.'

Jack wasn't completely sure what happened either. There were two possibilities. 'I've always had a connection with animals ever since I was a child. I've befriended foxes, badgers, and even rats in the past. I looked into the stallions' eyes and for a second it was as if we knew each other.'

Stran lit his clay pipe with a burning twig from the fire and leant back against a rock in front of Jack. He created clouds of grey smoke around him and spoke in his usual matter of fact way. 'I've never known anyone befriend animals. They don't have feelings like us, only instincts. I think another explanation more likely.'

'And what would that be exactly,' said Rory testily.

'I don't think Jack's magic has totally left him.'

'And you would be the expert now,' said Rory not attempting to hide his contempt for Stran.

'He may have a point,' said Jack surprisingly. 'I held my Bloodstone in my fingers as they approached. The herd parted at the last minute and galloped either side of us.'

'It looked like you'd both been trampled to death from where we stood,' said Roger. 'I couldn't believe my eyes when you were both left standing there unscathed.'

'Well whatever it was you're both OK,' said Elensar. 'We will camp here for the night and give Rory's ankle a chance to heal. We can resume our journey tomorrow morning.'

*

They set off early the next morning and were relieved that the weather held. The cloud was low and the temperature still below zero, but there was no biting wind and no rain or snow. The strapping on Rory's ankle did its job and they made good progress during the morning. They were all a little anxious when they set off and kept their ears alert and eyes peeled for any sign of stampeding horses. But as the day wore on, Rory's incessant light-hearted banter soon took their minds off their concerns and the previous day's trauma was forgotten.

It was as evening approached that Elensar stopped and peered ahead into the grey gloom ahead of them. The others exchanged concerned looks. Jack joined him.

'What is it, Elensar? You look concerned.'

'Don't worry,' said Elensar. 'I'm sure I can see the grey and white peaks of mountains in the far distance.'

'And that would be the Dwarf Mountains?' asked Rory optimistically.

Elensar looked down at him and smiled. 'Let's hope so. I think we should push on and made camp at the foot of them tonight. It shouldn't take any more than a couple of hours to reach them.'

'Well, let's hope the Dwarves are pleased to see us?' said Rory.

'I doubt that very much,' said Elensar as he adjusted his backpack and strode off across the plains.

The journey to the mountains was uneventful much to the relief of everyone and they arrived an hour after nightfall. They found plenty of dead wood and soon had a blazing fire.

'Won't that make it easy for the Dwarves to spot us?' asked Rory.

'They're going to find us anyway,' said Elensar. 'It may as well be sooner rather than later.'

'Well I just hope they give us time to eat first,' joked Rory.

'Dwarves are no joking matter,' said Stran in his usual blunt manner. 'You'd do well to take this more seriously.'

Rory was about to react, but Jack distracted him. 'Why don't you make one of your vegetable stews, Rory? I'm sure Roger would be glad to help you.'

Roger saw that Jack was trying to keep the peace. 'Of course – let me know what you want me to do.'

He and Rory peeled and chopped the vegetables while Jack, Stran and Elensar surveyed their surroundings.

'You have some knowledge of Dwarves, Stran?' asked Elensar. 'Is that from personal experience?'

Stran shook his head. 'I have never been this far east before. But I know of other mountain rangers who have.' Stran took his pipe out of his pocket and started to clean the bowl with a penknife, something he always seemed to do when he was uncomfortable. 'Some of them never came back … the ones that did vowed never to return.'

'It does not surprise me,' said Elensar. 'The Dwarves in my homeland have little to do with us. They live in the mountain region of the south lands and rarely venture out of them. I once bumped into a Dwarf patrol some years ago when we were tracking wood trolls in the forests of the south lands. They attacked us without warning, but we were on horseback and easily outran them.'

'The two Dwarves I met in Korrian's castle seemed hell bent on cracking open my skull with their axes,' said Jack. 'But they crumbled in front of my eyes when they saw my magic.'

Stran lit his pipe with a burning twig from the fire. Clouds of grey smoke filled the air surrounding him as he thoughtfully puffed on it. 'You're not going to have that luxury this time.'

Jack knew he was right. It made him feel vulnerable. 'So how do we approach them?'

'The only way we can,' said Elensar. 'With tact and diplomacy. We have to convince them of the great danger that Leah presents to us all.'

'And you think they will listen?' asked Stran, projecting his doubt as clearly as the thick grey smoke that surrounded him.

'We have to try as there are too few of us to engage them in combat,' said Elensar.

'It saddens me to see so much distrust and fear in this Faery world that I've entered. I thought I'd left war and conflict behind me in my old life,' said Jack.

'There is conflict everywhere,' said Stran. 'It is the nature of being. It may surprise you to know that I too was young and idealistic once, but life soon washes that away with its cruelty and greed.'

Stran had given little of himself in all the time that Jack had known him. Maybe life had made him cynical as it did to so many people. Jack was determined to hold onto his idealism no matter how challenging his life became.

'I have to find a way to convince the Dwarves of the danger we all face. It is my Elven land that is currently under threat, but it is only a matter of time before this Leah threatens other lands. Dwarves are not stupid, they will surely understand that.'

'I admire your optimism, Green-Jack, but I think it may take more than a teenage Elf to persuade them,' said Stran.

Stran's indifference prompted an irate response from Elensar. 'You will not insult Jack in my presence. He deserves your respect and you will give it to him, ranger.' Stran didn't answer and stared coldly at Elensar. 'Don't make me repeat myself,' said Elensar squaring up to Stran.

Jack stepped in between them. 'It's OK, Elensar, it's just Stran's way. He makes a habit of underestimating people, don't you Stran.'

A trace of a smile crossed Stran's lips. 'You're right, of course, Jack. Pay no attention to me, Elensar. I'm tired from our long trek across the plains.'

The tension was interrupted by Rory's cheery voice. 'Right you three – the stew is nearly ready. Sit yourselves around the fire and Roger and I will serve it up.'

*

Jack woke to see the cheery, freckly face of Rory smiling down at him.

'Come on, Green-Jack, the tea is brewing, and breakfast is almost ready. It's a grand day in the making.'

Jack sat up in his sleeping bag and looked up at the tall grey mountains that towered over them. The bright winter sun hovered over the mountains casting its welcome light across the landscape. The mountains lacked any greenery or vegetation; the only contrast to the grey granite was the snow-capped peaks. But they made a welcome change to the dreariness of the plains that they'd just crossed. Jack pulled off his sleeping bag and stretched his tired body as Rory handed him a bowlful of steaming hot porridge.

'Get that down you, Jack lad. That will line your stomach for the day ahead.'

Jack smiled as they were the very same words that his grandfather used to say when he made porridge. Noah never strayed far from his thoughts, especially since his illness. He hoped that the Koehtia had extended his grandfather's life at least until Jack returned, however long that may be.

Elensar and Roger joined him as Stran sat on his own and smoked his pipe. The ranger rarely ate. Jack sometimes wondered how he managed to keep going as he consumed little more than a sparrow. Rory followed up the porridge with dry biscuits and Roseleaf, both served with his customary smile.

Once they'd finished their breakfast, they packed their rucksacks and prepared for the next stage of their journey. As they surveyed the tall grey mountains, the uncertainty and apprehension surrounded them all like a cloud. Jack looked at Elensar and could see the tension in his face. The Border Guard Captain rarely showed his inner emotions, but they were there for all to see today.

He turned to Stran and watched him as he cleaned his pipe. Once the cleaning ritual was complete, Stran placed the pipe in his inside breast pocket. He stood to the side of Elensar and cast his gaze towards the mountains.

'So, ranger, which route are we to take?' asked Elensar.

Stran thoughtfully rubbed the stubble on his chin as he considered his answer. 'I took the opportunity to check out our options at first light this morning. There is a concealed narrow pass to the left which seems to lead to the heart of the mountains. Other routes involve rock climbing and I don't think either Rory or Roger are able for it.'

Rory reacted instantly. 'Don't you worry about me, Stran. I can look after myself and I'm more than able to match any challenge you can throw at me.'

'We'll take the pass,' said Elensar before Stran could answer Rory. 'We're all tired after crossing the plains. It's the sensible course to take.'

They strapped their backpacks on and set off on the next leg of their journey with more than a hint of trepidation. Stran led them into a narrow pass that was almost impossible to see as you approached the mountains. As difficult as Stran could be, Jack was glad that the ranger was with them. Although he had no prior knowledge of these mountains his experience in travelling this type of terrain was going to prove invaluable, of that he was sure.

They walked single file into a narrow passageway barely two metres wide, that sometimes narrowed to half that width. The sheer granite walls stretched up for hundreds of metres. Jack's claustrophobia threatened to surface but he allowed the anxiety to trickle through him without resisting it.

Stran led the company, followed by Rory, then Roger and Jack, with Elensar bringing up the rear. Jack turned to the Captain and whispered, 'we are easy to attack here.'

'We are too few to fight back so it matters little where the Dwarves confront us.'

Jack smiled to himself. Of course, the Captain was right – they hadn't come here to confront the Dwarves, they'd come to ask for their help. It was diplomatic not warrior skills that were needed for this leg of the journey.

They continued along the narrow pass for around an hour, although to Jack it seemed much longer, and he was relieved when they came out into a wide stone valley. Stran continued at a relentless pace until they eventually came across a shallow stream that wound its way eastwards across the valley floor. They all took the opportunity to fill their water bottles and Jack washed his face for the first time since they'd left Waterswood. The cold mountain water felt good on his skin as it washed away the grime from his face and the grit from his eyes.

They followed the stream and reached the far end of the valley by midday and took the path through the scattered boulders into a narrow ravine that led onto a still mountain lake. The tall mountains reflected on the surface of the silver water and Jack thought that it looked stunning. He could hear Tyler's voice in his ear urging them to stop and absorb its beauty.

But Stran pressed on around the lake following the path at the foot of the surrounding mountains barely taking in the scenery. He didn't even stop for lunch and they ate dry biscuits that Rory handed out as they walked. Roger joined Jack for the first time that day and walked quietly beside him. A close relationship was slowly developing between the two of them. Jack hadn't realised how close until Roger thought that he'd been trampled to death by the stampeding horses. Roger had held onto him like a father holding his son.

And that's what they were – father and son.

'How are you bearing up?' asked Jack.

'OK,' said Roger hesitantly, 'although I'm a little concerned about meeting these Dwarves.'

'Don't be,' said Jack. 'Elensar is the complete warrior. It isn't just combat skills he possesses but diplomatic ones as well. I'm sure once they all understand the threat this Leah presents to us all, they will help.'

'I have had one or two hairy moments in the Amazon jungle. Some of the natives can prove to be a little hostile when you first meet them, but the guides normally mediate and a gift of a bottle of whisky can go a long way.'

'You're used to suffering the hardships of the outdoor life,' said Jack.

'I am indeed,' said Roger. 'I'm a little strange that way as I quite like it.'

'It's just as well you do,' smiled Jack, 'as I don't think we'll be finding any posh hotels on this trip … not that I've ever stayed in one.'

'They're very over rated in my view,' said Roger. 'Full of plastic flowers and plastic people.'

'I've always been comfortable sleeping in the outdoors,' said Jack. 'Although I have to admit that I didn't enjoy crossing the plains. I have this strange thing where I'm uncomfortable in open spaces as well as confined spaces. Forests are my favourite places although I do love mountain scenery too. Rory's home village, Cill-Arney, is surrounded by the most spectacular mountains.'

'I'd like to go there sometime,' said Roger.

Rory turned around and smiled. 'There'll always be a welcome in Cill-Arney for you, Roger me lad.'

They reached the far side of the lake by late afternoon and Elensar suggested that they stop and make camp for the night. Stran surprisingly agreed and they dropped their backpacks by the side of a solitary gnarled and naked alder tree at the lake's edge. As Rory and Roger collected wood for a fire, Stran, Elensar and Jack surveyed their surroundings.

The path carried on around the lake and split off in between two raised mounds of rocky shingle. It was impossible to see where it led to as they were on lower ground.

But Stran was clear on which route to take. 'We'll head east along that path through the shingle tomorrow. If nothing else, it is still taking us in the right direction.'

Elensar nodded his agreement as he removed his longbow from his back. Suddenly, Jack saw a flash of silver in front of his eyes followed by a dull thud to his side. They all looked around to see a metal axe embedded in the trunk of the alder tree.

They heard a deep, menacing voice from up above them. Jack looked up to see a short, stout bearded individual staring down at them. He was holding another axe in his right hand.

'If the tall blond Elf doesn't drop his longbow this second, my next axe will split his head.'

Jack didn't need either Stran or Elensar to tell him that they were looking at a Dwarf ...

*

Chapter Twelve - Gravelaxe

Elensar held his longbow firmly in his right hand and didn't move. His eyes locked onto the Dwarf like a laser beam.

'I think you might be either deaf or stupid,' said the Dwarf coldly, 'but either condition will prove fatal if you don't do as I tell you.' His eyes momentarily flashed across to the other mound of shingle before focusing back on Elensar. Several more axe wielding Dwarves appeared on top of the mound.

Jack knew that Elensar would weigh up all options. He didn't have to wait long for his response.

'We come in peace. We have no desire to confront you and we will not use our weapons.'

'I agree that you won't use your weapons because they will be on the ground as I instructed. Now do as I say and drop the longbow.'

As much as it went against the grain for Elensar he reluctantly dropped the longbow onto the ground.

'And now your sword,' said the Dwarf.

Elensar unclipped his sword from his belt and dropped it to the ground alongside his longbow.

'Let's not forget the dagger that's concealed in your boot.'

This Dwarf knew his adversary well, thought Jack. Elensar reached down and pulled the dagger from his boot and threw it on top of his other weapons.

The Dwarf switched his attention to the others. 'Place any weapons you have on the pile … including the concealed ones.'

They all did as he asked, even Stran, which surprised Jack as he didn't know he carried a dagger. The Dwarf signalled to his colleagues on top of the other mound and they scampered down the shingle and gathered up the weapons. He slowly and deliberately climbed down from the mound, not taking his eyes off them for a second. He strolled over to the alder tree and removed his axe from the trunk. He ran his finger along the blade.

'Wood always takes the edge off the blade, unlike Elf flesh …' He looked at Elensar as he said it, before placing it back in his belt on the opposite side to the other axe that hung there.

'So why would four Elves and a midget stray uninvited into Dwarf territory?'

Jack was about to answer but Rory beat him to it. 'I'll have you know that I'm a proud Leprechaun from Cill-Arney on Emerald Island and I happen to be nearly as tall as you.'

The Dwarf shifted his steely gaze to Rory and studied him for several seconds. 'What you are or who you are makes no difference to me. I want to know why you think you can trespass into my land.'

Rory was about to respond but Jack stepped forward. 'We are here to ask for your help. My name is Green-Jack and I come from the Elven village of Waterswood on the far side of the Fireridge Mountains.' He introduced his friends. 'This is Captain Tathar Elensar from the Elven city of Arminas in our homeland. Stran Vander is a mountain ranger from Mountpass. Roger Thorne is a human who has agreed to help us, as has Rory McNory who has already introduced himself.'

'And why would you think that any Dwarf would want to help an Elf,' he said narrowing his eyes.

Jack stood tall and straight and didn't flinch under his steely gaze. 'Our land is in great danger. My people are already lost to it and if we don't find the person responsible there will be no Elven civilisation the other side of the Fireridge Mountains.'

The Dwarf adjusted the axes in his belt and slowly wandered around Jack and his friends, studying each of them in turn. 'And why should that be any cause for concern for us?'

'Because your land could be next,' said Jack.

The Dwarf considered his answer for several seconds; his cold stare permanently locked onto Jack. 'We are more than capable of looking after our own affairs. We have no need of any outside help and would never lower ourselves to asking the Elves.'

Jack had suspected that this wasn't going to be easy, but it was proving more difficult than he anticipated. 'Then take me to the leaders of your community and I will plead my case with them.'

A smile bordering on a sneer crossed the Dwarf's lips. 'You are looking at the leader of our community. My name is Gravelaxe and I head the ruling council of this land. If I say no, then that's your answer.' He turned to one of the other Dwarves standing just behind him to his right. 'Grindell, organise the prisoners into single file. We'll take them back to Bellowrock for interrogation.'

Elensar stepped forward and confronted Gravelaxe. 'We are not your prisoners and we will not submit ourselves to any interrogation.'

Gravelaxe didn't respond verbally, he just flashed his eyes at Grindell who immediately removed his axe and hit Elensar a sickening blow to the back of his head with the blunt end. The Captain collapsed to the floor and lay there motionless in a growing pool of dark blood.

Roger immediately dropped to his knees and checked Elensar's pulse in his neck. He looked up at Jack. 'He's alive – his pulse is strong.'

Jack was horrified and turned on Gravelaxe. 'We come here in peace. There is no need for violence.'

'Peace!' spat Gravelaxe. 'What do Elves know of peace? You have slaughtered my people for hundreds of years. The only language you understand is violence – and the more brutal the better. Now if you don't fall into line, you will feel my axe, but unlike in your friend's case, it will be the sharp end!'

Jack looked at Stran, Rory and Roger and shook his head in disbelief. 'Do as he asks.'

They stepped into line as one of the other Dwarves picked up Elensar and threw him over his shoulder like he was carrying the carcass of a dead animal. Two Dwarves stood behind, and two either side of them with Gravelaxe at their head. He raised his right hand and waved them forward before striding off towards the path that led between the two mounds of shingle.

For someone whose legs were so short, Gravelaxe set a healthy pace. He was over a metre tall with broad shoulders and wore a thick grey jacket with woollen leggings and knee length black leather boots. His short legs gave him a low centre of gravity and Jack could tell he would be fierce in combat. Jack wasn't sure how old he was. His jet-black hair and beard were flecked with grey, but his physical strength and gait suggested he could have been younger than his hair colour suggested.

The path between the shale mounds led down into another valley and Gravelaxe soon turned off into a narrow pass concealed in between several huge granite boulders. The path dropped down very quickly at an incline at least forty-five degrees and Jack struggled to keep his footing. But Gravelaxe carried on at his relentless pace not even looking to see if they were OK.

He suddenly stopped at the bottom of the pass and turned sharp left into a narrow crevice in the mountain. They entered a tunnel that was lit by flame torches in metal holders on the wall. Jack looked behind to see the grim face of Roger staring back at him. What had he got him into? He knew that this quest would be dangerous but this Gravelaxe character seemed dead set against any discussion or compromise. The likelihood of him helping them looked remote but what concerned Jack the most was what had he planned for them?

The tunnel opened out and they were confronted by two huge wooden doors. Dwarf guards stood either side of them and saluted as soon as they saw Gravelaxe, before opening the doors. They followed Gravelaxe into a huge dome shaped chamber. It was like the inside of a cathedral. Dwarves swarmed around the place going on with their business.

Some cooked over fires; some worked over forges. Some

sat in small groups huddled together deep in conversation. But that all stopped when they saw Gravelaxe; it was like a switch being thrown. They all stood and turned towards him and bowed their heads in deference. This character was akin to a dictator, thought Jack, which didn't bode well for their future.

Gravelaxe summoned two guards over and barked his orders. 'Take the prisoners to the cells and chain them to the wall.'

The two guards saluted him before roughly pushing Jack towards the far end of the chamber. One of them shouted, 'This way!', as the other removed his axe from his belt and snarled at them as they passed by him.

As Jack and his friends walked in single file every eye in that chamber was focused on them. Young and old, male and female Dwarves studied them every step. Their faces contorted with anger as they walked amongst them. One elderly female Dwarf came up to Jack and looked him directly in the eyes and hissed the word, 'murderer' under her breath. He was relieved when they turned into a narrow dimly lit stone passageway.

They went down several flights of stone stairs before coming into a narrow passageway less than two metres high. Jack's head nearly touched the ceiling and if Elensar had have been upright, he would have had to stoop down to get through. The Dwarf stopped in front of a metal door and pushed it open. The hinges squealed as the door creaked open. The Dwarf stepped to one side and barked, 'in!'

Jack stepped into the dark cell, followed by Roger, Rory and Stran. The Dwarf who was carrying Elensar strode into the cell after them and dumped him in the corner onto a pile of damp straw. He clamped a metal brace onto his ankle before striding out of the cell again.

One of the guards stepped into the cell and clamped an ankle brace onto each one of them and followed his colleague out into the corridor. The door was slammed shut leaving them in almost total darkness. They sat quietly for several seconds before Rory broke the silence.

'Well, I've had warmer welcomes …'

'Why do you have to make light of every situation, Leprechaun?' said Stran acidly. 'Just in case you haven't noticed our lives are in danger and you make childish jokes.'

'I'd rather laugh than cry,' said Rory. 'And besides, what good did worrying ever do?'

'It's Rory's way to always look at the bright side,' said Jack, 'just as it's yours to look on the bleak side.'

'I would prefer to describe it as a realistic outlook,' said an irritated Stran.

'I think we'd all be better employed looking after Elensar,' said Roger. 'That was some blow he took to his head.'

'Roger's right,' said Jack crawling across to Elensar. He lifted the Captain into the recovery position and checked the wound on the back of his head. It was covered in congealed blood but had stopped bleeding. 'We need some water to clean this up.'

Stran reached inside his coat and pulled out his water bottle and a cloth. He dampened the cloth and handed it to Jack, who immediately went about cleaning up the wound. Once he finished he leant back against the wall and looked around the cell as his eyes adjusted to the shallow light. 'I see they haven't bothered to leave us any food.'

Rory reached inside his coat and pulled out a bag containing dry biscuits. 'These will keep us going for a while. Hopefully the Dwarves will bring us something later.'

'I wouldn't count on it,' said Stran dryly. 'I don't think we're going to see much hospitality from Gravelaxe.'

'Why do they hate Elves so much?' asked Roger.

'It's history,' said Stran. 'Elves and Dwarves fought each other for centuries. It only stopped a hundred or so years ago.'

'Was there some sort of peace treaty?' asked Jack.

'Far from it,' said Stran. 'In the end they just kept out of each other's way. They conceded territory to each other and then kept to their own.'

'But Gravelaxe seemed to think that Elves are murderers,' said Jack.

'And I know Elves who would say the same about Dwarves. They were bloody wars and atrocities were carried out by both sides.'

'But surely after one hundred years they could all learn to put it behind them,' suggested Rory.

'As simplistic as ever, Leprechaun,' said Stran. 'But, unfortunately wars leave scars that sometimes never heal. Take it from me, our lives are at risk here. I don't think Gravelaxe has any intention of letting us go.'

Jack leant back against the wall and let Stran's words sink in. As much as he didn't want to believe the ranger, he had a sinking feeling inside that was telling him that Stran was right.

*

Chapter Thirteen – The Trial

Elensar woke in the early hours and despite a painful lump and gash on the back of his head, he was otherwise unscathed. Sleep on the hard, damp floor, was sporadic so there was always one of them awake with him throughout the night. Guards brought bread and water in the morning, although calling the hard granite lumps bread may have been stretching the description somewhat.

Rory held a piece in his hand and tried unsuccessfully to bite into it. 'I think you will need one of those Dwarf axes to cut this!'

'Where are we?' asked Elensar.

'In caves under the mountains,' said Jack. 'It took us about an hour to get here last evening.'

'Have they said what they're planning to do with us?' asked Elensar.

'Not a word,' said Jack.

'How's the head, Captain?' asked Rory.

'It's been better. What did they hit me with?'

'The blunt end of an axe,' said Rory.

'Elladan always said that my skull was made of granite,' said Elensar forcing a smile.

'Jack cleaned up the wound for you last night,' said Rory. 'It looks like its healing OK.'

'Did you get to see how many Dwarves there are?'

'We saw around one hundred in a large cavern on the way here,' said Jack.

'And they didn't seem pleased to see us,' added Rory.

'Dwarves are known for their long memories,' said Elensar. 'The wars between us were bloody and cruel, but both sides were equally guilty.'

'I'm not sure they quite see it that way,' said Rory. 'Why can't they be more like us Leprechauns and forgive and forget? I don't see any point in holding onto grudges. They do themselves more harm in the end.'

Just at that moment they heard the bolts on the cell door

pulled back. The door creaked open and four grim looking Dwarves strode in carrying chains.

'Get on your feet!' snapped one of them.

Jack stood up and helped an unsteady Elensar to his feet. The Captain was still feeling the effects from the blow to his head. Once they were all standing, one of the Dwarves told them to hold their hands out in front of them. They did as he asked, and he clamped chains on each pair of hands while another Dwarf unchained their feet.

When the Dwarves finished one of them stood at the cell door and barked, 'follow me!'

Stran went first followed by Roger and Rory - Jack and Elensar came last. The Dwarf led them back down the passageway and up the two flights of stairs, but instead of going into the main chamber, the Dwarf took them into a room at the end of the passageway. Once inside the dwarf pointed to a long bench.

'Sit there.'

They all sat down and waited in silence as the four Dwarves scowled at them. Jack looked at his colleagues and shrugged his shoulders. Why had they been brought here? They didn't have to wait long to get their answer. Gravelaxe came striding into the room and stood alongside the scowling Dwarves and stared icily at Jack and his friends.

Jack thought of all the challenges he'd faced since he'd set off on his journey less than a year ago. He'd come through some almost impossible situations but this one raised the bar even higher. How where they ever going to persuade Gravelaxe to help them? But more importantly, how were they going to get away from him if he wouldn't?

Gravelaxe studied them all one at a time; his steely grey eyes finally settling on Elensar. 'I trust your head is healing?'

'No thanks to you,' said Elensar holding his gaze.

'If you wish to avoid such treatment again then just do as I ask.'

Elensar didn't give him the satisfaction of replying and looked at him with contempt.

Gravelaxe turned his attention to Jack, stroking his beard as his eyes dissected him. 'Are you the leader of this band of mercenaries?'

Jack almost laughed at his description of him and his friends. 'Why would you think we're mercenaries?'

'Because,' said Gravelaxe narrowing his eyes, 'you are Elves and you have deliberately entered Dwarf territory. You are obviously a reconnaissance party for an all-out invasion.'

Jack laughed in exasperation. 'I've already told you, we're here to ask for your help. How can we attack you when my people have disappeared back to the spiritual world? We are no threat to you and we have absolutely no desire to invade you.' Jack's eyes pleaded with him. 'We are desperate, Gravelaxe, and without your help my people are doomed.'

But Gravelaxe was unmoved. 'And why would you think we would want to help you when you've spent large parts of your past slaughtering us?'

'I think you'll find, Gravelaxe,' interrupted Elensar, 'that the Dwarves have done more than their fair share of slaughtering. The Elven people have made mistakes in the past but so have the Dwarves.'

Gravelaxe looked unimpressed and headed for the door. He hesitated before leaving the room and said, 'we shall see who's telling the truth. You will stand trial for crimes against the Dwarf nation. Proceedings will start and conclude this afternoon.'

*

'He's mad,' said Rory dunking a rock-hard chunk of bread in his watery soup in an attempt to soften it. 'How can he hold us responsible for things that happened hundreds of years ago?'

Elensar didn't even attempt to eat the so-called food they were served. He paced around the room dragging his chains along the floor. 'We need to get out of here, but I just wish

102

I knew how. We've got no weapons and they've tied us up in these,' he said holding up the chains. 'It doesn't leave us with many options.'

Roger sat quietly listening as he attempted to eat his bread. He'd said little since they'd been taken prisoner by Gravelaxe. Jack put himself in his shoes and realised just how surreal this must seem to him. He couldn't help feeling guilty for putting Roger into such an impossible situation.

Jack placed a friendly hand on his shoulder. 'I'm sorry for getting you into this mess. I will do my best to persuade Gravelaxe to let you go.'

Roger looked offended. 'You will do no such thing. I'm in this for the long haul. I will stay with you right until the bitter end, no matter where it leads us.'

'But …'

'No buts, Jack,' reaffirmed Roger. 'I'm not going anywhere without the rest of you.'

'Spoken like a true friend,' said Rory raising a soggy piece of bread to him.

'If I could just get him on his own,' said Elensar. 'I could wrap the chains around his neck and threaten to strangle him if they don't let us go.'

'They won't let us near him,' said Stran. 'And those Dwarves are pretty handy with their axes at close quarters.'

'So, what do you suggest, ranger?' asked an irritated Elensar.

'The best we can hope for is that they let us go.'

'And the worst?' asked Elensar.

Stran didn't answer and dropped his gaze to the floor. They all knew what the worst was, or at least they thought they knew.

The door opened, and the four burly Dwarf guards returned. 'The court is ready,' said one of them. 'Follow me.'

He strode out of the room while the other three scowled at them. They put their bowls down and one by one followed him out of the door. He led them back into the main cavern, but its appearance had totally changed.

Rows of empty wooden benches faced a raised platform, with several elderly Dwarves sat behind a long table. A brooding Gravelaxe sat in the middle of them. Dwarves congregated at the far end of the cavern observing the proceedings. A raised wooden dock sat to the right of the front bench at a forty-five-degree angle facing the chairs.

The Dwarf guards led Jack and his friends to the dock and they climbed the steps and stood huddled together facing the makeshift courtroom. Gravelaxe signalled to one of the Dwarf guards and he beckoned the waiting public to enter the makeshift courtroom and sit on the empty benches.

It struck Jack that they didn't make a sound. There was no background murmur like there had been in the Waterswood court. It was obvious that this Gravelaxe ruled these people with intimidation and fear. He was a smaller version of Willy Venn but equally nasty.

Once every seat was taken, the Dwarf guards took up positions surrounding the court. Jack expected the proceedings to begin but was surprised once again when they all sat in silence. Jack's attention was diverted by a lone Dwarf with a hunchback who hobbled towards the back of the court. He looked for a space to sit but the benches were full, so he leant against the cavern wall.

Gravelaxe eventually rose to his feet and scowled at Jack and his friends for several seconds before turning towards the assembled gathering of Dwarves.

'Citizens of Bellowrock, on behalf of the Governing Council, I thank you all for attending this court today. Our community, which lives under the constant threat of attack from Elves and their associates, has once again been forced to unite against these cutthroat mercenaries.

Throughout history, the Dwarf nation has fought for survival against the murderous Elven invader. We have fought bravely, and we have fought well. Despite the overwhelming odds against us, these invaders have never managed to break our resolve, and they never will. Our spirit and nerve remain resolute.'

Rory discretely whispered to Elensar as Gravelaxe

continued his sermon. 'Do you have any idea what he's talking about?'

Elensar continued to stare straight ahead. 'I don't, but it sounds to me like an attempt to stir up the feelings of the Dwarves in the courtroom.'

'Well it doesn't seem to be working,' commented Rory, 'as they're not reacting.'

'I can smell the fear in this cavern,' said Elensar. 'These poor creatures are totally intimidated by Gravelaxe.'

'The hundreds of years of slaughter and oppression never wore us down,' continued Gravelaxe. 'And do you know why?'

His question was greeted by total silence. It appeared that no one wanted to risk saying the wrong thing. 'It is because the will of the Dwarf race refuses to be broken. We will never be defeated, and we will never succumb to slavery. Our ancestors fought true and hard against the Elven invader and it falls on our shoulders to uphold our proud tradition as a free and independent civilisation.

All invaders to our land will be dealt with in the same uncompromising fashion that our ancestors dealt with the invaders in times gone by. It falls on our shoulders, my friends, to do our duty and send a clear message to anyone who wishes to threaten our way of life.

But we will not resort to the brutal methods of our enemies. We, the Dwarves, are a civilised race. We will put these mercenaries on trial – they will answer to the Dwarf people and they will be judged by them. They will be given a fair hearing and if found guilty, will be subject to our laws.'

Gravelaxe turned his attention to a Dwarf who stood quietly watching to one side of the front bench. 'Goring, start the proceedings.'

Goring turned towards Jack and his friends as Gravelaxe took his seat. He held up a parchment and read from it in a loud and clear voice.

'You are charged with planning an invasion of the Dwarf community of Bellowrock, with the sole purpose of enslaving the people of this community. How do you plead?'

Jack looked to Elensar for guidance. 'What are they saying? They can't be serious. There are too few of us to mount any sort of attack on them.'

'It's a complete fabrication,' said Elensar. 'But we must enter a plea.'

Jack stood tall and straight and looked Goring directly in the eye and said firmly, 'not guilty!'

Goring didn't acknowledge Jack's plea and returned to his position to the side of the front bench. Gravelaxe took over the proceedings but remained seated. His steely grey eyes narrowed as they locked onto Jack.

'Would you like to tell the court why you are here?'

Jack couldn't help himself and gave a frivolous answer. 'Because you took us prisoner.' Jack regretted the words as soon as they were out of his mouth.

Gravelaxe took the opportunity to make capital from Jack's words. He rose to his feet and addressed the assembled Dwarves. 'You see how they disrespect us and our court. They think they are superior and cannot contain their arrogance.' He turned back towards Jack. 'If you continue to refuse to answer my questions we can end this hearing earlier.' Jack saw the faint trace of a smile curl his lips. 'But I suspect you may not like the verdict.'

'I am happy to tell you why we are here, but first I have a question for you. Do we get the chance to defend ourselves?'

Jack could tell from Gravelaxe's facial expression that he didn't like the question. 'Answering my questions is the best way to defend yourselves.'

'But surely we must have the opportunity to question you? What sort of hearing is this if we don't get to put our side of the story?'

Jack saw Gravelaxe's mouth tighten. It was obvious he wasn't used to being challenged. He studied Jack in silence for several moments before answering. 'You will have your chance to ask your questions but first you must answer mine.'

Although it was only a small concession it was a victory of sorts, thought Jack. 'I agree.'

'I'll repeat my earlier question,' said Gravelaxe. 'Why are you here?'

'As I've already told you, we are here to ask for your help. My land is under threat and the seriousness of the situation calls for a united response. A mysterious character called Graydon Leah has stolen the gold dust that sustains our community. We must find him and return the gold dust to where it belongs. The Faeries have told us that in order to do this we need a coming together of all the races. They call it a 'Unification of a Common Purpose'. Today we are a human, a Leprechaun, and an Elf. We need a Dwarf and a Pixie to complete our company.'

A gratuitous sneer crossed Gravelaxe's lips. 'I have no idea who this Leah is and have no interest. We both know the real reason you have come here.'

Frustration enveloped Jack. He turned to his friends looking for inspiration, but none was forthcoming.

Gravelaxe continued to espouse his wild accusation to the Dwarves. 'Do not listen to his lame excuses. They have come to conquer us, my friends, to enslave us all.'

Jack shook his head in disbelief at the ridiculousness of his suggestion. 'There are five of us, and there are hundreds of Dwarves in your community. How exactly is it that we are meant to conquer you?'

'And that's what you want us to think, that you are just five strong, but we know that there are thousands of you waiting to attack us.'

This was getting beyond ridiculous, thought Jack. Gravelaxe was living in the realms of fantasy. Jack shook his head again but this time in bewilderment. 'I am all that is left of my community. I am here along with friends from other communities to ask for your help. There is no invasion; it is a figment of your imagination.'

'And that's what you would like us to believe,' retorted Gravelaxe. 'But we have seen your army massed on the plains to the west of these mountains. They are just waiting your instructions and they will attack us.'

Jack was momentarily lost for words. He regained his composure and continued. 'We have no army. We came here in peace to ask for your help. Why are you saying this?'

Gravelaxe called over to one of the guards at the back of the cavern. 'Grindell – tell the court what you saw from the mountains to the west of here.'

The Dwarf replied on cue and to the prearranged script. 'An army of at least one thousand Elves are camped on the plains. They are heavily armed.'

'But that's nonsense,' countered Jack turning to the Dwarves sat in the chamber. 'Don't believe them, they're lying to you. I can assure you that it is just us five and we come in peace.'

The Dwarves sat eerily silent. They showed no outward sign of any emotion or understanding of what had been going on. Jack could see that it was a lost cause appealing to them.

'Enough of this,' said Gravelaxe. 'You are testing my patience.' He addressed the Dwarves sat in the cavern. 'You have heard all you need to. It's now time for your verdict. Do you find these invaders guilty?'

They didn't hesitate – every Dwarf raised their right arm. Jack looked to the back of the cavern towards the lone Dwarf – he had not raised his arm, but that didn't bother Gravelaxe.

'So, we have our verdict, you are guilty of crimes against the Dwarf nation.'

Jack looked to his friends and they all appeared to be as shocked as he felt. Rory was shaking his head in utter disbelief.

'Yer one is mad.'

'He may be,' said Stran impassively, 'but at this moment he holds all the cards.'

For once Jack agreed with Stran's cynicism. They were at the mercy of Gravelaxe, not a place where you wanted to be. What was he going to do with them? They were about to find out.

Gravelaxe's eyes narrowed as he focused his attention on Jack and his friends. 'You came here with the sole intention of conquering my people and condemning us all to a life of slavery. Well, thanks to the vigilance of my guards, your nasty little plan has been thwarted. You will never break the spirit of the Dwarf people.' He hesitated for a brief second and drew in a deep breath. 'It falls on my shoulders to make sure that you never get the opportunity to threaten us again, which is why I have no hesitation in sentencing you all to death.'

Jack couldn't believe what he was hearing. This madness had gone far enough so he tried to climb out of the dock and confront Gravelaxe, but the Dwarf guards immediately restrained him. 'You can't do this!' he cried as he struggled with them. 'We came here in peace to ask for your help. This is insane!'

But Gravelaxe ignored him. 'You will be taken from here at first light tomorrow morning, to the cliff that overlooks Grimdon Valley … and one by one you will be thrown over the cliff edge by the guards.'

This was fast turning into a nightmare. Jack pleaded with Gravelaxe. 'Please don't do this. We will leave your land and promise never to return … just let us go.'

But Gravelaxe wasn't hearing him. He ignored Jack's plea and turned to Grindell. 'Take the prisoners back to their cell.'

*

Chapter Fourteen – Bumbleflunk

Jack and his friends sat in the almost total darkness of their cell in a daze. A tray of food lay on the floor untouched.

'He's completely mad,' said Jack. 'How can he sentence us to death when we're innocent?'

'There wasn't a trace of emotion in his voice or on his face as he gave the verdict,' said Rory.

'There's no point in dwelling on Gravelaxe's insanity,' said Elensar. 'We need to work out how we get out of this.'

'What do you have in mind?' said Stran coldly. 'Are we going to fight them without any weapons? They will gladly hack us to death with their axes.'

Elensar leant towards Stran and even in the dark Jack could see the passion in his eyes. 'I am not going to sit back and let them throw me over a cliff. If I am to die it will be with a fight, as a proud Elven warrior and Captain of the Border Guard!'

Roger surprised them all. 'I agree – we can't just let them take us without any resistance.'

Jack was learning that there was more to Roger than the mild-mannered man he first met in London. There was a steely determination there which was going to be vital if they were to escape from the mad Gravelaxe.

'We're not going to be able to do anything in this cell as we're chained to the wall,' said Elensar. 'But we will get our opportunity when they take us out into the open. Jack, you and I will wrap our chains around two of the guards. Once we have their axes, we will be able to put up a fight.'

'I will join you,' said Roger.

'And me,' chimed in Rory. 'I may be only small but I'm sure I can handle one of those hairy midgets.'

Jack smiled because the Dwarves were as tall as Rory, but he didn't doubt his Leprechaun friend's bravery for a minute. 'I've seen what you can do first hand in Lestrada, Rory, so I doubt those Dwarf guards will know what's hit them.'

Just making plans to fight back visibly lifted the tension in that cell, but it soon returned when they heard voices outside the door.

'It's still the middle of the night,' hissed Elensar. 'Gravelaxe said they wouldn't come for us until first light.'

'Who can believe a word that comes from his lips?' whispered Rory. 'But it makes no difference. We'll still give them a fight to remember.'

They waited for what seemed like hours but probably was only a matter of minutes before they heard the key in the lock. The hinges squealed in protest as the door slowly opened. A head appeared around the door, but it was impossible to see who it was in the dark. They heard a voice that they didn't recognise, in a manner they weren't expecting. It was respectful, almost timid.

'Do you mind if I come in?'

Whoever it was pushed the door open wider and held a flickering candle up to his face. Jack recognised him as the Dwarf with the hunchback and limp who stood at the back of the chamber during the hearing. He hesitated at the cell door and looked uncomfortable, even nervous, thought Jack.

'There's no need to worry about the guards, they're asleep.' His voice was high pitched and displayed a slight tremor.

'Asleep!' repeated Rory. 'What sort of guards are they?'

'Er, the sort that has just unknowingly taken a sleeping draught,' said the Dwarf coyly.

'I don't understand,' said Jack.

'I brought them some tea that was laced with a drug. It worked almost instantly and will make them sleep for hours.' He stepped forward and handed Jack a key. 'Now if you wouldn't mind unlocking your chains. We need to make the most of the opportunity and get away from here now.'

Jack and his friends exchanged uneasy glances. Elensar took the initiative. 'Why are you doing this?' he asked. 'How do we know we can trust you?'

The Dwarf fidgeted unsteadily on his feet. 'I can assure you that I've come to help. I can take my key back and go if you would prefer ...'

'He has a point,' said Rory. 'We don't exactly have many other options.'

Jack quickly unlocked his chains and gave the key to Elensar, who immediately did the same and helped the others. Jack held out his hand to the Dwarf. 'I am Green-Jack.'

The Dwarf grabbed his hand and shook it warmly. 'My name is Bumbleflunk, Bumble for short. We need to get you out of here so I'm afraid there's no time to exchange niceties.'

'We're going to need weapons if we're to fight our way out of here,' said Elensar.

'Hopefully there will be no fight. I will be taking you through secret passages of which Gravelaxe and his cohorts have no knowledge. Now we must go.'

He limped out of the cell and they followed him in single file. Both guards were sound asleep on the floor outside of the cell.

'They're out for the count,' said Rory.

Bumble put his finger up to his lips. 'I think it would be wise if we don't talk until we're in the secret tunnels,' he advised politely.

He led them further down the narrow passageway away from the main cavern. They came to a dead end, but Bumble reached down into the corner and pressed something in the wall. The granite wall suddenly swung open revealing a dark tunnel beyond.

'In here,' he whispered.

They filed past him and into the tunnel. Bumble followed them and pulled the door shut behind him. He pointed to several torches in metal holders on the wall. 'Light them with the candle. We're going to need to see more clearly where we're going. And be careful with your footing – there are lots of pot holes in the ground.'

He led them along the tunnel as it sloped gently

downwards. Jack, Elensar and Roger had to walk with their backs bent so their heads didn't hit the low ceiling. They walked in silence as Bumble took them down several flights of narrow stone steps, and through endless dark tunnels. Just as Jack was considering crawling on all fours because of the nagging ache in his back, they came out into a small chamber whose ceiling was thankfully a metre higher. Bumble held his torch into a corner revealing a pile of rucksacks and weapons. 'These are yours I believe.'

'But how?' asked Jack.

'No questions for now,' said Bumble. 'Just get your things and we carry on.'

They all strapped on their rucksacks and selected their weapons. Elensar placed his dagger back in his boot and strapped his sword to his belt. As he slung his longbow and quiver full of arrows over his back, he turned to Jack and said, 'now I feel complete again. It's a strange thing but when I have no weapons I feel almost naked.'

Jack smiled that he understood. Elensar was an instinctive warrior and weapons were an important part of his makeup.

Despite a pronounced limp, Bumble kept up a relentless pace through the dark and cramped tunnels deep in the bowels of the mountains. His conversation was sparse to say the least but they all understood that he wanted to get them away from Gravelaxe, so he didn't want to waste time on idle chat. But what they didn't understand was why he was helping.

Jack wanted to find out; he needed to find out. He wondered if Bumble was an outcast from the rest of the Dwarves because of his disability. Maybe it was a simple as that. But something else occurred to him as they shuffled along the narrow tunnels. Could he persuade Bumble to join them on their quest? That was going to have to wait until they were well away from the mountains, he thought.

They emerged from the tunnels into a huge cavern. Bumble stopped and turned to them.

'Stay close to me as we're going to follow the path

around the wall to our left.' He held his torch out towards the centre of the cavern to reveal a huge black hole. 'No-one knows how deep this is so please be careful. Can I suggest that you just concentrate on your footing and try to forget about the dark expanse to your right.'

'Easier said than done,' whispered Rory in earshot of both Jack and Elensar.

'Don't worry, Rory,' said Elensar. 'I'll follow you and catch you if you trip.'

'And I'll be in front of you,' reassured Jack.

They set off slowly and walked gingerly around the pathway. Despite his limp, Bumble stepped confidently around the gaping dark hole to his right. Jack could hear Rory coaching himself as he followed Jack and Stran.

'Just focus on the ground in front of you and don't look to the right. Keep breathing slowly and you'll be fine, Rory.'

The path was mostly two metres wide but narrowed to barely one metre in some places. Jack kept a watchful eye on Rory as did Elensar to make sure that he was OK. Jack tried to get some feel for the size of the cavern, but it was impossible. The light from their torches didn't reach either the ceiling or the floor. He decided that perhaps it was best to concentrate on the task in hand and that was to get around to the other side unscathed.

Time lost its meaning in the dark and Jack had no idea how long they'd been in the cavern when Bumble told them that they were nearly at the other side. Another twenty paces at the most he said, and they would turn into a tunnel, which caused a relieved Rory to thank his lucky coin. 'I held on to my gold coin the whole way around, so it's saved me once again!'

The words were no sooner out of his mouth when the piece of ledge he was standing on crumbled beneath his right boot. Rory tried desperately to step back onto firmer ground, but it was too late, he'd already lost his balance. He teetered on the edge for what seemed like forever but was only a second or two at the most and he started to fall head first into the dark abyss below him.

But Elensar was on his toes in an instant and sprang forward and grabbed the pack on Rory's back and held on with grim determination. He fought to keep his balance as the combined weight of Rory and his backpack threatened to pull them both down into the darkness below them.

It was Jack's turn to spring into action and he grabbed hold of Elensar's pack and anchored himself by holding onto a shard of rock on the cavern wall. He pulled Elensar back and he quickly regained his balance. Rory surprisingly hadn't made a sound throughout the ordeal as he was suspended upside down in mid-air over the ledge.

Elensar held on tightly to his backpack and slowly pulled Rory back up to the ledge. But worse was to come as he heard a tearing sound coming from Rory's backpack. The strap he was holding onto was coming away from the pack and Rory's slow ascent halted and he jerked back downwards. This did elicit a response from the Leprechaun and he shouted at the top of his voice, 'ELENSAR!'

The sweat ran down the Captain's face as he fought to hold onto Rory. Roger appeared from behind them and lay down flat on the ledge and reached over and caught hold of Rory's jacket and was able to pull him sideways towards the ledge. Elensar daren't pull any harder as he didn't want the strap to come away all together and just held firm.

Roger kept calm and slowly but surely manipulated Rory back up towards and then onto the ledge. Rory lay their motionless for several seconds before sitting up and grabbing Roger in a hug. Elensar slumped back against the cavern wall alongside Jack and mopped the sweat off his brow with his sleeve. Rory shuffled backwards and sat next to Jack and breathed a huge sigh of relief.

'I can't thank you enough. I thought I was a goner then.'

Stran knelt by his side with a bottle of Peardrop with its top removed. 'Here, drink this. You look like you need it.'

Rory didn't need any encouragement and took a healthy mouthful of the Peardrop and then handed the bottle back to Stran. 'Thanks – that's just what I needed.'

The ranger didn't respond verbally but nodded his acknowledgement. Bumble who had been a silent observer to what had just happened ventured a suggestion.

'I don't wish to sound insensitive, but I really think we need to keep moving. Gravelaxe isn't going to take too kindly to you escaping and will almost certainly pursue us.'

'I thought you said he didn't know of these tunnels,' growled Stran.

'He doesn't,' said Bumble, 'but we're going to come out onto a mountain trail to the east of Bellowrock and Gravelaxe will know that's the direction we'll be taking.'

'He's right,' said Rory climbing back to his feet, 'and the sooner I'm out of this place the better.'

A tentative Rory covered the last twenty metres or so in the cavern under the close attention of Elensar and Jack, before Bumble turned off into a tunnel. Much to Jack and Elensar's relief the ceiling was high enough for them not to have to bend their heads or backs and the floor was smooth and even.

They followed the tunnel as it wound its way slowly upwards and they eventually came out onto a trail high up in the Dwarf Mountains. Bumble hesitated briefly and turned to the others.

'There is still at least another two hours of darkness before daybreak, so we need to make the most of it. Gravelaxe isn't going to discover that you've gone until then as the guards aren't going to wake for hours.'

'What will happen to the guards?' asked Rory.

Bumble dropped his gaze to the floor and didn't answer immediately. He looked back up at Rory and the sadness in his eyes was there for all to see. 'I'd rather not dwell on that. I think we need to concentrate on getting away from these mountains.'

Jack looked along the jagged peaks of the Dwarf Mountains; they seemed to stretch on forever. The moon and stars shed their shallow light onto the grey granite stone giving it a luminescent glow. As mesmerising as it looked, the knot in Jack's stomach was tightening. Just thinking about what might have happened if Bumble hadn't rescued them made him feel physically sick. He took a leaf out of Bumble's book and focused on the journey ahead and putting as much distance as possible between Gravelaxe and their company.

Bumble led them along the trail and carefully down a steep path that fed into a barren valley. Jack sensed the tension within his friends and could tell they were as anxious as he was to get away from the mad Gravelaxe.

*

Chapter Fifteen – Ruthless not Mad

Jack sat alongside Elensar and Roger as he sipped his Roseleaf. Stran sat away from the others and quietly smoked his pipe as Rory took the opportunity for a quick nap. Bumble paced up and down as he anxiously looked back along the valley that they'd travelled that morning.

'I really don't think it's a good idea for us to rest too long as we must get away from these mountains. I won't relax until we are far away from here.'

'He had surprise on his side last time,' said Elensar. 'He won't surprise us again. We're all exhausted following our ordeal, Bumble. A few minutes spent taking some food and rest is time well spent.'

Bumble wasn't convinced and continued to pace up and down.

'How long will it take us to get away from the mountains?' asked Jack.

'At least another day,' said Bumble nervously.

'Gravelaxe is insane,' said Elensar. 'That is a severe limitation when it comes to conflict.'

Bumble suddenly stopped pacing up and down and sat on a small rock in front of the Captain. 'He is most certainly not insane. He is the cruellest and most ruthless individual you are ever likely to meet.'

'Then what was all that nonsense about us having an army waiting on the plains ready to attack Bellowrock?' asked Elensar.

'It was merely a ploy to make sure the poor Dwarves of our community backed his plan.'

'Plan? What plan?' asked Jack.

'Gravelaxe has met this character Graydon Leah several times.'

Jack nearly choked on the mouthful of tea that he was in the middle of swallowing. 'He's met Leah!'

'The last time was only a few weeks ago when he passed through with your gold dust.'

'But why would he want to meet Gravelaxe?' asked Jack.

'He knew that the Elves would come after their gold dust, so he bribed Gravelaxe to stop them.'

'That's why Gravelaxe made up a story about us planning an invasion so that he could put us on trial and sentence us to death,' said Elensar.

'Exactly,' said Bumble.

'And what did Leah use to bribe Gravelaxe with?' asked Jack.

'A cup of your gold dust. Don't underestimate Gravelaxe by thinking he's mad,' said Bumble. 'He is anything but …'

'But how do you know all this?' asked Jack.

'Gravelaxe thinks I'm a fool,' said Bumble, 'so he completely underestimates me. I follow him and listen to his conversations whenever I can. I knew you were coming so I planned how I would help you.'

Jack was fast learning that there was a lot more to Bumble than first meets the eye. 'And you will have our eternal gratitude for that, my friend.'

'Now do you understand why I know that Gravelaxe will come after us? He cannot afford for you to get to Leah … And now, we must go.'

*

They spent the rest of that day and the next morning on a relentless march through the mountains. Bumble reluctantly agreed to them using the darkness to rest, but he was constantly looking back along the paths they had taken. It was obvious to Jack that Bumble was frightened of Gravelaxe which made what he did by helping them even more heroic. And now it was down to Jack and Elensar to make sure that they protected their Dwarf friend.

Just as the sun disappeared behind the mountain tops to the west of them, Bumble pointed towards a pass that split two mountains to the east. 'Once we get to the other side, we are free of the mountains. There is a wide plain that will take us a further day to cross, and then we enter thick pine forests. It is very beautiful.'

They continued along the mountain path and into the plains beyond and made camp in a nest of boulders around a kilometre away from the mountains. Elensar chose the spot deliberately as it would be impossible for Gravelaxe and his Dwarves to approach them without being seen.

Bumble relaxed a little as they were now away from the mountains and didn't raise any objections when Rory suggested lighting a fire and making one of his legendary vegetable stews. 'You haven't lived, Bumble, until you've experienced one of my stews. I'll start chopping the vegetables if someone can make a fire.'

Roger and Stran gathered wood and soon had a blazing fire warming up a kettle of water for a cup of Roseleaf. The tea was served, and Rory placed his stew pot over the fire and sat back savouring the mouth-watering aroma that slowly filled the air around them.

Elensar sat next to Jack and placed his longbow against a boulder next to him. 'I agree with Bumble about Gravelaxe following us,' he whispered in Jack's ear.

'Me too,' said Jack.

'I'll take first watch tonight,' said Elensar. 'I want to make sure that there's a warm welcome waiting for him.'

Rory served up large bowlfuls of his stew along with chunks of oatmeal bread. Even Stran enjoyed his which was a first. Bumble finished his stew and cleaned the bowl with his bread. He turned to Rory and said, 'that's the first meal I've eaten that's been cooked by a Leprechaun and I have to say that it was delicious.'

'You're very welcome, Bumble,' said a cheery Rory. 'I'm sure you'll get to sample more of my culinary delights before this journey is at an end.'

'I most certainly hope so,' smiled Bumble.

Elensar doused the fire and took up his position within the boulders. 'I suggest you all wrap up warm and get some well-earned rest.'

'I'll take second watch,' said Stran. 'I only need four or so hours sleep a night.'

*

They set off early the next morning, rested after a good night's sleep – their first since they'd encountered Gravelaxe. Elensar set them a target of reaching the forest before nightfall and Bumble was confident they could meet it, weather permitting.

The plains were not quite as stark and bare as the Running Plains on the other side of the Dwarf Mountains. An occasional clump of trees and cluster of rocks broke up the monotony. The mild weather, although not sunny, made for a pleasant day's travelling. They easily reached the forest before the light faded and they made camp by a shallow stream on the forest's edge.

Elensar again surveyed the plains behind them searching for any sign of pursuit by Gravelaxe and his Dwarves and was pleased to report to the others that they were clear. Rory and Stran quickly made up a fire and they were all soon sitting in a circle sipping mugs of Roseleaf.

Jack felt the tension lift from his shoulders as he sipped his tea. They were at last free from that maniac Gravelaxe. As Rory speculated about what they should have for their supper they heard an unwelcome and familiar voice from within the forest.

'So, we meet again …'

Jack turned towards the forest, and there stood in between the trees on top of a raised grassy bank, was Gravelaxe and around a dozen or so Dwarves, all holding axes. A vicious sneer curled the lips of the Dwarf leader as he gloated at them. Jack looked across to Elensar for guidance, and the Captain calmly placed his tea on the grass next to him and focused his attention on Gravelaxe and his Dwarves.

'Lay down your weapons or my Dwarves will slay you where you sit,' commanded Gravelaxe.

121

Jack followed Elensar's lead and carefully placed his mug on the grass. His short sword lay on the ground next to him. He estimated that Gravelaxe and his Dwarves were around thirty paces away from them. They had time to ready themselves for an attack.

But without warning an axe came flying towards Bumble's head. He didn't move and looked paralysed by fear. Jack grabbed him and pulled him to the ground as the axe embedded itself in the soil behind them. He dragged Bumble behind a rock and grabbed his sword. Stran and Roger followed suit and also dived for cover behind rocks. Elensar was on his feet in an instant with his longbow primed and ready and unleashed three arrows in rapid succession. They whispered through the air and found the chests of three Dwarves who immediately dropped to the ground like felled trees.

Gravelaxe and his Dwarves looked on in wide eyed amazement at the devastation that flew from Elensar's longbow before taking cover behind the trunks of the pine trees on the edge of the forest. Elensar stood firm with another arrow primed in his bow. He didn't even bother to take cover. Jack could hardly believe what he'd just witnessed. Three deadly arrows released in as many seconds. Elensar truly was the consummate warrior.

'Gravelaxe! Throw down your weapons and come out from behind the trees. I promise you that no harm will come to you or your Dwarves if you cooperate,' ordered Elensar.

One of the Dwarves stepped out from behind a tree and before he could even raise the hand that carried his axe, an arrow cut him down.

'Gravelaxe!' shouted Elensar. 'I have over fifty arrows in my quiver – more than enough to despatch you all three times over. Do the right thing by your Dwarves and surrender.'

Jack focused on the trees and there was no sign of any movement. He quickly surveyed the open plains behind them and the surrounding trees and was as sure as he could be that there were no other Dwarves that were going to surprise them. Elensar stood rooted to the spot, longbow primed, eyes fixed on the trees where the Dwarves sheltered.

Jack instinctively knew that Gravelaxe wouldn't surrender. As much as he hated what Gravelaxe and his Dwarves had planned to do to them, he also desperately wanted to avoid having to kill them all. An idea suddenly flashed into his head.

'Grindell! If you're there, step forward with your friends and drop your weapons. I guarantee that you will be unharmed and free to return to Bellowrock. It is Gravelaxe that we want.'

Jack studied the trees again but there was no movement. He looked across to Elensar and saw the steely concentration on his face. These Dwarves were as good as dead if they didn't surrender. He tried one more time. 'Grindell – the Captain here will have no hesitation in cutting you all down if you refuse to surrender. Do yourself and your friends a favour and give yourselves up.'

Bumble lay shaking on the ground in front of Jack. He looked up at him and tried to speak.

Gravelaxe called out from behind his tree. 'Bumble, you are a traitor. You will be hanged for betraying our people.'

Bumble found some courage from deep down within himself and responded. 'It is you who has betrayed our people, Gravelaxe, by doing a deal with Leah. He will destroy us all if he isn't stopped.'

'Leah is a figment of the Elves imagination,' retorted Gravelaxe. 'I have never heard of or met him.'

'You met him as he travelled through our mountains some weeks ago,' said Bumble. 'You took the Elven gold dust as payment to kill these people.'

'You're lying, Bumble. Why would any honest Dwarf believe the words of a traitor?'

'Grindell, we've all been bullied by Gravelaxe for years. This is our chance to rid our community of him. These Elves are honest and good people. I know that Gravelaxe made you lie in the court hearing. There is no Elven army massing on the Running Plains. They are here to help us. Throw down your weapons and walk away from Gravelaxe.'

Bumble's request was greeted with silence. Jack looked across to Elensar and shrugged. Something needed to give if they were going to break this deadlock.

And then something did. Axes and various swords were thrown out from the trees and several Dwarves, led by Grindell, stepped from behind them. They walked slowly in a line towards Jack and his friends with arms raised but Elensar kept his longbow at the ready and studied them every step they took. Jack held his sword in both hands and breathed slowly as he fought an inner battle to keep calm.

Gravelaxe stepped from cover of the tree and raised his axe in the air and was about to hurl it at Grindell's back. But Elensar reacted in a flash and unleashed an arrow that skewered Gravelaxe's throwing arm and the axe dropped to the floor as the Dwarf leader cried out in agony.

Jack bounded towards the Dwarves brandishing his sword as Elensar reloaded his bow. He stopped in front of them and shouted, 'lay face down with your arms stretched out in front of you!' They didn't hesitate and dropped to the ground. Jack then ran over to Gravelaxe and held the tip of his sword to his throat. 'Your rule of terror is over, Gravelaxe. You are now our prisoner.'

Gravelaxe held his injured arm and scowled at Jack but didn't answer. Jack walked around him and jabbed his sword into his back. 'Join your colleagues and lay face down on the ground.'

Gravelaxe limped over to where they lay holding his injured arm, before laying down on the ground next to Grindell. He didn't even look at his fellow Dwarves as he lay there. Elensar lay down his longbow and took some bandages from his pack and walked over to Gravelaxe.

'Let me remove that arrow before it turns your arm sceptic.'

Gravelaxe ignored him. Elensar lifted his head.

'You can either cooperate with me when I remove the arrow or not – the choice is yours. But let me assure you the first option is the least painful.'

Gravelaxe reluctantly struggled into a standing position and scowled at Elensar but still didn't speak. Elensar examined the arrow and it had penetrated clean through Gravelaxe's arm. He decided to cut the barb off and pull the arrow out. That way it would do the least damage as he removed it. He turned around and lifted his pack to search for a small serrated knife that he carried.

As he did so, Gravelaxe reached inside his jacket with his left arm and discreetly pulled out a knife. He took a step forward and raised his arm in the air. Jack saw what was happening and tried to scream out to warn Elensar, but the words stuck in his throat. He was too far away to do anything and looked on helplessly as his friend was about to be murdered by the Dwarf leader.

Gravelaxe's face twisted into vengeful hatred as he went to plunge the knife into Elensar's back. But something unexpected happened and Gravelaxe's facial expression changed from hatred to shock – his eyes and mouth opened wide and he fell forwards with the knife still in his hand. Jack saw the worn brown handle of a dagger sticking out of the Dwarf's back as he slumped to the ground.

Stran stepped forward as Elensar turned around oblivious to what had just happened. 'Never turn your back on a snake,' growled Stran as he pulled his dagger out of Gravelaxe's back and wiped the bloodstained blade on the grass.

Elensar knelt by Gravelaxe and checked the pulse on his neck. He looked up at Jack with a solemn expression and said two words; 'he's dead ...'

*

Chapter Sixteen –
New Dawn, New Companion

It was the morning after the night before and Jack and his friends looked on as the surviving Dwarves paid their respects at the graves of their fallen comrades. They had made wooden plaques carved out of tree stumps to mark each of the five graves. Gravelaxe was buried in the middle of the other four as recognition of his position as leader of the Bellowrock Dwarves. Although Jack had no respect for Gravelaxe the Dwarf he accepted that his position as leader deserved to be acknowledged.

As the Dwarves came away from the graves, Jack and Elensar took the opportunity to speak with them before they returned to their home. Grindell seemed a much more reasonable character without the intimidating Gravelaxe at his side.

'I'm sorry that your colleagues died,' said Jack. 'We try to avoid killing at all costs.'

'You were left with little choice,' said Grindell. 'Gravelaxe would have fought to the last Dwarf if we hadn't surrendered.' He looked at Elensar with a mixture of envy and respect. 'The Captain here is truly a gifted archer - the best I have ever seen.'

Elensar nodded his acknowledgement of Grindell's compliment. Jack turned his attention to Bumble. 'Well my friend, it is time for us to continue our journey. I'm hoping that you will join our company and help us on our quest.' He turned to Grindell. 'I wish you a safe journey back to Bellowrock and good luck with building the new society that your people deserve.'

But Grindell surprised Jack. 'I'm going to suggest that Bumble returns to Bellowrock with my colleagues. He is much more suited to persuasion and diplomacy than I am. When it comes down to it, I am a warrior, built in the same mould as the Captain here. I believe that you are going to need my skills more than Bumble's on your quest.'

It made sense to Jack. They were undoubtedly going to come across dangerous situations and Grindell's warrior skills could prove useful.

'And I have met this Graydon Leah with Gravelaxe,' continued Grindell. 'He is a very imposing character, not just in physical size, but his presence also. I was ill at ease in his company.'

Elensar stepped up beside Jack. 'What was it about him that made you so?'

'There is an aura about him – an aura of mystery. A huge grey wolf accompanies him wherever he goes, and it is totally under his spell. I have never in all of my years seen anyone tame a wolf.'

'And neither have I,' agreed Elensar.

Jack turned to Bumble. 'And what do you have to say to Grindell's suggestion?'

'It makes sense. I am not physically able for long treks and I am most certainly not made for combat. I think Grindell's suggestion is a sound one.'

'Very well,' said Jack. 'Grindell will join our company.' He took hold of Bumble's hand and shook it warmly. 'I can't thank you enough my friend for what you've done for us. If it wasn't for you, we would have perished at the hands of Gravelaxe.'

'I was glad to help,' said Bumble, 'and I wish you well. We all need you to succeed in your quest.'

They strapped on their packs and Elensar showed the level of his trust in Grindell by handing him his axes. Farewells were said, and they set off in their respective directions. Rory and Roger had been particularly quiet during the confrontation with Gravelaxe and Jack took the opportunity to see how they were both bearing up.

'I've never seen anyone killed before,' said Rory. 'It just left me a little numb.'

'Same for me,' said Roger. 'But I totally back Elensar's actions. Humans have had more than their fair share of brutal dictators over the years but Gravelaxe is up there with the worst of them.'

'We're lucky to have the Captain with us,' said Jack. 'Without him we would have been recaptured and we all know what Gravelaxe had in store for us.'

'I'll drink to that later,' smiled Rory.

Jack joined Grindell at the head of the company as they followed a path that wound its way through the middle of the forest. Winter had stripped it of much of its undergrowth, with only the occasional holly bush and clump of pines offering some green in stark contrast to the cold greys and browns. Jack loved forests – they were his natural habitat, but he loved them just that bit more once spring had cast its magic and started to restore the colour and vibrancy that made them so special to him.

Grindell marched quietly at Jack's side and offered little conversation, but Jack needed to find out what he knew about the terrain they were headed towards.

'Have you travelled this far east before?' asked Jack.

'I have only come as far as this forest. I am told that there are vast lakes and rolling hills on the far side, but that is as far as my knowledge goes.'

'And do you know where we may find Pixies?'

'I'm afraid I do not. Gravelaxe was a very insular leader and made a point of keeping us away from other races. You are the first Elves I have met.'

'And don't forget a Leprechaun and a human,' chimed in Rory.

'Of course,' said Grindell nodding his acknowledgement.

Jack didn't press Grindell any further as he wanted him to get used to being with them all, but his initial impression of the Dwarf was a positive one. Despite all the trials and tribulations they faced in Bellowrock, he was starting to feel that things were slowly coming together. They only needed one further addition to their company and the 'Unification of the Common Purpose' was complete.

And Grindell had met Graydon Leah which was another bonus. He would bide his time before asking the Dwarf what he knew about their adversary.

Jack had learnt much about himself since he set out on this amazing journey nearly twelve months ago but was also learning about his friends. Elensar had the guile and skill that made him almost invincible as a warrior, which is why the Faery Queens chose him to be part of the quest.

Stran was as mysterious as ever but had proved his worth by stopping Gravelaxe from killing Elensar. Jack sensed that the ranger had many skills that would show themselves before this quest had ended.

Rory was as optimistic as ever. Even nearly falling into that black abyss deep in the heart of the mountains failed to dampen his enthusiasm. Of all the Leprechauns that Jack had met, Rory was the one that he would have chosen to join him.

But it was Roger who surprised Jack the most. He had been subjected to the most extreme weather conditions; had been sentenced to death and witnessed deadly combat at close quarters. None of which had seemed to faze him. He was learning that his father was a strong and adaptable character who would yet prove his worth to the company.

They spent the whole day journeying through the forest and made camp for the night by a shallow stream just as darkness descended. They soon had a fire blazing and Roger made a pot of Roseleaf as Rory prepared vegetables for one of his speciality stews. Jack watched Grindell as he sipped his tea. He'd taken off his axes and leant back against a tree stump.

He was the same build and height as Gravelaxe with a black bushy beard, but although his eyes were grey and steely just like the Dwarf leader's, there was also kindness in them. Jack was convinced that they had made a good decision in allowing Grindell to join their company.

'So how do you find our tea?' asked Jack.

Grindell nodded. 'It is sweet and refreshing; nothing like the tea we drink in Bellowrock.'

'What is it like?' asked Jack.

'Dark and very, very strong,' said Grindell.

'Sounds like the tea my grandfather used to make,' said

Jack grimacing at the memory.

Rory served up his stew and Grindell enthusiastically devoured two bowlfuls along with several chunks of oatmeal bread. As he placed his empty bowl on the grass next to him, he turned to Rory and said, 'that is a fine bowl of stew.'

'It's a recipe from a very special colleen back in Cill-Arney, called Auntie Bridie. I will pass on your compliment the next time I see her, or better still, you can come to Cill-Arney one day and tell her yourself.'

'I would like that,' said Grindell. 'I would like that very much.'

Once the supper things had been washed and tidied away, they sat in a circle around the campfire enjoying its warmth. It was still very cold but the biting wind that had plagued them on the Running Plains was thankfully absent. Jack and Elensar took the opportunity to question Grindell further about Leah.

'Did you meet Leah many times?' asked Jack.

'I first met him some months back. He and Gravelaxe had a private meeting as I stood guard. I was not party to their discussions. Then I met him again about a month before you arrived on our mountains. Again, I was excluded from their conversation.'

'Did Gravelaxe tell you anything about what they talked about?' asked Elensar.

'Only that a band of Elves would come to our mountains and that they would kill us all if they weren't dealt with. Leah had said that you would claim to have come in peace, but it was just a cover to destroy our people.'

'Bumble told us that Leah paid Gravelaxe to kill us,' said Jack.

'Nothing would surprise me about Gravelaxe,' said Grindell.

'Is there anything you can tell us about Leah that may help us? Do you know where we can find him?' asked Jack.

'He comes from the far eastern lands. It will take us many weeks to get there and many more to find him when we do. He has a very intimidating presence. We must approach him with great caution.'

'Is he an Elf?' asked Elensar.

Grindell shrugged his shoulders. 'It's hard to say. His hair is long and thick, and he is much taller than you, Captain. He wears a heavy fur coat and carries a broad sword strapped to his back. The wolf goes everywhere with him.'

Elensar turned to Jack. 'It sounds like he has very powerful magic.'

Jack nodded his agreement. 'And he will be even more powerful with our gold dust.'

Elensar placed a firm hand on Jack's shoulder. 'But I am sure that you will be more than a match for him when the time comes.'

'You have magic?' asked a surprised Grindell.

'I did until Leah stole our gold dust,' said Jack. 'My whole community has faded back into the spirit world as there is no magic to sustain our land. As I tried to tell Gravelaxe, this Leah is a threat to us all and must be dealt with otherwise we are all doomed.'

Grindell held is hand out in the manner of a warrior and Jack clasped it firmly. 'I pledge to you my loyalty and that of all of the Dwarves in Bellowrock. Gravelaxe was a fool to trust this Leah and I will do my best to help you bring him down.'

*

Chapter Seventeen – Gwendolain

The following weeks were spent trekking through forests, climbing hills and mountain trails, travelling ever eastwards. They camped in sleepy hollows; by mountain streams, and sometimes under the stars in open fields. The terrain, although at times rugged, was always beautiful. Rory remarked as they gazed down at the silvery surface of a mountain lake; 'if only Tyler were here with his pencil and notepad to record this beauty.'

Just hearing mention of Tyler's name made Jack's heart ache. An overwhelming feeling of sadness threatened to engulf him. Tyler had been his constant companion on all his journeys except this one. He missed his old friend terribly.

Rory picked up on his mood. 'I'm sorry Jack. I should have thought before I opened my oversized mouth.'

'That's OK, Rory,' said Jack attempting a smile. 'With all that's been going on I haven't thought about him for a while. I miss his companionship and I miss his counsel.'

'Do you miss his moaning?' enquired Rory.

Jack laughed out loud. 'Would you believe me if I said yes?'

'I must admit that he did give us a good laugh on more than one occasion,' agreed Rory.

'I appreciate sentiment as much as the next person,' said Elensar, 'but we must keep going. I'd like to get to the far side of the mountains before dark.'

Elensar was right as always and they carried along the mountain trail in the opposite direction to the westerly travelling sun. Rory caught up with Jack and Elensar and whispered to them. 'I thought I should mention that we only have enough food to last five days at the most.'

'I was beginning to wonder if your rucksack was bottomless,' said Elensar. 'I was hoping that we would have come across some other communities by now.'

'Don't worry about it,' said Rory. 'Something will turn

up.'

'I hope so,' whispered Elensar, 'as we're not going to travel very far on empty stomachs.'

It was late afternoon as they descended the stony path from the mountains and followed a trail that led towards a dense green forest. A shallow, fast running stream joined the path just as they entered the forest and they all took the opportunity to fill their bottles.

Jack rinsed his face in the stream alongside Roger. His father had said little since they'd left Bellowrock and Jack was becoming concerned about him.

'Are you bearing up OK?' he asked.

Roger filled his canteen and took a mouthful of the cool stream water. 'I'm fine – a little tired, but fine.'

'That is hard terrain that we've just covered. Even Elensar is challenged by it.'

'I'm used to this sort of travelling. I thrive on it,' said Roger.

'Is it one of the others bothering you?'

'Not at all,' said Roger. 'What is there not to like about Rory? Stran doesn't say much but Grindell is fine, as is Elensar.'

'So, what is it?'

Roger didn't answer at first and took another mouthful of the stream water. 'What happened back there in Bellowrock unnerved me.'

'It unnerved us all,' said Jack. 'I've been in some tight scrapes but that was the worst.'

'I was frightened,' admitted Roger, 'even terrified …'

'We all were,' said Jack. 'But you stood your ground. Courage isn't the absence of fear; it's carrying on despite the odds stacked against you. If it wasn't for your quick thinking when we were in that cavern, we could have lost Rory. You helped him even though you were putting your own life on the line. I'm not sure it's happened by design, but this company has all the markings of a well-balanced group and you, Roger, are an integral part of it.'

Roger forced a smile. 'I just hope I don't let you down.'

Jack slapped him playfully on his back. 'As my grandfather used to say, you can only ever do your best and that is all that anyone has the right to ask of you.'

Roger's hunched shoulders lifted, and his body language looked more relaxed. 'I hope I get the chance to meet him one day.'

'I'll make sure of that,' smiled Jack.

'I think we should make camp in the forest,' said Elensar. 'We've still got another hour of daylight. Let's follow the path and see where it takes us.'

Jack had spent many hours walking through forests since he'd left his home in Heywood, and one thing he had discovered was that each one of them had their own distinct personality. Some were full of tall spindly pines with little undergrowth and a blue, grey light filtered by the green canopy. Some had such thick undergrowth that it was nigh on impossible to find a way through, and the density of the trees was such that it created an almost permanent dusk within the forest.

The forest they were entering was somewhere in between. There was some undergrowth but the paths through were wide and clear. The beech and oak trees were packed tight and held onto each other like needy lovers. The twisted shapes of the branches reached out like tentacles grasping their nearest neighbours. Jack marvelled at the natural beauty of their surroundings.

And then something strange happened. As they walked along the path the branches of the trees started to move. Elensar reacted instantly and reached for his longbow and primed it with an arrow as Grindell brandished an axe.

'What is it?' asked Rory.

Elensar scanned the trees and bushes looking for any sign of attack. 'I'm not sure but I've never seen trees that can move their branches before. Jack, can you detect magic?'

Jack was about to say no but suddenly felt a familiar tingle in the soles of his feet. 'Wait, I sense something.' He instantly knew it was Koehtia. It felt warm and comforting.

134

It slowly worked his way up his legs and into his body. Within seconds it was dancing on his fingertips. The elation he felt quickly disappeared when he thought of the reason why.

'Elensar! Koehtia is coursing through me. Leah must be near.'

The Captain peered deep into the forest. The branches on the trees continued to move. It was Rory who broke the silence.

'Look, the trees are forming an arch.'

Jack followed Rory's gaze and he saw that he was right. But more than that they were forming a corridor. Beech trees one side and oak trees the other. He called out to Elensar, 'do you have any idea what's going on?'

The Captain shook his head. 'I don't – but it could be a trap.'

'Or we're being invited in,' suggested Rory.

The Koehtia flowed through Jack like a raging river. His senses were on full alert. 'I'm not picking up on any threat. Maybe we should follow the path and see where it takes us.'

'I'll lead with you, Jack. Grindell, can you cover our rear?' said the Captain.

The Dwarf nodded and fell in behind Stran, Rory and Roger. Jack joined Elensar and the company cautiously followed the pathway that had opened out in front of them.

Elensar kept his bow primed and anxiously scanned the trees for signs of any threats. Grindell prowled like a leopard at their rear, ready to spring into action at the first signs of trouble. Jack kept vigilant and monitored his Koehtia. He looked around and smiled at Roger. He smiled back. Jack was confident that his father would be OK.

Elensar stopped suddenly and raised his right hand. 'Can you hear that?'

'Hear what?' asked Rory.

The captain didn't answer immediately and listened intently. 'It sounds like singing.'

They all joined him and quietly listened.

'Now I might be wrong, but I can't see this Leah fellow

greeting us with a song,' said Rory.

'Your flippancy is becoming very irritating, Leprechaun,' hissed Stran. 'We all need to keep focused not listen to you making needless jokes.'

'It isn't a joke,' said Rory indignantly. 'I'm saying that someone as ruthless and powerful as Leah who is hell-bent on making sure we don't find him isn't going to sing us a song, as opposed to someone that is genuinely pleased to welcome us to their land.'

Jack glared at Stran. 'Rory has a point and I'd prefer you didn't use that tone when you talk to him.'

Stran locked eyes with Jack but didn't respond. Elensar brought them back to the immediate issue.

'We proceed with caution. Let me know if you see or hear anything.'

They continued along the tree corridor looking for the source of the singing. Jack had to admit that it was beautiful, like a choir of angels serenading them. His Koehtia flowed through him but he didn't feel it was trying to protect him; it was like it was responding to the singing. He tried to keep his focus, but he had a feeling of calmness sweep over him and he had a sudden urge to dance to the music.

And that's what he did.

Jack danced around his friends as they looked on in stunned silence. The music carried him along – he had no choice but to dance to it like riding a wave to the beach.

'Er, Jack,' said Rory, 'as much as I like a good tune and I'm usually the first person to jig at a ceilidh, I'm not sure that this is either the time or place.'

But Jack wasn't hearing him and continued his dance. He tried to grab hold of Elensar by the hand, but the Captain resisted and grabbed hold of him and looked him straight in the eyes. 'Jack, what's happening to you?'

'It's the music Elensar – I just have to dance. Why don't you join me?' And carried on dancing around them.

''Look!' said Roger. 'There are blue sparks jumping between his fingers.'

'He's right,' said Elensar. 'I don't like this – I think the

Koehtia is deranging him.'

'Maybe your analysis is wrong, Rory. Maybe this Leah is cleverer and more devious than we think,' said Stran adopting a more conciliatory tone.

'You think he could be controlling Jack with his magic?' said Elensar.

'It's a possibility – that's all I'm saying.'

Just at that moment Jack stopped dancing around them and started to skip along the tree corridor.

Roger panicked. 'We've got to stop him! Who knows what's waiting for us at the end of that corridor.'

'We're going to have to find out sooner or later,' said Grindell.

'He's right,' said Elensar. 'Let's follow him.'

And they all ran after Jack as he skipped along the tree corridor. He was oblivious to them or for that matter anything else, humming to himself as he skipped in and out of the trees. He looked happy; he felt happy, he didn't have a care in the world. All his tension worries and tiredness had gone. He felt like that five-year-old boy who used to skip around Heywood Forest.

'What do you think is at the end of the corridor?' asked Rory as he jogged alongside Elensar.

'I don't know, Rory, but I won't be taking any chances. 'I'll keep this primed,' he said holding up his longbow.

And they didn't have to wait long as the pathway soon dropped down into a picturesque leafy vale. The company stood on the vale rim mesmerised by its beauty. At its centre, a shallow waterfall fed a clear blue pool amid a cluster of pink flowery shrubs. In fact, every bush, plant, tree or shrub in the entire vale was covered by pink flowers.

'I don't think I've ever seen anything quite so pink,' commented Rory. 'Not that I'm complaining as it looks amazing.'

'I have to agree with you for once, Leprechaun,' said Stran.

'And it's so warm,' said Rory, 'just like a summer's day.'

'Look,' said Roger, 'the path we followed has disappeared.'

They all turned as one and saw that Roger was right.

'Well I suppose there are worse places to be confined in,' said Rory.

'Maybe,' said Elensar, 'but I'll be a lot happier when I find out who's invited us in here.'

They walked down the path into the vale and by this time Jack had jumped into the pool and was splashing around like a young child.

Grindell stood by the side of Elensar and discreetly whispered to him, 'I don't like this, Captain. Something's not right.'

'I agree,' said Elensar, 'until whoever it is that lives here shows themselves, I suggest we keep vigilant.'

Just at that moment Stran called out. 'Look, there's something flying around the trees on the far side of the pool. Elensar raised his bow and looked in the direction Stran was pointing. He was right, and it started to fly towards them although not in a straight line. When it was around fifty metres or so away from them, it suddenly dropped to the ground.

It was a young girl ... with wings. The company stood mesmerised but Elensar still held his longbow to his shoulder and shouted out, 'who are you?'

She turned to Jack first and watched him for a few seconds before walking slowly towards them. She stopped ten paces away from them and curtsied. She was wearing a forest green suit with brown ankle boots and was around a metre high. She folded her wings down her back and turned to Elensar. 'I'd really like it if you lowered your longbow Mr Elf. I can assure you that I present no threat to you.'

Elensar checked the trees and bushes and as far as he could tell she was on her own. He whispered to Grindell, 'what do you think?'

The Dwarf shrugged his shoulders. 'She carries no weapons.'

Elensar lowered his longbow and removed the arrow.

She stepped nearer to them and curtsied again. 'Let me offer you a very warm welcome to my magical land of Gwendolain – the home of the flying Pixies.'

*

Chapter Eighteen - The Magical Land

'Gwendolain – that's a grand name,' said Rory.

'It's named after me. I'm called Gwendo, and I'm the Queen, so Gwendolain.'

'Makes sense,' agreed Rory.

'Could you tell us why our friend is acting so strangely?' asked Elensar pointing to Jack who was still splashing around in the pool.

'Ah,' said Gwendo, 'some people react that way to the magic.' She spread her wings again and rose gracefully into the air, flew over to Jack and hovered above him. She reached into her pocket and sprinkled some sparkling silver dust over him. His reaction was instantaneous. He stopped splashing the in water and sat still for a few seconds before looking around. He looked up to the others with a bewildered expression on his face.

'Where am I?'

Gwendo flew back to Elensar, hovered just above him for a few seconds before gently lowering herself onto the lush green grass next to him. She folded her wings behind her back and turned her attention to Jack. She curtsied again and introduced herself to him. 'I'm Gwendo - I'm Queen of the flying Pixies. This is our home, Gwendolain.'

Jack waded through the pool and climbed up onto the bank and shook the excess water from his clothes. 'How did I get here?'

'You reacted to our magic. We are quite playful here and you responded to that. But, no harm done, you're fine now. My Pixie dust saw to that,' said Gwendo.

Jack fought to recollect the events that led up to him splashing in the pool. His face lit up into a broad smile as he remembered. 'My Koehtia has returned!'

'It's always there; you just need the means to feel it, lovely Elf,' smiled Gwendo.

The Koehtia tingled the soles of Jack's feet. It felt good.

Gwendo walked around the company and looked each

one of them up and down. 'So, who have we here?' she asked as she stopped in front of Rory. 'A Leprechaun if I'm not mistaken.'

'I am indeed.' He bowed low before taking her hand and kissing it. 'Rory McNory and I come all the way from Cill-Arney on Emerald Island … grand to meet you.'

Gwendo giggled like a child, which was hardly surprising as she had the high-pitched voice of a little girl. Stran and Elensar introduced themselves before she settled in front of Roger. 'Well, well, I do believe we have a human in our midst.'

Roger shuffled nervously from foot to foot as Gwendo giggled again. Next up was Grindell; his gruff exterior didn't waiver as she gave him a warm hug. 'It's been a long time since I met a Dwarf.'

She returned her attention to Jack as he stripped off his dripping wet coat. 'And I sense you are no ordinary Elf.'

Jack laid his heavy coat on the grass and removed his jacket which was also wringing wet. 'My name is Green-Jack and I hail from Waterswood.'

'Mmmm,' said Gwendo as she nervously tucked her short brown hair behind her ears. 'I see some human in you. Elf and human, a very potent combination I would say.'

'Do you live here on your own, Gwendo?' asked Rory.

'I most certainly do not. I would go mad if I didn't have somebody to play with. 'She turned towards the trees on the far side of the pool and called out, 'Pixies – why don't you come and meet our new friends.'

The words were no sooner out of her mouth than a swarm of flying Pixies flew out of the trees towards them. They landed in a semi-circle around the company and giggled incessantly. They were all dressed the same as Gwendo and were around the same size. The energy level surged as they jumped up and down with the excitement at having guests.

'They're a bit noisy,' said Gwendo, 'but I can assure you that they will make you very welcome.'

'I can't believe it's still so warm and it should be dark

by now,' said Rory.

'And that's because it's always summer here,' said Gwendo. 'Who needs those dark, cold winters? Not me for sure.'

'One last question,' said Rory. 'We're tired and hungry after travelling all day. Can we find a nice spot to eat?'

'Of course. My lovely Pixies will see that you're all looked after.' She joined her Pixies and they all curtsied low. 'And once again, a warm welcome to Gwendolain.'

*

The company sat in a circle next to a dense cluster of pink flowery bushes as they ate their supper. Their winter clothing had been dispensed with and they sat in short sleeves on what could only be describe as a warm summer's evening. The Pixies had cooked them a delicious meal of potato stew with herbs and carrots accompanied by chunks of tasty oatmeal bread. They had a makeshift oven made from rocks and heated with white hot coals. The stew pot sat on top of an iron griddle and the delicious aroma of the stew wafted across them enticing them all to have second helpings, which of course Rory did.

Then the stew aroma was replaced with the sweet smell of apple pie cooking inside the stone oven. Rory's mouth was literally watering as he waited impatiently for his slice and when it came he wasn't disappointed. It was a large wedge covered in thick cream.

As he leant back against a tree stump patting his stomach, he said, 'Thanks Gwendo, that's the best meal we've had for weeks.'

'You've no need to thank me,' said Gwendo, 'it was Lilydrop and Roseleaf who did all the cooking.'

Rory raised his glass of pear juice and said, 'thank you lovely Pixies. That was a grand meal.'

As much as Jack and Elensar were grateful for the hospitality and food from the Pixies they were anxious to get on with the business of why they were there. As the

Pixies cleared up their supper things the two of them took Gwendo to one side.

'We need to talk with you Gwendo. We are in desperate need of your help,' said Jack.

'You're all tired from your travelling,' said Gwendo, 'so why don't you take the opportunity to get some much-needed rest. There'll be plenty of time tomorrow to talk.'

Jack looked at Elensar. 'She has a point. I'm exhausted from the last few weeks. Let's rest tonight and discuss the business tomorrow.'

'I knew you'd see sense,' said Gwendo. 'Now we sleep in the trees – we can make you beds up there, or if you prefer, you can sleep here.'

'I'll leave the trees to the birds,' chirped Rory. 'I like to keep my feet planted firmly on the ground.'

'Very well,' said Gwendo as she unfurled her wings. 'It's time for us Pixies to go to bed. Sleep well and we'll see you in the morning.' With that she rose up into the air and was joined by the other Pixies, before they all flew off into the trees together.

Jack and Elensar sat down with the others as they finished their drinks.

'Gwendo and the Pixies seem like nice sorts,' said Rory.

'That's one of the best vegetarian meals I've ever had,' said Roger. 'And the apple pie, well …'

'I feel at peace,' said Grindell. 'I haven't felt this relaxed for a very long time.'

'Hardly surprising living with that maniac Gravelaxe,' said Rory.

'I don't trust her,' said Stran changing the mood.

'You don't trust anyone, Stran,' said Rory. 'Sometimes I think you don't even trust yourself.'

The ranger scowled at Rory but Elensar backed him up. 'I agree with Stran – she's almost too friendly.'

'And she never looks you in the eye,' said Stran. 'Never trust anyone who can't look you in the eye.'

'Let's reserve judgement until tomorrow,' said Jack. 'We're all tired and will benefit from a good night's sleep.'

'You'll get no arguments from me on that score,' said Rory unpacking his sleeping bag.

*

Jack was woken by the delicious smell of breakfast cooking. He sat up to see Lilydrop and Roseleaf standing in front of the oven cooking tomatoes, mushrooms and eggs on the griddle. He extricated himself from his sleeping bag and joined them.

'Is there anything I can do?' he asked.

Lilydrop and Roseleaf didn't answer and just looked at each other and giggled.

'Can I make some tea?' suggested Jack.

'We don't drink tea,' said Lilydrop in a squeaky voice.

'Leave it to me,' said Jack as he reached inside his rucksack and pulled out a kettle and teapot. Within fifteen minutes he had a pot of Roseleaf ready and filled three mugs. 'Here, this is Roseleaf. Elves drink it all of the time.'

Lilydrop broke into a fit of the giggles again as Jack handed her the mug. 'Roseleaf, the Elves have named their tea after you.'

Just at that minute Gwendo landed next to them. 'I think you'll find, Lilydrop, that I named Roseleaf after the Elven tea.'

Lilydrop stopped giggling and returned to cooking the breakfast. Jack saw first-hand that Gwendo really did rule them.

'Did you sleep well?' asked Gwendo.

'I did indeed,' said Jack. 'I seem to sleep better when the Koehtia is with me.'

'And that's why you need to rest here a while, Jack. Take the time to build yourself up.' She looked at the others as they still slept soundly in their sleeping bags. 'You are all exhausted. I could see that the moment I set eyes on you. Take all the time you need to recuperate.'

'Unfortunately, one thing we don't have is time,' said Jack sadly. 'My home village is under threat – in fact the whole valley is under threat, which is why we must speak with you.'

'And speak we will,' said Gwendo as she unfurled her wings. 'But now I have other things to attend to.' And she flew off into the trees.

*

'That was a grand breakfast,' said Rory as he sipped his Roseleaf. 'I could get used to this pampering.'

'We're not here to enjoy ourselves, Leprechaun,' snapped Stran.

'I know,' said Rory equally testily, 'but I always appreciate a good meal and beautiful surroundings when they're on offer. This is what we all need after the stress we've recently been under, and I for one am going to enjoy it.'

Roger placed his hand on Rory's shoulder and gave it a reassuring squeeze. Rory and Stran were complete opposites when it came to their outlook on life and were never going to agree on many things. But Jack wasn't quite as relaxed as Rory was about their surroundings and took Elensar to one side.

'I tried to speak with Gwendo this morning and tell her about our predicament, but she was very evasive,' said Jack.

'What did she say?' asked Elensar.

'Not very much,' said Jack, 'before making an excuse and leaving. I haven't seen her since.'

'Well the next time she makes an appearance,' said Elensar, 'I'll make a point of explaining to her why we're here.'

They spent the rest of the day relaxing and getting to know their beautiful surroundings. Lilydrop and Roseleaf took care of their every need but Gwendo didn't make an appearance much to Jack and Elensar's increasing frustration. As Stran and Grindell took the opportunity to rest all day, Rory and Roger enjoyed the nature of Gwendolain.

145

'I don't think I've ever seen such brightly coloured butterflies,' said Rory.

'And the birds are unlike any species I've ever seen before,' said Roger.

'Are you an expert on our flying friends, Roger?'

'I spend a lot of my weekends bird watching in the country,' said Roger. 'I love to get out of the city as much as I can.'

'So, what does bird watching entail?' asked Rory.

'Er, watching birds,' said Roger.

'Ask a silly question,' laughed Rory.

Jack and Elensar wandered into the wood in the hope of finding Gwendo but she was nowhere to be seen. Enquiries as to her whereabouts to either Lilydrop or Roseleaf were met with blank expressions. As much as they both appreciated the beauty of their surroundings, feelings of concern started to surface as to why she was avoiding them.

As they all sat around the fire after their evening meal, Elensar whispered to Jack, 'I can't help getting the feeling that we're being held here.'

'But for what reason?' asked Jack.

'I wish I knew,' said Elensar, 'but Gwendo is definitely avoiding us and I want to find out why.'

An uneasy feeling surfaced inside Jack. As much as he didn't want to agree with the Captain, his gut feel was telling him that he was right.

*

Chapter Nineteen - Escape

Jack and Elensar's worst fears were confirmed when Gwendo didn't make an appearance for the next two days. Their agitation was being picked up by the others and they were now openly discussing why they were being held there.

'There's nothing to stop us just packing our things and leaving,' said Rory.

'Other than the fact that we're here to persuade a Pixie to join our quest,' said Stran pointedly.

'Fair point,' agreed Rory.

Elensar took Jack to one side out of earshot of the others. 'Time isn't on our side Jack. We may only have a matter of months to find this Leah and reclaim your gold dust. We have to leave, and we have to leave now.'

'But how are we going to persuade Gwendo to join us when she refuses to talk to us? We need a Pixie to complete our company.'

Elensar looked at Jack with an expression that suggested he wasn't going to like what he was about to hear. 'We could kidnap either Lilydrop or Roseleaf.'

Jack was horrified. 'Kidnap! How could you even suggest that? They are the most beautiful and innocent creatures I have ever met.'

'Have you forgotten why we're here, Jack? It's about the survival of your valley and the Elves that live there. We cannot fail … we must not fail.'

Jack knew he was right. But kidnap? It went against everything he believed in. 'Let me try to persuade one of them. If that doesn't work, then I'll reluctantly go along with your plan.'

They went back to the others and told them to pack and ready themselves to leave. Roseleaf was on her own washing up the breakfast things. Jack tentatively walked up to her and nervously shuffled from foot to foot.

She turned to him, her bright blue eyes shining like stars,

and her usual smile lighting up her face. 'Can I help you Jack?'

'Er, yes. We, er, we have to move on, Roseleaf and we need your help.'

Her smile widened showing her pearly white teeth. 'Just tell me what you want me to do.'

'Can you spare us some food?'

'Of course - we have plenty. I'll help fill your rucksacks.'

'And we're going to need you to come with us. I'll explain why later,' said a hesitant Jack.

'I'm happy to do whatever it is you want.'

'You'll come?' said a surprised Jack.

'Gwendo has told us to look after you in whatever way we can, so I'm just following her instructions.'

'Do you know where Gwendo is?' asked Jack.

'She said that she had things to attend to,' said Roseleaf.

Jack turned to the others. 'This may be a good time to go. Rory, can you help Roseleaf pack the rucksacks? I want to leave as soon as we can.'

They were all packed and ready within thirty minutes. Roseleaf stood innocently like a child alongside them. She didn't question them at all.

'OK, Roseleaf,' said Elensar. 'We're going to need you to show us the way out of here.'

She looked confused 'I'm afraid I can't help you with that.'

'Why not?' asked Elensar.

'Why would anyone want to leave here? It's beautiful, and none of us Pixies has ever tried. And besides, we don't know the way.'

Elensar turned to Jack and shrugged his shoulders. 'We'll head east. We're bound to find a trail out of here sooner or later.'

They followed the path around the pool and into the forest. There was a clear pathway through the undergrowth between the ferns and bracken, and that was the route they took. Roseleaf walked alongside them seemingly oblivious

148

to what they were doing. Sometimes she would suddenly unfurl her wings and rise up high into the sky. The first time she did it Elensar panicked and thought she was flying off, but she always returned.

She was just the most delightful companion and Rory had a soul mate with whom he could share his appreciation of their surroundings with.

'I love the forest,' said Rory. 'I don't think I've ever seen such colourful shrubs and bushes.'

'It's the magic of Gwendolain,' said Roseleaf. 'Our Queen created it for us all to enjoy.'

'And you don't mind leaving it?' asked Rory.

The question brought a disapproving scowl from Elensar and Rory looked embarrassed.

'I happily do what my Queen asks me to. Gwendo loves us all and will always look after us.'

Her words cut like knives through Jack. He was taking this beautiful Pixie away from her home and the only place that she'd ever known.

Elensar sensed his unease and whispered to him, 'we will bring her back when this is all over. We have no choice in this – it's what the Faery Queens have asked us to do.'

Jack knew that he was right, but it still didn't help ease his conscience. He was fast learning that leadership involved difficult decisions and he was glad he had the Captain to guide him.

The morning passed uneventfully as they followed the path ever eastwards. The forest seemed to stretch on forever but that suited them as Gwendo was less likely to be able to find them once she realised that they'd gone. They stopped for a brief lunch in the early afternoon and the ever-willing Roseleaf provided bread, cheese and dried fruit, all washed down with pear juice.

Following their lunch, they carried on along the same pathway and made good progress. As evening approached, Rory commented, 'we must be miles away from Gwendolain by now. We should be able to make camp for the night soon.'

149

'Can you still feel your Koehtia, Jack?' asked Elensar.

Jack stopped and searched inside himself. He felt the familiar tingle in the soles of his feet but the Koehtia no longer flowed through him. 'I think it's weakening – I can just about feel it in my feet.'

'There you are,' said Rory, 'we must have left Gwendolain way behind.'

And they all agreed. The tension that had surrounded them when they left in the morning had gone. They chatted between themselves as Roseleaf happily flitted in between the trees and shrubs.

Rory pointed to a clearing ahead next to a clear blue pool. Why don't we camp there for the night, Elensar? I could do with a nice soak in that lovely inviting pool.'

It was as they approached the pool that something very strange and unexpected happened. Lilydrop flew out from the trees and landed in front of them. Her bright blue eyes sparkled and she smiled broadly. She curtsied and said, 'did you enjoy your walk in the forest?'

The company surveyed their surroundings and soon realised that they were back at the place they'd left over eight hours previously.

'That can't be,' said Elensar disbelievingly. 'We've been heading east all day. It's …'

'It's Morning-Dew's forest all over again,' said Rory. 'The magic has duped us.'

And Jack knew he was right, but did he have the power to generate a 'Guiding-Light' like he used the last time? He searched for the Koehtia within him and had his answer – he barely felt it.

Lilydrop called over to Roseleaf. 'I was beginning to wonder where you were. Shall we make a start on this evening's supper?'

Roseleaf skipped over to her and together they started to slice vegetables. Elensar still shaking his head sat down on an upturned log and was joined by the others. 'I should have realised – our Artisans do a similar trick to deter people entering our land. Are you up to generating a 'Guiding

Light' again, Jack?'

He shook his head glumly. 'The Koehtia is very weak within me.'

'That surprises me,' said Elensar. 'You were buzzing with it when we first arrived here.'

'I know,' said Jack, 'but I can barely feel it.'

'I think we need to have a sit down with Gwendo,' said Rory. 'I have a feeling she knows exactly what's going on.'

'I'm sure you're right,' said Jack, 'but we need to find her first.'

'Can I suggest that we eat,' said Rory, 'and then turn our minds to what needs to be done. We all think better on full bellies, I know I certainly do.'

*

A very thoughtful company sat in a circle drinking their pear juice. Lilydrop and Roseleaf had served them up a delicious thick mushroom and herb stew. It was Jack's favourite and even though he felt disturbed about the day's events he enjoyed it greatly, along with the rhubarb tart for dessert. Rory ritually patted his stomach and sat back against his tree stump and allowed his meal to digest.

Grindell, Stran and Roger had been very quiet during the day and didn't venture any opinions on what had happened. Stran's only comment was that he left all things magic to those who understood it. Roger and Grindell sat quietly and listened.

'We need to find Gwendo,' said Elensar. 'She's the key to what's happening around here.'

'Easier said than done,' commented Rory. 'She's one very elusive Pixie.'

The words were no sooner out of his mouth when Gwendo glided down into the middle of the company and gently landed on her feet. She folded her wings and turned to Roseleaf and Lilydrop.

'Why don't you two take a well-deserved rest and leave our friends to tidy up?'

'But we really don't mind,' protested Lilydrop.

But a frown from Gwendo quickly changed their mind. 'Very well, Gwendo. Goodnight and we'll see you in the morning,' and the two of them flew off into the trees.

Gwendo helped herself to a glass of pear juice and sat on a log next to Jack and Elensar. 'I don't want them to hear what I have to tell you. They're already nervous enough.' She looked downcast, even depressed. Whatever it was she had to tell them caused her great pain. 'I'm afraid I haven't been very honest with you. All is not well in the land of Gwendolain. I have spent the last few days trying to put right what's been happening, but I've failed miserably.' Tears welled up in her eyes. 'My beautiful land is lost …'

'Lost? But why?' asked Jack.

Gwendo pulled a handkerchief from her pocket and dabbed her eyes and looked directly at Jack. 'I welcomed you to my land but for purely selfish reasons.'

Jack was still puzzled. 'I don't understand. You and your Pixies have made us very welcome.'

'I sensed your magic as you approached our borders which is why I welcomed you in. I thought you could save us, but I was wrong.' She dropped her gaze to the floor. 'I'm ashamed to say that I was planning to imprison you here. Please forgive me.'

Jack put his arm around her shoulder as she broke down and wept. 'Gwendo, there's nothing to forgive, but I wish you had told us what was happening as soon as we arrived. We are here to ask for your help but we're also here to help you.'

She looked up at Jack as the tears streamed down her face. 'There is a dark and terrible force that is draining my land of its magic. It has been steadily growing over the recent months. I have resisted it up until now, but … but I am all but drained. My land, the beautiful land of Gwendolain, is lost.'

'This dark and terrible force,' said Jack, 'would it be the work of a very dangerous character called Graydon Leah?'

Gwendo's tears suddenly stopped. 'How do you know of

him?'

'He is the reason we are here. He has stolen the gold dust from the Elven communities in Woodgate Valley far to the west of here. The magic that sustains these communities has all but gone. All my people have been temporarily lost to the spirit world. If we don't get our gold dust back, our land, and they, will be lost forever.'

Gwendo wiped her face, blew her nose and put her handkerchief back into her pocket. Her whole demeanour changed from one of defeat to indignation. 'So that's how he was able to break down my magic. He came to me many years ago to suggest that I could join him. He has a great lust for power and it is this, along with his thirst for magic, that has corrupted him. I of course rejected the idea, but I knew in my heart that he would come back one day.'

'Help us to defeat him,' urged Jack. 'Help us take back our gold dust so that we can help you to reclaim your land.'

'But you are just six. How can so few of you combat such power?'

'With you we will be seven. The Faery Queens have asked us to do this. They call us the 'Unification of a Common Purpose'. We need a Pixie to complete the company. Please say that you will join us.'

Gwendo stood up and stretched her wings. She wandered around them for a few minutes without saying anything, before stopping in front of Jack.'

'And they are confident that between us we can match this Leah's power?'

'They are,' said Jack.

'In that case,' said Gwendo, 'you have just found your Pixie.'

*

Chapter Twenty - The Wasted Land

Gwendo stood in front of a very tearful bunch of Pixies. She was doing her best to appear brave and confident, but Jack could see that her heart was breaking.

'I have no choice other than to join Jack and his friends. It is the only way that we will be able to rebuild Gwendolain.'

'But Gwendo,' said a tearful Lilydrop, 'you've always been here to look after us.'

'And I will be again,' said Gwendo swallowing down her sea of emotions. 'But I'm going to ask that you're all very brave while I'm away.'

'But the magic has gone,' said Roseleaf. 'How will we all keep safe?'

'By staying together and looking after each other just like we've always done. Don't stray far away from here and wait for me to return.' She took a deep breath and exhaled slowly. 'Now wipe away your tears my lovely Pixies and give your Queen a hug before she leaves.'

And that's what they did, each one of them in turn. Gwendo just about managed to hold it together and after the last Pixie had said her farewell, she joined Jack and his friends.

She looked up at Jack through sad, tear-filled eyes and said, 'I'd like to leave now if you don't mind. While I still can.'

If there was one thing Jack knew about, that was goodbyes. That feeling of leaving a part of you behind was familiar to him, but it still didn't make it any easier. It was the gravity of the situation they faced that forced them to take this path. This Leah had to be dealt with.

As they set off along the same path that they'd taken the previous day, Jack turned back to see the Pixies waving their Queen off, not that Gwendo looked or acknowledged them. Jack could see that it was breaking her heart to leave her beloved Pixies, so he nodded to Rory who walked alongside Gwendo and took her hand. He didn't say anything, but he didn't have to. His action spoke louder than any words. Roger walked silently alongside Stran and Grindell at the head of the company as Jack and Elensar brought up the rear.

Jack studied them all individually and then as a company. He'd achieved the first part of the task given to him by the Faery Queens. The 'Unification of a Common Purpose' was complete. They were presenting a united front and together they were going to confront this character Graydon Leah. They'd already faced enormous challenges to get this far on what was meant to be the easy part of the task. The next phase was going to be even more daunting. Leah wasn't going to meekly give up his new-found power without a fight, of that Jack was sure.

But Jack's grandfather had always taught him that anything worth achieving never came without a struggle and this surely was going to be the hardest challenge he had ever faced in his short life. He was very happy with the three new additions to the company. Roger, his father, had proved to be solid in the most difficult situations. Grindell's warrior skills were going to be invaluable and although he hadn't known Gwendo that long, his instincts told him that she was a formidable figure and her magic, when it returned, would be vital.

The Unification was complete and now it fell on their shoulders to find Leah.

They continued along the pathway through the forest in an easterly direction. Gwendo had assured Elensar earlier that the magic had faded and that they would soon be leaving the territory that was Gwendolain. Jack had so many questions he wanted to ask Gwendo, but knew that she was grieving for the loss of her land and her Pixies, so would wait for the right moment.

The day passed uneventfully. They stopped for a brief lunch early in the afternoon and continued through the forest and out onto rolling hills that stretched towards the fading horizon. Elensar found a suitable spot by an old oak tree and a shallow stream, to camp for the night. Stran and Grindell collected wood and soon had a fire blazing and Rory made them all a much-needed cup of Roseleaf.

Gwendo took her tea and found a spot on her own away from the others by the stream. Rory leant across to Jack and whispered in his ear; 'why don't you go over and join her.'

Jack wasn't sure if she needed the company. 'I think she wants to be on her own.'

'When I'm feeling down I'm always grateful for a sympathetic ear,' said Rory. 'If she doesn't want to talk, I'm sure she'll tell you.'

Maybe Rory was right thought Jack, so he strolled across to where she sat and squatted down next to her. 'Do you mind if I join you?'

She continued to stare into the stream and didn't look at him. 'I'm not very good company at the moment.'

Jack sat down on the grass next to her and sipped his tea as he watched the crystal-clear water of the stream slowly trickle by. 'I'm here if you want to talk.'

She sighed deeply. 'You and I have much in common.'

'In what way?' asked Jack.

'We've both lost our homes and our magic.'

And that was true albeit only temporarily hoped Jack. 'That's why it's important that you joined us. Together, we can confront Leah.'

Gwendo sighed deeply again. 'Do you really believe we can defeat him?'

Did he really believe it? Whether he did or not he had to give the impression that he did for the sake of the others. 'I wouldn't be here if I didn't.'

She turned towards him, her emerald green eyes seemingly devoid of hope. 'How do we challenge him without our magic?'

A fair question and one that Jack had an answer to, or at least he hoped he did. 'Morning Dew assures me that my magic will return the nearer I get to our gold dust.'

Gwendo smiled for the first time. 'Morning-Dew … the only one who spoke up for me.'

She knows Morning-Dew. He laughed to himself. Morning-Dew seemed to know everyone so why wouldn't she know Gwendo? 'How do you know her?'

Gwendo's smile disappeared and was replaced with sadness once again. 'I was a Faery Queen a very long time ago.'

Jack wasn't sure he understood. 'But why aren't you now?'

'Because,' said Gwendo, 'I was a little too unconventional for them. I challenged them too much to the point where they decided they could do without me.'

'And Morning-Dew was the only one who spoke up for you?'

Gwendo looked at Jack through misty eyes. 'She was a true friend.'

'What did you do when you left the Faery Queens?' asked Jack.

'I wandered aimlessly for a very long time. I didn't know where I was headed and didn't have any plans … That was until I met my lovely Pixies.'

'And that's when you created Gwendolain?'

Gwendo didn't answer but she didn't need to. It was obvious to Jack why she was so desperately unhappy to leave her Pixies and the beautiful land that she had created. He reached across and gently took hold of her hand. 'I promise you that I will do everything I can to help you.'

She smiled through a veil of tears. 'You can't do it on your own, Jack. I will be of no help to you.'

He squeezed her hand reassuringly. 'Oh, I think you will, lovely Pixie. I think you will …'

*

The next few days were spent trekking through endless hills and open fields. Gwendo's spirits lifted and together with Rory, she kept them all amused. That is, all except Stran. According to Rory, Stran had had a sense of humour bypass, although he wouldn't say it within his earshot.

157

The weather took a turn for the worse when they were hit by a cold snap. Sub- zero temperatures and biting winds which tempered Rory's good humour, but only slightly. There was no rain or wind to contend with and there was plenty of shelter at night, unlike the Running Plains.

Gwendo would occasionally unfurl her wings and fly high up into the sky and survey the horizon. It was after one of these jaunts that she gently landed next to Jack as he walked alongside Roger. It was early in the morning and they'd just set off from their overnight camp.

'Have you noticed anything strange about the landscape?' she asked.

Jack looked around the hilly field they were crossing and didn't register anything unusual. 'What is it that's bothering you?'

'The grass is brown and dry and look at the trees and hedgerows – they're lifeless and bare.'

'But we're still in the tail end of winter. You'll see it liven up in the coming weeks.'

'Spring would have normally started to take a hold by now. There's something not right – I can't put my finger on it but …'

'Can you sense anything through your magic?' asked Jack.

An expression somewhere between a smile and a grimace crossed Gwendo's lips. 'I haven't felt any magic since the day we left my Pixies. I've never felt like this before in my entire life. It feels like … it feels like I'm …'

'Naked and vulnerable,' said Jack finishing her sentence. 'I've felt the same ever since our gold dust was taken. It's strange because up until last summer I didn't even know about Koehtia or magic, but I always knew there was something there, but sadly no longer.'

'You are more than just your magic, Jack,' said Roger.

Jack turned to his father and looked quizzically at him. 'I'm not sure I understand.'

'You have amazing qualities of leadership. Every member of this company looks up to you, including Stran.

158

Elensar is a warrior but you are a leader. I could also list out your many other qualities if you want me to, compassion being top of the list. For someone who's still only fifteen years old that is amazing.'

'He's right,' said Gwendo. 'Perhaps you and I focus too much on what we don't have instead of what we do.'

'You have good instincts, Jack,' continued Roger. 'Follow them and I'm sure we will come through this challenge we face.'

'I need to hear all of your opinions,' said Jack. 'That's how you make good decisions.'

'And that's another of your qualities,' smiled Roger.

Their conversation was interrupted by a call from Elensar. 'Jack, can you join us?'

He stood on the brow of the hill they were climbing alongside Stran and Grindell. Rory was a few steps behind them. Jack, Roger and Gwendo slowly covered the hundred or so metres and joined the Captain. Jack's jaw dropped when he looked across the devastation that stretched out in front of them.

'That's what I was trying to tell you,' said Gwendo. 'There is something very badly amiss here.'

A forest covered the vale floor below them but there wasn't a trace of greenery to be seen. It wasn't just the deciduous trees and shrubbery that were bare, tall Pine trees were stripped of their needles and stood like spindly shadows of their former selves.

'Look at the grass on the hillsides,' said Gwendo pointing across the vale. 'It's brown and scorched.'

'Has there been a fire?' asked Rory.

Gwendo shook her head. 'I don't think so. There's something much more sinister going on here.'

'Sinister in what way?' asked Elensar.

'The forest looks like it's been stripped of all of its life,' said Gwendo.

'Let's go down and take a closer look,' said Elensar. 'I urge extreme caution as we approach the forest.'

Elensar removed his bow from across his back and

adjusted his quiver for easy access to the arrows it held. Grindell took out one of his axes and checked the blade's sharpness by running his finger along it. Stran remained his impassive self as Roger and Gwendo exchanged concerned looks.

Jack walked over to Elensar and whispered in his ear, 'what do you think is going on here?'

The Captain looked grim-faced across the lifeless vale. 'I wish I knew, Jack, I wish I knew.'

The company took a slow and sombre trek down into the vale, each keeping within their own thoughts. Jack tried hard not to let his mind run away with the endless possibilities of what may have happened to the forest. He needed to keep a cool head and make a judgement based on sound reasoning. But a nagging feeling persisted that this was something to do with Leah.

As they entered the forest Jack reached up and touched the naked grey branch of a beech tree that stretched over the path they followed. It was so brittle that it broke off in his hand and when it hit the ground it shattered into shards of rotten wood. The ground around the trees was littered with brittle copper leaves and dead pine needles. As bad as it looked from the top of the hill, close up it was even worse. Gwendo was right, thought Jack; the forest had been stripped of its life.

Nobody spoke as they absorbed the grim reality that confronted them. Elensar forensically studied the decaying scene looking for any clues as to what may have happened in the vale. It was Gwendo who was the first to venture an opinion.

'I think what we're seeing here is the result of the desecration that is going to slowly sweep across our land.'

'What do you mean, Gwendo?' asked Elensar.

'Leah is dark, Captain. He is the darkest individual I have ever had the misfortune of meeting and craves power for power's sake.' She sighed deeply; a grim expression cloaked her face. 'And now he has the Elven gold dust in his possession, he can wreak death and destruction wherever he chooses and there is absolutely nothing anyone can do about it.'

As much as Jack didn't want to hear those words he knew that there was a ring of truth about them. The task they had been set by the Faery Queens was beginning to look more and more impossible as they got nearer to their foe.

*

Chapter Twenty-One - Bleak Inn

'Do you really think that this is going to spread towards your land and beyond, Gwendo?' asked Rory.

'I sensed something was wrong weeks ago,' said Gwendo. 'I couldn't put my finger on the reason why, but my magic was fading.'

'And you think there's nothing that can be done about it?' asked Roger.

Gwendo didn't answer him and dropped her gaze to the floor. Jack answered for her.

'I can't believe that the Faery Queens would have sent us on a hopeless quest.'

Gwendo raised her eyebrows in response to Jack's comment. Her experiences at the hands of the Faery Queens obviously still scarred her but Jack trusted Morning Dew. He couldn't begin to believe that she would send him on a quest where he had absolutely no hope of succeeding.

'I understand your reticence, Gwendo,' said Jack, 'but I'm convinced my power will return the nearer we get to Leah. And as my power grows, his diminishes, which gives you the space to rediscover your magic.'

Gwendo gestured towards the dying forest. 'Look at it, Jack, the forest is all but destroyed and this is just the start. His power grows and the more it grows the darker he becomes. I fear we may be too late to stop this.'

'Are you saying we should give up?' asked Jack.

Gwendo's shoulders slumped and she dropped to the ground. 'I don't know what I'm saying … but hope is proving to be just a little elusive at the moment.'

'There's always hope,' chirped Rory, 'and besides, as disturbing as this is at least we know we're getting nearer to him.'

Rory's optimism struck a chord with Jack; they were getting nearer to their prey.

'I see no point in discussing this any further,' said Elensar firmly. 'We always knew the scale of the challenge we faced. Let's continue on our way and find Leah before he can wreak any more damage onto this land.'

'I agree,' said Rory. 'As Auntie Bridie always says, 'dwelling on a problem only makes it seem worse.''

And on that note, they continued their journey. Elensar and Stran led them into the dying forest. Gwendo said nothing and fell in beside Rory and Roger. Jack walked alongside a very quiet Grindell at the back.

The Dwarf hadn't ventured any opinion during the whole time he'd been with the company. His serious countenance revealed little of what went on inside of him. Jack thought it was a good time to ask him his opinion about their quest.

'You've been very quiet, Grindell. Do you have thoughts on our situation?'

The Dwarf carried on walking without replying and Jack was on the verge of repeating his question when he spoke. 'I understand little of magic. It's not something that was practiced in Bellowrock. I'll leave it to those who understand such things to guide me.'

'Does it make you want to abandon our quest?' asked Jack.

Grindell looked offended by the suggestion. 'I committed to joining your company and I will follow you to wherever it takes us.'

'But do you think we can succeed?' pressed Jack.

'My skills, as limited as they are, are at your disposal, Jack. But what I would say is that any individual who wishes to inflict such damage onto our land has to be stopped.'

Jack placed his hand on Grindell's shoulder. 'Your loyalty and skills are very much appreciated, my friend.'

Grindell's serious countenance cracked momentarily and Jack was sure he saw a trace of a smile.

The company left the dying forest behind by midday and entered a rock valley that stretched for as far as the eye could see. It was impossible to detect the effects of Leah's dark magic here but that did little to lift the unease that hung over the company. Elensar, stern faced and focused, continued to lead them on their relentless march.

They stopped for food mid-afternoon. The conversation was sparse; even the normally effervescent Rory was subdued. The sombre mood persisted for the rest of the afternoon and it was as nightfall approached that they came across something unexpected. Under the shadow of one of the many tall mountains to their right, far ahead in the fading light, several lonely grey buildings stood on the edge of the valley. It was the first sign of any civilisation they'd seen since they'd left Gwendolain.

Jack joined Elensar and Stran. 'Why would there be a town in such a remote place?'

'I'd hardly call it a town,' said Stran coldly. 'It's a few buildings that's all.'

'Whatever it is,' said Elensar, 'we need to be on our guard.' He turned to the company. 'Keep your weapons at the ready and be prepared for any eventuality.'

The sombre mood lifted but only to be replaced by tension. Jack removed his sword and held it in his right hand. A grim faced Grindell gripped his axe and scanned the landscape for signs of any threats. Jack, Grindell, Stran and Elensar led the company towards the buildings, followed by a very apprehensive Rory and Roger. Gwendo unfurled her wings and hovered just above their heads.

As they approached the buildings they noticed the faint flicker of candlelight in the window of the nearest one. The knot inside of Jack's stomach tightened; every nerve in his body was on edge. All his senses were signalling danger. He reached inside his shirt and held his Bloodstone in his fingers, more for comfort than protection. It had stopped Willy Venn from tearing him apart but that was when he could call on Koehtia. How would it protect him now?

They stopped outside of the door of the largest building. An old rusty sign hung down from an equally rusty bracket above the door. You could just about make out the words, 'Bleak Inn' written in large black letters across its middle.

'Not the most welcoming name I've ever seen,' said

Rory.

Stran glared at him but Rory just shrugged.

'Grindell and I will go in first,' said Elensar. 'Wait for our signal before following us.'

Elensar lifted the latch and pushed the door open. He took a tentative step inside and found himself standing in a dimly lit room. Tables and chairs lined the walls and a wooden counter with several hand pumps faced him. A damp, musty smell filled his nostrils – it wasn't the most inviting atmosphere he'd ever witnessed.

The bar area was empty except for him and Grindell. The Dwarf checked every dimly lit corner of the room to make sure they truly were on their own.

'It's empty,' he confirmed to Elensar. The Captain opened the door and beckoned the others inside.

Rory walked in and pointed to a brass bell on the counter. 'Why don't we ring it?'

Elensar picked up the small brass bell and shook it. A delicate ring echoed around the room. They waited for five minutes without a reaction when Elensar rang it again. The response was immediate.

'What's the rush?' shouted a gruff voice from an open door behind the counter. 'I'll be there when I'm good and ready.'

They heard footsteps and what sounded like something being dragged across the stone floor. An elderly male appeared at the doorway and he limped behind the bar. He supported himself with a walking stick in his right hand and rested his left hand on the counter. His wrinkled skin was pallid and grey; wispy, thin white hair barely covered a balding pate. His face contorted into a grimace as he eyed them all suspiciously.

'What do you want?' he snapped.

Elensar stood tall and looked down at the stooped figure behind the counter. 'We are looking for somewhere to stay the night.'

'Well you're looking in the wrong place! This is an inn – I serve ale.'

Elensar looked at the others and raised his eyebrows. Rory stepped forward and said. 'Well give us five tankards of your very fine ale, innkeeper.'

'And how are you going to pay for it?'

'Ahh,' said Rory. 'That might prove to be a problem.'

'No money, no ale,' said the innkeeper abruptly.

Grindell stepped up and placed several copper coins on the counter. 'That should cover it.'

But the Innkeeper wasn't impressed. 'Dwarf coin is worth nothing in these parts.'

Grindell responded by slamming his axe on the bar. 'This says it is.'

The innkeeper looked momentarily ruffled. He leant his walking stick against the wall and took a tarnished tankard off the shelf and proceeded to fill it from one of the pumps on the counter. After he filled five tankards he took the money from the counter and put it into his pocket.

He was about to leave but Rory called out to him. 'Do you have any pear juice or something similar?'

He didn't bother to turn around and answered gruffly, 'no,' and limped on his way.

Rory was about to protest but Jack said, 'don't worry, Rory. Gwendo and I can drink water from my canteen.'

They all sat around a table in the corner where Elensar had a good view of the door. Rory took a mouthful of his ale and smiled. 'Well he mightn't be the most hospitable innkeeper I've ever met but he serves a grand sup of ale.'

'It seems like he lives on his own,' said Jack.

'I wouldn't make any assumptions,' said Stran. 'If I've learned anything on my travels it's not to trust anyone or assume anything.'

'Sound advice,' said Gwendo. 'These are strange times. We need to keep our own counsel and not let on why we are here.'

'I agree,' said Elensar.

'But the innkeeper may be able to tell us what's been happening in the forests,' said Rory.

'Naïve as ever, Leprechaun,' said Stran dismissively.

'He looks like a man,' said Roger interrupting. 'He doesn't have the Elven ears.'

'I noticed,' said Elensar. 'But what business would a man have in a place like this.'

'If he is a man?' questioned Jack.

'Whatever he is and whoever he is, we need to keep our eye on him,' said Elensar.

The words were no sooner out of his mouth when the door opened. A tall hooded character walked into the inn and slammed the door behind him. He strode to the far side of the bar and threw himself down onto a seat behind a table. He kept his head hidden under his hood and didn't show any interest in the company. The cloak didn't disguise his heavy build; thick leather gloves covered huge hands and worn knee length black leather boots covered sturdy legs.

Uncomfortable looks were exchanged between the company. Elensar fingered his longbow which lay to his side and moved his quiver full of arrows to within easy reach. Jack and Grindell pushed their chairs back so that they faced the mystery guest.

The innkeeper suddenly appeared behind the counter again and filled a tankard. He limped over to the stranger and placed the tankard on the table in front of him. No words were exchanged, and the innkeeper limped back behind the counter and out through the door. The stranger didn't even look at his ale and continued to stare at the floor.

Jack felt the adrenaline running through him like a fast-flowing river. He breathed slowly and recalled the training that Elensar had given him all those months ago in Arminas. The stranger might not pose any threat, but they couldn't afford to take that chance. Roger appeared to be perfectly calm, as did Rory, but that could have been down to the ale he was gulping down!

Neither Elensar nor Grindell touched their ale. They were true warriors and needed to keep clear heads. Gwendo discretely studied the stranger trying to get a clue as to who or what he may be.

She didn't have to wait long. The stranger suddenly

167

removed his hood revealing the most disfigured and disgusting features. Jack thought he looked like a mutant but Elensar hissed one word.

'Goblin!'

The Goblin leapt to its feet, throwing the table and his ale across the floor. It raised its right hand which was holding a dagger and was about to launch it towards Grindell, but Elensar unleashed an arrow which hissed across the bar and thudded into the Goblin's chest making it gasp and it dropped to the floor along with its dagger. Grindell was onto his feet in an instant and covered the short distance in a few strides and dealt the Goblin a firm blow to the side of its head with the blunt end of his axe.

The Goblin lay motionless on the floor, dark red blood seeping from its chest and head. Grindell pulled its cloak back revealing an arsenal of weapons the like of which he'd never seen before. Several daggers and short swords hung from its weapon's belt. It had come prepared to slaughter them all.

Elensar ran across to the window and blew out the candle. He peered outside into the dark night.

'What is it, Elensar?' asked Jack.

'Goblins never travel on their own. There'll be more of them that's for sure. Let's get away from here before they turn up.'

'Wait!' said Stran. 'I'm sure the innkeeper told the Goblin we were here. I want to find out why.'

Before Elensar could protest, Stran had disappeared through the door behind the counter and a few seconds later raised voices were heard. Stran reappeared dragging the innkeeper by the scruff of his neck. He threw him onto a chair and stood over him.

'Why did that Goblin attack us?'

The innkeeper scowled but didn't answer. Stran grabbed him by his collar and half lifted him from the chair. 'How should I know?' he gasped.

Stran reached into his belt and removed the dagger that was hidden there. He held it up to the innkeeper's throat.

'Now I really don't care whether you live or die but if you don't answer my questions I'll make sure it's the second option.'

The innkeeper's sneer disappeared, and he swallowed nervously. 'Two Goblins have been staying in one of outbuildings for the last month. They told me to tell them if any Elves came into my inn.'

'Where's the other one?' barked Stran.

'He's … he's run into the mountains to warn the others.'

'How many?' asked Elensar.

'I don't know … they rarely come to my inn …'

'How far away are they?' asked Elensar.

'An hour at the most.'

'We need to get away from here,' said Elensar throwing his longbow across his back. 'If we're going to have to fight the Goblins, let's choose somewhere that gives us an advantage.'

*

Chapter Twenty-Two - Goblin Pursuit

The company travelled through the night not stopping to rest or eat. Unusually, there was no protest from Rory but there were good reasons for that.

'I'm in no hurry to meet one of those Goblin creatures again,' he whispered to Roger. 'They're ugly looking brutes and don't seem that friendly.'

'No argument from me on that score,' agreed Roger.

'We'll be meeting them again whether you like it or not,' snapped Stran. 'But we'll choose the time and place and make sure it suits us more than it suits them.'

Rory looked at Roger and raised his eyebrows, but he feared that Stran was right. As objectionable as the ranger could be, Rory would be the first to acknowledge that he was more versed in conflict than either he or Roger were. 'I'm sure you're right Stran. My comment was more in hope than expectation.'

A full, fluorescent moon lit their path as they relentlessly ploughed their way through rocky passes and clambered over narrow mountainside trails. Goblins were expert trackers according to Elensar, so he took every chance to put them off their trail by wading through streams whenever they came across them. But he knew that would only slow them down and was unlikely to make them lose their trail completely.

As they entered a long narrow valley, the first faint rays of sunlight peaked over the mountains ahead of them shedding its warm glow across the landscape. Jack joined Elensar at the head of the company and couldn't help but notice the tension in his face.

'We're going to have to rest soon,' said Jack. 'I think Rory's fit to drop.'

'I know, Jack,' said Elensar. 'But we need to find a suitable place where we can defend ourselves.'

They continued their march to the far end of the valley. Elensar led them up the mountainside and stopped on a sheltered plateau. 'This is as good a place as any to make a stand. We have a clear view of the whole of the valley. When the Goblins come we'll see them in plenty of time.'

'Can I light a fire, Captain?' asked Rory. 'I'm sure we could all do with a sup of tea.'

'I don't think so, Rory,' said Elensar. 'I don't want the Goblins to know we're here. Surprise is going to be a valuable weapon for us.'

'Understood,' said Rory. 'I've got some bread and cheese and dried fruit.'

Elensar took Jack, Grindell and Stran to one side. 'The Goblins are not going to be far behind us. They can march at a breath-taking pace, especially when they're tracking a foe.'

'It sounds like you've met them before,' said Jack.

'Briefly, some years ago.'

'Don't tell me, they hate Elves,' said Jack.

'They hate everyone,' said Elensar, 'including themselves. Folklore tells us that they are capable of some very dark deeds. They are ideal foils for a character like Leah as they will happily do his dirty work.'

'So, what's your plan?' asked Grindell.

'Surprise is our biggest weapon. They will think that we'll try to outrun them, so they won't be expecting an attack.'

'We're going to attack them! We have no idea of their numbers. Isn't that risky?' suggested Jack.

'We have no choice,' said Elensar. 'We're going to have to fight them at some point. Let's make sure it's to our advantage.'

'And your plan is?' asked Stran.

Elensar pointed to a ridge to the right of them. 'There are plenty of loose boulders on the edge of that ridge. As they approach, we'll wait for the right moment and then start rolling them down on top of them.'

'And the ones that survive?' asked Stran.

'I'll pick them off with my arrows.'

'What happens when they run out?' asked Jack.

'Then it's hand to hand combat.'

Jack stepped away from them and shook his head. 'I don't like it, Elensar. There are only seven of us and I don't think Rory, Roger or Gwendo are going to be capable of fighting a Goblin, especially if they're all the same size as that brute back at the inn. I think we should run.'

Elensar sighed deeply but kept his composure. Jack sensed his frustration with him.

'I would much prefer to avoid this but let me tell you something about Goblins. They will hunt their prey until they drop - nothing will stop them tracking us down, only death. The name Goblin originates from an old elvish word, Gobel. In tales of the old world, Goblins were always on the side of the dark forces. They were mutated from evil creatures and only understand death and destruction.' Elensar stepped forward and placed a firm hand on Jack's shoulder. 'If we run, they will pursue us to the point of exhaustion, and then we will be easy prey for them.'

'The Captain speaks wisely, Jack,' said Stran in his usual direct manner. 'He is the only one of who has experience of these creatures. We must listen to him.'

Elensar stepped away from Jack, and unusually Grindell offered an opinion without being asked.

'I agree with the Captain, Jack. His strategy is sound and gives us a fighting chance.'

He was outvoted. As uncomfortable as he felt about this battle, he couldn't go against the other three. 'Very well, we will do as the Captain asks.'

They re-joined the others and ate the meal that Rory had prepared. He sensed the tension in the air and, unusually for him, didn't attempt a conversation. As they finished their meal, Jack stood up and addressed them all.

'We have no choice other than to make a stand against the Goblins. The Captain has previous experience with them and has come up with a plan. Please listen to him very carefully.'

Elensar rose to his feet and nodded to Jack. 'I'm not going to lie to you, I would prefer that we didn't have to do this. But I can assure you we have no other option. If we all stick together and work as a unit, we may just come out of this alive.'

*

Jack, Elensar, Stran, Roger and Grindell all stood poised behind several huge boulders that were balanced precariously on the edge of the ridge. Rory and Gwendo stood to their side and scanned the far side of the valley looking for any signs of the pursuing Goblins. The tension in the air crackled like lightning.

'Are you sure they'll follow us?' asked Jack.

'I'm sure,' said Elensar.

'But it's nearly two hours since we arrived here.'

'They'll come. Just keep focused and push with all of your might when I say.'

Jack's mind drifted back to Lestrada when he and his friends were besieged by wave after wave of rabid wolves. The killing made him feel physically sick. But it was either kill or be killed, the same situation they found themselves in now. The size of the Goblin back at the Bleak Inn was intimidating - a mountain of solid muscle and sinew. How many were they about to be faced with?

He looked at Roger and his face displayed the same bewildered countenance he'd seen at Bellowrock when Gravelaxe pronounced the death penalty on them. How much did he regret dragging this kind and gentle man into this unreal world?

And what if one or more of them were slain in this battle? The Unification was broken and their quest over. Would he have set off on the quest if he'd have known the dangers they were going to face? He didn't have to answer that question, he had no choice. Once Leah had stolen the gold dust his future had been mapped out. It was either triumph or disaster that awaited him – there was nothing in between. The thought left him with a cold, icy feeling in the pit of his stomach.

Rory looked across and winked at him. He was small in stature but huge in spirit. Gwendo prowled behind the cover of the rocks forensically scanning the horizon for any sign of the Goblins. Stran was expressionless and emotion free. Roger looked pale and tense and why wouldn't he be? This was hardly the rush hour in London.

And then there were the two warriors in their company. Grindell, quiet and focused; he may have lacked height but he more than made up for it with raw strength and a steely determination that was written all over his face. Elensar, tall and willowy, analysing, planning every detail before the battle commenced. He drilled the Border Guard in Lestrada so well that despite wave after wave of attacks by the wolves, they never suffered one casualty.

Seven individuals who couldn't be more different and who together made up the 'Unification of a Common Purpose'. And the future of the Faery world depended on them.

Elensar climbed further up the cliff and looked back towards the valley entrance. It was quiet and unnervingly still. He returned to his position behind the boulders and breathed slowly. The moments before a battle were always the worst. Once hostilities commenced the tension disappeared and the adrenaline kicked in, arming his body for conflict. He was ready for anything that would be thrown at him and was determined to deal with this latest threat to their quest.

It was Gwendo who interrupted his thoughts. 'Captain, I'm sure I saw something at the far end of the valley.'

Elensar joined her and followed her gaze. Nothing moved – it was deathly quiet. He narrowed his eyes in concentration. Then he saw it, a flash of light. His instincts immediately told him what it was … sunlight reflecting off a sword blade. The Goblins were coming.

'Everybody take their positions and wait for my orders. We must roll the boulders at exactly the right moment to have the maximum impact. We have surprise on our sides so if we get this right we can devastate them.'

Elensar joined Jack and they both peered cautiously around the boulder focusing on the far end of the valley. Jack was shocked at what he saw. A wave of Goblins swarmed into the valley. They weren't marching they were running. Surely, they hadn't kept up that pace for over two hours, he thought.

'I told you Jack, they're relentless,' said Elensar reading his thoughts. 'They can run like that for days at a time.'

The Goblins continued at a pace towards the middle of the valley. Jack estimated there were at least two hundred of them. How were the seven going to defeat an army? As they drew nearer Jack could see that they were all heavily armed with an array of swords, axes and maces hanging off their belts. The deafening noise off their boots crashing onto the hard rock floor of the valley built to a nerve- shredding crescendo. The moment of battle was nearly upon them.

'Let's get our shoulders behind this first boulder,' urged Elensar. 'Shove with all your might when I say. Gwendo, shout when they are approaching the foot of the cliff.'

Jack's heart thumped in his chest as the noise from the Goblin army grew louder. As much as he didn't want to have this confrontation, he wanted it to start so they could get it over with.

'Now!' said Gwendo.

Jack and Elensar both heaved with all their might and the boulder teetered on the edge before slowly falling over. It rolled slowly at first but gradually built momentum as it crashed down the steep mountainside.

'And the next one!' screamed Elensar. Roger, Grindell and Stran pushed in unison and their boulder followed the other one over the edge and down the slope towards the approaching Goblin army. Elensar's timing was perfect as the Goblins reached the foot of the mountain the first boulder crashed into them.

They seemed oblivious to what was happening, and the boulder ploughed a furrow through them like a ball bowling over skittles. Goblins scattered in all directions, but the second boulder hit them as they ran. Their terrifying shrieks were hard to bear but Jack had seen first-hand that they were hell bent on killing him and his friends.

As the Goblins regrouped after the carnage and set to climb the mountain, the company sent another two boulders down onto them. The effect was devastating as they were crushed like ants under the enormous granite balls. But there were no more boulders and now it was down to Elensar to finish off the remaining Goblins with his longbow.

Jack did a quick count and estimated there were still fifty or more Goblins still standing and attempting to climb the mountainside. Elensar's devastating archery picked them off one by one. But they were too near for him to cut them all down, so it was about to come down to hand to hand combat.

Grindell suddenly broke ranks and ran down the slope towards the first of the Goblins and cut him down with a single blow of his axe. But there were too many for him to deal with on his own and Elensar drew his sword and joined Grindell's side and hacked away at the advancing Goblins.

But these creatures were strong and fought back fiercely. Jack withdrew his short sword and joined Elensar and Grindell. He confronted a nasty looking brute who was at least half a metre taller than him. It lifted its heavy axe and aimed a blow at Jack's head, but Jack was too quick and easily ducked out of the way. Jack thrust his sword through a gap in the side of the Goblin's leather jerkin and it fell to the ground writhing in pain.

Jack had no time to compose himself as another Goblin swung a heavy spiked mace at him but again he was too quick and easily jumped out of the way of the blow. But as he turned to face his attacker he stood on a small rock and fell backwards. He looked up just as the brute raised its mace and was about to deliver a fatal blow, when Roger appeared out of nowhere and plunged a dagger into the Goblin's belly.

Roger pulled Jack up before retrieving his dagger from the dying Goblin. There was no time for words as another

Goblin tried to jump onto Roger's back, but Jack was stunned when Roger threw the brute judo style onto the ground. Jack wasted no time and followed up by thrusting his sword into its belly.

Jack pulled Roger back from the melee and shouted in his ear. 'Thanks for saving me now go back and take cover. Leave this to Elensar, Grindell and me.'

'No chance,' said Roger. 'I'm not letting you do this on your own. I know how to handle myself. Let's stay close and cover each other's backs.'

Jack was about to argue but another Goblin flew at Roger catching him a glancing blow across the head with its mace, knocking him off his feet. Roger lay dazed on the ground as the Goblin stood over him and was about to deliver the killing blow when Jack hacked its arm off with his sword. The arm, still holding the mace, fell to the ground but the Goblin wasn't finished. It swung an axe with its other arm towards Jack, but he easily sidestepped the blow and thrust at the Goblin with his short sword. The Goblin deflected Jack's attack and once again swung the axe at him. Jack ducked under it and fell to his knees before plunging his sword under the Goblin's leather jerkin and into its belly. The Goblin shrieked in pain as it fell onto its back writhing in agony before dying.

Jack immediately ran to Roger's side and lifted him into a sitting position. 'Are you OK?'

Roger nodded. 'It just stunned me. My head is slowly clearing – just give me a few seconds.'

As Jack helped him to his feet, Roger suddenly shouted out, 'Jack!' and pulled him around. A Goblin stood over them with its axe poised to deliver a deadly blow. Jack had no time to avoid it or lift his own sword. He braced himself for the impact and his eventual death, when he heard a dull thud and the Goblin collapsed to the ground. Gwendo suddenly swooped down by his side and helped both him and Roger to their feet.

'What happened?' asked Jack.

Gwendo pointed to a rock to the side of the Goblin. 'I

dropped that on its head from way up in the air. I don't think he'll be waking up in a hurry.'

Elensar ran over. 'Are you all OK?'

'Just about,' said Roger. 'I have a lump on my head but that's all.'

'I think we've finished them off,' said Elensar. 'In all my years I've never seen anyone fight like Grindell. He was taking them down two at a time.'

Grindell ambled over to them as he put his axes back into his belt. 'I think they are all dealt with Captain. They may be big, and they may be strong, but they do not fight like warriors.'

Rory came running down with Stran. He was holding Elensar's longbow. 'Captain – two of the Goblins are making a run for it.'

Elensar took the bow and loaded an arrow before taking aim. He unleashed the arrow and it sped towards its intended target hitting the Goblin in its back. He'd fired the second arrow before the first Goblin hit the ground with the same outcome.

He slung his longbow over his back. 'We need to get away from here now. There are sure to be others and I don't want to be around when they find this carnage.'

As Jack walked back up the side of the mountain, he placed his sword back into his belt. As he strapped on his backpack he looked down at the carnage below. Mutilated and bloodied Goblin bodies were strewn across the mountainside and the valley floor. The sight didn't make him feel good; it made him feel sick to the stomach. But as he'd already acknowledged before the battle, it was a case of 'kill or be killed', and if they were to succeed in their quest, it had to be the former.

*

Chapter Twenty-Three –
Stranger on the Mountain

Jack sat back against a rock sipping water from his canteen. They'd marched relentlessly through tough mountain terrain for the whole day putting as much distance as they could between themselves and the valley of dead Goblins. Elensar left nothing to chance and covered their trail where possible, even when they were walking on solid rock.

'It's not as if you can leave footprints on rock,' remarked Rory innocently as he chewed on a piece of dried fruit.

'A good tracker doesn't need footprints to follow,' said Stran impatiently. 'They look for subtle signs like water drops from a canteen … Anyway, with the amount of noise you make Leprechaun, a deaf and blind Goblin would be able to track you.'

Rory looked at Roger and winked, whispering in his ear, 'Charm personified.'

Elensar had chosen another position high on a mountainside to camp for the night. They had a clear view of the trail behind them and any Goblin pursuers would soon be seen as they approached. Elensar was on watch as they all ate a cold meal of bread, cheese and dried fruit, much to Rory's frustration. It was another clear moonlit night and Elensar didn't want to risk lighting a fire for obvious reasons

Jack was struggling to get rid of the images of the day's battle from his mind. The sheer power and ruthlessness of the Goblins was sickening to see. They would have slaughtered the company without a second thought. He needed to talk to Elensar, so he screwed the top back on his canteen and called out to the Captain who was perched in a nest of boulders above them.

'Can I join you?'

'It's not very comfortable,' said Elensar. 'Find a spot as best you can.'

Jack climbed the short distance to the nest of boulders

and found a small gap to sit in facing Elensar and straightened his aching back. Elensar turned towards him but his eyes flashed back towards the pass every few seconds looking for Goblins.

'How are you holding up, Jack?'

'I'm fine,' said Jack not being completely truthful. 'I'm tired but that seems to have become a way of life.'

'I have been on some demanding sorties with the Border Guard, Jack, but nothing compares to what we have endured since we left Waterswood. You have every right to be tired.'

'I'm just amazed at how well Roger is holding up. The contrast in the life he led in London to this … the two couldn't be more removed.'

'They are a fine company, Jack. They've all responded well to the challenges we've faced.'

'I thought we were in trouble when I saw the number of Goblins that flooded into the valley today.'

Elensar looked across at Jack and half smiled. 'As did I, Jack. But the boulders did the trick, not only killing them also but causing chaos in their ranks. And Grindell fought like a demon. I would back my Border Guard against most opponents but if all the Dwarf warriors at Bellowrock fight like him then we may just meet our match.'

Jack nodded his agreement that Grindell was indeed an accomplished warrior, something that he suspected he would never be. 'I don't find killing people or for that matter any living thing easy to do.'

'And nor should you. We only do it when we have to. That is the true warrior's code. I have learnt to accept it over the years, Jack. You gain nothing by torturing yourself over it. You are a good young Elf with a strong moral compass and a fine ethic. You have been charged to save your world, Jack, and that is an onerous burden for anyone to carry.' He leant forward and clamped his hand on Jack's shoulder. 'And you carry it well, my young friend.'

Elensar didn't offer compliments easily and Jack was in no doubt that he was being sincere but there were times that he doubted his own ability to see the quest through to the end.

'But there's something more significant that we must take from the day's events,' continued Elensar.

'And what is that?'

'We are getting nearer to Leah.'

Jack wasn't sure he understood. 'But …'

'The devastation in the forests is gradually spreading outwards. We are heading towards the source of that devastation.' Elensar leant towards Jack; his voice dropped to barely a whisper. 'I believe those Goblins were his last throw of the dice to stop us getting to him. Leah is in these mountains somewhere … of that I'm sure.'

Jack could see the sense in what Elensar was saying, but he couldn't feel the Koehtia that he'd been told would surface as they neared Leah. Jack trusted Elensar. He was an experienced warrior and his instincts had served them well in the past. 'Morning-Dew told me that I would feel my Koehtia again as I neared our gold dust … I'm feeling nothing.'

'I can't claim to understand the ways of magic, Jack, but what I do know is that Leah does not want to face you.'

Jack was astonished. 'But he has the power. I have none. Why would he be afraid of me?'

'Because,' said Elensar, 'he has gone out of his way to stop you getting to him. Trust me - he's frightened, Jack.'

Jack pondered Elensar's words. Perhaps he was right? Maybe Leah was frightened of him … but he couldn't for the life of him think why.

*

They spent the following days hiking up and down mountain trails and through narrow rock-strewn ravines. The terrain was getting tougher and taking its toll on the company. Elensar was still alert to the possibility of Goblins tracking them and continued to make camp in places that were difficult to attack.

It was the fourth day after the Goblin attack when they

were faced with a dilemma. They stood at the foot of a tall rugged mountain range surrounded by thick, grey clouds. The only way ahead was either through caves at the end of the ravine or to follow a trail that led over the mountain.

Stran, Elensar and Jack considered their options.

'It will be very difficult to defend ourselves in the caves,' said Elensar. 'I would prefer that if we have to fight it's out in the open.'

'The mountain trail will be tough,' countered Stran. 'Those clouds are full of snow. We will have to contend with the weather as well as the physical terrain.'

'I just don't think Leah would skulk in a cave,' said Jack. 'I can't say why, it's just my instincts telling me.'

'And I agree,' said Elensar. 'I think we should follow the mountain trail.'

Jack and Elensar turned to Stran awaiting his response. 'I'm not saying we shouldn't choose the mountain trail – I'm just telling you that it will be more difficult than anything else we've encountered so far. The Leprechaun will struggle over such terrain.'

'Don't you be worrying about me, Stran Vander, I can handle any terrain that you can,' interrupted Rory.

Stran turned to him and said wearily, 'I'm not suggesting you can't, but it will be hard for you because of your physique and size.'

'I'll be fine,' said Rory indignantly.

'OK,' said Elensar stopping yet another argument escalating between Rory and Stran. 'We will go the mountain route.'

Elensar didn't want any further delay so, accompanied by Stran, he set off along the mountain trail. Grindell kept his own council as he always did and took his place at the rear of the company. Nothing seemed to faze him. He never argued with any of them and dutifully followed whatever lead he was given.

Roger walked with Rory and Jack joined Gwendo. The Pixie hadn't ventured an opinion about which way they should go. Jack took the opportunity to ask her.

'You didn't have anything to say about which route we should take?'

'The Captain understands these things far better than I do. I'm happy to be guided by him.'

Jack crouched down and whispered in her ear. 'Elensar is convinced that Leah lives on these mountains.'

She didn't seem surprised. 'And what do you think?'

He hesitated before replying as he already knew what her response would be. 'If he is here I would have thought I would feel my Koehtia by now.'

Gwendo looked up at him and raised her eyebrows.

'I'm sorry, Gwendo but I can't believe that Morning-Dew would lie to me. She's done so much to help me ever since I first met her.'

'I'm not suggesting she's lying to you, Jack. I just don't think the Faery Queens realise the magnitude of the task we face.'

'Why do you doubt our ability to challenge him?' asked Jack not disguising his frustration.

'How long is it since he took your gold dust?'

Jack thought for a moment. 'A few months at the most.'

Gwendo leant towards Jack and lowered her voice so that the others wouldn't hear what she was about to say. 'And in that time, he's destroyed my land. Ever since I created Gwendolain he's been trying to break it down. Once he had the gold dust from your valley, he was able to do in weeks what he'd been attempting to do for years. When I was exiled by the Faery Queens, they banished me to the eastern lands. It was largely waste land and uninhabitable, but I was able to create Gwendolain without theirs or anyone else's help. They have no influence in this land – it is largely unchartered territory and that is why they do not understand the challenge we face.'

Jack could hear the intensity in her voice. He was beginning to think she may be right but what choice did he have? If he abandoned the quest now, the whole of the Faery lands could be lost forever. He searched deep down inside himself again for any sign of Koehtia. There was nothing.

'We have to try, Gwendo. I love my home too much to abandon it to the despair that Leah would wreak upon it.'

'And I agree with you, Jack,' said Gwendo adopting a more positive tone. 'But let's not kid ourselves as to the task that confronts us. We face almost impossible odds – it's far better that we go into this with our eyes open.'

She was right of course, thought Jack. He placed his hand on her shoulder and looked deep into her crystal blue eyes. 'I believe in all the people on this quest. I believe in you, Gwendo. We shall not fail .... We must not fail.'

Gwendo placed her hand on top of Jack's. 'You have my loyalty, Jack, no matter where this challenge leads us.'

*

As the day wore on, Stran became more and more convinced that the snow would come. Dense, heavy, white clouds covered the mountain tops smothering the sun's rays, casting a shallow daylight across the mountains. On a quiet Sunday afternoon stroll along a mountain pass, it would have made for an enjoyable spectacle, but trekking on a mountain trail hundreds of metres above a deep valley to their right made it neither enjoyable nor a spectacle.

It was late afternoon as they searched for a suitable place to camp for the night that the first flakes fell.

'We need to find some shelter,' said Stran. 'Those clouds are full of snow and I don't want to be out in the open when the blizzard starts.'

'I agree,' said Elensar. 'There's been no shelter for the last hour, so I don't think there's any point in turning back. We'll have to plough on and hope we find somewhere.'

A light sprinkling of snow soon turned into a heavy blanket. And the heavy blanket soon turned into a full-blown blizzard as the wind gusted around the mountain. It was almost impossible to see for more than a few metres and the settling snow underfoot became treacherous. The company trudged slowly up the trail, but progress was severely hampered by the conditions.

Elensar stopped the company and gathered them together. 'The snow's getting worse. We'll stop as soon as we find somewhere suitable. Meanwhile take extra care as the trail is fast becoming dangerous.'

'I'm exhausted,' said Rory. 'Can't we rest here for a while?'

'If you want to freeze to death!' snapped Stran. 'We must keep going until we find shelter.'

Both Jack and Elensar agreed with him and urged the company onwards. Grindell walked alongside Rory and helped him the best he could. Roger held onto Gwendo's hand and kept her away from the trail's edge as the wind gusted around them. She was so slightly built that the strong winds could easily have blown her over the edge and even though she had wings it was unlikely that she would be able to fly in such heavy snow.

The snow was so dense that it was getting increasingly difficult for them to see each other. Jack followed Grindell and Rory at the back of the company and encouraged them the best he could, but it was difficult to make himself heard in the conditions. It was as he stepped to the side of Rory on the edge of the trail that his right boot slipped on some compacted snow. As he fought to keep his balance, a gust of wind blasted into him sending him teetering on the mountain edge. The combination of the howling wind and blanketing snow stifled his cries for help before his left boot also slipped sending him sliding over the edge.

He grabbed at a flimsy root that protruded from the snow, but as he held on for dear life trying desperately to get a foothold, the root came away from the earth and snapped, sending him skidding down the mountainside. His speed increased as the slope became steeper and the next thing he knew he was suddenly in mid-air. It felt like he was floating but that sensation was brought to an abrupt halt when he hit the branches of a densely packed cluster of Fir trees on the mountainside far below.

The branches slowed his momentum as he crashed through them, but he smashed his head and lost consciousness. His limp body bounced from the trees and ended up in a deep snow drift to the side of the trail hundreds of metres below from where he fell. Jack's lifeless body lay still, slowly getting covered by the falling snow.

Just as his whole body was about to disappear under the white blanket, a mysterious cloaked figure appeared on the trail and saw the top of Jack's head protruding from the snow drift. The stranger pulled his body from the drift and onto the trail. They knelt beside Jack and placed their fingers against his neck checking for a pulse. The stranger then lifted him up in their arms and slowly trudged along the trail struggling against the gusting wind and snow.

*

Chapter Twenty-Four – The Divided Unification

Elensar and Stran ploughed on relentlessly, unaware that Jack had fallen from the mountain trail. The snow lashed into them driven ever harder by the gusting winds. Communication between the company was almost impossible. It was two hours after Jack's fall when Stran grabbed Elensar and pointed to a narrow crevice in the mountain face.

He put his mouth up to his ear and shouted, 'I'm going inside to see if there is enough room for us all. Wait here with the others.'

Stran took off his backpack and squeezed through the small opening. He took several steps along a narrow passageway before it began to open out. It was pitch black and he had no feel as to how big the cavern was. He tentatively moved back along to the entrance and shouted to Elensar.

'It's too dark to see much but I get the feeling it could be big enough for us all. I've got some flints to make a spark, but I need some tinder to light.'

Elensar nodded that he understood and followed Stran into the narrow tunnel. He removed his backpack and took out a short stick with some fabric wrapped around one end and held it out to Stran. He flicked the wheel and sent several sparks into the fabric and it immediately burst into flame. Elensar held out the flaming torch in front of him and stepped further along the tunnel to where it opened out. He stood in the opening to a small cavern around ten metres across. It would be tight but just about enough room for them all to shelter from the snow.

Stran went back out onto the mountain trail and gestured for the others to follow him. Roger and Gwendo almost fell into the cavern quickly followed by Rory and Grindell.

'I don't think I could have managed another step in those conditions,' said Rory as he slumped down against the cavern wall.

As they all patted the snow from their clothes it was Roger who noticed Jack was missing. 'Where's Jack?'

'He was just behind Grindell and me,' said Rory. 'I thought he would follow us in.'

'I'm going outside to check,' said Roger as he stepped back into the narrow tunnel and out onto the trail. He peered back along the mountain trail but there was no sign of Jack, although he couldn't see for more than a few metres due to the falling blanket of snow. He briefly toyed with the idea of searching for Jack on his own but thought better of it and went back inside the cavern. 'I'm worried, Elensar – there's no sign of him.'

Elensar buttoned up his coat. 'He may have twisted an ankle or had an accident. I'll go back down the trail to see if I can find him.'

'I'm coming with you,' said Roger.

Elensar was about to argue but could see the determination in Roger's face. 'Very well but we must stay close together.'

Roger followed Elensar out onto the trail and the two of them tentatively walked side by side back the way they'd come. The conditions, if anything, were getting worse and their tracks on the way up were already covered which would make it almost impossible for Jack to follow them to the cave.

Their anxiety increased the longer they went without finding Jack. Roger constantly looked over the trail edge just in case Jack had slipped over the side and was maybe on a ledge and holding on for dear life. Elensar forensically studied the trail looking for any signs that may have given him a clue as to what had happened to Jack but there was nothing.

They'd been searching for over an hour when Elensar shouted into Roger's ear. 'I think the weather is getting worse. We'd better get back to the others while we still can.'

Roger shook his head firmly. 'I'm not going back until we've found him.'

188

'Roger, if we delay our return any longer we may not get back to the cave. We're not going to survive out here on the trail especially if the temperature plummets overnight.'

'But he's my son,' protested Roger. 'I can't just abandon him … I …'

Elensar could see the tears of frustration in Roger's eyes, but he didn't take his decision lightly. 'Jack is like a brother to me, Roger, so I do understand how you feel. But we need to wait until the morning before we carry on our search. Let's go back to the others - we're both tired and hungry.'

*

The ever-resourceful Rory had made Roseleaf and mushroom soup over a small fire while Elensar and Roger had been searching for Jack. Roger was in no mood to eat but eventually succumbed to Rory's persuasion and ate a bowlful of the delicious soup.

'We all need to keep our strength up Roger lad, especially as we're going to search for Jack when this snow storm finally stops,' said Rory trying to lift his spirits.

'There's no guarantees that the snow will stop anytime soon,' said Stran. 'I spend my life on the mountains and I've known it to snow continuously for months.'

'As optimistic as ever,' said Rory a little louder than he intended.

'Realistic, Leprechaun!' snapped Stran. 'What's the point of convincing ourselves that the snow will stop when the likelihood is that it won't?'

'OK,' said Elensar stopping another argument from escalating. 'We need to discuss what we do next. And that has to be in the context of our quest.'

Roger looked quizzically at the Captain. 'What do you mean by that?'

'What he means,' said Stran, 'is that we cannot lose sight of our main objective and that is reclaiming the gold dust from Leah.'

'I'm not going anywhere without Jack,' said Roger

189

indignantly. 'The quest can wait.'

'I'm not suggesting for a moment that we abandon Jack,' said Elensar. 'We will resume our search at first light in the morning.'

'Anyway,' said Rory, 'there is no unification of the races without Jack. We have to find him otherwise our quest is over.'

Stran removed his clay pipe from his pocket and went through his cleaning ritual before filling it with tobacco. He held it out to the others. 'Anyone mind if I smoke?'

When he received no objections, he lit his pipe from the dying embers of the fire and sat back against the cave wall. As the plumes of grey smoke surrounded him, he offered his opinion. 'That's not strictly true.'

'What isn't?' asked Rory.

'Your assertion that there is no unification without Jack.'

An already uncomfortable Roger shot Stran a withering look. 'I'm not going anywhere without Jack, so your unification is most certainly broken.'

Stran retained his impassive expression as he quietly puffed on his pipe. 'Our quest is bigger than any one individual. As important as Jack is, there is no reason why we still couldn't achieve our objective and reclaim the gold dust from Leah without him.'

'Are you seriously suggesting that we abandon him,' said an exasperated Roger.

'I'm not suggesting anything,' said Stran. 'I'm merely saying that we can still do what we set out to do, with or without Jack.'

'And who amongst us has the ability to confront Leah's magic?' asked Rory.

'I would have thought that even you could work that out, Leprechaun,' said Stran looking directly at Gwendo.

The Pixie had been quietly listening to the conversation up until that point but Stran's subtle suggestion prompted a response. 'My magic has gone, Stran. Once Leah broke down Gwendolain, my magic disappeared with it.'

'You were a Faery Queen once,' said Stran. 'That must

count for something.'

'I think your faith in me is misplaced,' said Gwendo.

'As much as I appreciate the importance of discussing our options,' said Elensar directly addressing Stran, 'I have no intention of abandoning Jack. As soon as the weather settles, we will resume our search for him.'

Grindell surprised them all by intervening in the discussion. 'Maybe Jack hasn't had an accident.'

Roger sat next to him looking confused. 'What else could have happened to him?'

The company listened in anticipation to Grindell's answer. 'He could have been kidnapped.'

'Right from under our noses? I don't think so,' dismissed Roger.

'Grindell makes a good point,' said Elensar. 'I told Jack earlier that I was sure we were getting nearer to Leah. I think it unlikely that wherever he resides he will be on his own. I'm certain he sent those Goblins to attack us.'

'And Jack was behind us all,' said Stran. 'None of us noticed he'd gone.'

Roger shook his head dismissively. 'There would have been a struggle – one of us would have heard something.'

'It' an option we shouldn't dismiss,' said Elensar.

'I'm going back to look for him just as soon as the weather clears,' said Roger. 'And I'll do it on my own if I have to.'

'No-one has to do anything on their own,' said Elensar firmly. 'We will all search for Jack tomorrow. Both Stran and I are experienced trackers and, between us, I'm sure we'll find some clues as to what's happened to him.'

'I won't give up until I do,' said Roger. 'As far as I'm concerned the quest is of secondary importance.'

'Are you saying you will abandon us instead?' said Stran pointedly. 'We are all inextricably linked to the success or failure of this quest and we must work as a team otherwise we are doomed to failure.'

'I see no point on speculating about what may or may not happen,' said Elensar attempting to dispel the growing tension between Roger and Stran. 'We are involved in a high stakes mission to reclaim the gold dust for not just the Elves in Woodgate Valley, but the survival of all the Faery races.'

'And don't assume, Roger, that the humans are immune to Leah's ambitions,' said Stran. 'He won't stop until he controls the whole world.'

Roger was about to respond but Gwendo stood up and stepped in between them. 'Roger, I'm sure we all understand your feelings for Jack. Everybody in this company has respect for him. Some of us love him very much.' She looked at Rory and Elensar in turn. 'We will never lightly abandon Jack to his fate, but we have to face up to what we do if we don't find him. These lands are being slowly destroyed. Do you think Jack would want us to abandon this quest because we lost him? His passion for his people and his land burns like a fire within him – it's plain for all to see.'

She unfurled her wings and stretched them out to their full span before folding them down her back again. It was as if she was attempting to release the tension within her.

'We must follow this quest through to the bitter end regardless of what happens to any of us. We owe that to ourselves and to each other.' She swallowed deeply and took a long and slow deep breath. 'And we owe it to all the Elves in Woodgate Valley who have been abandoned to the spirit world … their lives depend on us.'

She turned her attention to Stran. 'And a little more sensitivity wouldn't go amiss from you. Roger is understandably frightened that he may have lost his son, and Rory and the Captain are missing a very close and dear friend. We need to explore every option fully before making any decisions.'

She looked at them in turn and they all nodded their agreement. The stakes on their quest had just got considerably higher. Not one of them would have chosen to confront Leah without Jack as their leader, but the unthinkable had to be addressed if they were going to save the Faery lands from destruction.

*

Chapter Twenty-Five –
An Unexpected Friend

Jack opened his eyes – he was lying flat on his back with a blanket covering him. A flame flickered in the distance. He tried to sit up, but his body felt like it had been trampled by a herd of wild horses. Each in breath sent painful spasms searing through his chest and back.

Then he remembered falling from the mountain trail and hitting the trees but nothing after that. How had he got here? Had his friends come to rescue him? A familiar voice in the distance told him they hadn't.

'You're awake.'

Although Jack knew the voice he couldn't place it. 'Who are you? And where am I?' he croaked.

Whoever it was walked over and knelt in front of him. Jack's vision was still blurred from the concussion he'd sustained from the fall. He lifted his head and blinked his eyes. As his vision cleared he looked up at the stranger and his mouth fell open.

'You don't seem pleased to see me, Green-Jack.'

Pleased was a word that Jack had never associated with the Elf sat in front of him.

It was Grimley.

Jack slumped back down. Was he hallucinating because of the bang to his head? Perhaps he was still unconscious and this was some sort of weird dream.

'I have made tea and there is soup in the pot.'

It couldn't be Grimley – he was being friendly.

'I'm sure you haven't broken any bones, but you've sustained some serious bruising to your back and chest. You need to rest a while.'

Jack checked out his surroundings. He was in a small cave. A fire in the corner cast dark shadows over the wall as the stranger sat back down just across from him. *It couldn't be Grimley ... could it?*

'I'm guessing you fell from the trail high up in the

mountain. The fir trees on the mountainside would have broken your fall and your rucksack probably cushioned the impact.'

Jack tried to pull himself into a sitting position – shards of pain stabbed his back and ribs. The stranger picked up his backpack and placed it behind him. Jack looked up into his face. His vision was now clear and had adjusted to the firelight. He recognised the intense grey eyes and long, silver hair tied back in a pony-tail. It was Grimley – but how?

Grimley poured tea into a tin mug and handed it to Jack. He sipped it, the taste was unmistakeable, it was Roseleaf. Grimley filled a bowl with chunky soup from the pot and placed it to the side of Jack. 'Let it cool a while – it's vegetable.'

Jack still wasn't convinced he was fully awake. Grimley would have faded into the spirit world along with the rest of Waterswood. But even if he hadn't, what would he be doing on this mountain? And the most puzzling question of all, why was he helping him? None of it made any sense.

Jack placed his mug on the floor and picked up the bowl of soup. He took a spoonful and blew on it before carefully placing it in his mouth. It tasted good. The warmth flowed through him nourishing his tired, aching body. He didn't speak as he ate; he didn't even look up. Grimley was also quiet, but Jack sensed he was watching him closely.

As Jack's head cleared the negative thoughts surfaced. Grimley was being his usual devious self, trying to put Jack at his ease waiting for his opportunity to kill him. But that didn't make any sense. Grimley had found Jack following his fall. If he wanted him dead all he had to do was leave him in the snow, he would surely have died from hypothermia.

Jack finished his soup and placed the bowl to his side and picked up his tea. Grimley continued to study him as he sipped it.

'Where are we?' asked Jack.

'We're in a cave I found at the foot of the mountain. The

195

snow is still very heavy. We will be better off staying here until the morning.'

'And what about my friends?'

'They will also be taking shelter if they have any sense.'

Jack remembered that they were high up on the mountain trail when the snowstorm hit. They were looking for shelter when he fell. The driving wind and snow made it almost impossible to see and to walk. He hoped that they found somewhere as it wasn't a night to spend out in the open.

Jack finished his tea and placed his mug alongside the empty bowl. 'How did you find me?'

'You were buried up to your neck in a snowdrift to the side of the trail. You would have died from exposure if I hadn't have come along.'

If anyone else had said that he would have been showering them with gratitude. *But Grimley?* 'I don't wish to sound ungrateful, but you did try to have me killed in the past. Why the sudden change of heart?'

Grimley didn't offer an answer immediately. His cold, grey eyes forensically studied Jack. 'Things have moved on since then. We are both victims of Graydon Leah and have scores to settle.'

'And why didn't you fade into the spirit world along with the rest of the Elves in Waterswood?'

A sneer never seemed to be far away from Grimley's lips. Again, he didn't answer immediately. 'You don't understand the workings of our land quite as well as you would like to think, Green-Jack.'

Grimley wasn't going to make it easy for Jack. They were still adversaries even though Grimley had saved him. Game playing was what he was all about and Jack had little choice other than to go along with it. He struggled into a more comfortable position despite the sharp pains stabbing him in the chest.

'Why don't you educate me?'

'There are Elves still loyal to me in Waterswood despite your best efforts to mislead them with your lies and propaganda. They helped me to escape from the gaol and I was far away from Waterswood by the time my people were taken.'

Jack was amazed at Grimley's arrogance. He still called the Elves of Waterswood his people. All he ever did was subjugate them to his tyrannical rule. But Jack needed to find out as much as he could about Leah so decided against confrontation. 'So where did you go?'

Grimley had an irritating habit of not answering questions immediately. He looked blankly at Jack before filling a tin mug with tea. He held the pot out, but Jack shook his head. Grimley replaced the teapot by the fire and took a sip of his tea before placing his tin mug by his side.

He turned his attention to Jack. 'I went to the Redwood's village in the Fireridge Mountains. I stayed there for some weeks before returning to Waterswood.' Grimley fell silent and lowered his gaze. Jack thought he looked pained.

'You didn't know, did you?'

Grimley offered no answer. Jack leant towards him despite the pain in his ribs. 'You had no idea what had happened to the Elves of Waterswood, did you?' pressed Jack. 'It was your blind prejudice and stupidity that caused our people to fade away to the spirit world.'

Grimley looked uncomfortable. The sneer momentarily absent from his lips. He raised his eyes to Jack.

'It was when I returned to the Redwood village that their Elders told me that Leah had used their guards to take the gold dust from the other communities in Woodgate Valley.' Grimley hesitated. It was if he didn't want to say the words that were in his head.

'Go on,' pressed Jack.

'When they sent their guards back some weeks later, they found each village deserted.'

Grimley diverted his gaze, looking into the dying embers of the fire. Jack could see the guilt written all over his face, if indeed it was possible for Grimley to feel such an emotion.

'He never told me …'

'Who never told you?' interrupted Jack.

Grimley swallowed deeply before answering. 'Leah.'

Jack was confused. Why would Leah have had to tell him? Unless … 'I thought Leah stole the Waterswood gold dust.'

Grimley picked up his tin mug and sipped his tea – he was in no hurry to answer.

Jack could see Grimley's discomfort, but he didn't hold back. 'You let Leah take our gold dust. He didn't steal it, did he? You handed it to him on a plate. What possessed you to do such a stupid thing?'

Grimley drained his mug before slamming it down on the ground. 'I'll tell you what possessed me, Green-Jack, it was you!' He leant towards Jack, his eyes blazing. 'Everything was absolutely fine in our village until you came along.'

Jack couldn't believe what he was hearing. 'The only reason I found out I was an Elf and even thought about finding Waterswood was because you tried to have me killed. You sent Vilner and the LEOs to burn down my cottage.'

But Grimley wasn't backing down. 'The moment you stepped into our village you sowed unrest. In a matter of two days you disrupted our whole community and even while you were away you instigated lore breaking and dissent.'

'I was living a simple life with my grandfather in the forest. I had no idea I was an Elf, and in the main I was happy and contented. But that all changed when you tried to kill me.' Jack tried to bite down on his anger. He wanted to stay in control and make sure Grimley knew just how reckless he had been with the Waterswood gold dust. 'You tried to have me killed because I was half-human. How sick and twisted is that?'

Grimley countered immediately. 'As distasteful as that is to me and many Elves, it wasn't that.' He leant forward stabbing his index finger towards Jack. 'I saw you … I saw you bring that girl back from the dead in the human forest!'

Jack was momentarily stunned into silence. He tried

desperately to gather the thoughts spinning around his head. Grimley wanted to kill him because he saved Becky's life? He wasn't just power crazed he was inhuman.

'I saved a beautiful young girl's life and you wanted to kill me. That's insane … Don't you see that?'

'What I saw, Green-Jack, was an irresponsible use of Elven magic. You had no idea what you were doing, and I couldn't risk you finding your way to Waterswood.' He sat back and seemed to catch himself. He lowered his gaze momentarily before looking back at Jack. 'You were a danger to Waterswood … You could've destroyed us all.'

Jack couldn't find the words to tell Grimley what he felt at that moment. After all this time he found out the reason why Grimley wanted him dead and it was all because he saved Becky's life. Grimley's madness knew no bounds. He thought Jack was a danger to Waterswood when all the time the only real danger that it ever faced was from Grimley himself.

Grimley sat back and breathed deeply as his anger slowly subsided. 'I have known of your whereabouts for some years. I had you watched.'

'No doubt by Finn Tarr, that human mercenary you employ to terrorise runaway Elves.'

'What I did was for the safety of the Elves of Waterswood. Every Elf who lived in the human world presented a risk to us all. I asked Finn Tarr to bring them back but always insisted that he did them no harm.'

'Something he didn't always manage, Grimley, as you well know,' spat Jack. 'But you always took good care of them in Darkenwold just like you would have taken care of me.'

'Being head of a community sometimes means that you have to take difficult decisions for the greater good. I made sure that I was aware of all Elves in the human world, which is why I kept you under regular surveillance. I didn't consider you a threat unless Ciara returned; that was until that irresponsible display of magic. I've seen the damage that magic can do. Darkenwold is full of demented Elves who thought they could handle it. I didn't take the decision lightly to ban its use in Waterswood – it was for the safety of the wider community. Your arrival in Waterswood could have threatened the stability that I had taken years to create – I couldn't risk that.'

The contempt that Jack held for Grimley was growing by the second. He oppressed the whole community for his own selfish reasons but the bare-faced stupidity he showed regarding the practice of magic was breath-taking.

'It's because of your ignorance that the people of Waterswood have faded away to the spirit world. You gave away the gold dust that sustained our Elven land.'

'None of this would have happened without your interference,' said Grimley. 'If you had have stayed away, we would still be living our contented lives that we had enjoyed for years.'

Jack shook his head in disbelief, Grimley was bordering on delusional. 'I don't think many of your fellow Elves would agree with your description of their lives as being contented. Oppressed would be the more appropriate word.'

Grimley fell silent. His failure to answer spoke volumes.

'Leah played you for the fool that you are, Grimley. It breaks my heart that the people of Waterswood have suffered because of your incompetence yet you are still here. You haven't shown one ounce of contrition throughout our conversation.' Jack leant forward again and looked directly into those cold, grey eyes. 'You have let down every Elf in Waterswood by your actions and they will never forgive you for that.'

Grimley hesitated for a second before responding, his arrogance on hold. 'As pious as ever, Green-Jack, but you ignore the fact that I'm here.'

'And why are you here?' asked Jack pointedly.

Grimley swallowed deeply. He studied Jack carefully for a moment. 'I'm here to offer my help.'

Jack burst into mocking laughter. 'You expect me to trust you after all you've done?'

Grimley's gaze settled on Jack and didn't waiver.

'Maybe trust is too strong a word, but I can help.'

'How exactly?' laughed Jack sarcastically.

'I know where to find Leah – his castle is on this mountain range.'

So Elensar was right. We are near to our prey, thought Jack.

'And there's something else that might interest you,' said Grimley pointedly.

Jack studied Grimley's face for any signs of duplicity.

'Leah is frightened of you …'

*

Chapter Twenty-Six – Unwanted Companion

Jack slept fitfully. Partly due to his aching ribs and bruised body. But meeting Grimley had unsettled him. Never in his darkest dreams did he think he would come across Grimley on this journey let alone that he would owe his life to him. And just to further complicate matters he was offering to help him find Leah.

Elensar had been right about Leah's whereabouts. His instincts had told him that they were nearing their foe and Grimley confirmed that Leah did indeed reside on this very mountain range. But Jack was disturbed. He was disturbed for a very good reason. His Koehtia was still absent. He'd tried several times during the night to connect with it but felt nothing.

He was about to confront Leah with no magic and a battered and bruised body. He smiled to himself – the odds weren't exactly stacked in his favour. And there was Grimley – could he trust him? He already knew the answer to the question, but he was in a predicament where he at least needed Grimley to help him find his friends. He decided to leave any decisions on hold until he was reunited with them. Elensar would know what to do.

Grimley came back into the cave carrying a bundle of wood that he'd collected from outside. He placed it on top of the ashes from the previous fire and retrieved some dry tinder from his pack and lit it with sparks from a flint wheel.

'The wood is damp from the snow, so it will be a bit smoky at first, but it will soon dry out. I'll boil some water and make tea.'

'Is it still snowing?' asked Jack.

'Just a few flakes,' said Grimley. 'The snow's very deep so it's going to make walking difficult.'

'I need to get back out on the trail and find my friends.'

Grimley had his back to Jack as he tended the fire. 'I would've thought they'd be looking for you.'

'I was at the rear of the company when I fell – they may not have even been aware until they found shelter and realised I wasn't there. The conditions during the night would have made it impossible for them to search for me.'

Grimley turned around and looked quizzically at Jack. 'So, they have no idea what happened to you?'

Jack felt uneasy at the question. Did Grimley sense an opportunity to permanently separate him from his friends? 'They will come looking for me which is why I need to get back on the trail.'

'We need to eat first and you're going to need some strapping on your chest before you go anywhere. You have cracked your ribs thanks to your fall.'

Grimley showing concern was a new experience for Jack. He decided to take it at face value. 'I have some bandages in my pack – they should be adequate.'

Jack struggled onto his feet. His back was sore but flexible. Shards of pain shot through his chest – Grimley was right, he'd damaged his ribs in the fall. He took out the bandages from his pack and removed his coat and shirt. Just as he was about to wrap them around his chest Grimley walked over to him and held out his hand.

'It will be easier if I do it for you. The tighter the strapping the better.'

Jack handed him the bandage. 'I never had you down as a Healer.'

Grimley didn't look at him as he tightly wrapped the bandage around Jack's chest. 'I worked with Crystal in her clinic as a young Elf. There was a time when we were friends but that changed when I joined the Council of Elders.'

Grimley fastened the bandages and stepped back from Jack. 'How does that feel?'

Jack twisted in both directions and was pleasantly relieved to find the pain was bearable. 'That feels much better – thanks.'

Grimley returned to the fire and filled the teapot with the boiling water. As he stirred the pot he said, 'I have cheese and dried fruit if you would like to share it?'

Sharing food and pleasantries with Grimley – this was getting more and more bizarre by the minute, thought Jack. 'If you can spare some.'

Grimley handed Jack a mug of tea and a plate with the food on. They both sat across from each other around the fire. Jack was hungry – he hadn't eaten since the previous evening. Grimley also gave him a chunk of oatmeal bread. It was a little dry and hard, but Jack was still grateful.

Jack placed his plate by his side when he finished eating and sipped his tea as he watched Grimley eat. As helpful as Grimley had been, Jack still didn't allow himself to relax in his company. He'd seen a different side to him but too much had happened between them for Jack to change his opinion of him. And there were questions that needed answers.

'You said last night that Leah was frightened of me. What makes you think that?'

Grimley carried on eating. Jack was about to repeat the question when Grimley laid his plate on his lap and looked across at him. 'He doesn't seem in any hurry to confront you.'

Jack was beginning to wonder if Grimley was game playing again, but he offered an explanation. 'Although I have met Leah several times over the years I could not claim to know him well. I doubt if anyone knows him well. He makes a point of cloaking himself in mystery.'

'As interesting as this all may be, it doesn't explain why you think he's frightened of me.'

Grimley finished his food and put his plate down by his side. He picked up his tea and slowly sipped it. 'I was persuaded to let him take our gold dust because he said that it would make you very powerful and enable you to take over Waterswood. He said that he would look after it until it was safe for me and the Council of Elders to return.'

Jack shook his head in exasperation. 'And you believed him?'

Grimley offered no answer.

Jack was seething. He couldn't believe that Grimley

could be so stupid. 'He wanted the gold dust to enhance his own power. You must have seen the desecration in the forests to the west of here. You gave him the means to carry out his ruthless ambition to control the whole of the Faery lands.'

Grimley rested his elbows on his knees and looked up at Jack. He appeared genuinely contrite. 'You think I don't know that now?'

'You were so hell bent on stopping me from coming back to Waterswood that you would have done anything, including abandoning the people of Waterswood to the spirit world.'

Grimley's contrition didn't last. He sat up straight and glared at Jack. 'I didn't know that would happen. Do you think I would have risked it if I did?'

'You could have consulted Lomund. He would have told you the huge risk you were taking.'

'Lomund!' Grimley said his name as if it offended him. 'All he ever did was undermine me. He opposed all of the measures I took to secure the safety of the Elves of Waterswood.'

Jack couldn't believe what he was hearing. 'It was your actions and your actions alone that saw our people fade away.'

The air crackled with the tension between them. Jack was in no mood to listen to any of Grimley's lame excuses. 'It was your obsession with me and your total incompetence that doomed the Elves of Waterswood to their fate. What angers me the most is that I haven't heard one word of regret from you about what has happened.'

Jack's anger momentarily overwhelmed Grimley. His sneer disappeared. 'Of course, I have regrets. Leah misled me. I was distraught when I realised what had happened. And that is why I'm here, to facilitate the return of our gold dust.'

As much as Jack might agree with his intentions he was surprised at his naivety. 'And how exactly is it you plan to do that?'

205

Grimley didn't answer and diverted his gaze away from Jack. It was obvious to Jack that he had absolutely no idea on how he was going to persuade Leah to return the gold dust. He was here on a whim and Jack feared that Grimley would get in the way of the serious business of dealing with their foe.

'You have seen for yourself the devastation in the forests as you approached these mountains.' He leant towards Grimley. 'You do realise that it's spreading out across the land? If Leah's power is left unchecked, that devastation will reach Woodgate Valley.'

Grimley turned towards Jack but offered no response. It was obvious to Jack that he was totally out of his depth. Leah had played Grimley for a fool. It was all part of his plan to enslave the Faery world.

'Leah is never going to give up the gold dust, we're going to have to take it from him … by force.'

Grimley looked quizzically at Jack. 'But there are only a handful of you. Leah's castle is guarded by mutant Goblins. They will cut you down before you get anywhere near him.'

Jack wasn't sure that he wanted to reveal any of their plans to Grimley. He half-smiled to himself. What plans? They had no idea of what they would do when they confronted Leah other than hope that his magic miraculously returned.

'We will deal with whatever threat we encounter,' said Jack trying to convince himself as much as Grimley. 'But what I must do first is find my friends.'

Grimley stood up and picked up the two plates and cups they'd used for breakfast. He lit a candle from the fire and placed it on top of a ledge before stamping out what was left of it. He opened his backpack and put the plates and mugs into it. 'Even though the snow has stopped, the mountain terrain is treacherous. You are not fit enough to trek in such conditions.'

There was almost concern in his voice, but Jack was already on his feet and fastening his coat. 'I have no choice – I must find my friends and then carry on the search for

Leah.'

Grimley fastened his own coat and threw his pack over his shoulder. He picked up the candle and stood in front of Jack. 'I can take you and your friends to Leah's castle – it is a two-day trek from here at the most.'

Jack studied his face in the candle light. He looked like he was being serious. 'Why would you do that?'

'I would have thought the answer was obvious. I may not like the fact that you use magic but unlike Leah you are no threat to our valley. I will help you in whatever way I can.'

Did Jack really want Grimley to join the company? How could he trust him? He already knew the answer to that question – he couldn't. But he would find it almost impossible to walk in the snow and up the mountain trail on his own. And there was something more obvious that confronted him. If he refused Grimley's offer, then he would almost certainly go directly to Leah and tell him where they were.

Jack went to lift his backpack but as he went to throw it over his shoulder, a sharp pain shot through his back and ribs almost taking his breath away. He dropped the pack onto the floor and tried to steady his breathing. Grimley stepped forward and picked up the pack and gently placed it over Jack's shoulder.

Grimley being helpful was becoming an uncomfortable habit. Jack nodded his appreciation and followed him out of the cave and into a narrow twisting tunnel. It was only a few metres before they emerged into the bright, cold daylight. As Grimley had said, the snow had stopped, but it was bitterly cold. Jack hesitated by the cave entrance as his eyes adjusted to the bright sunlight. The snow crunched under Grimley's boots as he trudged slowly back towards the trail.

Grimley stopped just short of the trail and turned to Jack. 'We'll take the easy route up the mountain – it's not so steep. I'm assuming your friends will come back down towards us to look for you. We should meet them sometime during the daylight hours. Then I can take you to Leah.'

207

Jack nodded his agreement but still felt uneasy relying on an individual who had tried to have him killed in the past, but what choice did he have? As Grimley set off along the trail, Jack followed and hoped that it wouldn't be too long before he was reunited with his friends.

*

Chapter Twenty-Seven –
The Search for Jack

The company began their search for Jack early the next morning. Roger barely slept during the night and was anxious to leave at first light. He was persuaded to eat some breakfast by Rory but was packed and ready to leave within minutes after he finished. Elensar and Stran led the group out into the deep snow and they both forensically scanned the trail for any clues that would tell them what had happened to Jack.

Their job was made even harder by the heavy snow fall over night, but they were both experts in tracking and they would spot things that the ordinary eye would miss. Rory sensed Roger's anxiety and did his best to reassure him but most of what he said fell on deaf ears. Roger was eaten up with worry about Jack and no words were about to put his mind at ease.

The freshly fallen snow was crisp and deep and slowed their progress considerably. The trail narrowed to less than a metre in some places and a combination of unsure footing and the steep drop to one side of them made progress even more difficult.

'I never noticed just how high it was on the way up here,' said Rory. 'I've never been great with heights if I'm honest.'

'Don't worry,' said Grindell. 'I'll keep close – you won't be falling with me around.'

'Thanks, Grindell,' said Rory. 'I've always hated heights ever since I was a young Leprechaun. My friend Seamus used to tease me about it.'

'That's what friends tend to do in my experience,' smiled Grindell.

Two hours after they began their search, there was still no sign of what had happened to Jack. And it wasn't just Roger who was visibly worried. Elensar stopped the company and spoke with Stran.

'Have you seen anything that would give us any sort of

a clue as to what happened to him?'

The ranger didn't have to think about his answer and shook his head. 'Not a thing.'

Elensar addressed the others while Stran stood on his own staring over the trail ledge. 'I'm not sure how long we should carry on the search.'

'I am,' said Roger interrupting him. 'We carry on until we find him.'

'But anything could have happened to him,' said Elensar. 'Jack would want us to focus on the quest above all else.'

Roger was about to argue when Stran called across to Elensar. 'Come over here – I've found something.'

Stran was kneeling by the trail edge looking over. Elensar joined him and followed his gaze.

'What is it, Stran?'

Stran pointed to a tree root that was hanging in mid-air. 'Lower me down, I want to have a closer look.'

Elensar took some rope from his pack and tied it around Stran's waist. He anchored himself against a rock and slowly lowered him down the mountainside. Stran stopped by the root and examined it. He took out his knife and cut around a metre off and called up to Elensar to hoist him back up.

Once he was back with the others he showed them the root. 'This has been pulled from the ground recently and if you look at the end you can see that it's been snapped.'

'Is this meant to mean anything?' asked Rory innocently.

Stran shot him a look of pure scorn and carried on his explanation. 'If I slipped over the edge of the trail on the ice and snow, the first thing I would do as I fell would be to grab a hold of something.'

Elensar took the root from him and studied it. 'So, Jack slipped over the edge and grabbed onto this. His weight would have pulled the root from the ground and it snapped.'

Every one of them looked over the edge and took on board the distance that Jack would have fallen. No one spoke as the horror of the circumstance sunk in. Roger stepped back from the edge shaking his head. Rory followed him but didn't offer any words of comfort. Instead he reached out and tenderly touched his arm.

'Nobody could survive that fall,' said Stran. 'That's a shear drop down to the fir forest at the foot of the mountain.'

Rory instantly turned on him. 'For just once in your life Stran, can you show a bit of sensitivity. Roger has lost his son! Doesn't that mean anything to you?'

Stran was about to react but Roger beat him to it. 'I don't accept for a minute that he's dead.' His whole body shook with emotion. 'Until I find his lifeless body then I carry on the search.'

Gwendo stepped forward. 'Let me fly down there and have a look. I'll be back before you know it.'

'What if the snow comes in,' said Elensar. 'You'll be stranded.'

'Even with my lack of sense of direction I think I can find my way back up the trail,' she smiled.

Before Elensar could respond she unfurled her wings and flew gracefully into the air. 'Wish me luck.'

Gwendo swooped down the mountainside scanning the thick snow searching for any signs of Jack. Although the slope was steep, she was sure that Jack wouldn't have come to any harm as there were no nasty rocks or tree roots protruding. But the slope petered out into a sheer drop after around one hundred metres and Jack would have found himself falling through the air. She stopped and hovered for a minute and looked immediately below her onto a strip of densely packed fir trees and tried to work out the trajectory of Jack's descent. He would have almost certainly hit the trees below at speed. Could he survive such an impact?

She flew down to the trees and landed just beyond them and took her bearings. The mountain trail was several paces below her and the snow all around was deep and crisp. A thought flashed into her mind – could Jack be buried in the snow? As she mulled over the idea something on the trail below caught her attention. The snow was too deep for her to walk easily so she rose into the air and flew down to the

211

trail. As she landed, her heart leapt in her chest. There were two sets of footprints in the snow side by side. She momentarily considered following them but hesitated. Maybe it wasn't Jack. It would've been a miracle if he'd survived that fall. But who else could it be? She decided to go back to the others. Elensar would know what to do.

The adrenaline flowed through her like river rapids and she flew back up the mountain with ease. She landed back amongst the company and could barely contain herself. 'I found tracks on the trail below.'

Roger was in front of her in an instant. 'Where were they?'

'I followed the trajectory of what would have been Jack's fall from the mountain. I'm certain that he would have hit a dense patch of fir trees just above the trail at the foot of the mountain.'

'How could he possibly survive that fall?' asked Stran.

Roger and Rory turned on him and glared but Gwendo continued. 'I found two sets of footprints on the trail. I'm not sure which direction they were headed.'

'Two sets?' asked Elensar. 'If Jack survived that fall he would have probably needed help so it makes sense.'

'It could be anyone,' said Stran.

That was too much for Roger and he exploded at the ranger. 'That's my son we're talking about here, Stran. If you can't find something helpful to say then keep your thoughts to yourself. I'll go back down the mountain on my own if it's too much trouble for you.'

Elensar stepped in between them. 'Nobody's going on their own … we'll go together. Stran, do you have a problem with that?'

Stran locked eyes with Elensar but didn't offer an argument. Elensar turned away from him and addressed the others. 'We'll go back down the trail towards where Gwendo saw the tracks. If it is Jack, then we will meet him on his way back up.'

Roger didn't need any encouragement and immediately set off followed by Rory and Gwendo. Elensar was quickly after him. 'Roger, I understand your anxiety, but the trail is deadly. It's not going to help Jack if you go tumbling over the edge as well.'

Roger turned on him and looked as if he was going to argue but his expression softened and he nodded to Elensar. 'I'm sure that Jack is OK. Look how he survived that Stallion stampede on the Running Plains.'

'I was right there next to him,' chimed in Rory. 'I was convinced I was a goner.'

'That jewel around his neck will keep him safe,' continued Roger. 'I'm not saying that I understand why but it's done it once and I'm sure it will do it again.'

'Elensar and I saw Jack taken away by a huge flying bird when we were searching for his mammy. We were all frantic with worry and Elensar searched for him like an Elf possessed. But two days later there comes Jack on the back of a flying horse and he's only rescued his mother and my two friends, Seamus and O'Reilly, from a mad sorcerer.'

Roger forced a smile. 'I'm realising what a resourceful young man he is.'

'Resourceful young Elf,' corrected Rory.

Despite the deep snow and ice, the company made good progress back down the trail. The snow thankfully held off and by midday they were soon approaching the point where Gwendo had seen the footprints in the snow.

'We should have seen Jack by now if he was heading back up the trail,' said Elensar as he turned to find Stran.

The ranger lagged behind the rest of the company and stopped once he caught them up. Stran stood there impassively and didn't offer a response.

'Where was it you saw the tracks, Gwendo?' asked Elensar.

Gwendo pointed towards the fir trees on a downward slope a few hundred paces from where they stood. 'They were just beyond those trees.'

'Tell me if you see anything,' said Elensar, 'and I mean anything, no matter how insignificant it may seem.'

He led them down the slope towards the trees. Nobody

spoke as they crunched their way through the thick snow. Roger looked visibly edgy as he followed the Captain down the trail. As they rounded the trees, the two sets of tracks were easily spotted by them all, but there was one thing that concerned them. The tracks headed off in a different direction - they followed a line around the mountain instead of the trail they'd just come down.

Elensar and Stran both knelt by the tracks and studied them for a few seconds. Stran stood up first. 'They're heading around the mountain for sure.'

Elensar stood up beside him. 'I agree – we should follow them.'

Stran shook his head. 'I'd like to go back a bit further and see where they came from.'

'Why waste any more time?' asked a clearly frustrated Roger. 'Jack will be wondering where we are.'

'We don't know that it is Jack,' said Stran. 'But if you give me just a little time, I may be able to prove beyond any doubt that it is.'

Roger was about to argue, but Elensar stepped in. 'Stran has a point, Roger. It may be worth going back to the exact spot where Jack would have landed. We could find some clues as to what has happened to him.'

Roger reluctantly nodded his agreement and followed Stran and Elensar back along the trail. As objectionable as Stran could be, there was no doubt about his tracking skills. He stopped by the trees and carefully looked them up and down. He pointed to two tall trees on the end. 'Notice that several of the branches at the top are broken. They are thinner than the lower branches and would have cushioned Jack's fall considerably without doing him any serious harm. He would have almost certainly ended up in the snow drift to the side of the trees.'

'Then what?' asked Rory.

'That, Leprechaun, is what I hope we're about to find out.' And carried on back down the trail.

'On my life,' whispered Rory to Roger, 'he almost sounded pleasant.'

The trail narrowed slightly as it passed along the side of a craggy rock face. The snow on the ground thinned and the footprints weren't quite so clear but Stran was still able to follow them. It was only a few hundred metres further when the tracks turned off towards a narrow entrance in the rock face. Stran hesitated and waited for Elensar.

'Can you light your torch so we can look inside?

Elensar stepped out of the wind and retrieved his torch and lit it with his flint wheel. He entered the narrow entrance followed by Stran and they tentatively walked along a tunnel that opened out into a small cave after a few metres. They stood in the middle surveying the scene. It was Stran who spotted the remains of a fire and knelt down and placed his hand over the ashes.

'I can feel just a trace of heat. I would guess that whoever was here left this morning.'

They walked around the cave searching for clues but nothing caught their eye. Elensar led them back outside and went to speak to the others while Stran studied the entrance to the cave.

'Did you find anything?' asked Roger.

'We found the remains of a fire,' said Elensar. 'Stran is pretty certain they left this morning.'

'Do you think Jack is one of them?' asked Rory.

'There's nothing that suggests it,' said Elensar.

'There is now,' said Stran walking over to them. He held up a tin mug in his hand. 'The initials GJ are inscribed on the bottom.'

'That's Jack's alright,' said Rory. 'He did that before we left Waterswood.'

Roger was barely able to contain his excitement. 'Where did you find it?'

'It was on a ledge by the cave entrance.'

Elensar smiled. 'Jack knew we'd come looking for him.' He looked up over the fir trees towards the trail they'd just descended. 'Somehow Jack survived falling from that trail half way up the mountain … But I wonder who the other set of footprints belong to?'

Chapter Twenty-Eight –
A Question of Trust

The conversation between Jack and Grimley had been sparse to say the least. Partly because Jack had little to say to him but also because his ribs were so sore it was as much as he could do just to breathe. Walking and talking at the same time wasn't an easy option. The strapping around his chest helped but it was still an effort to walk without stabbing pains running through his chest and back.

He'd agreed with Grimley that they should take the shallower climb up the mountain, not that he was aware of any trails other than the one he'd taken with his friends the previous day. Doubts constantly circled his mind about Grimley but he had little choice other than to follow him for the time being.

In the end, it all came down to trust and he most certainly couldn't bring himself to trust Grimley. Yes, he'd saved Jack's life when he could easily have walked away. And he fed him and bound his ribs to enable him to walk. But too much had happened between them in the past. It was difficult to get beyond the fact that Grimley had tried to kill him and his grandfather. Caution was the only logical way ahead for Jack.

Grimley stopped and pointed up to the sky. 'Those low white clouds are full of snow. I think we need to look for somewhere to shelter.'

Jack agreed that another snow fall was imminent, but he really didn't want to leave the trail.

'If your friends are looking for you they will also have to shelter from the snow. They will have little choice,' said Grimley sensing Jack's unease.

'I was hoping we'd have met them by now?' said Jack.

'I told you that we needed to take the shallower trail because of your injuries.' He pointed to a trail further up the mountain. 'That is the trail we could've taken but as you no doubt found out yesterday it is much steeper. I suspect that is the route your friends will take. They will see our tracks clearly in the snow so they will find us … that is if they are looking for you.'

Jack looked quizzically at Grimley. 'Why wouldn't they be looking for me?'

'If they've worked out that you fell, and that is a big if, they may draw the conclusion that you didn't survive it.'

As much as Jack didn't want to agree with Grimley, he had a point. Elensar was the consummate leader – the quest would always take priority over any individual. He had little choice other than to go along with Grimley … for now.

'OK, let's find somewhere to shelter from the snow.'

As Grimley turned away and continued along the trail, Jack took a spare glove out of his pack and placed it over the end of a fir branch on the edge of the trail. If the snow covered his tracks, and his friends came looking for him, Stran was sure to find the glove. Jack looked hopefully up towards the mountain trail above them but it was empty. An eerie silence gripped him. He turned back and reluctantly followed Grimley.

It wasn't long before the snow came – just a few flakes at first but it soon turned into a full-blown blizzard, with the wind lashing wave after wave of white flakes into them. It occurred to Jack that Grimley was more than a little familiar with the route as he found a concealed cave entrance that was impossible to see from the trail. It was hidden behind a clump of fir trees, but Jack was just relieved to be out of the driving snow.

Grimley gathered some dead wood and soon had a fire blazing. He filled the kettle from a water canteen and made them both a cup of Roseleaf. Jack's injuries had eased considerably over the day and that was helped by Grimley's tight bandaging of his chest. His head had cleared and he felt far more alert that he did the previous night. He had questions that needed answering and he was ready to confront Grimley with them.

'I have some dried mushrooms to make soup,' said Grimley. 'I trust that will be acceptable to you?'

Jack heard a trace of sarcasm in Grimley's voice. 'I've always liked mushroom soup,' said Jack. 'My grandfather made it regularly for me.'

Grimley appeared uncomfortable at the mention of Jack's grandfather. He retrieved a pot and a bag of dried mushrooms from his rucksack and filled it with the mushrooms and water and placed it over the fire. He focused his attention on the soup and ignored Jack.

'It was only my grandfather's alertness that saved our lives that night you tried to burn our cottage down.'

Grimley sat down opposite Jack and looked sheepishly at him. 'I acted in what I thought was the best interests of our community. You would have wreaked havoc in Waterswood if I hadn't intervened.'

'Do you regret what you did?' asked Jack staring deep into those cold grey eyes.

Grimley lowered his head and stared down at the floor. 'Of course, I have regrets …'

Jack shook his head in disgust. 'Your only regret is that the bungling Vilner screwed up. You think that without me your life would have carried on as before.'

Grimley raised his eyes and looked at Jack but didn't answer.

Jack smiled sarcastically. 'Has the penny finally dropped? Leah was always going to take the gold dust regardless of me. You would have been abandoned to the spirit world along with the rest of the Elves of Waterswood.'

'There are many things I find irritating about you, Green-Jack, but none more so than your piety. You look down on me and so many others. What must it be like to be so perfect?'

Grimley's riposte momentarily shocked Jack into silence giving him the chance to continue.

'Yes, I have made many mistakes, none more so than trusting Leah. I was wrong about the practice of magic but there was nobody within our community who had the skills to teach us. Any decision I made was for the good of us all. I know that Lomund and his friends branded me a dictator but it's not easy being the head of a community. You have everybody's interests at heart not just a few.' He dropped his head into his hands and rubbed his face as if trying to erase uncomfortable memories. He sat up and looked directly into Jack's eyes. 'I sincerely regret what has happened but I did my best. If I could turn the clock back and do things differently, I would.'

Jack studied Grimley's face and thought he saw genuine regret there. But this was Grimley. He decided to leave the past where it was and focus on what lay ahead. The confrontation with Leah was looming and he needed to find out as much about him as he could.

Grimley sat forward and slowly stirred the mushroom soup. He added some herbs and stock and replaced the lid on the pot. 'I will let it simmer for a while before we eat.'

Jack adopted a more conciliatory tone with Grimley. 'We must leave the past where it is and concentrate on the future. I need to know that you recognise that things will be different in Waterswood … that is assuming that we can reclaim our gold dust from Leah.'

Grimley fiddled nervously with his mug. Jack watched him carefully as he waited for a response.

'I accept that there will be changes. The Elves of Waterswood will demand them following their experiences that led them to the spirit world. It has knocked us all – we must rebuild our society and learn from our mistakes.'

'I'm glad to hear it,' said Jack. 'We must create a fully democratic and accountable system that we all can participate in.'

Grimley drained his mug and placed it on the ground next to him. 'Why are you so convinced that democracy is the only way forward? I have studied the human system and it brings nothing but weak leadership and confusion. Firm leadership is what's required.'

Just when Jack thought that Grimley's attitude was softening, he reverted back to type. 'Democracy may have its flaws but it beats the alternatives. If a government is ineffective, or weak, or worse corrupted, then they can be voted out. What you presided over, Grimley, was a dictatorship.'

'Your piety surfaces once again, Green-Jack,' said Grimley pointedly. 'Tell me, on how many occasions have you been involved in governing a community?'

'You know full well that I haven't, Grimley, but that doesn't mean to say that I don't recognise injustice when I see it. What happened in Waterswood was wrong. You stepped on any dissent and incarcerated our people in Darkenwold. That's not to mention that you employed Finn Tarr as a mercenary to terrorise our people.'

Grimley sighed deeply. 'How are we going to rebuild our community if you are just going to sit in judgement on me?'

Jack leant towards Grimley to make sure he could see the passion in his face in the firelight. 'Until I met you on this mountain, Grimley, you and the Elders were never going to be allowed in government again. You were to be put on trial and punished for your crimes.'

A self-satisfied smile adorned Grimley's lips. 'I find it amusing that you are capable of vindictiveness, Green-Jack. In fact, I find it reassuring.'

Jack did his best not to be indignant but failed miserably. 'It's called justice, Grimley, something that you know little about.'

'So, let me make sure I understand this, Green-Jack,' said Grimley smugly. 'You have already decided that the Elders and I are not fit to govern Waterswood and therefore cannot stand for election to the institutions you're planning to create. Perhaps you could explain to me how that is democratic?'

Jack drained the last drop of tea from his mug and placed it on the ground next to him. As reluctant as he was to acknowledge it, Grimley had a point.

'It will of course be up to the people of Waterswood to decide whether you are fit for government. Lomund will head an interim assembly until elections can be arranged. It will be that government that will decide on your fate and that of the Elders.'

'Very noble of you,' said Grimley his voice thick with sarcasm. 'But let me ask you a question. Do you know how the Council of Elders came into being? Do you even understand how it works?'

As much as it pained Jack, he had to admit that he didn't. 'I know little about the Council of Elders but my one and only experience of it was not a good one.'

'Elven culture has always valued our elderly citizens, unlike the human race who discard their old people as soon as they are perceived to be of no further use.'

It was a sentiment that Jack had heard from his grandfather on many occasions. Again, he had to admit that Grimley was right.

'Many years ago, in the early days of Waterswood,' continued Grimley, 'the community decided it needed some form of government. Various systems were tried until they eventually settled on the Council of Elders. Once an Elf reached a certain age he would become eligible for nomination to the council.'

'Two things,' said Jack. 'Why is that only the male Elves are eligible and who does the nominating?'

Grimley sighed in frustration and seemed genuinely irritated by Jack's question, but he composed himself before responding. 'Aelves have always taken a more caring role in our society and left the government to the males.'

'Well it's about time that changed,' interrupted Jack. 'Aelves like my mother, Lilac and Crystal could make positive contributions to the way our community is run.'

Grimley didn't respond or even acknowledge Jack's suggestion and continued. 'As one of the Elders decides to step down from the Council, he will nominate his replacement. This is subject to approval by the other members.'

'And there lies the problem,' said Jack. 'The character of the Council will rarely change. As much as I appreciate the wisdom of elderly people, they can become set in their ways. What is needed is a more balanced council that

221

consists of Aelves and Elves both young and old. And if they are subject to elections every so many years, they are more likely to take notice of the people they represent.'

Grimley lifted the lid off the pot on the fire and stirred the soup. His face showed his frustrations with what Jack was saying. He replaced the lid back on the pot and turned his attention back to Jack. 'What you're suggesting is a recipe for disaster. There will be constant disagreements and nothing will ever get done.'

Jack resisted the urge to laugh. 'And are you seriously suggesting that what has happened in Waterswood wasn't a disaster? Our gold dust has been stolen and our people have faded into the spirit world. Just how much worse can it get?'

Grimley grimaced at Jack's words. He had no constructive suggestions to offer but that still didn't stop him from disagreeing. 'I'm not saying that mistakes weren't made but I don't think it's right to completely dismantle a system that in the main has worked well for many years.'

Jack leant forward and was about to disagree but Grimley held his hand up.

'But I'm not saying that we shouldn't review our system and put it to the people. These things need to be debated and all strands of opinion heard. But I urge caution and strongly suggest we don't make any hasty decisions that we will all live to regret.'

He lifted the lid of the pot and filled two bowls with steaming hot soup. He handed one to Jack along with a chunk of oatmeal bread. Jack took a spoonful of the soup and blew on it before tentatively taking a sip. It was good – nearly as good as his grandfather's which surprised him.

Once he finished his soup he placed his bowl on the floor next to his mug. Grimley finished his and did the same. He rinsed out the teapot with water from his canteen and put a heaped spoonful of Roseleaf into it. He filled it with hot water from the kettle before stirring it and leaving it to brew by the side of the fire.

'The soup was good,' said Jack. 'I appreciate what you've done for me since you found me in the snow.'

Grimley nodded his acknowledgement but didn't say anything. Jack had questions he needed to ask about Leah.

'Is there anything you can tell me about Leah that may help when I confront him?'

Grimley thought for a moment before answering. 'He is a formidable character but like all of us he has his weaknesses'

'And they are?' asked Jack.

'The most obvious is his arrogance. He is clever and powerful, but he underestimates people.'

'You said that he fears me. Why do you think that?'

'You are an unknown, Green-Jack. And of course, he has heard the stories about your magical powers.'

Jack was confused. 'What stories?'

'I told him that you brought the girl back from the dead. And there was the incident with the Redwoods in the human world.'

Jack leant back against the cave wall and digested what Grimley had said. So, Leah knew of Jack's abilities with Earth Magic. But what about his? 'I know that Leah has great power, especially since he stole the gold dust from Woodgate Valley. He must think that he has more than enough power to deal with me.'

'And that goes to the heart of his dilemma. His arrogance tells him that he can defeat you, but he isn't going to know for sure until that moment of confrontation.'

Jack felt the discomforting flutter of anxiety in the pit of his stomach. Was he ready for this encounter when it came? The doubts that had been lingering on the edge of his awareness were beginning to surface again. He slowed his breathing in an effort to compose himself. He needed his friends to find him ... and soon. The thought of a confrontation with the enigma that was Leah, accompanied only by Grimley, was just too terrible to contemplate.

*

Chapter Twenty-Nine – Death in the Snow

Buoyed by the find of Jack's tin mug, the company continued the search with a renewed vigour. Elensar, Stran and Roger ploughed on relentlessly despite the thick snow. Rory, Gwendo and Grindell followed, albeit a little slower due to their shorter legs, although Grindell's body strength more than made up for his short stature but he stayed with the other two to make sure they didn't get left behind.

Elensar and Roger were so focused on catching up with Jack that neither noticed the thick snow clouds overhead. Stran tried to bring their attention to them but neither were listening. The pursuit of Jack continued at a pace. The first few flakes of snow were barely acknowledged and even when it became heavier they didn't slow. It was as the winds picked up and the snow fall became a blizzard that Stran grabbed a hold of both Elensar and Roger.

'We must take cover. We're going to become totally disorientated in this blizzard and end up losing our way,' he shouted.

'No way!' said Roger. 'We'll lose the tracks if we stop.'

Grindell, Rory and Gwendo struggled to their sides. Grindell joined the debate. 'We could barely see you from just a few strides away. If we don't stop, we stand a good chance of losing each other.'

Roger was about to argue but Elensar stepped in. 'He's right, Roger. It's getting too dangerous. Jack and his companion will almost certainly be taking shelter, so we won't lose any time.'

'OK,' said Roger reluctantly, 'but as soon as the snow eases we get straight back on the trail.'

Elensar tied a rope between them all to make sure that they lost no-one and led the search for shelter. The conditions made it almost impossible to walk any distance, so he settled for assembling a make-shift shelter under a clump of fir trees. They sheltered under the branches and used the canvas windbreaks that had proved so useful on the

Running Plains.

They huddled together using their combined body heat to keep each other warm. It was Rory who came up with his familiar suggestion and provoked an equally familiar response from Stran.

'Why don't we gather some wood and light a fire? I can make us all a nice mug of Roseleaf …'

'Do you ever stop thinking about your belly, Leprechaun?' barked Stran.

Rory winked at Roger and said, 'come to think of it, no, not very often.'

'Let's sit tight for a while,' said Elensar, 'and see how the weather pans out. If the temperature drops as it did last night, then we're going to need a fire to survive the cold.'

'You'll get no arguments from me on that score,' chimed in Rory. 'And I always think …'

Elensar suddenly clamped his hand around Rory's mouth and pointed towards the trail. Despite the thick and heavy snow, they could make out tall figures trudging towards them, coming from the direction they were headed. Elensar took his hand away from Rory's mouth and crouched behind the canvas windbreak and peered through the blanket of snow. The clumsy gait of the strangers and their sheer physical size told him all he needed to know.

He turned to the others and hissed one word, 'Goblins!'

Grindell and Stran were by his side in an instant, both with weapons drawn.

'How many?' asked Stran.

'It's difficult to see through the falling snow, but I'd guess at least twenty.'

'Not too many for us to deal with,' said Grindell slowly running his finger down the blade of his axe.

'I want to avoid any confrontation in these conditions,' said Elensar. 'They are tall and strong and will be difficult to engage in close combat.'

'Then let me handle them on my own,' said Grindell. 'I have surprise on my side. They won't know what's hit them.'

225

Elensar half smiled. 'I'm sure you're right, Grindell, but I don't want them to know we're here. We're well covered by the tree branches so we're safe for now.'

'They're looking for us,' said Stran through gritted teeth. 'They know we're on the mountain.'

'Now that wouldn't take a genius to work that out,' said Rory, 'especially after the carnage we left in the valley.'

Stran shot Rory a sharp look but didn't respond.

'It seems that Leah relies on the Goblins for his security,' said Elensar. 'Not the most reliable beings I could think of.'

'Wait a minute,' said Gwendo. 'They've come from the direction in which Jack was headed.'

She didn't get to finish her sentence as Roger was already ahead of her and leapt to his feet. 'They must have captured Jack. We need to help him.'

'I think that's unlikely,' said Stran. 'If they'd captured him then why were they headed further back down the trail.' He shook his head. 'No, Jack and the stranger have taken shelter somewhere. They are safe, for now.'

'How can you be so sure?' asked Roger.

'I can't be sure,' said Stran, 'but Jack and the stranger sheltered in that cave further down the trail when the weather closed in last evening, so I think it's likely that they will do the same again.'

Grindell and Stran sheathed their weapons and sat back down. Elensar kept the Goblins under surveillance until they were out of sight. He turned to the others. 'We're going to see more Goblin patrols as we near Leah's lair. It's vital that we remain vigilant. We'll resume our pursuit of Jack as soon as the weather eases, but I want to avoid any confrontation with the Goblins.'

Stran raised his eyebrows. 'Do you think that's possible?'

'I don't know,' said Elensar, 'but we have to try.'

'They are cumbersome warriors,' said Grindell. 'They may be big in stature, but they are slow and predictable. We will deal with them if the need arises.'

Elensar smiled at Grindell. He knew that the Dwarf was

more than capable of handling himself against any foe.

'I suppose there's no point in asking if we can light a fire,' said Rory more in hope than expectation.

'No point at all,' snapped Stran.

*

As darkness fell, the wind dropped, and the snow eased slightly. Elensar left the makeshift shelter and scouted the trail for any signs of Goblin patrols. Once he'd satisfied himself it was clear, he returned to the others.

'We'll have a cold snack and get on our way before the Goblins return.'

'Ah Elensar, I'm freezing. Can't we have something hot to warm us all up?' pleaded Rory.

'There's no time and the Goblins will see our fire if they're anywhere near,' said Elensar.

Rory and Gwendo unpacked some stale bread and cheese and handed it out to the others. As hard as the bread was it filled their empty bellies and pacified their growing hunger. They were packed and ready within twenty minutes and warily made their way back to the trail. Elensar scouted ahead as Stran went back down the trail to make sure that there was no sign of the Goblin patrol that had recently passed them. They both returned to the group at the same time and nodded to each other.

'Remember to keep your eyes and ears open. If you hear or see anything unusual let me know immediately,' said Elensar.

He set off along the trail followed by Rory, Gwendo and Roger. Grindell and Stran brought up the rear. The snow had stopped, and the temperature had dropped noticeably. The only sound you could hear was the crunch of their boots through the deep snow. The snow was nearly half a metre deep in some places which slowed them down considerably. Gwendo struggled the most as she was only a metre tall and the snow was up to her waist but Grindell was on hand when it became too much and lifted her through the worst drifts.

The snow clouds cleared to reveal a dark jewelled night-time sky and a luminous, milky-white moon that shed its bright light across the landscape making the crystallised snow on the fir trees sparkle like diamonds. In any normal situation it would be a sight to behold but the threat of being attacked by Goblins set the company on edge.

Progress was painfully slow but there was little they could do other than plough on the best they could. They came to an exposed part of the trail and Elensar was concerned that they could be seen from a distance. He urged the company forward, but the snow had drifted in places and Gwendo and Rory struggled to get through.

Roger picked up Gwendo and sat her on his shoulders and Elensar lifted Rory and held him in his arms.

'I can manage!' protested Rory, but Elensar ignored him and continued to wade through the deep snow.

Stran dropped back and spoke with Elensar. 'I'm not sure this is such a good idea. We're very exposed out here and we've got little room for manoeuvre if we're attacked.'

Elensar didn't stop and carried on wading through the snow. 'It's only going to get worse, Stran. We've got to keep moving the best we can.'

Stran was about to respond when something flashed past his head and buried itself deep in the snow. Grindell sprang forward and retrieved it. It was a half metre mace complete with ugly metal spikes. They all looked in the direction it came from and a lone Goblin stood on the trail around 100 metres ahead of them.

Elensar immediately dropped Rory into the snow and removed his longbow from his back. He loaded an arrow in an instant and unleashed it in the direction of the Goblin. It sped towards its intended target and hit the Goblin full in its chest sending it crashing to the ground like a felled tree.

Elensar turned to the others and shouted, 'it won't be on its own. We need to choose a place we can defend. Follow me!'

But before he could react, Stran shouted at him. 'Elensar – in the trees.'

Elensar turned towards the trees to see at least a dozen Goblins running towards them, maces in hand. He unleashed a burst of arrows at them and four of them instantly dropped to the ground, but the others were on top of them before he could reload.

Grindell threw off his pack and launched himself into the heart of the Goblins with both of his axes slicing through them like a warm knife through butter. Another four were vanquished in the blink of an eye and Elensar dealt with the remaining Goblins hacking them to death with his broadsword.

Rory, Gwendo and Roger stood rooted to the spot; almost hypnotised by the sudden killing spree they'd just witnessed. Stran scanned the trail in both directions looking for more Goblins. But Elensar was in full warrior mode and rallied the company to pick up their packs and take refuge in the fir trees that overlooked the trail.

'We must find cover! We're too exposed if more Goblins come. We need to regroup on the higher ground behind the trees.'

The words were no sooner out of his mouth when he heard a shout from Stran. 'The Goblins we saw earlier are coming back, and they're moving fast. We won't have time to get there, Elensar. We're going to have to fight here.'

Elensar dropped his pack and primed his longbow. He unleashed a succession of arrows and each one felled a Goblin but there were at least a dozen left on their feet and they didn't slow in their rush towards the company. With all his arrows used, Elensar dropped his longbow and took out his sword and joined Grindell and Stran.

Roger dragged Rory and Gwendo away from the trail and up the bank towards the fir trees. 'Shelter in the trees. I'm going to join the others.' Rory had no time to protest as Roger leapt through the snow and back onto the trail with his dagger in his hand.

But Elensar shouted at him and Stran. 'Drop back and protect Rory and Gwendo. You don't have the weapons to fight Goblins.'

Roger was about to protest but Elensar shouted, 'now!'

Stran pulled Roger back just as Grindell engaged the first of the Goblins. He was less than half their size, but his axes easily found their intended targets and sliced into the bellies of the huge brutes. Elensar's sword cut down the Goblins like a scythe slicing through corn. His speed and agility were too much for them. The Goblins had brute strength but limited fighting skills and were easy prey to a Dwarf and an Elven warrior.

Roger watched the slaughter and it made him sick to the stomach. As brutal as the Goblins were they all fell blindly to the joint onslaught of Grindell's axes and Elensar's sword. Even the last few who were left standing didn't take the opportunity to run away and threw themselves into certain death.

But Roger's attention was distracted by a shout from Rory and he turned around to see a huge Goblin, mace in hand about to attack Gwendo. Rory's reactions were lightning fast, and he managed to pull Gwendo away. This turned the Goblin's attention towards him and he swung the huge mace at his head, but Rory jumped to the side and the mace hammered into the ground.

Rory took out his dagger in the hope that the Goblin would lose its balance and give him the opportunity to plunge it into his belly, but the Goblin came at him again. Rory dodged the blow but slipped in the snow. He lay helpless on his back as the Goblin raised its mace again as it prepared to land the killer blow.

Stran sprang forward and threw his dagger at the Goblin. It hit the Goblin in its left arm and it screamed out in pain. The Goblin turned towards Stran and roared in anger. It took a step towards him and raised its right arm holding the mace. Stran had no weapons to fight with and attempted to step backwards but the Goblin didn't hesitate and brought the mace crashing down onto Stran's head. The sound of the metal mace smashing into his head was sickening. Stran collapsed onto the snow, his skull crushed and bleeding. The thick, dark red blood from his wound coloured the snow around him. He lay there motionless.

As the Goblin towered over Stran and prepared to finish him off, Roger ran forward and launched his dagger at the brute. It thudded into its chest – the Goblin gasped at the impact and staggered backwards before falling into the snow next to Stran. Elensar ran over and thrust his sword deep into the Goblin's chest until it stopped struggling. He removed the blade from the Goblin and wiped the blood off in the snow.

Elensar sheathed his sword and knelt down by Stran and lifted him in his arms. He placed two fingers on his neck looking for a pulse and concentrated for several seconds.

Grim-faced, he turned to Rory. 'He's dead.'

*

Chapter Thirty – Castle in the Sky

Grimley returned to the cave carrying some deadwood. 'The snowstorm is easing. Maybe we should think about getting back out on the trail.'

'Even in the dark?' said Jack.

'Once the clouds clear and the snow stops, it's going to be a bright night. It will be cold, and the snow will be frozen on top, but it will still be possible to make progress.'

'I thought we were going to wait for daylight before we continued.'

'We can still do that,' said Grimley, 'but I assumed you were in hurry to find your friends.'

Grimley made a good point, thought Jack. 'I'll pack my things and be ready in five minutes.'

As Jack buttoned up his coat he wondered about where his friends might be. Were they looking for him or did they think he was dead? It was a question he couldn't answer but could only put himself out there and hope. He lifted his pack and winced with the pain in his ribs.

Grimley held out his hand. 'I can carry that.'

Jack was struggling with a Grimley who helped him. The nasty version was the one he was more familiar with. Had that person gone? Jack very much doubted it. He handed over his backpack and said, 'thanks.'

He followed Grimley out of the cave and into the cold night air. The snow had stopped and as Grimley had suggested, it was a clear, crisp night. They re-joined the trail and Jack looked either way for any sign of his friends but was disappointed when he saw nothing but an untouched landscape and snow laden trees. He sighed in frustration before trudging along the trail after Grimley.

Leah was near but Grimley had been vague about just how near and where he was. Jack had learnt precious little about Leah from his chat with Grimley and still did not know what to expect when he confronted him. The Faery Queens were sure that Jack needed his friends from different races. They called it the 'Unification of a Common Purpose' but Jack still didn't fully understand just how it would help him defeat Leah.

And there was still no sign of his Koehtia.

He was about to face the biggest challenge of his life without the Earth Magic that had saved him on so many occasions. His only magical defence was the Sarmondian Bloodstone that hung around his neck. It had protected him during the combat with Willy Venn, but that was a physical challenge. The magical properties of the stone were still largely unknown. Even the Artisan Meredin knew little about it.

Grimley walked silently by his side. Jack didn't sense any unease in him. In fact, he seemed incredibly relaxed. There was a time when Jack thought that Grimley cared for nobody but himself but his experiences over the previous day had thrown doubt on that. Grimley had saved his life and had done nothing but help him since. It just didn't make any sense, but Jack decided not to dwell on it and turned his mind to finding his friends.

They made steady progress over the next hour despite the snow drifts that crossed the trail. At some points there was as much as a half metre of snow to wade through. Jack's ribs ached at the extra exertion, but he still managed to keep going. The shallower trail had indeed made his journey easier and he doubted whether he could have managed the steeper trail that he'd followed with his friends.

It was as they emerged from a dense cluster of fir trees that they saw the company of Goblins coming towards them. They stopped instantly and assessed the situation. Their options were limited to say the least. The Goblins were no more than a hundred paces ahead of them and must have seen them.

'Let's retreat back into the trees,' said Jack.

Grimley remained calm and watched the brutes as they slowly made their way towards them. 'They've seen us, Green-Jack, and will soon find us. It will be all the worse for us when we're captured.'

'I have a sword – I can fight them.'

'Against twenty or more Goblins. I think not. They are murderous brutes and would take great delight in killing us both.'

'Then what do you suggest?' asked Jack getting more and more anxious by the second.

'We surrender ourselves to them.'

Jack was horrified. 'And just let them kill us anyway?'

Grimley shook his head. 'They won't kill us, they will take us prisoner.'

The Goblins continued their approach. They didn't run or increase their pace – it was a slow relentless march towards them. A knot tightened in Jack's stomach. The thought of handing himself over to those brutes made him feel physically sick. 'And then what happens?'

'They'll take us to Leah.'

Jack looked quizzically at Grimley. 'Why are you so sure?'

'Because,' said Grimley as the Goblins closed in on them, 'Leah uses them as his servants. They are totally under his control.'

Before Jack could answer, the leading Goblin took a short sword out and marched up to him and pointed it at his chest. The brute was another half a metre taller than Jack and nearly twice as wide. Its face was hideous; a high forehead, bulging eyes and discoloured crooked teeth. It made no attempt to talk to him but just grunted.

Jack had no idea what it was trying to say so just stood there. The brute reacted by landing a stinging slap across Jack's face that sent him sprawling across the snow. Then it leant over him and pulled his sword and dagger from his belt before dragging him back to his feet. The Goblin turned to his companions and threw the weapons onto the snow. One of them picked them up and placed them on an already full weapons belt.

The Goblin then turned his attention to Grimley and held out his hand. Grimley removed the packs he was carrying and handed them over. It snatched them from him and threw them over to his companions. One of them picked up the packs and tore them open, emptying all the contents across the floor. Anything that wasn't edible was discarded starting a free for all as the brutes grabbed at the food and shovelled it into their mouths. There was no waiting their turn, they pushed and pulled each other out of the way to get their hands on the food.

Once they'd finished, the Goblin who had slapped Jack, pushed him and Grimley into the midst of the group and marched back along the trail. Jack and Grimley were surrounded with no chance of escape and had no choice other than to follow. The Goblins paid little attention to either of them and set a brisk pace despite the conditions.

How Jack prayed that Elensar and his friends would find them before they reached Leah's castle. Although there were twenty or so Goblins, the Captain's skill with a longbow would make short shrift of them. And those that were left would be easily dealt with by Grindell. That thought momentarily lifted him but the imposing presence of the huge brutes that escorted him brought him quickly back down to earth with a bump.

Jack turned to Grimley. 'Are we far from Leah's castle?'

Before Grimley could answer, Jack felt a blow to the back of his head from the Goblin immediately behind him. It seemed that they didn't want them to speak.

They turned away from the mountain trail they'd been following and took another path down towards a sheltered valley in between the two adjoining mountains. The snow wasn't quite as deep allowing the group to march a little faster. They followed the path along the valley floor for over an hour. Pine and fir trees lined the valley walls and the bright moonlight sparkled upon the snow-covered branches highlighting the path through them.

It was as they followed the path through the trees that Grimley discretely nudged Jack and raised his eyes towards the mountain to the right of them. Jack looked up but didn't see anything at first but when he looked further along the valley where it narrowed, he saw an arched bridge that crossed from one mountain to the other. It was as he gazed at the bridge that he saw it, on the mountain across the far side of the valley.

A tall castle was built into the mountainside, whose pointed spires reached so high they seemed to pierce the sky. Sheer rock faces surrounded the castle making the only way in across the bridge. Leah had built a fortress that was almost impossible to attack. How could Elensar and the others possibly force their way in to such a place?

The moonlight illuminated the stone walls creating the impression that it was a magic castle. It looked impregnable. A part of Jack couldn't help but admire the ingenuity that had gone into the design of that castle, but his task was to defeat the incumbent of that imposing place. A task that was always going to be difficult suddenly looked impossible.

The Goblin commander veered off to the left and led them onto stone steps that climbed their way up the valley wall towards the arched bridge. Grimley gestured for Jack to go ahead of him and they slowly climbed the steps one by one. The bridge was easily 500 metres above the valley floor and Jack's legs ached after the first hundred or so steps, but the Goblins ahead showed no signs of slowing.

The stone steps were thankfully wide enough so that Jack wasn't close to the edge and didn't have to look down towards the valley floor which was by now a good fifty metres below them, but the Goblins marched relentlessly upwards. Jack's ribs still ached from his fall and each step brought a stabbing pain through his chest.

As they approached the halfway mark Jack had to rest. He was exhausted and in considerable pain. He sat down on a step and turned to Grimley. 'I've got to rest. My legs are shaking from the constant climbing and my ribs are agony.'

Grimley didn't have a chance to respond when a Goblin pushed past him. It pulled Jack up by his coat and lifted him off his feet and held him over the edge of the steps. Its mouth contorted into a vicious sneer as it held Jack in mid-air with a two hundred metre drop below him.

Jack was too terrified to scream. He felt the fabric of his

coat tearing and could tell that the Goblin couldn't give a damn. The Goblin pulled him back onto the steps and dropped him. As Jack tried to regain his feet he felt a sharp blow to the back of his head that sent him sprawling head first into the hard stone. He just about managed to put his hands up in time to protect himself and Grimley helped him back to his feet.

He whispered into Jack's ear. 'Just try to keep going. They won't care what state you're in when they hand you over to Leah.'

Jack somehow managed to find the energy deep within him and continued the climb. If he stumbled or slowed, Grimley discreetly helped him not giving the following Goblin any further excuses to inflict its callous violence. It was another twenty minutes before they reached the top by which time Jack's legs had all but gone. Despite Grimley's age, he somehow weathered the climb much better than Jack.

Grimley walked by Jack's side and supported him as they crossed the arched bridge. The downward slope to the gates at the castle entrance was a welcome relief for Jack and his fear at the prospect of meeting Leah on his own was lost within his exhaustion.

As they approached double heavy iron doors they were pulled open by the Goblin guards that flanked them. The Goblin company marched into a vast marble hallway and stopped in the middle. The doors slammed behind them, confirming Jack's predicament. He was now held a prisoner in Leah's fortress with little prospect of his friends coming to his aid.

As they waited, Jack took the opportunity to study his surroundings. This was no medieval castle; even by modern standards it was palatial. Marble floors and walls were complimented by a wide marble staircase at the far end. Leah hadn't spared any expense in building his fortress. But that was easy to do when you weren't paying for it yourself, thought Jack.

Two Goblins grabbed him and Grimley and marched

them down a long passageway at the far end of the entrance hall. Was this it? The moment when he finally met Leah. He was soon to find out. The Goblins bundled them both down some stairs and into another narrower passageway that was not as palatial as the upstairs. Flame torches burnt in metal holders on the grey stone walls casting a shadowy light along the passageway.

They stopped outside a heavy wooden door and one of the Goblins opened it. He grabbed Jack by the arm and unceremoniously threw him into the room, slamming the door behind him. Jack sprawled across the floor and was surprised to find himself laying on a thick fur rug.

He pulled himself to his feet and was surprised all over again. There was a huge four poster bed covered with a heavy silk eiderdown sat against the far wall. There was bread, cheese and dried fruit on a small table by the side of a blazing fire. A porcelain teapot sat on the grate next to the fire. He walked over and picked it up and filled an empty cup on the table – it was Roseleaf.

Jack sat on the chair by the table and nursed the cup in his hands – the warmth soothed him. He had been expecting a cell – this was more like a guest's room in a hotel. And it seemed that Leah was expecting him. He pondered his situation as he sipped his tea. Now how would he know his arrival was imminent?

*

Chapter Thirty-One – The Findra

Rory cradled Stran's dead body in his arms as the tears streamed down his freckly cheeks. The ranger's blood stained his coat, not that he noticed. 'I can't believe he's dead. He gave his life for mine – I didn't think he even liked me.'

'I've known many rangers over the years,' said Elensar. 'They're all like Stran. It's just their way – they don't believe in small talk.'

'But to give your life for someone else … I'm lost for words,' said Rory shaking his head.

'Stran knew that if you'd got killed then that was the end of the Unification. He gave his life for the cause, and for that we should all be eternally grateful,' said Elensar attempting to console Rory.

'He paid the ultimate price,' said Roger solemnly. 'I just hope he finds peace.'

Gwendo laid her hand on him and mouthed some silent words. 'He will be in the spirit world now with the Faery Queens. They will look after him well you can be sure of that.'

'I'm sorry to have to return to more practical concerns,' interrupted Elensar, 'but we can't afford to wait here any longer than is absolutely necessary.'

'Elensar!' The Captain's attention was caught by Grindell who'd been keeping watch while the others tended to Stran. 'We have more company.'

Elensar looked up to see Goblins approaching them from two directions. He was already exhausted as was Grindell – now they would have to split up to fight both groups. How long could they hold out?'

He quickly sized up their options. Could they make a run for it? Unlikely – the Goblins were physically stronger and bigger. They could travel much quicker than he and his friends. No, they had no choice other than to fight.

'I can handle the largest group, Captain,' said Grindell

as he limbered up by swinging his axes around his head. A broad grin covered his face as he turned back towards his foe. This was Grindell's reason for being – he was the consummate warrior. As he prepared to launch himself into another attack he heard a fizzing sound by his ear and an arrow hit the lead Goblin in the middle of its chest. The force of the impact sent the brute staggering backwards. As it fell on its side, Grindell saw the arrow had gone clean through the Goblin's chest and was sticking out of its back.

Two more arrows fizzed past the company taking down another two Goblins. Elensar and Grindell looked at each other in surprise and then checked the fir trees behind them for the source of the arrows. A Dwarf appeared in between the trees and ran towards the company. He screamed at them, 'throw yourselves to the ground and let my warriors deal with the Goblins!'

They didn't hesitate and threw themselves onto the snow as a hail of arrows whispered over their heads and cut the Goblins down as they approached. The attack lasted only a matter of seconds, but it was devastating, at least thirty Goblins were left dead or dying, turning the snow around their bodies a deep crimson.

The Dwarf jumped back to his feet and shouted to the company. 'Let's get out of here now! The mountains are swarming with Goblin patrols.'

'Who are you?' asked Elensar.

'There's no time for that now,' said the Dwarf curtly. 'We must get you to safety.'

As the others went to follow him, Rory called out, 'what about Stran?'

'We'll have to leave him, Rory. I'm sorry but we have no time to bury him,' said Elensar.

'I'm not leaving him,' said Rory firmly. 'He saved my life, the least I can do is give him a decent burial.'

The Dwarf turned to the trees and shouted, 'Stimta! Pick up their dead friend and carry him!'

Another Dwarf appeared out of the trees and took Stran from Rory. He threw him over his shoulder and bounded back towards the trees.

'Now we must go!' shouted the Dwarf.

He led the company into the midst of the fir trees where they were joined by another dozen Dwarves. The snow wasn't as deep so they were able to travel quicker than they could out on the trail. Each Dwarf had what looked like a miniature bow strapped over their backs. Elensar was amazed at how they generated so much power with such a small weapon.

He had a chance to study their rescuers as they made their way under cover of the Fir trees. He was sure they were Dwarfs, but they were at least a head and shoulder taller than Grindell. They were stocky but also nimble on their feet. They all wore thick fur coats and fur hats on their heads. They were obviously highly skilled warriors and had intimate knowledge of the mountains.

They made their way steadily up the mountainside, only breaking cover from the trees when they had to. Two of the Dwarves hung back to make sure they weren't followed. Whoever they were, Elensar knew that they owed their lives to them. He and Grindell could never have dealt with all the Goblins that attacked them.

The journey was intense and hard, and within an hour they arrived in a small encampment hidden by thick clumps of fir and pine trees. Unless you had prior knowledge, you would never know that it was there. Around a dozen or so heavily camouflaged canvas tents were carefully hidden beneath the trees. They were met by another two Dwarves as they approached the camp.

One of them addressed the first Dwarf who come to the company's aid. 'Where have you been, Casdilian, we were becoming concerned for your safety.'

'There are Goblin patrols everywhere. We saved these people from almost certain death.'

The other Dwarf eyed the company suspiciously.

'It's OK, Sharnan, they are not from the castle. Any enemies of the Goblins are friends of ours.'

Elensar stepped forward. 'I am Captain Tathar Elensar

from the great Elven city of Arminas.' He pointed to his friends in turn. 'This is Gwendo a flying Pixie from her own land to the west of here. Rory McNory is a Leprechaun from Emerald Island.' Rory bowed low as he always did when meeting people for the first time. 'This is Roger Thorne – he is from the human world.'

He turned to Grindell and beckoned him over. He placed his arm around his shoulder. 'May I introduce Grindell from Bellowrock - the finest warrior that I have ever fought alongside. He is a Dwarf like yourselves.'

Casdilian smiled. 'Why do you think we are Dwarves, Captain?'

'I, I assumed you were because of your physical stature and your warrior abilities.'

Casdilian removed his fur hat and pulled back his thick dark hair to reveal pointy ears. 'And how many Dwarves do you know with ears like this?'

Elensar was genuinely shocked – he and Grindell exchanged puzzled looks.

'We are the Findra,' continued Casdilian, 'and Captain, we are neither Dwarves nor Elves … We are Dwelves.'

'Dwelves?' repeated Rory. 'Is that a cross between a Dwarf and an Elf?'

'It is indeed,' smiled Casdilian. 'Our forefathers come from the mountains and valleys far to the west of here. They were outcasts by their people. Neither Dwarf nor Elf wanted them. They travelled east until they eventually found these mountains, and this is where we have always lived. We live simple lives, Captain, and in general we don't interfere in anyone else's, but we saw you were about to be overwhelmed by Goblins and we will never sit back and allow that.'

Elensar bowed his head. 'We are indeed grateful for your help. Grindell and I were on our last legs when you came.'

'You all look cold and tired,' said Casdilian. 'We will make you some hot food and give you warm beds to rest in. But first, we must give your friend the burial that he deserves. There is no better death than when you sacrifice your own life for the sake of a friend's.'

*

The company stood around the grave that was to be Stran's final resting place. It was on the side of the mountain with a view across a picturesque valley. It was a setting that he would have appreciated. The Findra made a plaque out of pinewood and Rory carved his memorial: -

'Stran Vander, Elf and mountain ranger. Rest in Peace with the knowledge that your sacrifice saved the Unification'.

Rory gave a very brief but sad eulogy. 'I know we might not have been close friends, Stran, but I like to think there was a healthy respect for each other. You were indeed a fine ranger and there is no doubt in any of our minds that we wouldn't have got to where we are now without you. We will all do our best to make sure that we complete this quest and return the gold dust to their rightful owners. This will indeed be a fitting epitaph to your life. And for my part, Stran, I owe you my own life and I will honour that sacrifice for the rest of my days.' He held up a small glass of Peardrop; 'To Stran Vander, mountain ranger, friend to the Leprechauns, may you rest well my friend.' Then he drained his glass.

A solemn company returned to the camp to find that the Findra had cooked them a huge breakfast of scrambled eggs, mushrooms, a potato and vegetable pancake and something they called flatbread. This was washed down with herbal tea which Rory was very complimentary about.

'That was a grand breakfast, Casdilian, and this is a fine sup of tea,' he said as he held his mug out for a top up.

'You are very welcome, Rory,' said Casdilian.

Most of the rest of the day was taken up by sleep. For the first time in weeks they had warm soft beds inside the canvas tents. Exhaustion had finally caught up with them but Elensar was angry with himself when he woke as he felt

243

he had wasted the day sleeping when they could have continued their pursuit of Jack.

'Don't beat yourself up Elensar. We all needed that rest, especially you,' said Rory as he sipped from a mug of herb tea that the Findra had made them. 'You're going to be much more help to Jack now you're rested.'

Casdilian joined them by the fire. 'Who is Jack?'

'He's a young Elf who is the leader of our company. We lost him when he fell from the mountain trail two days ago,' said Elensar.

'How do you know he survived the fall?' asked Casdilian.

'We found a trail the morning after he fell,' said Elensar, 'but there were two sets of tracks, so he must have had assistance.'

'Did you say there were two of them?' asked Casdilian.

'Yes, I did,' said Elensar. 'Why is that important?'

Casdilian sighed deeply. 'I'm afraid your friend was captured by a Goblin patrol during the night. It was only an hour or so after we came across you.'

Roger sprang to his feet and confronted Casdilian. 'Did you say captured? Was he harmed?'

'There was no fight,' said Casdilian. 'There must have been at least twenty Goblins, so they had no choice other than to surrender.'

'Where did they take him?' pressed Roger. 'We must go there now.'

Casdilian's expression turned sombre. 'They took him to the castle. Once inside, you're never seen again.'

'Who was with Jack?' asked Elensar.

'There were two Elves – one very young and the other much older. They seemed like they were friends.'

Elensar turned to Gwendo, 'Any ideas?'

Gwendo shrugged her shoulders. 'You are the only Elves I've seen in years.'

'I'm more interested in this castle,' said Roger, 'and more importantly, how we can get in there.'

'Wait,' said Elensar. 'Before we decide that – do you

know who lives in this castle?'

'We know who it is,' said Roger impatiently. 'It's Graydon Leah and the more time we waste discussing things, the more danger Jack is in.'

'He is an Elf,' said Casdilian. 'And he possesses great powers that we do not begin to understand. We make sure we keep out of his way on the few occasions that he leaves the castle.'

'We're wasting time, Elensar,' said Roger impatiently. 'We must leave now.'

'The castle is well defended,' said Casdilian. 'You will not get near it without encountering the Goblin patrols.'

'The longer we delay, the more danger Jack will be in. We must go,' urged Roger.

'As much as I understand your anxiety about Jack,' said Grindell, 'it would be sheer madness to walk into more Goblin patrols. There are only two warriors in our group – we would be slaughtered.' He turned to Casdilian. 'Tell us about the castle; where is it in relation to where we are now?'

'It's around half a day's trek to the east of here,' said Casdilian. 'It's high up on the next mountain but you have to cross a bridge to get to it.'

'How easy is it to cross the bridge undetected?' asked Elensar.

'Impossible,' said Casdilian. 'The only access to it is via a narrow stairway that climbs the side of this mountain. There are always Goblins at the top. You could never get enough warriors up there in time to mount a serious challenge.'

But Roger was still determined to go to the castle. 'We have to try – we can't just leave Jack at the mercy of Leah.'

'I would ask what brings such a diverse group onto these mountains?' said Casdilian. 'We rarely see strangers here.'

'We have come to reclaim something that Leah stole from our friend Jack's community. But it's more complicated than that,' said Elensar.

'I'm listening,' said Casdilian.

'He has stolen the gold dust that sustains an Elven community far to the west of here. That community has now faded back into the spirit world because there is no magic to sustain it. Leah now has great power because of it and from what we've seen on our travels here, he intends to destroy the lands and any civilisations that get in his way.'

Casdilian looked confused. 'How can so few of you expect to challenge this Leah and take this gold dust back?'

'The Faery Queens call it a 'Unification of a Common Purpose'. Which is why we are an Elf, a Dwarf, a Pixie, a Leprechaun and a human,' said Elensar.

'So where does your friend Jack fit into this?' asked Casdilian.

'He is half Elf and half human. Roger is his father which is why he's so anxious to rescue Jack, as we all are. But there is another reason why we need to join Jack.'

'And that is?' asked Casdilian.

'Jack can muster powerful magic, but he can't do it without the gold dust. We need to help him find this, so he can take on Leah and defeat him … because if he doesn't, then the whole of the Faery world is lost … forever.'

Casdilian thoughtfully rubbed his chin as he considered his response. 'Well I may be able to help you. This Leah may have built an impressive fortress, but he doesn't know these mountains as well as the Findra.'

'What are you saying?' asked Roger.

'I'm saying there are a network of caves under the castle that he may not know about, and that, my friends, is how I can get you into that castle undetected.'

*

246

Chapter Thirty-Two – Graydon Leah

Jack woke from a deep sleep that he didn't want to have but exhaustion had won the day. He sat up on the side of the bed and rubbed his tired eyes. A sharp pain in his chest reminded him of his cracked ribs. Bright sunshine flooded the room from a window to the side of him. He looked out across the snowy mountains and saw the sun was high in the sky. He'd slept for nearly half the day.

His thoughts were interrupted by a knock at the door. He sat back on the bed waiting for the door to burst open but it didn't. Whoever it was knocked again, and Jack walked over to the door and pulled it open expecting to be confronted by the grotesque features of a Goblin but was pleasantly surprised to find a tall Aelf with long dark hair standing in front of him holding a tray of food.

'I came earlier but you were asleep,' said the Aelf.

Jack stepped back from the door. 'Please, come in.'

She walked past Jack and placed the tray on the table next to the fire. She pulled the cover off one of the plates. 'It's a vegetable pie with mashed potato and a cream cheese sauce. I hope you like it.'

Jack was starving and would have been grateful for anything at that moment. He sat down at the table, picked up the fork and cut the corner of the pie and placed it in his mouth. It was delicious, although to be frank, he was so hungry at that moment anything would have tasted good.

Jack turned to the Aelf. 'Are you joining me?'

She shook her head. 'The Master doesn't allow us to eat with the guests. I eat with the other servants in our quarters.'

Master? Jack didn't need to guess who that was. 'That would be Graydon Leah.'

'Yes.'

'Please, call me Jack. And your name is?'

'Savia, although the Master doesn't like us to talk to our guests.'

'Well I won't tell him if you don't,' smiled Jack.

Savia smiled back but didn't answer. She was young, thought Jack, maybe around his age. She wore a long dark blue gown that nearly reached to the floor. She stood to his side gazing downwards. Jack sensed her anxiety – she was obviously frightened of Leah. He took a mug from his bedside table and placed it alongside the mug on the tray and filled them both with Roseleaf and handed one to her.

She stepped back. 'I'm not allowed to drink with the guests.'

Jack pulled up a chair. 'Sit down Savia and share a mug of Roseleaf with me as I eat … please.'

She hesitated at first but eventually took the mug and sat down by Jack. He finished the pie and mashed potato in just a few forkfuls and ate some dried fruit in a bowl. He sat back and sipped his tea.

'That was delicious. I haven't eaten a decent meal in weeks.'

Savia nodded.

'So, how long have you lived in the castle?'

Savia hesitated before answering. 'I'm not allowed to converse with the guests. I'm meant to serve you your food and take the tray back.'

'Are you frightened of Leah?'

She nervously sipped her tea. 'He looks after us all.'

'There are more Elves in this castle?'

She nodded.

'Are you prisoners here?'

'The Master looks after us all. We want for nothing.'

Jack drained his mug of the Roseleaf and placed it back on the tray. 'Where do you come from?'

Savia shrugged her shoulders. 'I do not know. I can only ever remember living in the castle.'

'How many servants are there?'

Savia stood up and placed her mug on the tray alongside Jack's plates. 'I must go.'

Jack was about to ask another question when the door suddenly burst open and a Goblin guard came striding over to him. It grabbed him by the scruff of the neck and dragged

248

him out of the room and along the passageway. It marched him back up the stairs and towards the marble hallway by the castle entrance. Two large wooden doors that had been previously closed were now open and the Goblin unceremoniously bundled him into the room beyond. As he left he closed the doors behind him.

Jack ended up face down on a thick red carpet. As he pulled himself up he heard a voice from across the chamber.

'I apologise for my guard's lack of finesse. I've tried to refine them but I'm afraid you can't polish a piece of dirt … but they do their job.'

Jack climbed to his feet and looked across a large square chamber towards a tall Elf standing in front of a dais. A regal gold chair sat upon it. The red carpet on which he stood led up to the dais. Jack didn't need to be told that he was face to face with Graydon Leah.

A white wolf lay on the carpet next to him baring its teeth, a low growl emanating from its throat as it suspiciously eyed Jack.

'Shadow can be a little nervous the first time he meets strangers, but there is no need to fear him, he is totally under my control.'

Jack took the opportunity to discretely observe Leah. He was taller than him and wore a long, dark fur-trimmed robe. His long black hair hung loosely on his shoulders and a neatly trimmed beard covered his sharp face. His eyes were dark and menacing. Jack could smell the power oozing from him. He reeked of magic.

Jack searched within himself for any sign of Koehtia. There was none. How could this be? The gold dust had to be within the castle surely.

'You're very quiet, Green-Jack. I had expected a more vocal introduction from you.' He stepped onto the dais and sat down on the gold chair. The wolf didn't move and kept his eyes locked onto Jack. Leah waved Jack forward like he was summoning a servant.

Jack walked forward and stopped a few metres short of the dais.

'Have you not been taught how to show reverence to a King?'

So, Leah thinks he is a King? He was no King Erenin that was for sure, but Jack didn't want to antagonise him unnecessarily and dropped down to one knee and lowered his head. He stayed like that for several moments.

'Please, Green-Jack, back to your feet.'

Jack stood up and studied the chamber. Dark blue velvet drapes adorned the walls and an open fire burned in the grate in the far corner. Paintings of wolves and Leah covered every bit of bare wall not covered by the drapes.

Leah poured red liquid from a decanter into a silver goblet and nodded towards Jack. 'Wine?'

Jack shook his head. 'I never touch it.'

Leah raised his eyes in surprise. 'I can send for water if you prefer.'

'I'm fine,' said Jack. 'I was very well looked after in my chamber.'

'I'm very pleased to hear it. I like to think of all my guests being comfortable.'

Jack sensed Leah was playing with him, but he had little choice other than to go along with it.

'I'm wondering what brings you to my castle?'

'I was given little choice in the matter … Your guards saw to that.'

A self-satisfied smirk crossed Leah's lips. He picked up his wine goblet and raised it to his nostrils and gently sniffed. 'Southland wine – I make a point of bringing several cases back with me on the rare occasions I travel there. Full bodied and strong tasting, just the way I like it.' He took a mouthful and swilled it around his mouth before swallowing. 'You should learn to enjoy fine wine, Green-Jack, as you're missing out on one of life's greatest pleasures.'

He put the silver goblet back on the table next to him and turned his full attention onto Jack. 'You're here Green-Jack because you think I stole the gold dust from Waterswood.'

Jack knew full well that he hadn't stolen the gold dust –

the fool Grimley had given it to him. But he didn't want to overly antagonise him. He held all the cards at that moment.

'I had no need to steal the gold dust, I was given it to look after.'

'So I believe,' said Jack. 'Does the same apply to the other communities' gold dust in Woodgate Valley?'

Leah's cold dark eyes locked onto Jack. 'I don't think that's any concern of yours, Green-Jack, do you?'

Jack didn't answer but held his stare. Leah took another mouthful of his wine. 'I imagine you're wondering about your friends?'

Jack didn't answer. He didn't want to give him any clues about the company.

'You can stop wondering, Green-Jack, because they're all dead.'

Jack's chest tightened, a sharp spasm of pain shot through his ribs like a burning arrow. His heart pumped rapidly as the adrenaline rushed through his body. He fought not to show any outward reaction. He studied Leah's countenance for any sign of duplicity, but he was like a closed book.

'They died in battle during the early hours of this morning. My Guards tried to take them prisoner, but they were foolish enough to resist. Don't get me wrong, Green-Jack, they put up a fierce fight, but in the end, they were overwhelmed by the sheer weight of numbers.'

Jack felt numb. *Could his friends really have been slaughtered that morning?*

'Two Elves, a Dwarf, a Pixie, a Leprechaun and a human all perished.'

He knew the makeup of the company, but did that necessarily mean he was telling the truth?

'I find any violence unpleasant, Green-Jack, but I can assure you my guards were left with little choice. You must be feeling distraught at this news and I wish I didn't have to tell you, but you deserved to know the truth.' He pulled a long red sash that hung next to his throne.

A few minutes later the door opened and Savia appeared.

'Savia, take our guest back to his chamber. He has just had a terrible shock. Please make sure he is comfortable and that he has anything he wants.' Leah rose from his throne and walked over to Jack. He towered over him and placed his huge hands on Jack's shoulders. 'I'm sorry it had to come to this, Green-Jack. Go back to your chamber and rest. We can talk again tomorrow. Be secure in the knowledge that I will offer what help I can.'

Jack was in a daze and didn't react. Savia gently took him by the arm and led him from the chamber. He said nothing until they got back to his room.

'Savia, can you close the door?'

She did as he asked and he beckoned her over. He whispered in her ear, 'I need you to find out if there has been a battle on the mountains. I need to know if there were any Goblin casualties and if any strangers were killed.'

She pulled back from Jack and looked genuinely scared. 'I cannot do that – if the Master finds out he will punish me.'

Jack grabbed her hands and pulled her too him. He could see the fear in her eyes. 'Please, Savia, this is important. I'm not asking you to take any unnecessary risks, but I need to know if my friends are dead or alive. You do understand, don't you?'

She nodded reluctantly. 'I will come back later with food for you. I will do my best.'

*

Jack lay on his bed for what seemed like hours, turning events over and over in his head. The thought of his friends being slaughtered by Goblins filled him with despair. But he couldn't imagine the scenario where that could have happened. Elensar was too good a warrior for that, but …

He had to consider all the options. If he truly was on his own, then the Unification was over. He would have to find a way to escape. But where would he go? He would summon Troy and travel to the homeland. King Erenin would know what to do.

But it wasn't just about accepting the death of his friends. There was the death of his father. He had taken Roger away from a secure existence in the human world. How would he ever come to terms with that? Just as the despair was about to overwhelm him, the door opened and Savia came into the chamber holding a tray. She set it down on the table and turned to Jack.

She whispered in his ear. 'There was a bloody battle on the mountain this morning. Several Goblin patrols were slain. That is all I know.'

Jack slumped in his chair. That must have been his friends. Who else could inflict such casualties? But had they survived the battle? He had no way of finding out, but he couldn't bring himself to believe Leah. He had no choice other than to go along with him – at least it gave him time.

*

Chapter Thirty-Three –
Terror Under the Castle

Casdilian and Elensar looked up in awe at the moonlit castle from the base of the valley floor. The rest of the company stayed back in the shadows as the two leaders discussed their next move.

'That is a magnificent structure,' said Elensar. 'It's almost impossible to mount any sort of serious attack.'

'Like all seemingly impregnable things, it has its weaknesses,' said Casdilian. He pointed across the valley floor. 'There is a trail that leads around the foot of the mountain. That's where we'll find the concealed cave entrance.'

'You know these caves well?' enquired Elensar.

'I explored them many years ago,' said Casdilian. 'To claim I know them well would be an exaggeration.'

Casdilian saw the look of concern on Elensar's face. 'Don't worry, Captain, I know them well enough to get us into the castle. And you have a Dwarf and a Dwelf in your company – we both thrive underground.' He turned to Stimta. 'Keep us covered as we cross the valley floor. Cut down any Goblins you see.' Casdilian removed his short bow from his shoulder and primed it with an arrow.

Elensar was fascinated by the weapon. 'How do you generate so much power with such a small bow?'

'It's a crossbow,' said Casdilian. 'The cord stretches when we prime it – that's where the power comes from.'

Elensar nodded his approval. 'I'm impressed.'

Casdilian turned to his warriors. 'Return to our camp once we've safely reached the other side of the valley. Wish us well and should anything happen that means I may not return, you Stimta, will take command of the Findra.'

The Dwelf didn't respond verbally. He nodded his acknowledgement and discreetly returned to the shadows as he primed his crossbow.

Grindell, Rory, Roger and Gwendo joined Elensar and

Casdilian as they furtively made their way across the valley floor keeping to the shadows wherever possible. Once on the other side they joined a narrow trail through the rocks that led around the foot of the mountain. Nobody spoke within the company as the tension increased. They all knew that they were getting close to their journey's end. What was waiting for them inside the castle? What had happened to Jack? Was he still alive? They would soon have answers to their questions.

Casdilian proved to be a worthy guide and expertly led them around the many boulders strewn across the trail. They couldn't risk lighting any torches for fear of attracting unwanted attention from Goblin patrols. It was as the sun appeared over the mountains to the east that Casdilian indicated with a wave of his arm for them to stop.

He gathered the company together and whispered, 'I'm sure there is a concealed entrance along this rock face. It's a narrow crevice that is difficult to see, especially in this light. Wait here while I search.'

Elensar turned to the others as Casdilian went ahead on his own. 'Remember what I said earlier – vigilance is the key. We have encountered and survived many impossible situations. We near the endgame of our quest. Everything that has befallen us up to this point has prepared our company for this moment. Grindell and I will do our best to deal with any threats as they arise.' He looked at each of them in turn. 'I have no doubt we possess both the skills and resolve within this company to meet the challenge the Faery Queens have set us. Let us go about this task united and with our heads held high.'

Casdilian returned just as he finished. 'I've found it – follow me.'

He led them along the trail before taking a detour around the back of several large boulders. He stopped by the last one and pointed behind it. 'This is the cave entrance. I'm going to need some help moving the boulder.'

Grindell and Elensar joined him and leaned into the boulder with their shoulders. They pushed with all their might against the large round lump of granite. It took several tries, but it eventually moved just enough for them all to squeeze through. Once inside Casdilian lit a torch with a flint wheel. They stood at the foot of a narrow tunnel.

'It's good that the boulder didn't move much as any prying Goblins won't even notice the entrance behind it,' said Casdilian. 'We follow the tunnel upwards. Stay close and let me know if you hear or see anything.'

He set off along the tunnel followed by Gwendo, Rory and Roger. Elensar and Grindell, weapons at the ready, brought up the rear. The tunnel slowly and deliberately climbed upwards. Any time they came to a fork, Casdilian always chose the upward path.

They continued along a series of endless tunnels before eventually coming out into an enormous cavern. Casdilian held his torch out in front of him but the light couldn't reach the ceiling or the foot of the cave.

'Oh no,' said Rory. 'Please tell me that we're not going to follow a narrow path around a bottomless cavern again.'

Elensar stepped up by his side. 'The ledge is much wider this time, Rory. I'll be behind you all the way, so you will be safe my friend.'

Rory nodded unconvincingly. 'Just make sure you stay close.'

Casdilian led the company slowly along the ledge making sure there were no stones or holes for them to stumble on. He was an expert guide and as they made steady progress around the ledge, they all began to relax, even Rory. It was difficult to gauge just how big the cavern was in the pitch black but they all kept focused on the task ahead. The challenge of taking the gold dust from Leah was what dominated their thoughts at that moment. The confrontation with this unknown person was getting nearer and they were ready to deal with whatever confronted them.

Time lost its meaning in the dark as they edged carefully around the cavern. Nobody spoke, and the only sounds were the clatter of their boots on the stone ledge and their tense breathing. Elensar and Grindell constantly checked behind them for any signs of pursuit, while Casdilian forged ahead.

It was as they stopped to rest that Grindell grabbed Elensar by the arm. 'Did you hear that?'

'Here what? asked Elensar.

'Listen!' urged Grindell.

Casdilian joined them and held the torch out into the cavern. 'I can't see anything.'

'Shush! scolded Grindell. He removed both axes from his belt and held them at the ready as he forensically scanned the cavern.

'I can't hear anything,' whispered Elensar.

Just as he spoke he saw something move out in the cavern. It was nothing definite, but it was just a flash out of the corner of his eye. He took out his sword and crouched into a combat position. Casdilian handed the torch to Roger, unstrapped his crossbow from his shoulder and primed it with an arrow. As he held it up an ear-piercing squeal resonated around the chamber. Rory and Gwendo crouched down low against the cave wall behind the others.

'W-what in the name of the great Leprechaun was that?' said Rory.

Elensar felt the cold clammy sweat run down the back of his neck. He was a warrior who had faced many different enemies in his time, but he had always been able to see them. Whatever it was out there was hidden in the inky blackness.

'There's something flying around the cavern,' said Grindell. 'I can hear its wings.'

Another shrill squeal echoed around the cavern, but they still couldn't see anything. Tension gripped the company as they peered into the impenetrable darkness. Grindell tuned his ears and eyes to the conditions. This was his territory – deep caves are what he knew best. He turned to Casdilian. 'It might be the flame that's alerted whatever it is out there to our whereabouts.'

'But we can't fight in this darkness,' said Elensar. 'I wouldn't even be able to see the sword in my hand.'

Before Casdilian could answer, a huge, dark, winged

creature swooped into the light from the darkness and headed straight for them. Casdilian knelt down and unleashed the arrow from his crossbow but the creature changed direction in the blink of an eyelid and disappeared back into the darkness.

'On my life!' said Rory. 'What was that?'

Elensar looked to Grindell but he shrugged his shoulders, as did Casdilian. It was Roger who ventured an opinion.

'It looks and flies like a bat, but its wingspan must be at least two metres. I've never heard of a bat that size before.'

'It's the dark magic,' said Gwendo joining him. 'Leah's magic is distorting nature. It's just one of the many abominations that he has unleashed on these lands.'

Casdilian quickly reloaded his cross bow and readied himself for another assault. Elensar and Grindell stood several paces either side of him, weapons at the ready. Rory crouched against the cavern wall as Gwendo remained by Roger's side. Each one of them watched and listened with every shred of their awareness.

Another shrill squeal echoed around the cavern. It was almost impossible to tell where the giant bat was. Roger waved the flaming torch towards every area of the cavern, but the bat remained out of sight. This game of cat and mouse continued – it was only the bat's cry that told them it was still out there.

It was almost impossible to maintain their high levels of concentration in the darkness and it was as if the bat sensed its moment and dropped towards them at high speed. Casdilian unleashed an arrow but the bat dodged it once again. He immediately reached for another arrow and was priming his crossbow when the bat attacked from below and swiped at the company with one of its huge wings. Gwendo was knocked off balance and teetered on the edge of the dark abyss. It was as she fell forward that the bat took its opportunity and grabbed at her with its mouth. It caught hold of her thick coat and turned away from them to fly back into the darkness.

Casdilian quickly cocked his crossbow and unleashed an arrow that flew directly into the beast's belly. The force of the impact shocked the bat and it let out a shriek of pain, dropping Gwendo from its mouth and she fell into the blackness as the shrieking bat corkscrewed down into the dark cavern. Rory was on his feet in an instant and screamed, 'Gwendo!'

'Don't worry,' said Elensar trying to reassure them all. 'She'll be able to fly back up to us. Roger! Keep waving the torch over the edge so that she can see us.'

Roger did as he asked and looked down into the black abyss but there was no sign of Gwendo or the bat.

'What if the bat damaged her wings with its mouth?' said Rory.

'Let's not jump to any conclusions,' said Elensar. 'She's one very tough Pixie – she'll find her way back.'

Casdilian looked dumbstruck. He dropped his crossbow onto the ledge and slumped back against the cavern wall. 'It's my fault. I shouldn't have fired an arrow at that thing.'

'Nonsense!' said Grindell. 'That creature would have almost certainly killed her.' He slapped a consoling arm around his shoulders. 'No, my friend, what you did gave her a chance.'

'He's right,' said Elensar. 'We'll wait for her.' He sheathed his sword and sat next to Casdilian. Rory, Grindell and Roger continued to hang over the edge looking for any sign of the Pixie.

*

The company stayed in the same spot and continuously scanned the cavern for any signs of Gwendo. A grim-faced Elensar paced up and down as the others took turns in hanging over the ledge and peering into the darkness below. Casdilian was subdued and quiet as he cleaned his crossbow. Rory had convinced him that he'd done the right thing by Gwendo, but the guilt still gnawed at him.

Roger handed the flaming torch to Rory and joined

Elensar. 'We could walk further around the cavern,' he suggested. 'We may find a way down to the bottom.'

Elensar turned to Casdilian. 'What do you think?'

'It's worth a try. Gwendo will see the flame from a long way off in this pitch black.'

Grindell agreed and they picked up their packs and continued around the ledge. No-one openly showed their anxiety but it was there. The bat was wounded but they didn't know how badly. There was a chance it would come back. Rory was unusually quiet as they wound their way around the ledge. He hadn't mentioned his fear of heights or the darkness since Gwendo had fallen into the cavern. He'd taken her disappearance very badly.

First Jack and now Gwendo had been lost. The two key players in the company because of their prowess with magic. Elensar, Grindell and Casdilian undoubtedly were excellent warriors but they would be no match for Leah and his magic. Nobody in the company spoke the words but they were all thinking it. Without Jack and Gwendo the quest was doomed.

Casdilian called across to Elensar. 'We're coming to the far end of the Cavern. If my instincts are right, we're directly under the rear of the castle. The front of the castle is well defended, but they won't expect an assault from the rear as it's almost impossible to reach across the mountains.'

'So how do we get up there?' asked Elensar.

'There are passageways that lead to the rear of the castle. I'm sure that they are in this cavern,' said Casdilian.

'We have no option other than carry on around the ledge,' said Grindell.

Elensar agreed and they continued to follow the ledge with Rory at the front with the torch. Even his optimism was on the wane since the disappearance of Gwendo. It was hours since she'd fallen into the darkness and although no-one said it, they all feared the worst, that she was lost to them.

They'd eased their way half way around the cavern when

Rory stopped and turned to Elensar. 'Captain, I'm just about out on my feet. Can we please rest and eat something?'

Elensar nodded his agreement. 'You're right, Rory. We need to eat.'

'Wait,' said Grindell pointing out into the cavern. 'I'm sure I saw something.'

Elensar and Casdilian were by his side in an instant following his gaze. 'What was it?' asked the Captain.

'I'm not sure, but there was definitely something moving.'

Elensar turned to Casdilian. 'Load your crossbow. We can't take any chances.'

Casdilian took his bow from his shoulder and primed an arrow. He pointed it to the floor. 'I'd prefer it if you told me whether or not to fire, Captain.'

Elensar put a reassuring arm around his shoulder. 'Your instincts are fine and every one of us trust you to make the right decision.'

Rory held the torch out as far as he could and they all peered to the edge of the light it shed. It was Roger who reacted first.

'I saw something lower down in the cavern.'

Grindell strained his Dwarf vision to its limits and peered into the darkness below. His gruff Dwarf countenance suddenly broke into a smile as he saw a small flying creature break into the edges of the torch light. 'It's Gwendo!'

The Pixie hovered a few dozen metres below them and didn't appear to be gaining height.

'Gwendo!' shouted Rory. 'It's us. Come on you brave little Pixie Queen – just a few more metres and you'll be safe with your friends.'

But there was no answer from her. They instinctively knew she was exhausted. Casdilian dropped his crossbow on the ground and took out a long rope. He uncoiled it and threw it out into the cavern towards Gwendo. 'Grab the rope Gwendo – I can pull you up.'

She didn't react at first but eventually moved towards

the rope and grabbed it with both hands. She kept her wings moving but only just and Casdilian was able to pull her slowly towards the ledge. It seemed to take forever, and the others watched in silence as he slowly brought her towards them.

Elensar reached out as she was just a few metres away and grabbed her hand and pulled her to him. She fell into his arms and he cradled her like a child. She said nothing as he lay her against the cavern wall. She had no coat on and was so exhausted she couldn't even fold her wings.

Rory threw a blanket around her and held her in his arms. He was crying tears of joy and his previous exhaustion had gone. 'Am I glad to see you, little Pixie?'

Roger knelt down and held his canteen up to her lips. She took a few tentative sips and laid back in Rory's arms. It was several minutes before she spoke. She looked across to Elensar who was kneeling in front of her. 'Captain – I think I know what's going on here.'

He placed his hand on her shoulder and gave it an affectionate squeeze. 'Don't worry about that for now. Just rest and get your strength back.'

She took another sip of water. 'And I know how to get into the castle.'

Chapter Thirty-Four – Confrontation

Jack sat at the table sipping a mug of Roseleaf. Savia had left him a breakfast of porridge, toast and fruit. He'd slept fitfully during the night because Leah's news from the previous day had played on his mind.

Were his friends really dead?

Leah had seemed sorry that his Goblins had killed them in battle but was that regret genuine? He was on his own. There were no friends to discuss this with. This person had stolen all the gold dust from the communities of Woodgate Valley. He'd broken down the magic that sustained Gwendolain. But worst of all he was gradually destroying the land to the west. And this was going to spread across the whole of the Faery lands.

Jack had to keep an open mind and consider all possibilities. Leah held all the cards and Jack's options were limited to say the least. But he'd managed to get out of many impossible situations. The sorcerer Korrian had great power but he was still able to defeat him. Jack shook his head. But then, he had his Koehtia to call on.

Come on think, Jack. Just because a situation looks impossible doesn't mean it is. He smiled to himself. It was one of his grandfather's expressions, one of many that had stayed with him on his travels. He looked up at the mirror in front of him. Tiredness lined his face and dark rings circled his eyes. He'd aged ten years since he set out to find his mother all those months ago.

There was a knock at the door and Savia came into the room holding an empty tray. She walked up to Jack and put the tray on the table.

'Did you sleep well?' she enquired.

'Not really,' said Jack. 'But the breakfast was just what I needed.'

She smiled. 'I am glad you enjoyed it. The master is in his reception chamber and asked if you would like to join him?'

'Do I have a choice?'

Savia didn't respond and put his dirty plates onto the tray. 'I can take you there now if you wish.'

Jack drained his mug and put it onto Savia's tray. 'I'm ready when you are.'

The young Aelf took Jack back along the passageway and up the stairs towards the main castle entrance. She placed the tray on a table outside the large double wooden doors that led to Leah's chamber. She knocked twice and opened the doors beckoning Jack inside the room. He walked in to find Leah sat on his throne and Grimley stood to his left. The wolf was on his right laying on the floor. It eyed Jack suspiciously but it didn't show any other outward sign of hostility.

Leah waved Jack forward as Savia shut the heavy wooden doors behind him. Jack stopped a few paces short of the throne and bowed his head.

'Welcome again to you, Green-Jack. I hope you slept well?'

'I've slept better.'

'And I trust my servants are looking after you?'

He nodded. 'Very well.'

Grimley didn't make eye contact with Jack. He stared down at the floor. Jack thought he looked uncomfortable.

'You and my friend Grimley are already acquainted I believe. I'm hearing that you and he are getting along better since you met on my mountains.'

'We didn't exactly have the best of starts to our relationship,' said Jack, his voice heavy with irony.

Leah burst into raucous laughter, his deep voice echoing around the chamber. 'I like a sense of humour in an Elf.' He stood up and put his arm around Grimley's shoulder and guided him towards Jack. 'Let's put the original altercation down to a misunderstanding. You two should be friends. Please, shake hands.'

Grimley reluctantly offered his hand as did Jack and they partook in what could only be described as a token handshake.

'There,' said Leah, 'that wasn't so bad.' He turned to a table to the side of his throne and picked up two silver goblets. He handed one to Jack and one to Grimley. 'Water for you, Jack, and wine for Grimley.' He picked up a third goblet and turned back towards them. He raised his goblet and said, 'a toast – to new found friends.'

He lifted his goblet to his mouth and took a healthy mouthful of wine, while Jack and Grimley barely sipped their respective drinks. Leah sat back down on his throne and Grimley returned to his side. He placed his goblet back on the table and set his dark eyes on Jack.

'I hope, Green-Jack, that you have had time to come to terms with the loss of your friends. This ridiculous idea that the Faery Queens had of sending a small band of mercenaries to destroy me has failed. Not that it had ever had any chance of succeeding.'

'What makes you think they wanted you destroyed?'

His dark eyes tried to penetrate deep into Jack's soul. Jack remained impassive and gave his adversary little to work with. 'They see me as a threat. They have no power in the eastern lands. Make no mistake Green-Jack, they wanted you to destroy me.'

'My friends and I came here with only one purpose, and that was to return the gold dust to its rightful owners.'

Jack noticed a flicker of anger flash into Leah's dark eyes. His lips tightened momentarily but the fake smile soon returned. 'Then you are mistaken as the rightful owner is standing on my left. He willingly gave me custody of the Waterswood gold dust because of the threat you presented to that community.'

Jack fought to keep his composure. They both knew full well what had happened. Why did he insist on this charade? 'It wasn't Grimley's to give to you. It's owned by the Elves of Waterswood as the other gold dust you stole is owned by those communities.'

This time Leah's anger broke through. 'You are nothing but a child, Green-Jack – how dare you speak to me in that manner? You will remember in whose presence you are!'

Shadow suddenly lifted his head at his master's anger. He looked at Jack, growling and baring his teeth. Jack kept his calm. 'I'm sorry that the truth angers you but it needs to be said. You cannot keep what doesn't belong to you.'

Leah stood up and took a menacing step towards Jack. He looked down on him and gritted his teeth. 'If it's truth you want then I will give you truth. I've known about your ridiculous Unification since before you left Waterswood. I have had you followed the whole time and I've been kept informed by your new-found friend here.'

Grimley guiltily dropped his gaze to the floor. Jack looked at him with scorn. 'I have my answer as to whether I could trust you, Grimley. You are beyond contempt.'

Leah looked pleased that he'd provoked a reaction from Jack. He stepped back and sat down on his throne. 'Doves are very reliable message carriers. Grimley informed me as soon as you literally dropped in front of him. And then it was just a simple case of my guards finding you.'

Jack's rage started to build within him. He was as angry with himself as he was with Grimley. But what to do next? He decided to test Leah. 'If you do the right thing and return the gold dust to its rightful owners, I will make sure that you are left in peace. There will be no repercussions.'

Leah looked at Jack with a mixture of disdain and contempt. 'You forget, Green-Jack, that it is I who have all the power. As we both know, you have none.'

Jack needed to provoke him but not too much. 'That may or may not be true, but your power cannot harm me. I am the heir to the House of Sarmondian.' He reached inside his shirt and pulled out the blood red jewel.' This is the Sarmondian Bloodstone and protects me from danger. You may know the House of Sarmondian is the Elven house of magic.'

Leah stroked his beard thoughtfully as he looked at Jack. He slowly stood and walked over to him. He looked at the jewel in Jack's hand and then without warning unleashed a heavy blow with his fist into Jack's midriff. The goblet Jack was holding flew out of his hands and clattered onto the marble floor. The pain coursed through Jack's body like a lightning strike and he fell to the ground in agony.

'It would appear that the jewel doesn't protect you from all danger.' Leah looked down on Jack not attempting to hide the triumph he felt. Jack was no threat to him and he was making sure he knew it. Leah picked up the goblet and placed it on the table and sat back down on his throne.

Jack was already suffering with his cracked ribs. The blow from Leah had compounded that pain. He thought he was going to be physically sick. His situation was getting worse by the minute.

For the first time since Jack had entered the chamber, Grimley spoke to Leah. 'Can we talk about the return of the gold dust to Waterswood?'

Jack looked at Grimley with pure contempt. He'd been used by Grimley as a bargaining chip for the gold dust. He needed Koehtia; he needed his friends.

'Let's not get ahead of ourselves, Grimley. You gave me the gold dust for safe keeping and it is indeed in a safe place. There is still too much potential danger out there to risk taking it back to Waterswood. We will reassess the situation when the time is right but until then it stays here.'

'But you promised me that as soon as you had Green-Jack in custody that I could have the gold dust back and resume the governance of Waterswood.'

Leah picked up his silver goblet and noisily drained it. He slammed the empty goblet onto the table and boomed, 'When, and if it goes back depends on me, Grimley! Do you understand?'

The power of Leah's response caused Grimley to take a backward step. The wolf looked up and growled menacingly at Grimley. The former head of the Waterswood Council of Elders shrank into the corner. Leah turned his attention back to Jack.

'So, Green-Jack, where do we go from here?'

Jack was on his knees holding his stomach which was still hurting from Leah's blow. He didn't offer an answer, not because he didn't have one but because he was having trouble breathing.

Leah rose from his throne and walked over to Jack and helped him to his feet. 'I apologise for striking you, Jack. That was wrong of me. I should've considered your lack of years. Please forgive me.'

Jack looked up into his face and saw what looked like genuine contrition. But Leah was a great actor. He'd learned that in the short time he'd spent with him. He nodded his acknowledgement.

'Good,' said Leah as he walked back to his throne and sat down. 'I really think that we could be a good team, Jack. You and I can control the whole of this land then start thinking how we can expand our empire to the other magical lands.' He turned to Grimley. 'And our friend here can keep an eye on things in the Woodgate Valley.'

Jack managed to straighten himself and rubbed his abdomen. The pain from Leah's blow was easing slightly. 'Who is it exactly he's going to keep an eye on? All of the people have faded into the spirit world.'

A forced smile crossed Leah's lips. 'A temporary situation, my young friend. Once I have established my power I will, how can I phrase it delicately so as not to offend you?' He filled his goblet with wine as he pondered his response. 'I will dispense with the Faery Queens and make the conditions right for the people to return.'

Dispense with the Faery Queens? Jack was horrified because he knew exactly what he meant. His situation was getting worse by the second. He had to get away so that he could warn Morning Dew and her colleagues. But he couldn't afford to upset Leah again. If he had any doubts previously about his sanity he now knew for sure that Leah was mad. He needed to play along with him until he decided what he was going to do.

'And what about the people from the valley. What plans do you have for them?'

'They will live peaceful lives in their former homes. But this time they will have the magic to sustain their land.' He turned to Grimley. 'As we both know our friend here made

268

a huge mistake when he banned the use of magic in Waterswood.'

Jack didn't believe a word of it. He'd already seen the devastation wreaked on the lands to the west of Leah's castle. And he was sure in his own heart that he planned slavery for the people of the valley.

'And there is something else that we need to address,' said Leah. 'Your assertion that you are the rightful heir to the House of Sarmondian isn't true.'

Jack studied his face carefully. What was his game now? 'Why would you say that?'

'Because,' said Leah, 'that honour and privilege belong to me.'

*

Chapter Thirty-Five –
Heir to the House of Sarmondian

Jack wasn't sure that he'd heard Leah correctly. Surely, he didn't really believe that he was the heir to the House of Sarmondian? Jack knew that wasn't true. The Bloodstone hung comfortably around his neck. If he wasn't the true heir to the Sarmondian line, the stone wouldn't allow it. This was another one of Leah's games, but Jack didn't want to provoke another blow to his already aching body. He calmly repeated his question.

'I'm interested in why you would say that?'

Leah looked all around the chamber and spread his arms wide in a gesture of pride. 'Look at these surroundings, Green-Jack. Wouldn't you agree that this is a castle fit for a King?'

Jack didn't respond. He knew that Leah was trying to provoke him.

'And remind me where it is you hail from, Green-Jack? A hovel in a human forest.' He smirked triumphantly. 'Hardly a fit abode for the heir to a high Elven family.' Leah shook his head nonchalantly. 'No Green-Jack, it is I who head this ancient Elven house. I am merely following the destiny that was written for me many years ago.'

Jack needed to breathe deeply but he couldn't because of his cracked ribs. He fought within himself to keep calm. 'Written by whom?'

Leah didn't respond immediately. He stroked his beard and studied Jack intently for several moments. 'My mother and father travelled far across the magical lands. They told me stories of our homeland on Emerald Island. About how the other high Elven families isolated the Sarmondian House for being too powerful. The dispute escalated to the point that my ancestors left their home and they travelled as far away from the homeland as they could. They came to this part of the world and created these lands with their magic.'

Leah knew some of the history of the Sarmondian House but had fabricated his own version of what happened after they left the homeland. Jack was sure that Woodgate Valley and the surrounding communities were created with the help of the Faery Queens. They looked after the lands as best they could within the Faery lore. As much as they may have disapproved of what Grimley was doing they couldn't intervene. Leah was rewriting history, but Jack wasn't about to challenge him.

'You are uncharacteristically quiet, Green-Jack. Do you doubt my word?'

'It's a different version of what I was led to believe,' he said diplomatically.

Leah smiled. 'You have had your head filled with the Faery Queen's propaganda, Jack. You must not believe their nonsense. I have plans for these lands that are far more ambitious than anything those Faeries could ever contemplate. We will have a land that thrives with riches for all and we can plan how we rid the planet of these primitive humans.'

Now Jack was sure of his madness. Leah's plans would destroy them all. He searched deep inside of himself for any sign of his Koehtia, but it was futile. There wasn't even the slightest sensation in the soles of his feet. He was on his own, no friends and no Earth Magic. The only thing that could protect him was his Bloodstone. He had to get away from the castle. On an impulse, Jack foolishly turned around and ran towards the doors. He opened them and attempted to run through but felt a strong hand grip him by the arm and looked up into the grotesque face of a Goblin, who took great pleasure in throwing him back into the chamber and closing the doors. Jack ended up in an undignified heap on the floor.

Leah walked over to him and helped him back to his feet. He looked down at him and said, 'oh Jack, how am I going to learn to trust you when you do such foolhardy things?' He placed his hands on Jack's shoulders and gripped them tightly. Jack thought he was going to crush his bones, but

271

then he loosened his grip and stepped away.

Leah held out his hand. 'I think the time is now right, Jack, for you to return the Sarmondian Bloodstone to its rightful owner.'

The last thing Jack was going to do was hand over the Bloodstone. His mother's words from the confrontation with Korrian were still fresh in his mind. The Bloodstone was his and his alone until he chose to give it away. And that was never going to happen. He needed to think, and think quickly, he sensed that Leah's patience was wearing thin.

'If what you say is true,' said Jack, 'and the Bloodstone is yours by right, then you will be able to take it from me and there is nothing that I can do to stop you.'

Did Leah know about the history of the Bloodstone? He knew a little about the House of Sarmondian, but did he understand the vagaries of the Bloodstone ownership? Leah's dark eyes bore deep into Jack. It made him feel increasingly uncomfortable.

Leah turned to walk away and then without warning he lunged at Jack, grabbing the Bloodstone chain hanging loosely around Jack's neck with his right hand. Almost instantly he screamed out in agony and sharply withdrew his hand which was now covered in a ball of bright yellow flames. He ran from Jack bellowing at the top of his voice and grabbed the wine decanter and poured its contents over his burning hand. The flames reduced slightly but flared up again, but then Leah poured a jug of water over the hand and this time the flames were extinguished. He dropped to his knees and rested his head on the seat of his throne. He couldn't speak as he struggled to catch his breath.

Jack knew that the Bloodstone was protecting him, just as it did when Willy Venn inadvertently grabbed it, proving beyond any doubt that Leah didn't have any claim to be the true heir to the House of Sarmondian. But now he had an angry adversary to face and no Earth Magic to help him. Jack suffered no harm from his Bloodstone; the chain and stone felt cool against his skin. The raw power that emanated from the stone was impressive. Meredin told him that the Bloodstone was made long ago in the days of the ancient Elves and was hewn from crystals mined deep under the city of Arminas. In truth, their power wasn't understood but those who had witnessed if first hand where in awe. Was there a way for Jack to use the power to attack Leah? If there was it was beyond him.

Grimley stood open-mouthed watching the scene unfolding in front of him. Shadow rose to his feet and slowly withdrew behind the throne. He sensed his master's anger and didn't want to be the object of his uncontrolled ire when it erupted. Jack saw Leah's shoulders tighten and he knew his anger was going to be brutal once it surfaced.

Leah climbed to his feet and slowly turned towards Jack. His mouth twisted in anger, or maybe it was pain? His dark eyes focused on Jack and without warning he raised his right arm and sent a sheet of white fire towards him. Jack was ready and dived to his side, rolling over to his right as the fire hit the marble floor and fizzed past him, colliding with the stone wall in a shuddering explosion, sending shards of stone and mortar all over the chamber.

The pain of Jack's cracked ribs seared through him like razor-sharp knife blades. Not only didn't he have any Koehtia, his physical mobility was badly impaired by his rib injury. It would be easy for Leah to attack him at will.

'You have gone too far, boy! I have given you the best of my hospitality and extended the hand of friendship towards you. But how do you repay it? By throwing my hospitality back in my face and deliberately attacking me.'

Jack was still lying on the floor. He couldn't even lift himself up. 'I didn't make that happen. If you knew anything about the Bloodstone you would know that it protects its legitimate owner.'

Leah's attention was distracted by a disturbance outside the door. He angrily cried out, 'desist immediately, or feel my wrath!'

As Leah returned his attention to Jack, the double doors to the chamber burst open and someone came running into the chamber. Jack turned his head and he thought his heart would sing with joy. A tall Elf with shoulder-length blond hair and striking blue eyes stood there. It was Captain Tathar Elensar from the Elven Border Guard. He was quickly joined by an axe wielding Grindell, Roger, Gwendo, Rory, and another slightly taller Dwarf joined them holding a small, strange looking bow.

But Leah's reaction was instant, and he roared. 'One more step forward and I will destroy you all!' The wolf who had been sheltering behind the throne sprang to its feet, teeth bared and snarling.

Casdilian unleashed an arrow towards Leah's chest but he raised his arm and sent a flash of red fire across the chamber and the arrow evaporated into a ball of red flame and ended up as a pile of ashes on the floor. Leah looked furious and took a threatening step down from the dais. 'That was a very, very, stupid thing to do.'

But as he raised his hand Grimley grabbed a marble figurine from a shelf next to the dais and hit Leah a sickening blow on the back of his head. Leah staggered forward and fell to his hands and knees. Elensar saw his opportunity and ran over to Jack. He picked him up in his arms and carried him back to the others.

Gwendo immediately sprang into action. 'Captain, you stand one side of Jack. Roger, you the other. Grindell, stand next to the Captain. Rory, you and I will stand to the side of Roger.'

Casdilian looked lost. 'What should I do?'

'Stand the other side of Grindell.' Then she addressed them all. 'Now link arms - we must be as one.'

They did as she asked, and the Unification was complete, with Roger and Elensar either side of Jack supporting him. Leah slowly climbed back to his feet but ignored the company and left them under the watchful eye of Shadow. He instead turned his attention to Grimley who was still holding the marble figurine. Leah didn't speak as he rubbed the back of his head. When he looked at his hand and saw the blood he let out a scream like a Banshee.

Grimley looked terrified and took a step backwards, dropping the figurine on the floor. His rash attempt at killing Leah had failed and Grimley knew that his retribution when it came would be brutal. He didn't have to wait long. Leah raised his right hand and sent a flash of red fire towards Grimley. When it hit him, he let out a shriek that sent shivers down the spine of everyone in that chamber. But Leah didn't stop there and sent bolt after bolt of red fire slamming into Grimley's writhing body, the force lifting him off his feet. He kept him suspended in mid-air as the red-hot fire burned Grimley's limp body. And when he stopped, Grimley's lifeless, charred body slumped to the floor, the fetid stench of burning flesh filling the chamber with its nauseating odour.

Leah smirked in triumph as he studied his handiwork before slowly turning towards the company. He stared at them without speaking. His upper lip curled in contempt. Shadow stood by his side snarling at the company. 'Is this the best the Faery Queens could muster? Four midgets, an Elf, a human and a half breed mongrel.'

Gwendo whispered to Jack. 'Search for your Koehtia, Jack. I can assure you it's there.'

Jack's body was still wracked with the pain from his ribs and stomach. His head ached, and he would've fallen over if his friends weren't holding him upright.

'So,' sneered Leah. 'Please tell, just how are you proposing to take the gold dust away from me?'

'Concentrate, Jack,' whispered Gwendo. 'Feel the magic, it's waiting for you.'

Jack tried to breathe and straighten, but the pains in his chest and midriff stabbed through him like burning spikes.

'Throw down your weapons,' commanded Leah. 'Or it will be all the worse for you. I may take pity on you if you cooperate - or I may not. You saw what I did to Grimley. You will be next.'

Roger whispered in Jack's ear. 'It's me, your father. Listen to Gwendo. Search for your magic, it's there.'

Jack turned towards him. It was the first time Roger had

used the word father. His heart smiled. He tried to take a deep breath, but the pain stopped him. He needed to lie down – he needed rest.

'My patience is wearing thin. My friend here,' Leah pointed to Shadow, 'hasn't eaten all day, so a Dwarf or a Pixie would make a very satisfying lunch for him.'

Jack turned to Elensar. 'Please, let me lie down.'

Elensar whispered in his ear. 'Let your Koehtia heal you Jack. Remember what Meredin told you in Arminas.'

Leah raised his right hand and sent a red bolt of fire over the heads of the company, that flew through the open doors and blasted lumps out of the far wall in the entrance hall, scattering stone rubble across the marble floor. 'The next one will be aimed at you. Now drop your weapons.'

Elensar nodded to the company and they all did as he asked but quickly linked arms again. Something stirred deep down within Jack because of the red fire. He felt a knowing tingle in his feet. Could it be? It had been so long that he couldn't be sure. *Let it build, Jack. Don't rush it. The Koehtia will find its own way through your body.*

And it did. The once familiar sensation moved slowly and deliberately up his legs and into his midriff. The pain dissolved in warmth. Then his cracked ribs – they healed one by one. Before he knew it, his whole body was teeming with Koehtia. He stood up straight and took his first pain free breath in days. He felt vibrant – he felt alive. He squeezed Roger and Elensar's hands and winked at them both in turn. He unlinked his arms and stepped in front of his friends.

Leah watched him in silence. He sensed that Jack had found his magic. Jack saw the menace in Leah's eyes suddenly joined by a flicker of fear. Despite all Leah's bluster about his magical powers, he knew that Jack's prowess with Earth Magic could threaten him. They stood facing each other without speaking for several moments. It was like two prize fighters sizing each other up. Jack's mind slipped back to his fight with Willy Venn. He was frightened then; now he felt calm and ready for the battle ahead.

'It's over, Leah. Back down before anyone else gets hurt.'

The sneer returned to Leah's lips. 'You are no match for me, Green-Jack. If you don't surrender this instant I will kill you all!' He thrust his right hand out in front of him and threw a searing red bolt of fire directly at Jack.

It crackled across the chamber, but Jack reacted instantly, raising his right hand and easily deflecting the red fire bolt towards the ceiling above Leah's throne. It hit the ceiling with a shuddering explosion, cascading large fragments of falling stone all around Leah, sending him staggering backwards. The whole castle felt as if it shook under the impact. Shadow cowered at the foot of the dais and howled in fear. Jack dropped to his knee and called out. 'Shadow – come to me. I will look after you.'

The wolf hesitated for a brief second before suddenly dashing across the rubble strewn floor and hiding behind Jack. He stroked his ears and whispered, 'it's all right boy. You're safe now.'

Leah recovered his composure and screamed in fury, hurling another red bolt towards Jack, but he was ready and easily deflected it with his hand again, exploding it back into the wall behind the throne, once again showering Leah in stone dust and rubble. The sheer power of Leah's magic shook the castle to its foundations every time it impacted the walls.

Jack settled Shadow with his friends and told them to step back towards the entrance to the chamber. Elensar was about to protest but Jack reassured him. 'Don't worry, he can't harm me.' Reluctantly, they did as he asked, and Jack turned back towards Leah. His Koehtia was by now flowing freely through his body. His relationship with it was so strong that he knew that he was untouchable by anything that Leah threw at him. 'You cannot harm me … Stop this before it goes too far.'

Leah was coughing and choking on the dust cloud that surrounded him. Covered from head to foot in stone dust, he looked nothing like the imposing figure that Jack had first encountered. But he was far from giving up. He turned to Jack, his face twisted with fury. 'You will never defeat me, Green-Jack. You are just a child. I have command over more magic than you could ever imagine. I would have been merciful if you hadn't challenged me, but now I will destroy you all.'

Jack shook his head. 'That's just it, Leah, you don't have control of your magic. You're calling on more and more and it's starting to consume you. Stop now while you still can.'

But he wasn't listening. He hurled another bolt of red fire towards Jack who raised his right hand and effortlessly deflected it to the floor in between them. Shards of white hot marble shattered like shrapnel all over Leah, setting fire to his robe. He screamed out, more in rage than pain and tore off the flaming robe and threw it on the throne. Leah's anger was now out of control and he threw bolt after bolt of red fire across the chamber towards Jack, who was easily able to deflect them all back towards him with a mere flick of his hand. Jack was seriously beginning to worry about the wall behind the dais collapsing with the force of the exploding red fire bolts impacting the masonry.

The ferocity of the attack forced Jack to take a step back and he stumbled on a large shard of stone. Jack momentarily lost his balance and fought to stay upright. Leah saw his chance and leant forward throwing a red flash of fire at Jack. A flaming red ball slammed into Jack's chest sending him flying backwards into the arms of his friends at the back of the chamber.

Roger screamed, 'Jack!' and grabbed a hold of him and tried to help him upright.

But Leah wasn't going to waste the opportunity and gloatingly said, 'I warned you Green-Jack that I was too powerful for you. And now you're going to pay the price for not joining forces with me.' He raised his right arm high into the air and launched another red bolt of fire at Jack who was lying helplessly in the arms of Roger.

Jack struggled up into a sitting position and held his hand

out in front of him, more as a protection than consciously trying to deflect the red fire. It hit Jack's hand and rebounded directly back towards Leah, hitting him full in his chest, lifting him off his feet and backwards, leaving him sprawling over the dais. He lay there dazed for several moments before pulling himself up onto his throne. He slumped back into the chair breathing heavily, the sweat dripping down his face.

The continuous effort required from Leah to control the magic had taken its toll on him. Jack climbed back to his feet with the help of Roger and took a long deep breath. He staggered towards Leah who was still lying on his throne, panting like a tired dog. Jack sensed something was about to happen and appealed to him once more. 'Leah! Listen to me. The magic is going to destroy you if you don't pull back now. It's not too late to save yourself.'

But it was too late. A red mist started to engulf Leah. It seemed to be coming out of every pore of his body. It hung around him like a cloud and he started to gasp for air. Jack moved towards him to see if he could stop what was about to happen, but Gwendo grabbed his arm and pulled him away.

'It's too dangerous, Jack. Leah is lost to us.'

She pulled him to the back of the chamber along with the others and they all crouched down and winced at the spectacle unfolding in front of them. Leah started to writhe around uncontrollably. He tried to pull himself off the chair, but he fell onto the floor in a crumpled heap. A heart-rending cry for help sprang from his lips before he was engulfed within a ball of red fire. One last anguished scream filled the chamber as he disappeared into a red haze. When it eventually cleared all that was left on and around the throne were the charred remains of his bones and his robe.

Jack turned away and felt physically sick. Two arms wrapped around his shoulders and turned him around. He looked into his father's eyes. Roger held his face and kissed him firmly on his cheek. He hugged him and Jack hugged him back. No words were said; no words were necessary.

Chapter Thirty-Six –
Quiet after the Storm.

Well, I thought we'd lost you for a horrible moment there, Jack lad,' said Rory taking a sip of his tea.

Jack sat at a small round table surrounded by his friends. They all nursed mugs of Roseleaf. Savia had taken them to the servants' quarters in the lower castle. Jack wanted to get away from Leah's throne room. He couldn't stay there – the stench of death filled the air and he needed to get away.

'I'm not sure what happened when that red fire bolt hit me. The force knocked me backwards, but it didn't feel as if it harmed me other than the physical shock. Maybe my bloodstone was protecting me?'

'Or your gold coin?' suggested Rory.

Jack reached into the breast pocket of his shirt and withdrew two flattened pieces of jewellery. The gold coin that Cara had given him all those months ago in Cill-Arney had been spread even thinner. And the silver ring Becky had given him was just a mangled mess.

'There you go,' said Rory, 'your Leprechaun gold coin saved you again.'

Jack smiled. 'I'm just relieved to still be here and sharing a much-needed mug of Roseleaf with the truest friends an Elf could ever wish for.'

'I'll drink to that,' said Rory raising his mug.

The frightened servants had hidden downstairs once they heard the company fighting with the Goblin Guards as they entered the castle. Elensar and his friends had surprise on their side and easily dealt with the initial resistance they encountered. The Goblins were no match for the combined warrior skills of Elensar, Grindell and Casdilian.

Jack went to find Savia and her friends immediately after his confrontation with Leah and reassured them that they would all be safe. But she was understandably distraught when she heard of the demise of her master. They served Jack and his friends' soup along with the Roseleaf which was just what was needed. Rory noisily slurped his soup as he recounted the company's adventures since they lost Jack.

The light-hearted moment was tinged with sadness when he told Jack about Stran's death. 'He died saving me, Jack. Who'd have thought it? I always thought he disliked me.'

'It was just his way, Rory. He sacrificed himself for the Unification and we should all thank him for that,' said Jack.

Rory raised his mug. 'To Stran Vander – a fine Elf and a fine ranger.'

'And we owe a great debt of gratitude to Casdilian and his Dwelves,' said Grindell.

'He's right,' said Elensar. 'Without them we would have perished on the mountain under the weight of Goblin attacks.'

'Thank you, Casdilian,' said Jack raising his mug. 'You and your people are true friends and I hope you will be a part of this new Faery world we are building.'

Jack turned to Gwendo. 'I also believe that we all owe you a huge debt of gratitude.'

Gwendo blushed slightly. 'It was luck, Jack. If I hadn't fallen down that cavern, I'd never have found the gold dust hidden at the bottom. I sensed the ancient magic that was protecting it and realised why you and I weren't feeling it. That's why the Faery Queens suggested the Unification. We had to pool all our resources to enable us to break that spell. I have had reason to criticise them in the past but they were right when it mattered.'

'But I don't understand what happened to yer one Leah,' said Rory.

'As I repelled his attacks he called upon more and more magic,' said Jack. 'It got to the point where he could no longer control it. In the end, it destroyed him. I was lucky to have worked with Meredin in Arminas. He warned me of such dangers.'

'And we owe Grimley for attacking Leah when we first arrived,' said Elensar. 'That gave me the chance to get to you, Jack, so that we could form the Unification.'

'Why would he have done that?' asked Rory. 'I thought

he'd tried to have you killed in the past.'

'He did,' said Jack. 'Grimley saw me as a threat because of my Earth Magic. I think Leah may have helped convince him and offered to take the gold dust and keep it safe for him until I was imprisoned in Darkenwold. But that was just an excuse to take the dust for his own ends. Grimley only realised he'd been used just minutes before you burst into the chamber. Maybe anger got the better of him, or perhaps it was just impulse. We will never know.'

'Well, I'm just glad that my son survived the most horrendous ordeal,' said Roger. 'I never imagined in my previous life that I could be a part of something so vital to the survival of our world. I've seen and experienced things that I only thought existed in fairy stories.' He raised his mug, 'To true friendship.'

Savia quietly walked up to Jack and stood next to him looking uncomfortable. 'Jack, may I speak with you.'

'Please, speak freely Savia. You are amongst friends.'

'We, my people and I, have only ever known the castle. The master always provided for us. We are frightened, Jack. We do not know what the future holds for us.'

'There is no need to be frightened, Savia. You can come back to Waterswood with us.'

She didn't answer. She looked troubled. 'What is it, Savia? Did I say something wrong?'

'It's just that … it's just that these mountains are our home. We've never known anywhere else.'

'Then stay with us on the mountain,' said Casdilian. 'You will be very welcome.'

'Why don't you all stay in the castle?' suggested Rory. 'It seems a shame to waste such comfortable surroundings.'

Jack looked to Casdilian. 'Well?'

'I've never known anything other than a tent on a mountainside. I'm not sure.'

'At least move your people nearer to the castle so you can help and support each other,' suggested Elensar.

Casdilian nodded. 'I will put it to my people.'

Jack looked to Savia. She smiled. 'I would like that very

much.'

Shadow sat next to Jack quietly observing proceedings. He nudged Jack's arm as if to let him know he was still there. Jack affectionately stroked his neck fur.

'And what of our friend here? I suspect he is too tame to return to the wild. Maybe I could take him back to Waterswood?'

Casdilian wasn't so sure. 'I agree he's too tame to release into the wild, but he's a mountain wolf, Jack. He needs to live in a cold terrain. Your valley will be too warm for him.'

'Then maybe he should stay here with you,' suggested Jack.

Casdilian nodded his agreement. 'We will look after each other, I'm sure.'

*

The following days were spent moving the gold dust up from the caves below the castle. Horse-drawn carts were arranged by Savia and her friends. It was Casdilian that noticed a subtle change in the weather.

'The snow is starting to thaw. In all the time we've lived on these mountains we've never known that.'

Jack and Gwendo stood alongside the Dwelf leader at the castle's entrance staring out at the mountain tops across the valley.

'Leah's hold on the environment has gone with the breaking of his magic,' said Gwendo. 'The natural balance of nature can be restored. We are all creatures of Faery and are at one with our world. It mystifies me as to why anyone would wish to destroy such beauty.'

'I've witnessed the corruption of power before,' said Jack. 'Magic is a wonderful gift but there is a tremendous responsibility that goes with it. If you are not careful it can consume you.'

Gwendo looked up at him and smiled. 'So wise and yet so young.'

The carts were assembled at the bottom of the valley and

loaded with the gold dust. Five days after Leah's demise the company set off on their long journey back to Waterswood. The mood was light, yet subdued. They all realised how close they had come to the end of the Faery world as they knew it. Rory called it a time for reflection and that is what they all did.

*

Chapter Thirty-Seven – The Healing Land.

The journey back home proved to be uneventful. Even the Bleak Inn wasn't quite so bleak this time although the inn-keeper's demeanour hadn't improved much since their last visit. But what really gladdened their hearts was that the desecration that Leah had wrought on the forests was healing. Streams that had dried now had water trickling through them and buds were forming on some of the trees and bushes.

Gwendolain had reclaimed its magic and the vale was pink and glowing just as it had been in its prime. But the welcome for Gwendo from her Pixies was truly something to behold. They didn't stop crying and laughing for the whole day after they arrived.

Gwendo volunteered her Pixies to take the gold dust back to the villages in Woodgate Valley. Her reasoning was sound as she said that they could all carry a small sack each and make much quicker progress than a horse drawn cart.

'I think those people have spent more than long enough in the spirit world. They need to get back home and the sooner the better,' said Gwendo.

'But how are you going to know which community the gold dust belongs to?' asked Jack.

Gwendo smiled. 'We're Pixies Jack – we'll know.'

'I don't think it's a good idea to put the gold dust back into the wishing-well, said Elensar. 'You need a new, more secure place to hide it.'

'He has a point,' agreed Gwendo.

Jack thought for several moments. He leant over to Gwendo and whispered in her ear. She smiled back instantly, and said, 'the perfect place.' And with that the Pixies rose into the air like a pink cloud and flew westwards towards the Woodgate Valley.

The company arrived in Bellowrock a week later and were impressed and relieved in equal measures to find a new regime in place. Bumble had arranged democratic elections and they now had a fully elected Council running the community. Grindell glowed with pride at the changes made by his people and he was even more made up when they appointed him head of the Bellowrock Guard. It was decided that Grindell and several of his guards would join the company on the final leg of the journey back to Waterswood.

After a night's rest in the Dwarf Mountains the company set off across the Running Plains. Their experience on the outward journey was still fresh in their minds and there was a noticeable tension within the company during the first day. They were all pleasantly relieved to find that the biting winds and the constant rain and snow were absent.

The running horses showed up on the third day but not en masse like they did on the previous occasion. They stopped with the company and grazed with them as they carried on their way.

'Is it me, or is there a totally different atmosphere everywhere we go,' chirped Rory.

'It would seem that Leah's influence stretched much further than we thought,' said Elensar. He slapped Jack playfully on his back. 'I think, my young friend, that your land has made a huge step forward in the last few weeks. It bodes well for the future.'

*

Some six months after the company left Waterswood, they stood as a group on the path that led down from the Fireridge Mountains. Jack was at their head and looked down on his home village. The emotions that swam through him at that moment were too overwhelming to describe.

Rory grabbed his hand and urged the others to join them. 'Come on my lovely lads, we set off as a unifying force for the Faery races, lets walk back into Waterswood as one.'

Roger stood the other side of Jack and grabbed his hand, as Elensar took hold of Rory's. Grindell and his Dwarves stood either side of them and linked hands as the Unification set off on the last few hundred paces of what had been an epic journey into the unknown.

As they entered Waterswood Jack squeezed Roger and Rory's hands and they both smiled back at him. They walked along the path that opened out onto the village square and Jack was surprised and disappointed to find it empty. He was sure that they all would have gathered there to meet him.

He let go of Roger's and Rory's hands and walked over to the wishing-well. Where were they all? He turned back towards his friends and shrugged his shoulders. The disappointment threatened to swallow him. Rory raised his right hand and pointed across the square.

Jack turned around and saw a lone Aelf walking slowly towards him. She was barely one and a half metres tall and her long dark wavy hair rested on her shoulders. Her long green gown trailed across the cobble stones behind her. Jack was rooted to the spot – his feet wouldn't move. His eyes misted with tears as she stopped in front of him.

He involuntarily dropped to his knees as he fell into her embrace. He felt her moist tears on his hair and neck and they didn't speak for fully five minutes. Roger walked up to them and helped Jack back to his feet. He looked down at her and said, 'we have a fine son, Ciara.'

She looked up to him through a veil of tears and reached for his hand and said, 'the finest.'

Roger wrapped his arms around the two of them and held them close. As Jack savoured the embrace, he heard a familiar voice from behind him. 'Have you got a hug for me?'

He thought his heart would burst when he saw Noah standing there. His grandfather looked tanned and well. He opened his arms wide and beckoned Jack to him. Jack let go of his parents and engulfed his grandfather in a back-breaking embrace. He stepped away and studied him for a second.

'You're looking … you're looking … so well!'

Noah nodded his agreement. 'All thanks to you, Jack

lad.'

'How did you manage to get down the well and through the stream?' asked Jack.

'That's down to me,' said another voice from behind him.

He turned around to see Morning-Dew walking towards him. 'That entrance was very old hat. I thought it was time we updated it. You can enter through the Faery trail in Heywood Forest now. The door is the same but it saves all that clambering up and down well shafts.'

Jack heard a bark from across the square and an excited golden retriever came bounding towards him. He knelt down as Sonny-Boy leapt on top of him and smothered him in wet licks. 'OK boy, it's good to see you too.'

Jack suddenly became aware of someone standing to his side. He looked up into the most dazzling blue eyes and a smile that warmed his heart. Becky stood in front of him looking radiant in light blue shorts and a lilac top. Her legs and arms were tanned and her hair was bleached from the sun. His emotions were running at fever pitch as his heart thumped in his chest. How long had he waited for this moment, to be reunited with the girl he loved?

He stood up and she almost melted into his arms. They held each other without speaking. It was as if either of them weren't sure that each other was real. He could feel her heart beating in her chest and smell the summer in her shiny hair. When they finally let go she stood back and looked deep into his eyes.

'I'm so glad you're safe. You've been away for so long I was beginning to worry.'

He put his finger to her mouth. 'I'm here, that's all that matters.' They embraced again as Sonny stood at their feet, his tail wagging frantically. Jack stepped back from her and refreshed his memory of the girl who had stolen his heart. 'You're looking very tanned. What month is it?'

'It's late August,' said Becky.

Jack turned to his friends. 'I forgot to celebrate my birthday while I was away. I was sixteen on April the second.'

'And that my young friend, is as another good reason to have an even longer celebration.' Jack turned around to see a rather rotund Elf with a red blotchy face to the side of a tall blond Aelf with short swept back hair and striking blue eyes walking across the square. An elderly Elf with long wispy grey hair with half-moon glasses perched on his nose walked with them. The three of them wrapped Jack and Becky in a warm embrace and held them for several minutes.

As Jack stepped back he saw the tears in Lomund's eyes. Lilac and Tyler had broad smiles that lit up their faces. Becky held Jack's hand and Sonny-Boy sat at their feet looking at all the people that surrounded him. Lomund looked like he'd lost the power of speech as he was overcome with emotion but managed to utter a very emotional, 'well done Jack. We're all so very proud of you.'

Jack's heart sang with joy all over again. All the pain and fear had evaporated to be replaced by love and happiness. Before he knew it, the whole square began to fill with the good folk of Waterswood all desperate to thank the small band of friends who had saved their land. Kardan and Mildun lifted Jack onto their shoulders and paraded him around the square before standing him on the wishing-well wall.

Cries of 'Speech! Speech!' echoed around the square. Jack raised his hands in an effort to quieten the crowd. It took several minutes before they eventually did. Jack looked around the smiling faces that surrounded him and contrasted the scene with the last time he'd stood there, where fear was the overriding emotion. Shane and his guards stood proudly at the square perimeter and saluted Jack. His attention was diverted by Gwendo and her Pixies flying over the square and landing on top of one of the buildings. They had done their job with the gold dust well. Each one of them bouncing up and down with joy.

He swallowed and breathed deeply. His throat was dry but he started to speak anyway. 'My friends, it's been a long, hard road but we came through in the end, and I have many people to thank for that.' He turned to the company and indicated for them to join him. Rory, Grindell, Roger and Elensar stepped up onto the wall. He waved Gwendo over and she flew down and landed deftly on the wall by Rory.

'People of Waterswood, please give a loud cheer and show your appreciation for the bravest, most loyal bunch of friends an Elf could ever wish for.'

The crowd replied with interest. They gave a rousing reception unlike anything that square had ever witnessed in its entire history. It took fully five minutes for the crowd to quieten but they eventually responded to Jack's plea to listen.

'It's my sad duty to tell you my friends that one of our company did not return. Stran Vander perished at the hands of an attack by Goblins on Leah's mountain. He was a citizen of Mountpass and a very fine mountain ranger. I don't think it's an exaggeration to say that we wouldn't have succeeded in our quest without him.'

The crowd listen respectfully to Jack. They sensed the moment.

'As a mark of respect to Stran, I would like us to erect a statue of him on top of the Fireridge Mountains. I believe that would be a fitting memorial to him as he would always be overlooking Woodgate Valley. He gave his life for a cause that he truly believed in.'

The respectful silence continued. They all recognised that Stran's sacrifice helped ensure their freedom.

'I would also like to thank the five friends who are standing with me.' He introduced them one by one. 'Rory McNory, a Leprechaun from Cill-Arney; Grindell, a Dwarf from Bellowrock; Gwendo, a flying Pixie from Gwendolain and Captain Tathar Elensar, from the great Elven city of Arminas. And last but not least, may I introduce my father, Roger Thorne, from the human village of Grasslake.'

The crowd once again erupted into rapturous applause. Roger, Grindell and Elensar looked a little embarrassed but

Rory and Gwendo grinned broadly and enjoyed the moment.

'Together we represented a unification of the Faery races and it was because of our combined strength that we were able to eventually defeat Graydon Leah. And because of this I would like you all to grant them the freedom of Waterswood and may they always be welcome here.'

He received a unanimous 'Yes!' from the crowd and they all jumped up and down in excitement.

'And now my friends,' continued Jack, 'it falls upon us all to rebuild our community and engage with our neighbours. Never again must we fall into the trap of isolation. Together we are stronger, and we will build a fair and just society that treats everyone with the respect they deserve. Thank you, my friends, and I wish you all health and happiness.'

Jack and his friends stepped down from the wishing-well wall and were instantly mobbed by the gathered throng of people who all wanted to show their appreciation for the company. In all its history, Waterswood had never experienced a day like it and probably never would again. A huge street party, or as Tyler more aptly named it, a party in the lanes started in the early evening and didn't finish until the next morning.

I'm not sure I could do justice to the celebrations from that memorable day and night, so I've reprinted the relevant extracts from one Tyler Goldsmith's journal: -

'So, he did it, young Jack, not that I ever doubted he would. At an age where most Elves are still establishing their own identity, our Jack has vanquished a sorcerer when saving his mother, toppled an unjust and corrupt regime that had run Waterswood for years, and to cap it all off, he saved the Faery lands from death and destruction and dealt with a powerful and dangerous foe, Graydon Leah.

And that's why every Elf in Waterswood wanted to shake his hand and personally thank him. Jack as usual took it all in his stride and refused every offer of a Peardrop with which the grateful residents wanted to ply him. It was wonderful to see him with his grandfather and parents – I'm not sure who was the prouder. But Jack seems very taken with the young girl Becky. Being a poet, I look for beauty in most things, but I didn't have to try too hard with that young girl. She truly is charming and it was obvious to all who were there that she thinks the world of our Jack.

Now I've never been that keen on animals, but I made an exception with Becky's dog, Sonny-Boy. He seems to have an appetite even bigger than mine and took great delight in licking my face at every opportunity. Of course, Lilac had to comment that I'd found someone who liked me at last. What would I ever do without her?

Rory was in top form and together with the Pixies provided great entertainment for us all. He played his tin whistle and the Pixies danced. Gwendo is a real character and she had me in fits of laughter with her flying antics and her banter with Rory.

I found the Dwarves a surly bunch at first but they all mellowed following several glasses of Peardrop. Grindell even surprised us all with a song and his colleagues joined in with the rousing chorus. I'm looking forward to a trip over to Bellowrock to meet them all.

Lomund was a little overwrought by the occasion and had to go to bed early, but he was delighted when Jack told him he wanted to share his cottage with him. The strain over the recent years has taken its toll on Lomund and he is in desperate need of some peace and rest. But having Jack stay with him will give him some focus and I'm sure we'll see the old Lomund back with us again soon.

Jack told me about Grimley and I was at a loss to explain his actions. On the face of it, it appeared like he was up to his old tricks when he seemed to help Jack and was only leading him into the hands of Graydon Leah. But then he went and confounded us all by attacking Leah and giving the others the chance to get Jack back into their midst. I suppose we'll never know …

So, now the task falls onto all our shoulders to rebuild Waterswood and to engage with our neighbouring communities. Jack needs peace and calm for the first time since he discovered us, and together with Ciara, Crystal, Lilac and Lomund, we will make sure that happens. We are so lucky to have this fine young Elf in our midst and even luckier still that he is our leader. But I'm mindful of the fact that Jack is like a precious jewel and must be looked after, and let me assure you, my friends, that is exactly what's going to happen.

Finally, some thoughts on this long, drawn out and painful saga. It began with Grimley forcing Ciara to leave Waterswood. She conceived her son with a human and in Grimley's eyes that was an unforgiveable crime. And then young Jack saved Becky's life. In any humane society that would be considered to be worthy of the highest praise but in Grimley's mind that was an even bigger crime than Jack's conception.

And that is where Grimley was so badly wrong. Both of these so-called crimes were acts of love, and that my friends, can never be a crime. Is there a higher power than love? I think not. Love is what makes our world such a wonderful place to be … And long may that be so.

Good health and live long and happy love-filled lives,

Tyler Goldsmith, Resident Poet of Waterswood Village.'

The End

Epilogue

A voice whispered in his ear; 'Green-Jack – we're waiting…'

Jack rose from his bed and quickly dressed. He crept out of Lomund's cottage, being extra careful not to make any noise as he closed the front door and headed towards the Waterdown Hills. He looked back towards his beloved Waterswood and smiled. Candles flickered across the sleepy village; a full moon rested over the Fireridge Mountains shedding its luminescent glow across the valley. His heart was so full of joy that he felt like it would burst into song at any moment.

They were sure to dance this night …

As he approached the brow of the hill, he saw Morning-Dew and Gwendo waiting for him.

'Where have you been?' asked Morning-Dew as she enthusiastically grabbed his right hand. Gwendo grabbed his other hand and the three of them skipped towards the forest at the top of the hill. He heard singing and laughter in the distance. As he reached the hill summit he saw them dancing in a circle in front of the Tickle Tree. They were all dressed in silver-white gowns that flowed like sails in the wind behind them.

Jack felt like a young child again as he watched them. The Tickle Tree was more animated than he'd ever seen her. Her branches moved in time to the rhythm of the dancing. As soon as they saw Jack they stopped and ran over to him. They joined hands and formed a ring around him and began dancing and singing again.

Morning-Dew whispered in his ear. 'I think they're pleased to see you.'

When the singing stopped, they led him by the hand to the Tickle Tree. Jack couldn't tell how but he knew she was smiling as she wrapped him in her soft, feathery branches like she was embracing a long lost child. As he stepped away from her embrace, she lifted her lower branches, and there safely hidden, were the barrels of Waterswood gold dust. Gwendo and her Pixies had done their job well.

The Faery Queens formed a semi-circle around Jack as Morning-Dew and Gwendo stood either side of him. The Tickle Tree rested a slim, feathery branch on his shoulder – it was as if she didn't want to let him go.

'My, my, we're quiet tonight,' said Morning-Dew. 'I usually struggle to get a word in edgeways when we're together.' She turned to Jack and smiled. 'Which may come as a surprise to you.'

Jack returned her smile before studying each of the Faery Queens in turn. They were tall and lithe like Morning-Dew, with long dark hair that rested loosely on their shoulders. Their eyes were dark and soulful and looked upon him with warmth and affection. A strange feeling came over him – it was as if he'd met them all before …

*

Lightning Source UK Ltd.
Milton Keynes UK
UKHW040603141218
333964UK00001B/48/P